Martin Stephen is High Master of The  School and author of fifteen titles on military history.

Praise for *The Desperate Remedy*:

'Breathtaking plotting and delightful characterisation in a Jacobean tale of murder and political intrigue - a pyrotechnic, explosive rocket of a book' JENNI MURRAY

'Martin Stephen takes a refreshingly different approach in his Jacobean thriller . . . Dastardly political and religious manoeuvrings, footpads, trollops and demented Catholics, all add up to a terrific book, the first of a long series, we must hope' SPECTATOR

'Intrigue, high life and low life are brilliantly woven in a thriller which has a compelling vividness and pungency. The historical details are utterly convincing; one can see and smell Jacobean England and hear its inhabitants speaking. I do hope Sir Henry Gresham has a long life' LAWRENCE JAMES

'A historical thriller that brings early sixteenth-century England vibrantly alive . . . a first novel full of impressive contemporary detail . . . (Stephen) sweeps us through the intricately woven plot of this well-told spine chiller' THE GOOD BOOK GUIDE

Also by Martin Stephen

The Conscience of the King

THE

DESPERATE
REMEDY

Henry Gresham and
The Gunpowder Plot

Martin Stephen

timewarner
paperbacks

A *Time Warner* Paperback

First published in Great Britain in 2002
by Little, Brown
This edition published in 2002 by Time Warner Paperbacks

Copyright © Martin Stephen 2002

The moral right of the author has been asserted.

A CIP catalogue record for this book
is available from the British Library.

ISBN 0 7515 3259 2

Typeset by M Rules
Printed and bound in Great Britain by
Clays Ltd, St Ives plc

Time Warner Paperbacks
An imprint of
Time Warner Books UK
Brettenham House
Lancaster Place
London WC2E 7EN

www.TimeWarnerBooks.co.uk

ACKNOWLEDGEMENTS

I am extremely grateful to Graham Seel for his historical advice, and to Sonia Land, Tara Lawrence, Ursula Mackenzie, Philip Franks and Jenny Stephen.

I would like to thank Cambridge University Library, the Bodleian Library, Oxford, the John Rylands Library, Manchester, and Fitzwilliam College, Cambridge, for research facilities, and the Royal Exchange Theatre, Manchester.

'*È necessario a chi dispone una repubblica, ed ordina leggi in quella, prassuppoie tutti gli nomini rei, e che li abbiano sempre a usare la malignità dello animo loro, qualunque volta ne abbiano libera occasione.*'

('It is necessary for him who lays out a state and arranges laws for it to presuppose that all men are evil and that they are always going to act according to the wickedness of their spirits whenever they have free scope.')

NICCOLÒ MACHIAVELLI, 1469–1527

PROLOGUE

It was a murderer's moon, with dark, scudding clouds hiding the stars. The soldier moved quickly but silently through ebony night, his stride confident and determined. London was deserted this long after midnight, yet still he was careful, gliding close by the sides of the darkened buildings. He had no fear of the Watch, feeble and infirm as it was, but on his business all complications were best avoided, however minor. Tall, dark and powerful, his mop of red hair was invisible beneath the hat pulled firmly down across his brow.

He arrived at the place, and drew back into an opposite doorway, waiting. He heard the courtier long before he saw his shadow arrive at the door, panting with exertion. The storm lantern was shaking in the courtier's hand. He moved out from the shadow of the doorway and heard the other's indrawn breath of fear, before recognition struck. The courtier might be the finest of servants at Court, bowing and scraping his way up the arse of his masters. He might be lord of all he surveyed below stairs. He was certainly a trusted secretary of one of the most powerful men in England. Yet here, in this place, he was a frightened little man, on his master's orders, in a dark cloak and borrowed boots. He paid for his pleasure and his vanity by this meeting in a dark place.

1

The soldier smelt the familiar stench of fear on the courtier, who scuttled to the door like a frightened rabbit, but he did not show his contempt. He had made a career of hiding behind the bluff manner of a simple man. Deceit was second nature to him. He was even sympathetic to the stinking wretch, enquiring solicitously in a hoarse whisper if he was ready to enter the cellar. A curt, nervous nod was the answer to his pains.

It was a marvellous thing, the soldier's lantern. Its flame had been lit in the man's lodgings, and then locked away behind the ingenious shutters. The flame could breathe, but yet it could not be seen. He opened one of the shutters, and the thin light gleamed on to the lock of the ancient oak door. He drew the key from his purse, and the well-greased tumblers moved solidly and silently back.

The courtier gagged as their feet kicked up the dust of ages. He cursed under his breath as he cannoned into one of the stone pillars that held up the cellar, feeling the fear in the pit of his stomach. He fell back on to a pile of ancient hangings, discarded since Henry VIII's days and left to moulder. More dust rose up and coated their dry tongues. The soldier paused, courteous as ever, his thoughts hidden behind the craggy, pleasing mask of his face.

They reached a pile of faggots and brushwood.

The soldier opened the other shutters on his cloaked lantern. He placed it on the floor. His shadow and the courtier's shadow danced briefly on the ancient walls, elongated, cutting through the mingled smells of fresh wood and decay. He cleared a path through the wood, revealing a stained barrel. Its lid had already been prised open and lay, resting loose, across its top. He took his dagger and flipped the lid to one side. He spoke in a low voice, for all that they were alone.

'Here, you see it?'

There was the tiniest of echoes through the long vaulting. He reached his left hand into the barrel and drew out a handful of the gritty powder within it, holding out his hand to the courtier.

The courtier looked nonplussed.

'It's decayed,' the soldier explained, as if to a child. 'If gunpowder's badly stored, or if it's stored too long, the elements disperse. If they do, it won't explode, but only burn with a fierce fire.' He looked at the cringing figure of the courtier, his face dripping with sweat. 'Fades away. Like a man with too much ale in him,' he added unnecessarily.

The courtier reached out, taking a pinch of powder between shaking finger and thumb. He looked at it, pretending to a knowledge he did not have. He had eagerly claimed to know of gunpowder, to have experience of it, seeing advancement and the favour of his master by his pretence of knowledge.

'Yes,' he muttered, 'I see. In faith, in true faith, I see.'

He looked up into the soldier's face. It was impassive, as ever. Faith, the soldier was thinking, true faith, is something you will never have.

'I shall tell my master so.'

And what is it that you see? the soldier thought. A fine new robe, perhaps, or a jewel to adorn your finger, or even a purse with thirty pieces of silver in it? Or a bucking whore beneath you in your fine bed? Whatever you see, it is not the powder thrust in your face. Nor, in mercy to your miserable little soul, do you see or even dream of the truth. Because if you even wondered at it, your soul would shrivel in the flames of Hell. He kept his thoughts silent, as always. He merely nodded. He flicked the lid back on the powder barrel with the dagger held in his right hand. He looked down at the courtier.

'I must check the other doors. Will you cover the barrel with the wood? I'll leave you the lantern.'

The courtier had no option. As he scrabbled to replace the faggots, the soldier retreated to the nearest archway, resting his body behind it. Let the popinjay put back the wood. Let him experience servitude. What matter if he did it badly? His master was hardly likely to order the cellars searched. Or at least, not yet.

3

He emerged when the scrabbling noises ceased and the courtier's shadow calmed down from its avid dance on the walls. He closed the lantern down to one shutter.

He bade the courtier farewell by the open door of the cellar, hearing him squelch, stumble and mutter his way home through the pitch-black night. He waited until the noise of his going faded into echoes and then died completely. He listened then, in total silence, for a full quarter of an hour. Not a dog howled, not a mouse stirred. There was only the thin whistle of the wind in the eaves. He was safe.

He bent down and silently inserted key into lock. He turned it, securing the house and its cellar behind him, and with the same hand drew down the last shutter on the lantern. He listened in total stillness for a further five minutes or so.

The soldier opened up his clenched left fist. A thin, sharp residue of powder lay within it, stuck to the sweat on his palm. Not decayed powder. Not separated powder. Not powder ruined by damp. Wholesome, fine-ground powder. Powder in prime condition. The best powder. Powder ready to blow to Hell or to Heaven those above it when it was lit.

Guido Fawkes, or Guy Fawkes as he was known in England, made his way silently homeward through the dark streets, allowing a rare, thin smile to cross his lips.

CHAPTER 1

Will Shadwell froze in terror. There was the noise again. Behind him, somewhere in the enveloping and impenetrable dark. He had heard it once before, a tiny crack like a twig breaking and the briefest rustling. Imagination? A cow, a sheep? Some idiot peasant's hog stirring in the field? Or men with knives destined for Will Shadwell's back, creeping up on him through the black silence?

He had trudged on, as the sun had hung like a raw orange ball over the horizon's razor edge, taking an age to set. The sense of danger, the fear, were ever present, tingling his bones. Something was wrong. He knew it.

Hot tears of self-pity welled up in him, burnt his eyes against the cold of the night. He was crouched low in a dry ditch, the dust in his nose and mouth, the debris of a country track already working its way inside his doublet and scratching against his skin. He had never felt more alone or more in terror of the nameless things hidden in the vast sweep of the flat countryside. He was holding back his breath, despite the red-hot iron bars in his chest, the impossible urge to scream and run. He had never meant to be on the road in the middle of the night. It was the horse's fault, that damned animal. He knew nothing of horses, could hardly ride. It had looked as good as any other in the dim light of the early morning, rolled its mad eyes at him like any other horse. He had thrashed it into action, hurling it towards Cambridge and the only man to whom he could turn, the panic driving him on and communicating itself to the animal beneath him. He had to see Henry Gresham. Gresham. The only man he could turn to, the only man who would know what to do with the terrible secret Will Shadwell had stumbled on, the secret he carried only in his head. The only man who might stop this terrible pursuit, take the wolves off his back.

The night spread round him, silent, still. There had been nothing now, no noise, for five minutes or more. Hope flared up in him. He knew every noise in London's mean streets, could interpret every sound. Here in the country the night spoke a different language, every sound of it in his heightened state of terror a possible death threat. Had it been some animal, treading lightly over the ground? Surely no men could be so silent. His breath was starting to come to him normally now, his heart thudding less against his eyes.

The horse had foundered outside Royston. He knew they would come after him, expected someone to notice his sudden run from London. With the horse under him he could at least match pursuit. With its useless carcass dead on the road he had had to branch off to avoid pursuit, on to the side roads and tracks. It had been a mistake, dull-faced peasants eyeing him as the only thing of interest to have passed that way in years, noting his progress and all too willing to tell it to whoever came behind. If only he could have hidden the horse, instead of leaving its lathered hide as a sign to any pursuer.

Dare he move? If there were pursuers still out there they might walk past him in his ditch. They were showing no lantern, lighting no flares, if even they existed. He knew he stank, but if they were there they had no dogs, that much he was certain of. He was lost, of course. The tracks he had taken weaved their way through the

6

Flatlands, but the stars stayed where they had always been. He reckoned he was upstream of Cambridge, knew if he kept on he would meet the slow, flat river. Gresham would be in bed now in his College rooms, simple and book-furnished for all the man's impossible wealth, a world apart from the magnificence of the house on the Strand and the whore who kept it for him. He would know what to do. Gresham always knew.

He was feeling drowsy, despite the cold that was starting to penetrate the thin, ragged cloak that was all he had time to grab when he fled London. Perhaps he would sleep here in the ditch, wait until morning . . .

He did not hear or even sense the man. He felt his hot breath against his cheek, heard the words cut through the night in his ear, had time to note the almost caressing husky tone.

'Will Shadwell . . . a fine dance you've led us.'

He screamed then, a spasm tearing through his body and hurling him up out of the ditch. He dimly saw three, perhaps four vague shapes where the night was blacker. He twisted away, felt a thorn tear at his boot and into the soft flesh above his ankle. He felt a thud in his back, was knocked forward, and looked down startled at the blade that had appeared through his flesh, just beneath his ribcage. He opened his mouth, and the warm, salty taste of his blood hit him at the same time as the tearing agony of the pain. He felt himself falling, heard rather than felt himself thud into the soft ground. Gagging, gasping, drowning in his own blood, he felt a boot kick him over. The last thing Will Shadwell saw on God's earth was the thin blade driving down towards his eye socket.

'You'll pay me the usual?' sniffed the miller, who seemed to have a permanent cold.

Henry Gresham prodded the dead face with his boot.

'I've told no-one else . . .' the miller added morosely, wiping his nose.

Gresham cut a fine figure by the riverside. Tall, strongly built, there was an inner fire in his eyes and a slight smile that suggested he found the world both ludicrous and amusing.

The body bobbed gently up and down in the tiny ripples that lapped the edge of the millpond.

'I turned 'im over for you,' the miller said, half bowing and putting his head between Gresham and the corpse, demanding attention yet being sycophantic at the same time. The drowned always lay face down, as if turning their heads from the sun for the last time. The body was swollen, white with corruption, but still recognisable.

It was Will Shadwell. A murdered Will Shadwell.

Spy, informer, double-dealer, whoremonger, pimp, thief, gambler, sodomite, drunkard, occasional follower of Satan when the money was good – and one of Gresham's best men. He had possessed no morals, and so could not be suborned by a good cause. He was utterly selfish and ruthless, and therefore a thoroughly known commodity. He was greedy beyond belief, and hence utterly reliable, provided Gresham paid him more than anyone else.

Once, in a Southwark stew, Shadwell had falsely claimed that someone else was paying him more. Gresham had nailed his hand to the table, sinking his dagger through the soft flesh of the palm he was holding out for more money.

'I've given you a good dagger as well as your gold, Master Shadwell,' Gresham had commented mildly, leaving the room with the screaming and impaled man gaping at the blood seeping into the timber. 'Come back to me when it's spent up.'

And because Shadwell was all these things and yet a coward, he had come crawling back to Gresham three weeks later. He did not lie again about how much others were paying him. He appeared to bear no grudge. Violence was nothing in his world. Mastery and power had to be proven. If proven, they were acknowledged, as much a fact of life as lechery or drunkenness. The mark of the dagger was still visible now on the puffy flesh of his right hand. It waved liked a dead weed in the water.

Now he was dead, hunted down, a town creature flushed out of its habitat and hounded to death in the broad sweep of the country-side. Even the water damage could not disguise the tears the brambles and thorn had made in what looked like a pell-mell chase. Something or someone had torn off a boot. He had been skewered from behind, enough to kill him in time. The actual killing blow, the knife thrust, had gone in through the eye socket and upwards, with so much power that it had broken through the top of the skull. It was a classic thrust, requiring pinpoint accuracy.

Gresham nodded distantly to the miller, and again to Mannion, his servant, who was behind them both. He heard the clink of money as Mannion drew a purse from his belt and started carefully to count out coins. The miller slavered over the sight, his eyes fixed on the money and his greed only thinly cloaked by a ragged air of servility.

'Thanks, master,' said the miller, who would have tugged his forelock had there been any hair left on his greasy pate. He gave a curt order to his lad, who started to drag the body out of the water. The miller was turning away to go back to the screaming wife and screaming brood who were warming up for the day in the stone-built mill when suddenly he paused. A thought must have struck him, Gresham realised, an event so rare as to stop him in his tracks. 'Why is it you're the only genl'man who pays to see corpses?' the miller asked, daringly. He sneezed, and a globule of something white shot from his nose and lay on an uncomplaining reed. Gresham turned to look at him.

'Why, a man must keep his finger on the pulse,' he replied, straight-faced, gazing down at an entirely pulse-free corpse. The miller, not surprisingly, failed to get the joke. As a trade millers were universally corrupt and oafish. All within a ten-mile radius of the city were bribed by Gresham to report any bodies in the water to him. Except babies. Gresham did not require to be shown the babies, unless, that was, they were finely dressed. The bodies always ended up in the millstream. At least Shadwell's had not been pounded to a pulp by the great paddle of the millwheel. It was no consolation to Shadwell, who was past caring.

As he went to mount the fine grey mare for the short ride back to Cambridge, Gresham halted, and went back to the corpse. Something had caught the light, glinting fitfully inside a tear in Shadwell's tattered doublet. He motioned to the miller's lad to halt his labours, and bent down to feel inside the sodden, stinking material.

A bead. A single rosary bead, from a string of such beads that sold in their thousands in Europe. A dangerous item for a man or woman to wear openly in Protestant England, where to be a Catholic was all too easily seen as being an enemy of the state. The tear in the doublet looked new enough. Had Shadwell's flailing hand caught at the rosary as he fell to the ground? Well, one thing was sure. Gresham would never find out the truth from Will Shadwell.

A thick mist still clung to the river and its banks, reaching head height in the lower meadows. The dew clung to the ground and the heady smell of wet grass was everywhere. The towers of the great King's Chapel towered above Cambridge in the distance, and the pall of smoke was already beginning to cling to the town from the early-morning fires.

Henry Gresham saw none of it. He was preoccupied with his thoughts.

Why kill Will Shadwell? He and his kind lived in a raw, violent and a brutal world, yet even there the game was usually played by certain rules. Who among the vagabonds and thieves, the beggars and the rogues, the cutpurses and the pimps he called his friends would kill him? An argument over an unpaid bill? Some story of treachery? A whore who had caught the French welcome from him, paying him back as he sweated inside her spread legs? Or some noble Lord who had attended one too many Masses or plotted once too often to restore the true faith to England? Yet for someone as base as Shadwell there was no need for high treachery to explain his death, no need even for low drama. His death could be about nothing more than a debt that had gone on too long, or simply an opportunist robbery in a dark country lane.

It was possible, simple robbery, yet it stuck in Gresham's gullet. Shadwell's killing was a professional's work. Someone had wanted Will Shadwell dead, and had been willing to follow him to Cambridge to see it done. Will had never worked in Cambridge, and had never been there long enough to make an enemy want him dead. That argued for a bigger secret than a debt or the wrong woman bedded. Had he sluiced a rich man's wife or daughter? Or had he latched on to something that the new government in London had decided should remain secret? Or was it the Catholics he had offended, the same Catholics who still carried huge power and influence for all that their faith was unfashionable?

The time was when a self-respecting assassin would never have travelled beyond Deptford. Yet these were troubled times, so early in the reign of King James I. How could they be otherwise? It was Scotland's King who now ruled England, and Scotland was England's oldest enemy. To add spice to the novel situation, the mother of the new King, Mary Queen of Scots, had been put to death on the order of the previous holder of the English crown, Queen Elizabeth, only a few years earlier. Men still alive had signed the death warrant of King James's mother. Henry Gresham had been in that business up to his neck and, in the final count, her neck as well. It was best to hope that King James had not been told of *that* side of his mother's death, for all that there had been no love lost between them.

A bird flew up from under the horse's hooves, with a sudden clatter of wings. Well trained, the mare took stock for a second of the irritating thing, decided it posed no threat and went calmly on its way. Gresham's hand, which had instinctively moved to his sword, relaxed halfway along its travel and returned to his side, his left hand continuing to take loose hold of the reins.

There had been a strange optimism two years ago when the new King had ascended the throne. It was already fraying at the edges, with mutterings in the streets and at Court. His Royal Highness's retinue of Scots Lords were as willing to take any money on offer as they were unwilling to wash, and their rapaciousness was becoming as legendary as their stench. James had offended the Puritans by having a Popish wife, and offended the Papists by declaring them excommunicate and appearing to go against his early promises of tolerance. The majority of the country, who wished nothing more than to be left in peace to procreate and earn a decent living, increasingly went in fear of a Catholic uprising, or a rebellion from the English establishment against the Scottish upstart.

Gresham almost found himself yearning for a return to the days of Good Queen Bess, the arch-bitch. Gresham had learnt the art of survival in part from her. She was an actress of unequalled power, and a ruthless whore who would have murdered her own mother without even a momentary qualm if need dictated it. She was also a Queen who would have wept bitter tears in public afterwards, whipped herself with barbs that, strange to say, seemed to leave no mark and provoked numerous plays as a result, as well as more sonnets than there was paper on which to print them. Queen Elizabeth I may have been so corrupt as to make Beelzebub turn in his grave, but somehow that corruption had never broken through the façade of the Virgin Queen, the pure preserver of the State. It had been true of her chief minister as well. Old Lord Burghley had made enough money to buy the Armada whilst producing an English fleet so decrepit that it might as well have farted as fired at the Spanish. With the Devil's own luck, the wind had farted instead, bringing Burghley the victory his ships could never have done. As one of Gresham's old informers had cheerfully stated, old Burghley may have knifed you in the back, but somehow you always felt it was being done by a gentleman. Burghley's son and successor, the wizened Robert Cecil, had a corrupted body that told all too well the tale of his corrupted soul. The double-dealing, the murders and the struggle for power might still be the same. The sense of style had gone, and there was a rawness to the brutal world of 1605 that had not been seen since Good Queen Bess had herself ascended the throne half a century ago.

Gresham's scalp itched, under his hat. He had a full head of hair, as yet not ravaged by the pox, and it was well washed. It always itched when there was trouble around. He had endured a lifetime of trouble. He neither feared nor welcomed it. It was simply a part of life, like the footpad on the road, the poison in the wine or the first spot that signified the plague. The particularly virulent itching suggested significant trouble. Well, trouble was a normal part of Gresham's life, and had been so for as long as he could remember. What was unusual was his inability to explain his chronic sense of foreboding, his inability to trace the sense of danger to its source.

It was all most irksome, and most inconvenient. Gresham flicked at his reins. The horse picked up a little speed, then deciding its rider's heart was not in it slowed down again to an easy amble. Gresham had lost a good worker in Will Shadwell. Will Shadwell had been Henry Gresham's creature. An attack on Will Shadwell was an attack on Henry Gresham, yet the reason was a mystery. Gresham did not like mysteries. They disturbed him. They cried out in the night to be explained. They threatened his survival. Survival, Henry Gresham had decided long ago, was all one had. Ruthlessness was required to survive. That, and a sense of humour, a dash of loyalty and a measure of courage.

The mystery was still crying out in his brain as he rode into the inner courtyard of Granville College. He had time still to go to his room, change from his riding clothes into suitably sombre doublet and hose and don the long gown of the MA or Master of Arts.

They gathered in the Combination Room, Gresham and the fifteen other Fellows, before going in to High Table. It was panelled, as was the Hall they were about to enter, very much in the new fashion. Gresham loved the depth of the wood, the changing pattern of its rich colour, but a part of him yearned for the ancient stone that lay behind it. The contrast of rough stone with rich hangings draped over it, hard against soft, wild colour against sombre grey, warmth against cold seemed an emblem for life. Contrast, change, the clash of ideas, these were what made Cambridge breathe and live.

'Well met, Sir Henry,' said Alan Sidesmith, the President Gresham had placed in nominal charge of the unruly crowd that went to make up Granville College. 'Was your ride restorative?' Gresham had never seen Alan Sidesmith drunk, nor ever seen him without glass or even tankard in his hand. Alan knew more of Gresham's other business than Gresham had ever told him, but Sidesmith was one of the few men in whom Gresham had complete trust.

'I've a good horse, good health and will soon have a full stomach. And it's summer in Cambridge . . . how could I not be restored?' Gresham replied lightly.

'That would depend, I suppose,' said Sidesmith equally lightly, 'whether a certain miller who sent you a message this morning was wishing to display to you his corn, or whether he had something else in mind.'

Gresham knew better than to be drawn.

'Yes,' he said, as if debating a matter of great significance, 'that would depend, wouldn't it?' He grinned at Sidesmith, who grinned back.

'Now, Sir Henry,' announced Sidesmith in a businesslike tone. 'Those newly knighted such as yourself are best placed to advise me on a tricky question of etiquette. Over *there* . . .' he pointed to a large and prosperous man whose desire to show off expensive clothes had overcome his reluctance to boil alive in the summer heat, '. . . we have a rich London merchant, a Trinity man, who wishes to transfer allegiance for his son to Granville. However, over *there*, we have a new Scottish Lord from Court who claims to have a degree from Europe. Who shall have the seat of honour on my right-hand side – Mr Money In The Bank and a good degree, or My Lord Influence At Court and probably not much else?'

14

'There is no choice, old friend,' announced Gresham. 'The Scottish Lord already smells to high heaven, whilst the merchant will take a good hour or so to do so despite all he sweats now.'

'Thank you, Sir Henry,' said Sidesmith. 'So helpful, as ever. Perhaps you would care to tell the noble Lord that he has been relegated because he stinks?' He moved off with a smile. The merchant gained the seat of honour on the President's right-hand side, the given reason being that he had his degree from Cambridge.

The great gong struck, and they processed into the Hall. Gresham's money had refounded Granville College, one of the most ancient and derelict in the University, yet he took his place on the High Table in strict order of seniority and the timing of his Fellowship, making him one of the most junior. The students in their gowns shuffled to their feet, benches scraping on the cold floor, as the President and Fellows entered. A student, a thin-faced boy with a face pockmarked from smallpox, came nervously forward, bowed to the President, and recited the long Latin grace. There was a subtle chorus of shuffling and, from somewhere among the depths of the student body, a hurriedly suppressed squeal as an arm was pinched. More bowing, and the business of the meal was allowed to continue.

Gresham's companion sniffed as he sat down.

'Out of sorts, Hugo?' asked Gresham, taking his own linen napkin from his sleeve.

The Fellow in question was a huge man, slobbering rolls of fat hanging over his neck and bulging out his thick arms into rotund sausages of flesh.

'I approve of tradition,' the man replied, grabbing at the warm bread that had already been placed on the platters in front of the Fellows. 'If three tables was good enough for this College in all its history, it's good enough for me.' He was already looking hungrily for the servant to bring in the first trenchers of food, and a glass of wine had already gone into the cavern he called his stomach.

'Ah,' said Gresham, 'but you didn't have the task of telling the eminent citizen of this town that he was good enough only for the second table, or telling that same to a man with an excellent degree who sees some jumped-up favourite of Court dining here on high.' It was an old argument, and Gresham did not offer it to convert, but merely to annoy. It worked. Hugo spluttered and sent dangerously large lumps of bread firing from his mouth across the table.

'It is a *nonsense*! A *nonsense*! I firmly believe . . .' Dinner at High Table was started, and would proceed along its normal path. Gresham had insisted that Granville College have a High Table for Fellows, guests and those with BAs and above, and the remaining tables for those studying for their first degree or those with no degree. He had proposed the abolition of the second, intermediate table to the President.

Alan Sidesmith had smiled.

'It'll cause a rumpus, you know,' he had said, with no sign that it concerned him at all. 'The young men of pleasure we seem to be receiving at this University in such large numbers will dislike a College where they can't buy their way into higher fare, and out of the company of the poor students.' Under the old system, the third table had been reserved for 'people of low condition'.

'What a great pity,' Gresham had replied. 'We'll just have to make do with taking students who wish to learn, instead of those who simply wish to play tennis, get drunk and swagger that they've done their study in Cambridge.'

'Now that would be something new,' Alan had responded, a mischievous twinkle in his eye. 'But I do hope it won't restrain you personally in pursuing those noble aims.'

In fact the young and the rich had flocked to Granville in its new foundation. Its High Table was frequently extended to several tables as it was besieged by the rich and the famous, its simple rule that no man without his Bachelor of Arts could sit there giving it an unexpected prestige. The fact that the rule had been waived

16

only once, for Her Majesty Queen Elizabeth I, had added to rather than taken away from the distinction.

The heady smell of fresh-baked bread and roast meat mingled with the sharper tang of the wine on High Table and the ale and beer cheerily being consumed by the students. Granville College ate a good dinner, the platters loaded with meat and fish and the game pies being offered first to High Table, and then taken down to vanish into the gaping mouths of the students. A senior student was reading aloud from the Bible, one of many monastic traditions the Colleges had absorbed. The difference was that whilst total silence would have greeted the reading in the monastery, here a burble of conversation was allowed to accompany it.

Hugo was denouncing the decline of logic in favour of rhetoric to his other neighbour at table. Gresham turned to the man on his left. A man after Gresham's own heart, he had been fighting for a greater musical element in the Cambridge course.

'How goes the new material?'

Edward smiled at Gresham.

'Slowly, but surely. Master Byrd presents challenges to those who try to do justice to his music.'

'Musical challenges, or other challenges?' Gresham asked innocently. William Byrd was widely believed to be a committed Papist. He had published a book of sacred songs in 1575 which had circulated among Papists and found their way into Gresham's hands, and from thence to the man who ruled over the choir of Granville College.

'Challenges of all types,' answered Edward, with no sign that he wished to relinquish any of them. 'Firstly, it's a matter of debate whether or not the songs should be performed in a chapel at all. Secondly, singing them seems tantamount to declaring an allegiance to Rome. Thirdly, it's the Devil's own job deciding if they need an organ alongside them.'

'So in summary,' Gresham answered, 'their forthcoming presence in our order of service will result in the musical director being excommunicated for singing secular work in God's chamber, burnt alive for being a Papist and beaten by the Chapel organist for doing him out of a job?'

'Sir Henry,' answered Edward with a mock bow of his head, 'how can I challenge the wit and judgement of one so distinguished?'

'Not at all, if you know what's good for you,' said Gresham cheerfully, draining his glass. He was looking forward to the performance. 'But I wonder you bother with that music. There must be easier pieces.'

'When I meet music in which I hear God's hand,' said Edward sombrely, 'I'll risk the judgement of God's emissaries on earth to hear it played.'

There would be another stir when Edward believed he had the music to his standard, and allowed it to be sung. Accusations would fly back and forth, perhaps even the odd pate would be broken. Gresham ran his eye over the Fellowship of Granville College. One Fellow was a sodomite, making a play at every pretty boy who joined the College. Two others were bedding every serving girl who offered herself. Times being hard, there was no shortage of offers of either kind. Another had the pox, and had been seeing a local quack to little effect. Dipping the genitals in a mess of white vinegar was one of the least painful remedies, and the Fellow in question had been coming to dine for weeks smelling like a barrel of wine that had been allowed to go off in the sun. The newest Fellow was involved in a ruinous lawsuit, chasing an inheritance that an older brother would grab, at dreadful cost to the younger sibling. Two of them were Catholics to the core, two of them fierce Puritans. They sat at opposite ends of the table, and a pair of them had nearly come to blows in a recent public debate.

Opposites attract, thought Henry Gresham, and from the clash of opposites comes new ideas. He gazed contentedly, as much as his restless spirit could ever be content, over his High Table and the college he had refounded. He had no children that he knew of. He seemed destined to be barren. In the meantime, the 135 students and Fellows made a contented burbling noise in the Hall Gresham had built. It could hold two hundred with ease, and would do so before too long. His children? Possibly. His Foundation? Certainly.

The meal over, he had two reasons to retire to his rooms. The first was a letter written in his best handwriting, a letter which had been returned to him a few days previously by a man called Tom Barnes. Its style was faultless, and Gresham could only marvel at the sharp logic and intelligence that shone through the written words. There were only two problems with the letter. Firstly, Gresham had never written it, despite what seemed to be his handwriting and signature, and secondly, its content was sufficient to have him hung, drawn and quartered were it ever to reach any member of the Government. There could be many reasons for the existence of such a forgery, and Gresham needed time at least to eliminate from his mind some of the least likely. When that reading was over, he had his copy of the English translation of Machiavelli's *The Prince*, obtained from St Paul's for a King's ransom on his last visit to London. He had read it in the original Italian, of course. He was fascinated to compare the original with the translation. It was not to be.

The knock on the door was loud, insistent. Gresham slipped the letter through the gap in the floorboards beneath his feet, and shouted for the visitor to enter.

The courier stank of horse piss and sweat. He had arrived long after supper, his leathers stained with mud up to his armpits. Cambridge was at its most dank and dark, the Fenland mist swirling round the gates of the Colleges like a miasma of plague, waiting to strike. The feeble flicker of candle from the latticed and barred windows in the inner court hardly dented the blackness. The courier had arrived after nightfall. Every tongue would wag in the morning. Gresham called away 'On His Majesty's business', again. Some would snigger, nod knowingly, and gaze down in their tankards as he strode past to his place at table in the morning.

The Porter ushered the courier into Gresham's rooms. They were on the first stairway, built in the fourteenth century. He was Cecil's man, of course, and exuded a sense of menace. Silently he handed a package to Gresham. The Porter hovered over his shoulder, drunk, inquisitive.

'Time you kept your watch, old Walter,' said Gresham to the grizzled old man. 'Who knows how many fresh young virgins are queuing by your gate to test if men are like wine, better when they're old?'

Old Walter grinned, and clumped down the stairs. Gresham could just as easily have kicked him down the stairs, or snarled at him to mind his own damned business. As it was, Gresham saw nothing but an accident of birth in their different station in life. He treated Walter as he treated all people. God persistently refused to treat all people as equal until they proved otherwise, but that was no reason for Gresham to follow suit. As a by-product, old Walter would continue to tell Gresham everything that went on in the College. As far as most of the Fellows and the students were concerned, old Walter, the drunken sot, was invisible. Gresham had been using his sharp eyes and ears for years.

Gresham did not need to ask who the letter was from. There were only a small number of men in England who had couriers willing to ride through the night. The seal on the letter was far more ornate than the content. Come to London. Immediately. No formal greeting, no 'To that most beloved servant, Sir Henry Gresham . . .' Merely a blunt message. Come. Come now.

Gresham sighed. He sighed again as he turned to his purse, took out a small coin, remembered the courier, and chose a larger one. It was accepted. Without thanks, but with the merest nod of the head.

'Tell him yes. Soon.'

The courier nodded again. It was all that was necessary.

Cambridge was a haven. Its conflicts were explicable, its double- and triple-dealing following a strange local logic. True, its townspeople were low and squat, hating the University that gave them their living. A riot was never far away, which was why the Colleges were built like domestic castles, facing inwards into their courts and quadrangles and with a towered Lodge as their entrance. Yet the sense of power those buildings gave was illusory. The power in London was the power of life and, more frequently, death. The power in England was very simple, for all the puffed-out vainglory of the Cambridge Fellows. England's power was the power of the Court, nowadays the Court of King James I of England, erstwhile King James VI of Scotland.

So now Henry Gresham would have to drag himself out of the parochial world of Cambridge, back to the dark, brutal and blasphemous underworld of London, a world only recently rid of yet another outbreak of the plague.

He was rather looking forward to it.

Jack Wright sat in the darkest corner of the room, pushing the remnants of his meal idly around the edge of the wooden platter. The air in the room was greasy, stale. There were eight of them in all, in a room that would have more easily coped with four or five. The Catherine Wheel in Oxford had been chosen for recruiting the newest conspirators. It was safer than London, and Oxford was less full of Government spies than Cambridge. It was as safe as anywhere for a group of men for whom life would never be safe again. Jack could not stop himself looking nervously at the door every minute or so. He saw in his mind the soldiers bursting through it, the yelled commands, the kiss of iron round his wrists as he was led away. He shook his head, as if to clear it of the image. His nervous glance returned to the door. Part of him was trying to listen to his friend, but he had learnt at times to let the impassioned words of Robert Catesby flow over him, as unmarked as a stone in the river with the clear water washing over it.

John Wright, or Jack as he had been known since his early childhood, had taken his usual seat at the back of the room. He was a stocky figure, his apparent heaviness deceptive. His sword arm was lightning fast, his agility with a blade in his hand legendary. It was a skill he had tried to use much less since God had called to him and he had answered. Would that his mouth had the same skill as his arm. It was not that he lacked thoughts or ideas, but somehow the link between brain and mouth had eluded him all his life. For years he had felt the frustration of hearing the nonsense others talked, seen the strike of wit that won the applause and the adulation, felt the ideas seething in his head but stumbled at the final hurdle of their expression. As a child he had been laughed at and mocked when the few words he could muster had tumbled out and dried up, like an empty barrel with a hole knocked in it. That was where he had learnt his agility, turning to his fists in those days to make sure that his school fellows paid his body the respect they would not give his words.

He had known Catesby casually for years, in the way that all the sons of the oppressed Catholic families banded together and knew each other. They had attended a Mass together, in the small hours of the night when the fewest servants would see and hear and the risk was reduced. The priest had been impassioned, the liturgy powerful beyond faith. Afterwards, Jack Wright had been moved to tears, and Catesby had turned to meet him.

'It's a thing to die for, isn't it, as Our Saviour was willing to die?' he had said, a fierce light in his eyes.

'It is . . .' Jack Wright had started to say, wanted to say that it was more than life, that it was the source of life, a faith and a beauty so poignant yet so tragic . . . but the words had dried up, as they always did, and the red flush of embarrassment crept up on his face as his eyes dropped.

He felt Catesby's hand on his shoulder.

'We don't need words, do we? The words have been written for us. But we know the beauty. We of all people know the terrible beauty. To feel is enough, isn't it?'

Jack Wright looked up. Was it his imagination that a light pulsed from Robert Catesby's eyes? As if a tide of lovingly warm water had been released to sluice through his mind, the tears came to Jack's

22

own eyes. Here was a man who knew, who understood. Here was a man who needed no words. From that moment in a cold chapel was the bond struck between Robert Catesby and Jack Wright.

Catesby's personality shone like a second sun, filling every corner of the tavern's room.

'Men have a *right*, a *right* given by God and by nature to defend their own lives and freedom, a right that no earthly power can take away,' he was arguing passionately, the light of martyrdom in his eyes, thumping the table for effect. 'We Catholics in England are mere *slaves*.' He dwelt on the word, drawing it out in all its shame. '*Lower even than slaves*. We're free men, yet we allow our lives and our freedoms to be removed without law, without reason and without authority. Our very life, our vigour, is being sapped by this passive resistance, this feebleness, this palsy of fear and cowardice that's all we seem able to muster in the face of persecution. We're the laughing stock of Europe: despaired of by our friends, and despised by our enemies as God's lunatics!'

Despite the familiarity, the power of Catesby's personality tugged at Jack Wright's soul. When Catesby talked to you, you felt that you were, for him, the most important person in the world. Catesby could reach into men's souls. His audience stared in rapt silence, almost adoration, as he reviled the King, whipping them up into a frenzy of self-justifying anger against the monarch and Robert Cecil, his Chief Minister. It was a brilliant performance. Jack had seen it many times, yet still it held a measure of magic even for his cynical eyes and ears. For a moment, for all of them, the fear retreated, the gnawing, bitter fear that governed their every step, their every breath.

'And is there hope? *No!*' Catesby spat out the negative, as if it were a red-hot pip from a sour cherry he had just eaten. 'With Robert Cecil pouring poison into the ear of the monarch, turning his eagerness into hate? *There is no hope unless we ourselves create that hope!*'

King James had seemed well-intentioned to the Catholic cause before his accession, and his wife was known to be Catholic. Cecil, the King's Chief Secretary, was widely credited with turning the mind of the King against English papists whilst at the same time toadying up to the Spaniards.

They needed some of Catesby's magic. At the mere thought of the tunnel Wright's flesh began to crawl and a spasm ran through his muscles. It had seemed easy enough. Hire the house, dig through until they were under the House of Lords, plant the powder. Yet before they were six feet into the tunnel they were gagging for air, their sweat turning the loose earth beneath them into greasy, salty mud. There was hardly room to move, the candle guttered and died in the rancid air and terror closed in with the darkness. The arm with the pick or shovel could only move back so far, the picking at the tunnel face tearing the same muscles time after time, reducing them to red-hot strings of pain. Their beards, hair and mouths became encrusted, unwashable, the dirt pitted into the skin. They felt the dust coat the inside of their lungs, their breath foul for hours afterwards, their racking coughs depositing a scummy yellow layer like vomit. They had reached the foundations after a lifetime of effort, half mad with the pain of their bodies, half mad with the thought of the soft, suffocating fall of earth and a hidden, slow and secret death. The ancient stone had seemed to bounce their feeble blows off its surface. They were tired, all of them. In time they would need money, horses, weapons, armour. Now their greatest need was for more brute strength and muscle. The two new conspirators would give them that at least.

Catesby finished his oration with a final flourish, and sat down, draining the tankard to its dregs in one huge gulp. Catesby did everything, from talking to drinking, as if he had half an hour of life left to him, and had to cram a lifetime's experience into a few minutes. He was a meteor in a dark sky. Jack could not help wonder how long that meteor would sustain its light, before it crashed to earth.

'Well spoken, Robin,' Jack said, going up to Catesby and taking his hand. Catesby had slumped down on a stool, as he sometimes did after one of his orations, as if his job was now done and the effort of speaking had drained him of his life force.

Catesby glanced up at his old friend, and smiled. It was a smile of total warmth that lit up Jack Wright's soul.

'I hope it was well spoken. But it's more than words we need now, Jack, much more than words.'

'We have a plan, don't we?'

'We do indeed,' replied Catesby. 'And there'll be those who'll seek to stop that plan before its rightful conclusion. They must be stopped, Jack. Stamped out like vermin . . .'

It was easy in talk to make a death seem nothing more than stamping on an insect. It was different when you forced the steel into the soft flesh, heard the shriek of pain, felt a man's dying breath on your face, saw the light fade from his eyes.

Wright shook the new recruits, Wintour and Grant, by the hand, and made his apologies. Both men were well-dressed, obviously prosperous, but both looked dour, old before their time. Jack hoped their muscles were more vigorous than their manner. The presence of the priest, with all the makings of a Mass, made him nervous. They were hunted men, these priests, hiding from one house to another, facing the rack and their innards ripped out if they were discovered, and bringing the same threat to those who hid them.

He slunk out into the late afternoon, feeling the bite of the wind on his flesh through the loose cloak, hand comforted by resting on the hilt of his sword. It would be more than the bite of wind he would feel if they all played the wrong hand in this particular game of cards.

CHAPTER 2

How could you live and not be excited by London?

It was eternal damnation, a smoke-filled Hell and a cauldron for the plague. And it was deliriously, amazingly and ecstatically exciting. The stench of the shite on the streets and the heavenly smell of a fresh-baked loaf. The waft of the wind bringing the sweet-fresh smell of meadows from outside the city boundaries, and the stink of the open sewer they called the Thames. Everywhere people screaming their wares, a city turned into a multitude of salesmen. A heaving, sweating multi-coloured multitude with their feet in mud and their eyes raised towards the stars. It was a raw, violent and often brutal melting pot, but with all the filth and the putrid vapours of too many people and animals crowded on top of one another came an unequalled excitement. The city had grown in recent years out of all control, the higgle-piggle of streets growing more dense and narrow by the week, spilling out beyond the old walls. Yelling builders and ramshackle scaffolding seemed to clog the routes, fighting with the men, the women and the horses, the sheep and cattle on their way to slaughter, and the open-eyed yokels so busy looking up that they could not see the midden at their feet.

For all the excitement, a nagging question bit at the mind of Henry Gresham. Why was he here? It was not his time to be in London. Yet he had answered the summons, knowing he had no choice.

He had ridden hard. He was a very rich man whose wealth was spent very carefully. One of its objects was horseflesh. Another was Mannion. Mannion, good soldier that he had been, oversaw the stables between Cambridge and London that kept a good horse on permanent standby for Henry Gresham. Mannion also kept an eye on the men who would take Gresham's windblown mount from him, wash it down and give it the love that Gresham, already on his next mount, could not.

He need not have hurried so. Robert Cecil, Viscount Cranborne, soon to be Earl of Salisbury and the youngest man ever to be sworn in as a Privy Councillor, would have waited. As the inheritor of Europe's largest and most efficient network of spies and informers, Cecil spent his life waiting, like a spider at the centre of his web, and watching.

Yet riding as if life depended on it, feeling the rush of wind through his hair, knocking the startled farm traffic aside, the pounding of the horse beneath him on the rough tracks . . . this was life itself, this was oblivion and fulfilment all in the one moment. Cecil could control elements of Gresham's life. No-one could control that wild, rough ride to London.

Previous meetings between Gresham and Robert Cecil's kind had resulted directly or indirectly in Henry Gresham being shot at or lunged at with sharp metal on innumerable occasions, seriously wounded on two occasions and shipwrecked, mercifully only once, on the wild Irish coast. Cecil's instructions had also resulted in Gresham being sentenced to be hung (twice), sentenced to be hung, drawn and quartered (once) and, on another memorable occasion, actually being roped to the rack in the Tower of London.

Yet Gresham kept coming back.

How on earth had he got himself involved in this lunatic world where power was the only morality, and where nothing was as it seemed? It was as if it had been that way for ever, from the moment when as little more than an overgrown boy he had been dragged in to play such a deciding role in the tragedy of Mary Queen of Scots. He had made no conscious choice to become involved. In Gresham's experience, Fate did not consult with humans before deciding the course of their lives, or if they were to have life at all. Falling initially in the way of the Queen's spymaster, old Sir Francis Walsingham, Gresham had increasingly found himself taking his orders from Robert Cecil, the self-appointed heir apparent to Walsingham's vast complex of spies, agents and informers. Gresham and Cecil had loathed each other from the first moment of their meeting. Yet the danger, the excitement and the risk were a heady mixture, and Gresham had carried on, playing the great game until it had seemed that he had pushed his life to the edge and that by then he owed God a death. Then Cecil had summoned him, years ago, wanting him to go on some pitiful and dreary expedition to see informers in Spain. Gresham had refused. Cecil had looked at him, and drawn out of a wallet a piece of writing, carefully copied in a clerk's hand.

'You might care to read this, Master Gresham, before you make any final decision regarding your acceptance of my request.'

Cecil was cool, calm, measured as he always was.

Gresham read it. In a lesser man the colour would have drained from his face and the hand reading the paper shaken. Instead Gresham made himself read it once, twice and a third time, his hand rock steady.

'Yes?' he had said, gazing calmly, matter-of-factly into Cecil's eyes, revealing none of his inner sickness.

Cecil had stolen Walsingham's papers, the complete record of his spy network. Somewhere in those papers had been details of the affair that had blighted Gresham's life, the only thing he had done of which he was ashamed. Cecil had found it out. It was there, written in a neat hand on the paper.

'It would be a pity if this paper were to become known, would it not?' asked Cecil, in a silky voice. 'Known to a wider public, I mean.'

'Why, sir,' Gresham replied, no sign of his fear in his voice, 'the truth will always out. The Bible tells us so, does it not? And what is one man's vanity and reputation against the call of truth?'

'Will it suit you to go to Spain, Master Gresham, as I have asked?' Was there the tiniest hesitation in Cecil's voice, along with the aggression?

It was a deciding moment, Gresham knew. If he conceded the power of Cecil's paper against him now and obeyed, he would never be his own master again. Yet if he resisted, Cecil could provoke his ruin. It was folly to resist, madness. And so because he was who he was, he chose to fight.

'No, my Lord, I cannot go.' *Cannot*, he was careful to say. 'Cannot', not 'will not'. 'I have the strongest personal reasons for requiring to be here in England at the moment. Of course, were the matter more urgent, or were your Lordship's life to depend on it, then I would go at your Lordship's command, without hesitation. I ask to be relieved of this duty, by your gracious mercy.'

By your gracious mercy. That made it Cecil's decision to absolve him from the mission, a favour granted from on high. Yet it also meant that he, Gresham, had not bowed to pressure, had not given in to blackmail.

Gresham carefully took the paper and placed it on the table, among the mass of papers that always surrounded Cecil, midway between them. He had given a form of words that allowed Cecil to save face. Would he take it?

There was a long silence.

Genuine thought, Gresham wondered, or enjoyment of the pain he knew he must be inflicting, for all the calm of the young man before him?

Cecil finally moved, taking the piece of paper carefully with forefinger and thumb, as if it was something faintly distasteful.

'A pity, sir. You would have been an excellent choice. Yet there will be other opportunities, that I do not doubt. Ones you will be more advised to accept, as I choose to exercise my "gracious mercy". As you so gallantly describe it.'

'Your Lordship is indeed most merciful,' replied Gresham, and seeing the expression in Cecil's eyes of the hawk looking down on the mouse, 'most merciful.'

Gresham had not won a victory, that much he knew. The sword was poised, hung over his head, not back in its scabbard. He had merely negotiated an armed truce, and risked being played with by Cecil, as a boy tortures a fly. So Gresham had accepted with enthusiasm several other requests from Cecil, all of them dangerous. As he had done so he had made notes not only of those missions with Cecil, but of his involvement going back years to the days of Walsingham.

The climax had come with the Essex rebellion. Cecil had a habit of triumphing over those apparently better suited than he for survival. For years he had been locked in mortal combat with the dashing and handsome Robert Devereux, second Earl of Essex. Essex had the ancient lineage, the charm and the body that had bowled over every woman at Court, including the Queen. It had done him no good. Cecil's wits, the animal and immoral way in which he fought, had overcome his rival, as they overcame all rivals. The idiotic, ill-fated Essex rebellion had sent Essex to the block, leaving Cecil in total power at Court. Essex's head was still there, picked bare, on London Bridge. There was only one Robert now. Robert Cecil.

The walls of London were ahead of him, and Gresham eased his pace as more and more people appeared on the roadway. He grinned inwardly as he remembered his own decisive part in the Essex rebellion – or, rather, the decisive role he had played in making sure that the so-called rebellion never even spluttered into danger, but fizzled out with hardly more noise than a musket shot. It had made interesting reading, when he had written it down and had it copied, and if Gresham's version had become known he felt it likely that Cecil's thin head might be joining Essex's on a pike. It had been one of his better moments when he had presented a copy, the true account of the Essex rebellion with proof of Cecil's treachery, to Cecil himself. He had trumped it, if it needed doing, by the casual mention of the fact that copies of that and numerous other papers, as well as being lodged in a variety of secret places dotted around England, could also be found in the Papal archive. They were to be held in secret until removed by Gresham himself, their early release authorised only if Gresham were to die. Cecil blanched at that, showing emotion for almost the first time since Gresham had known him. The cellars below the Vatican were one of the very few areas Robert Cecil knew he would never penetrate, and there was a delicious touch of spice in the business by virtue of the fact both men knew that Gresham's access to this unique repository of documents had come through his having done some of Cecil's dirty work in Italy. It was poetic justice.

There was another reason for Gresham's hatred of Cecil, if another was needed. Two years ago Cecil had testified against and betrayed the friendship of the one man Henry Gresham had ever called master. Sir Walter Raleigh was the greatest man Gresham had ever known, a scholar poet, soldier, sailor, courtier and wit. He had saved Gresham's life. When the great wheel of fortune had seemed destined to plunge Raleigh down to the depths, and he had looked to his friends to rescue him from the sucking bog of Court politics, Cecil had betrayed him. Raleigh had been convicted on a trumped-up charge in a court hearing so biased it had shocked Europe. Now Raleigh, larger than life and leader of leaders, was languishing and ague-ridden in the Tower. Raleigh's wife had helped bring up Cecil's ailing child, taking him in alongside her own lusty, bawling brat and seeming to breathe life into his thin frame. This was how Cecil rewarded those who preserved his life blood, by imprisoning them in the Bloody Tower. Gresham could understand a man who betrayed his principles. He could never forgive a man who betrayed his friends.

The towers and roofs of Whitehall Palace were ahead of him

now. Whitehall was Cecil's home, its labyrinthine passages an emblem for the devious and complex mind that dominated the Court more than any other. This was the moment of calm before the storm, the moment before a great venture when time froze and the last chance to turn away beckoned. Gresham's horse had come to a halt. Gently, he urged it forward. In an uncertain world, Gresham knew only two things. He despised Cecil, and whatever task Cecil had for him would bring grief and hardship in its trail. He also knew that he could not refuse the excitement of what Cecil might offer, or run too freely the risk of what he might reveal.

A surly groom took his horse, and Gresham stretched his muscles as he stood on the cobbled courtyard. Gresham was sure it was going to be Catholics this time round. He dreaded Catholics. They were what he did least well. The woman who had brought him up, raised the bastard son of Sir Thomas Gresham, was a Catholic. With her breast milk had come the rosary bouncing off his infant nose. He hated the Catholic business more than any other. The Marlowe business, the Essex rebellion, that tragic creature Mary and most of all his dealings with the Armada had seemed real. His dealings with the Catholics had seemed sad by comparison. Early on in his accidental career he had met a Catholic priest who had seemed to him the nearest thing to a saint on this earth that he would ever know. Months later he had watched that saint hung until near gasping dead, seen his heart cut out of his body and that long-suffering and frail body chopped into four pieces. To Gresham, who was no longer sure that there was a God, the shrieks a man uttered in his death throes were a single language, spoken alike among Roman or Protestant. The mutilation of human flesh in one cause or another seemed just another form of human sacrifice, the practice so widely condemned by Christianity.

Cecil was courteous, as ever. Grey-haired, the rich clothing he wore could only partially hide the deformity in his spine. His desk was littered with papers, and the paintings on the wall showed both his passion for art and his ability to pay for the best.

'Good morning to you, sir,' he had intoned, motioning Gresham to a stool.

The voice was flat, expressionless. The eyes were gimlet-hard, like a rat's. Cecil had a thin, mean figure, and a thin, mean face. His long cloak hid the ludicrously short legs that were such a joke in the marketplaces. There were many who saw a warped body as testimony to a warped mind. How right they were, thought Gresham, who had met many with both afflictions but never anyone who combined them to such effect as Robert Cecil. He moved in a manner that gave least cause to show the wrench in his neck, hidden by an exceptionally large collar on the cloak and an extravagant ruff. He seemed permanently cold, yet he met his network of spies in the largest and coldest room in his Palace. A huge, carved stone fireplace held the most meagre of fires, spluttering to cope with the cheapest of sea coal in the early morning and producing far more smoke than heat.

'How go your affairs in Cambridge?' enquired Cecil solicitously.

'Well, my Lord,' replied Gresham, outwardly deferential and inwardly impatient for the fencing to end. 'The College grows by the month.' Cecil was Chancellor of the University; another power base.

'So good to hear!' mused Cecil with total insincerity, pouring wine into a goblet and pushing it across the table to Gresham. The goblet was gold. It shone forth in this dreary room like sunshine after rain. The wine was cat's piss. Cecil only spent money on things that lasted, like the goblet or fine paintings. On something like the wine, that would be urine in a matter of hours, he spent as little as possible.

Gresham smiled, took the goblet and raised it in a toast. In doing so, he sniffed the wine, and without his smile shifting at all put the goblet down in front of him, its contents untasted. They would remain so throughout the meeting. Even a badly brought-up dose of the pox would have revolted had the liquid in the glass been poured over it.

Cecil's expression did not change, though he certainly noted the rejected goblet. He sat back in his splendid chair, gazing out through the narrow window with its view of the river. His guest sat on a bare, three-legged stool, with one leg shorter than the others. It was all there was to sit on, except the near-throne in which Cecil sat upright.

'We live in wicked times, Sir Henry. Wicked times.' Cecil sighed. There was no goblet or wine for him. In all their meetings Henry Gresham had never seen food or drink pass Cecil's lips.

Well, mused Gresham, you should know, as having created no small measure of that wickedness yourself.

'There are those in our midst who seek to deny the most basic, the most central commandments of Our Lord. Those who seek to do so whilst holding positions of very real power. Wicked men, Sir Henry. Truly evil men. Do you not agree?'

Catholics. It had to be Catholics. Damn, Gresham thought, anything but Catholics.

'You know of Sir Francis Bacon, I believe?' Cecil enquired, responding to Gresham's silence, leaning forward. It was his most beguiling gesture. In leaning forward the collar of his cloak drooped and the ruff dropped slightly, revealing his warped neck. 'Indeed, I think you have dined with him?'

Bacon? Bacon? Gresham's mind, behind its public mask and the half-smile, was in a turmoil. Bacon had been accused of most things, except being a Papist. Bacon's intelligence was matched only by his ambition. He had spent a lifetime trying to get inside the Queen's linen and was now trying to get inside the King's. Gresham hoped it was cleaner than the outside of the monarch. Bacon was just another man of talent trying to compensate for a lack of birth, driven by the same ambition that drove all those who came to Court. What had Bacon to do with the state of the nation?

'He has been to College, my Lord,' Gresham replied light-heartedly. 'He talks well,' he added dismissively. Let Cecil make the running.

'It is not his talk that concerns me, Sir Henry,' replied Cecil. He was sitting back now, ready to launch the blow.

'It is his sodomy.'

Gresham's face did not flicker. His expression did not falter. His pulse missed not a beat. He held down a massive urge to burst out laughing.

'Is it proven, my Lord?' enquired Gresham, his expression serious.

'No,' replied Cecil, looking coldly at Gresham. 'It is not. Yet if it is true, I must have it proven. I believe you to be the man to find such proof.'

Sodomy was a capital offence, certainly. The growing band of Puritans shouted the evils of fornication at an increasing number of street corners, to the hilarity and amusement of the populace. When they denounced the double sin of sodomy, the crowds ceased their laughter and joined in the shouting. Yet more and more the fashionable end of society was turning to experiment, be it with the new weed tobacco, strange concoctions of wine and herbs or the practice of sex. Sodomy was ill-advised. It was hardly the stuff of which the survival of nations was composed.

'I hope, my Lord,' responded Gresham carefully, 'that I have some experience of finding proof. Yet are you not better advised to set one of similar inclination on to this project? Why not set a thief to catch a thief? Am I to believe this is an urgent matter?'

'You might consider my example, Sir Henry. I *believe* very little.' Cecil's eyes bored into Gresham. Gresham did not flinch, the infuriating half-smile still on his lips. 'I *observe* a great deal. I merely use that which I have.'

Touché, thought Gresham. Or if not that, stalemate.

All in all, it left them in their usual state of even balance. Both despised each other, yet had need of what each other had to offer. Each one could destroy the other, but knew the destruction was likely to be mutual. In that room Gresham was in the presence of raw power, pure and simple, and Henry Gresham could not resist the taste and smell of it.

Yet to be set on to determine the destination of Bacon's prick? After a frantic summons to travel without delay and post-haste to London? Bacon was fiercely ambitious. That much was widely known. He was in debt. That was also widely known. And most known of all was the fact that he had one of the best brains in Christendom. He was related to Cecil, but the relationship, complicated by too many embattled women, had not been easy. It was also rumoured that, in common with Kit Marlowe – an earlier tragedy – he thought those 'who liked not boys were fools'. It was all good stuff for gossip in the ordinary and the tavern, but even if Bacon was proven to have buggered every boy in Europe it would hardly set England tottering on its constitutional heels. Essex had been Bacon's patron, of course, before Bacon had turned against him and even helped in his prosecution. Was this Cecil paying back an old debt, slowly destroying the last vestiges of those who had supported his old enemy Essex?

His scalp started to itch unbearably, even though he would swear no flea had made its entry to his head. He refused the overwhelming urge to scratch his itch.

'I will do as you ask, my Lord,' said Gresham calmly. 'It is *my* choice to do so.' Their eyes locked for a brief, fiery clash, and then both went dark. 'Yet I think there are greater issues than one man's buggery, in the present times.'

Cecil mouthed an insincere farewell, failing to rise to show Gresham to the door. There had to be a deeper reason for all this, thought Gresham as he left. At a guess, Bacon had offended Cecil, or was coming to be seen as a threat to Cecil's power in some way. This had to be personal. Would Gresham help destroy the man if it were so? He would see. He had felt no compunction working against Essex and bringing him down, not least of all because he saw Essex as both a threat to the nation and a lifelong enemy of Sir Walter Raleigh. If Bacon seemed a fly not worth the squashing, Gresham would leave him in peace and return an infuriatingly bland report to Cecil.

A servant appeared from nowhere and held open the carved and varnished door. As he passed through Gresham felt a distinct increase in temperature. Was it the room? Or was any room occupied by Robert Cecil colder and darker by virtue of its occupant?

'God's blood!' yelled the informer.

The cheap red wine had spilled out of his mouth and across one of the weeping ulcers that ringed his lips.

If Gresham was disturbed by the blasphemy, he did not show it. He leant casually back in his chair and motioned invitingly to the jug and the man's half-empty tankard. He carefully laid his arm in between some of the more poisonous stains on the table and gazed at the half-drunk informer.

'So *have* you news of Bacon's household?' asked Gresham patiently. Gresham's enquiries after Bacon had coursed out through the underworld of London. This was the latest lead that had emerged from its sewers.

The informer grunted, reached for the jug and poured himself a life-threatening dose of vinegar. He drew back on it, careful this time to make no spillage. He made as if to wipe his lips, remembered in time the damaged flesh thereabouts, and poked out instead a thick red tongue to gather up the residue.

'Yes, I do. Truthfully, I do. The little man has . . . visitors. *Young* visitors.'

The conspiratorial tone he sought to adopt was spoilt somewhat by the vast belch of foul breath that ended his sentence. The explosion of air seemed to rock him back, like a loose-shotted cannon.

Little man? Sir Francis Bacon was not particularly short, though certainly no giant. Those who envied the size and scope of his brain tended to vilify his build, as if the latter reflected the former. It was a common mistake of the time. If it had been true, the pathetic stunted and warped figure of Robert Cecil would not contain the most powerful brain in the country.

'The names of these young visitors?'

The informer's eyes were still glazed with the shock of his own eruption. God forbid he might fart next, thought Gresham. If he did it was likely to have lumps in it.

'Names? Names?' The man took another swig. 'These things have no names. They're sweepings, sweepings. Bastards taken at birth from a whore's bed, or saved from the river.'

The brown and swirling waters of the Thames bore a frequent cargo of new- or still-born children. They were meant to be from the loins of the whores who had matched London's stupendous growth. Gresham cared not to think how many well-born casement windows had seen a private cargo despatched into the waters of Lethe. All new-born appeared alike when swelled by their feast of filthy river water.

'If not names, then witnesses. Who witnesses this nightly progress?'

The informer allowed an expression of alarm to cross his eyes and ravaged face. He took another half-swig, his moderation reflecting a new sense of danger.

'Why, the servants, of course. All the servants.'

'And the Gateman will testify to this? The other servants will testify?'

'Why . . . why . . . they may, of course. Of course they may.'

Gresham's voice was at its most silky soft. He placed his other arm between a stain that might have been blood and one that was certainly grease, and leant forward.

'Without testimony those visitors are phantoms, just ghosts upon the wind.'

His voice turned from summer sun to the glint of blade in passageway.

'As you, my friend, are so much piss and wind.'

He came to his feet. He was an impressive figure, five foot eight or so and with an easy muscle rippling below the superbly tailored doublet, hose and cloak.

His figure, clothed all in black, loomed over the informer like Death himself. And now the voice became ice, cold beyond belief. It froze the informer, even as it released him. As Gresham spoke, he heard the tinkle of urine falling to the floor from the terrified man, smelt the hot, raw stink of steaming piss.

'You will return here, a fortnight from now. You will bring names, names of young sodomites or names of servants who will testify against their master. Or you will bring nothing. On what you bring you will be judged. Leave. Now.'

Gresham sank back in his chair, a black mood of despair threatening to overwhelm him. The informant, humiliated by his wetting himself and terrified beyond belief, fled, muttering incoherently.

This was going nowhere, Gresham thought. I am facing a man of unbounded intelligence, and all I have to question is fools.

'More work for the laundress.' The gruff voice was Mannion's. Built like a Cathedral, he had stationed himself just outside the door, opening it to let the informer out and himself in.

'More work for the chambermaid,' muttered Gresham, nodding to the steaming yellow pool on the floor beneath the table. He doubted she or the landlord would bother. The floor had seen much worse. There was a virtual history of London drunkenness etched on to the worn boards.

Mannion waited. If his master wished to talk, he would do so. Mannion would listen. Sometimes his master needed to talk and hear no reply. Sometimes he spoke and needed to debate. Mannion would respond, in kind. He would know which it was and, if it seemed proper to do so, would speak.

There was silence, Gresham sipping thoughtfully at his own goblet. As ever he had made sure he had his own wine, not the spew served to the informer. It was the best the inn had to offer, which was not very much. Like much of the City, it was brash, and new and quite raw, and like the City it had a taste of something much older, something sweetly rotten, beneath it.

So there was to be no talking, Mannion reflected. So be it.

'Shame about the candles,' Mannion muttered as they left the room. Gresham had left them burning, most of them not yet half done. The landlord would gratefully snuff them out and use the remaining half, charging Gresham for the whole candle. Gresham did not respond. It was an old joke.

It had been years ago. They had just started campaigning after a dreadful winter. The canvas of the tent had seemed as if it was just drying out, in the rare sun of a Flanders spring. The soldiers had come in silent, angry. Usually an action cleared the blood, exhilarated them. This time the pathetic Spaniard in charge of the troop had not only been concealing the gold they had been sent to rob, but concealing his wife. She was a pretty girl, not yet nineteen years of age. Hidden in a baggage cart, they would probably have left her, heavily pregnant as she was, if they had found her. Even a scream would have caused a laugh and no more. It was early in the campaigning year, they were fat with an idle winter and there were no grudges to pay back as yet. Instead she had climbed out of her hiding place silently, seeking to rush out of the wagon and into the shrubbery surrounding the ambush. The youngest recruit had heard the rustle of clothing behind him and swung round with sword outstretched. His mother had obtained the sword for him. God knew – or so Gresham hoped – how the Toledo steel of a Spanish grandee had found its way into the hands of a woman who had proudly borne six fiercely Protestant sons in an East Anglian farmhouse. The sword was sharp as a razor, despite the youngest son's crude attempts at sharpening it. Its curving arc, powered by all the untrained force of a healthy and terrified eighteen-year-old, had sliced neatly through the stomach of the pregnant woman.

It had also sliced into the unborn boy, so that it was bleeding to death even as it flopped to the ground. It had an audience fitting for such an end in Flanders mud. Its mother saw it bleed to death in front of her, as her frighteningly red hands clawed at her own gut. So did its father and its murderer, and an assorted troop of Protestant and Catholic mercenaries and volunteers.

The young man skewered himself on the sword his mother had given him. He did it badly, of course. He would take days to die as the horrific wound in his belly and bowel suppurated and led to its inevitable conclusion. The problem was, he would scream.

So they came into the tent in varying moods and set about getting as drunk as possible in as short a time as was possible. Henry Gresham was a veteran of two years' standing. Having seen so much, he was later to the bottle than many of the younger ones. He saw the outstretched hand knock the lamp and its oil off the empty barrel and fling its contents against the canvas of the tent. He saw the oil sink into the canvas, inert. He saw the wick, still flaming, sail through the air as if the world had slowed down and God declared a war against time, towards the canvas. He saw the wick hit the canvas, flicker as if ready to die, and then burst out anew on the oil-soaked cloth.

They should not have stored powder in the tent. There was a store for it, only a few hundred yards away. Yet they were veterans, survivors of a war that seemed endless. They knew the perils of powder that had separated through old age, of powder that was damp or badly mixed. They preferred to keep and tend their own, and despite their every precaution the fire reached it.

Henry Gresham never knew what object, flung out by the blast, gouged his leg and thigh to near pulp. He did know the sight of his erstwhile commander, screaming for light with a boiled face and eye sockets permanently burned out. The last thing he remembered was Mannion, reaching out as if to stop him connecting with the ground.

So it was that Henry Gresham commanded candles, not lamps, in his house and in the rooms he hired. A candle, if knocked over, tended to go out. If not, its flame was a slow, friendly kind of fire. Oil simply wished to ignite. He could bear lamps, of course. Indeed, in strange rooms and strange houses where he had no control he hardly even noticed them. Henry Gresham had long ago lost any belief that a human being could control their life. All one could do was to control it where one had power, that being a very small portion of the whole.

'I'll have what's left of those candles snuffed out and in my bag in seconds,' Mannion grumbled. 'You've paid for them, haven't you?' Mannion never ceased to mention the waste of candles. By reminding Gresham, he made the fear normal.

'View it as my gesture of protest against the dominance of night in this world of ours,' Gresham said loftily, and swept out of the room.

'View it as a damn silly waste of money, more like!' muttered Mannion, closing the door behind him.

Mannion also had a sense of humour. By comparison with many other men's sense of humour it was odd in the extreme. What Mannion found funny, and what could not produce even the tiniest stretching of his craggy features, never ceased to fascinate Gresham. Boots, for example, were endlessly funny to Mannion. It was as if he deemed mankind to have been born with feet the aim of which was to trudge through whatever muck God chose to put at ground level. He would accept clogs or the most basic leather footwear as a reasonable recourse against the elements on the part of the dominant species, but in the face of the finery the gentry put on their feet he was reduced to hopeless laughter.

A gentleman would don boots as a matter of necessity. A courtier would like people to believe that his fine shoes would never need to meet muck or mud, unless one was riding, of course. Henry Gresham was a gentleman, fabulously rich and a courtier when he chose. He was also an agent for King James I of England and King James VI of Scotland. So it was that he was planning to walk home from The Mermaid Inn after his rather fruitless conversation. Gentlemen and courtiers rode horses or had carriages. Gentleman courtiers who were spies tended to avoid both, as drawing attention to themselves.

Mannion eyed his own stout leggings, and the supple leather of his master's fine boots.

'Shame about the boots,' he muttered with a grin. Mannion had no fear for the armed gangs who roamed the streets after nightfall. He was highly amused by the prospect of what the walk would do to his master's fine boots.

There was something about London muck that did for fine leather. Too much of Gresham's time was taken up in walking back from shady rendezvous. The worst times were early morning, and late at night. During the day it was not too bad. A veritable army of men scurried to shovel up every human, horse, cattle and dog turd that lay steaming on the streets. There was money to be made from shit, but to make it you had to see it. At night it was invisible, and ever present.

'Remember that dream you told me about once?' said Mannion, as they walked through a street with a particularly narrow overhang.

Gresham had once had a nightmare where he was leaving one of Bankside's most unsavoury taverns and his way home was lit by endless torches. The dim and flickering light illuminated thousand upon thousand of straining arses, perched over the narrow and overhanging streets and each delivering their message to the street with a hollow thud.

He shook his head, and the image vanished. A grinning Mannion led him down the rickety stairs and through The Mermaid, full as was usual with its theatrical crowd and some of the more daring socialites, tasting a bit of rough and arty for the night. The air was thick and unpleasant, the dancing light revealing the sweat on the fevered brows. Men dealing, men stealing, men intriguing and whores selling. It was a foetid mix, and Gresham could not wait to be out of it.

Gresham's eyes flickered round the room, seeming to see nothing, noting everything. He noted a dour, stooping figure, clearly the worse for drink, sitting alone at a back table. Gresham scrabbled in his memory for the man's name. It would come. They emerged into the black streets. The muscularity of their walk, and the ease with which their hands rested on the swords in their belts, caused the ways to part in front of them. They were the source of menace, not its victims.

'That man, seated in the corner,' Gresham said, 'the one on his own and worse for drink; do you recognise him?'

'Should I?' replied Mannion. 'Shall I go back in and ask?'

'No, not yet at least. I remember him from somewhere. It'll come back.'

As they passed an 'ordinary', light spilled out from the door, and two men fell brawling into the street. There were shrieks and yells, good-natured laughter. Out of the dark a crowd gathered, egging the two on. Gresham and Mannion looked away, preserving their night vision. Inside that same tavern Gresham knew a man could be reading exquisite sonnets to his friends. Shortly after, they were plunged into darkness, the huge overhang of the half-timbered buildings closing over them like a black cloud. It was a residential area. The doors were closed and bolted this late in the night, and only the feeble light of an occasional candle or guttering lamp behind closed shutters showed that some merchant was still up, counting his credit or bemoaning his losses. Or, as a shriek from behind followed by the thuds of two or three blows suggested, a wife was being taught what a man thought was good manners.

It was then that a moment for Heaven came, a moment that summed up for Gresham the magic of London. Shortly behind him two men were fighting, cheered on by a drunken crowd, and a wife was being beaten for doing no more probably than trying to be herself. And then, from a high window, came the breath of Heaven.

Music had always inspired Gresham. It was his greatest regret that he could not find in himself the means to produce what so inspired him from others. *O Jove, From Stately Throne*. That was it. Gresham had met the composer. Farrant? Yes, Richard Farrant, no less. Perhaps it was Farrant, his face ravaged by smallpox, leading the small *ensemble* in the upstairs room, playing and singing beyond all reasonable time, desperately trying to compensate for the ugliness of his own face by the beauty of his music.

The voice of Heaven filtered out through the shutters and on to the dark street, dropping like gentle rain on the heads of Gresham and Mannion. As a man they stopped, raised their faces, and let the beauty fall on their upturned visages like a summer shower.

It was high summer. Even here, in the great city, the sense was in the air. With the warmer evenings fires were lit later and left burning shorter. The smoke that hung over London on a still day like a funeral pall was visibly less. The cattle driven through the streets were fat and full of milk.

The most dangerous thing they met on the journey was a dog, half wild with hunger and trailing a leg damaged in a fight, or in a collision with a cart. It slunk away down an alley.

He had worked himself back into a good humour by the time he and Mannion reached home, his mood generated by what awaited him there. Known simply as the House, the London home built by Gresham's father was situated in the highly fashionable area of the Strand, and with its own landing on to the River it was a prime site. His father had bought it when the monasteries had been dissolved.

The House was well-run. That much was clear. The two well-built men who acknowledged their master as he trudged through the mud to his own doorstep recognised him, but would have recognised an enemy just as clearly, and sounded the alarum. Their pleasure in seeing their master was in no small measure related to the fact that Henry Gresham showed pleasure in seeing them.

'Good evening, Matt, good evening, Will,' he muttered as he passed them by. Mannion grunted at them.

The entrance hall was of marble, brought over at fabulous expense from Italy. The statues and hangings were also Italian. The woman was English.

Jane Carpenter was nearing twenty-three years of age, and was the most beautiful woman in London. She had a face of stunning beauty, cheekbones pushing up round the roundest and darkest pair of eyes in Christendom. Her body lacked the plumpness of many Court ladies, but she had the grace and strength of a young colt, and legs beneath her dress that seemed to cross counties. Yet it was her eyes that commanded attention, extraordinary eyes, with dark lights seeming to flash beneath their surface. Gresham grinned at her as Mannion struggled to pull off his boots, replacing them with soft shoes. She grinned in return. With him she dropped the rather aloof distance she maintained with all people of social standing, the faint tone of terrible boredom.

'Are London's problems solved, my Lord, and can innocent maidens go safely now to our beds?'

'Firstly, I don't solve problems but rather create them, I think. Secondly, I am not nor ever will be "Lord" to anyone. Thirdly, you are not innocent, and fourthly, in your bed no-one is safe.' Feeling rather proud of his grasp of numbers, he reinforced the words, as soon as Mannion had left the room with his boots and cloak, by flinging out an arm, gathering her up and delivering a kiss that shook the fine plaster on the walls.

'Ouch!' she exclaimed truthfully, the hilt of his sword banging into her just under her ribcage. 'Why do men always have to bang at everything?'

'It's in the nature of men to give, and women to receive,' muttered Gresham, nuzzling her hair.

'As gifts go, what men give tends to be rather single-minded and very repetitive,' Jane replied, pushing him away and laughing up at him. 'Must I expect to endure receiving you tonight?'

'If I choose to honour you with my gifts, then yes. Yet as you've always been such an obedient servant, I don't doubt your instant bending . . .' She raised both her eyebrows. '. . . or whatever,' he added lamely, 'to my will.'

She dropped her hands to her sides and looked at him with that rare mixture of exasperation and love.

'Do be quiet, Henry Gresham. And come to your bed.' Your bed? For a brief flicker of a moment, Gresham was taken back to the time when he had first set eyes on this woman. Was it the timbre of her voice that sent him back, or that strange mixture of something brazen with something vulnerable and defenceless?

It had been on one of his first journeys from the calm of his Cambridge College to London, in 1590. He was still hobbling from his wound, and was without the relay of spare horses that Mannion was establishing for him. His horse had thrown a shoe just outside Bishop's Stortford. He had been left to his own devices in a village that did not even boast a poor inn, whilst Mannion saw to the horse and a replacement.

As he sat, picking at the rough grass and throwing it into the dank pond, he became aware that a pair of eyes were gazing solemnly at him from in between some bushes.

He gazed back. The two gazes locked, and held.

A thin, piping voice came from the bushes. 'First one who blinks loses.'

Gresham was so surprised that he blinked.

'There, you've lost. You must pay me a forfeit.'

The accent was thick but the diction clear.

'Well, young madam,' said Gresham as the painfully thin figure of a six- or seven-year-old girl climbed out of the bushes and into full view, 'I've no recollection that I ever agreed to your terms.'

'But you didn't refuse them either, sir, and therefore as a gentleman you're bound to agree with me.'

The logic was somehow faulty, in a way that Gresham could not quite fathom.

'And what if I don't agree?' The girl's eyes seemed to occupy her whole head. They were the darkest blue Gresham had ever seen, with flickering sparkles hidden deep inside them.

The girl shrugged. 'Then I suppose you'll beat me.'

'Do many beat you?'

'All the time. You see, I'm a bastard, and bastards deserve to be

47

'beaten.' The little girl said it as if it was a litany she knew off by heart.

'How often are you beaten?'

'All the time. Here, you may see.' The girl dropped her loose tunic over her bony shoulders, down to her waist. Seven or eight red stripes marked her back, with the older blows turning to dull and dark bruises. She turned to look at him, over her shoulder. There was no coyness in her posture or voice, merely a statement of fact.

'They go on further down, but you're a man, so I can't show you my secret places.'

She carefully drew up her stained tunic, and sat on her haunches, looking at him. 'May I have my forfeit now?'

Gresham had often wondered what would have happened then, were it not for the interruption. He suspected he would have given this little vixen a few coins, and shooed her on her way. It was still his time of darkness, not a time when he had a care for any other living creature, being too full of mourning for those he had loved and betrayed.

Yet at the word 'forfeit' there was an outraged yell from one of the hovels overlooking the pond, and an elderly man erupted from the ill-shuttered door.

'You bitch! You brazen whore's whelp! Where've you been, you little whore, when your duty called? I'll teach you your duty . . .'

The girl might have been quick enough to evade the blow, had she not been rapt in her attentions to Gresham. As it was, she was a split second late and caught the blow square on her back.

It was not much of a back, as these things went. It was only seven years old, it had never been properly fed or properly clean. Yet it could bleed like any other back, if a witch-hazel stick whipped across it.

Gresham broke the man's arm. It was easy enough, for a soldier. As he raised it for the second blow on the prostrate little figure beneath him, Gresham sprang up, finding his sword in his hand without consciously willing it there or even knowing it had

48

happened. He brought up the sword arm, with its extra weight of metal, just behind the man's wrist, a split second before he brought down his other arm with terrible force on the outstretched arm 'twixt wrist and elbow. The crack of bone would have shattered ice.

The peasant was bellowing on the ground, his arm smashed. The girl had vanished back into the bushes, nursing a new welt but not, Gresham noted, making a sound. Neighbours were rushing out on to the green to see the cause of the entertainment. In very short order they surrounded the gentleman and demanded reparation not only for the damage done to the man, but for disturbing the peace of the whole village. After all, a sword could only kill one man, and there were ten or more of them there in the space of three or four breaths. There was money in this business, and they knew it, peasants that they were.

Then Mannion loomed over the rise that surrounded the pond, and things became calmer. Things usually did become calmer when Mannion arrived on the scene. The villagers who had been feeling their cudgels with enthusiasm suddenly thought it better to put them behind their backs. A rather more civilised process of negotiation assumed pride of place. The man on the ground howling in his agony – 'William', it would appear by all counts – was a labourer. Well, William would not be labouring for a month or two, that was clear. William was also the nearest thing this village had to a saint, that much was also clear. Taken on his daughter's bastard, he had, that same daughter who had caught God's justice when she died in childbirth with no man to call her proper husband.

Looking at William, Gresham wondered how the bastard girl had ever survived. The midwife must have spirited the poor wean away and presented it back to William when the lump it might have made in the pond would have been too obvious even to the other villagers. Come to think of it, there was a fretful old woman hovering at the back of the gesticulating villagers.

It took precious little money to calm them down. Yet what took all of them aback, including Gresham, was his final question.

'How much for the girl?'

Mannion looked up, startled, at his master, and wondered for a brief moment if he liked fucking children. God knows, enough did. And, Mannion decided almost instantaneously, his master didn't. Yet he too had seen the child sliced out of its mother's belly, and knew that taking on this child might somehow claw back some of the despair from that dreadful day.

And the child could always be handed over to someone else to bring up, when Gresham returned to emotions more proper for a man.

In the final count, the amount paid for the girl was paltry. The expression in William's eyes suggested that his arm was well broken if this was the reward. Gresham had visions of him erupting into the path of every gentleman who rode by, demanding that they break his arm.

She had shown no emotion until the time of their leaving. A mere piece of property, she had been bartered and sold, with no-one thinking to ask her opinion. She vented it, forcibly, when she was seated behind Mannion the servant on his horse, as was only proper.

She screamed and shrieked and pummelled and yelled, causing even Mannion's horse to buck and to rear in protest.

'What is wrong with you, girl!' Gresham exploded.

'You bought me,' the thin, shivering Eve proclaimed through gritted and tear-stained teeth. 'I shall ride on no horse except your own.'

Gresham had killed more men than he cared to count. He had witnessed the person he most loved in Creation die in agony before him, and because of him. He had suffered in a few months more pain than most men underwent in a lifetime. He had a fortune to his name, he cared for no man and he cared for nothing . . . Why, then, thought Gresham, am I riding at a sedate pace and freezing to death, whilst a seven-year-old bastard girl sits behind me in state, wearing my fine cloak?

If he had been able to answer that question, then perhaps he would really have been God.

There was a vestige in him of his own childhood. He too had known what it was to be the bastard.

'Find me a woman to care for this . . . minx,' he had said to Mannion as they arrived in London. The girl had been restored to rude good health by a substantial meal. If her eyes had opened any wider on their entry to London they would have consumed her face.

'Find me someone who won't just care for her. Find me some servants who'll love her, as if she were their own.'

And Mannion, as he always did, found what his master wanted.

Jane had fallen in love with the House only slightly less than she had fallen in love with the strange and darkly dressed man who had rescued her from abuse. It had been a dark, dreary and a sad place she had come to, still in mourning for the death of Gresham's father and an heir who seemed determined to neglect it. As a child she had haunted its every nook and cranny, and as she grew older and into womanhood she seemed to light up the building with her love for it. Nominally under the care of the elderly Housekeeper, Jane had grown into that role herself so gently that no-one could point to the exact time when she became the acknowledged mistress of the House.

The House was the best-run house in London. No wine was drunk, no food eaten and no clothing for footmen paid for without Jane being convinced that the expenditure was proper. There was a part of Jane that was the feral cat, a part Gresham knew would never leave her. It accounted in part for her raw sexuality, her enjoyment of the physical act. The servants saw the untamed Jane if they cheated their master, the House or her, and felt it. Gresham had seen her turn on a thieving servant with a cold fury, and a ferocious concentration of anger that was almost tangible. Yet months later she had waited most of the night by that same serving girl's bed when she seemed as if she would die of a fever, and fed her beef tea. That same woman he had seen when a sudden downpour had flooded the hall, her skirts tucked up to her knees, laughing and joking with the servant girls as they all joined to swoosh the filthy water back out into the street. The men servants may have leered at her behind her back, for all Gresham knew. To her face they were strangely protective, their visible respect tinged almost with a certain fearfulness. All the servants spoke in awe of her, grumbling as servants did. Yet it was her food that was the freshest, her room the most clean and her bed linen the most virgin-white. In a way Gresham did not understand, they took an immense pride in her. He knew and accepted almost with complacency that many of them would die for him. It surprised him how many he thought might die for her. Then again, he lived in a world where if the master or the mistress sinned, the servants received an equal or worse punishment. Dying for your master or your mistress was not a choice for the servants of the well-born. It was a condition of service.

Gresham still did not know how the irritating, obnoxious foundling, the by-blow of a hasty assault on a peasant common, had become his mistress.

He had come to the House late one night, obsessed with business. The thin-boned foundling had turned into a strikingly beautiful seventeen-year-old with an imperious will. She had strode about his chamber, showing real anger as she explained the various frauds upon his money that his servants had perpetuated.

'And furthermore, my Lord, there's one even greater crime to which you must answer!'

'And what's that?' said Gresham, wearied beyond belief by decisions that affected all Christendom, not to mention his supposedly immortal soul. How was it to him if a cook was ordering extra chickens?

She stood there, tall and straight as the bolt from an arrow, flashing radiance in the room. 'You, who have every right to claim me as your own, have never looked at me as a woman!'

Well, he had been taken by a fit and had done more than look upon her as a woman that night, to their apparent mutual satisfaction. Yet when he woke, he was more than a man with the edge taken off his carnal hunger by a fine night of lovemaking. More scared than he had been in the face of a Spanish cannon, he realised with an almost sickening fear that he was in love. He knew that he had signed his will away. He had not sought it. He had even tried positively to avoid it, or any other entanglement. It had done him no good.

Yet Jane had steadfastly refused to marry him. He had pleaded with her.

'You seem to have claimed ownership of my body, and doubtless wanted my soul since I first saw you by that cursed pond! I've said I love you, haven't I? Why won't you make a proper woman of yourself, and a proper man of me, by being my wife? Am I fat and stinking of grease? Am I not rich enough for you?'

She had turned away that night, after their lovemaking, peaceful and contented. She let his ranting pass over her, with the inner calm that drove him to even greater fury. She turned round to face him, letting cold air into the bed.

'I've said my thanks with my body. It's all I was gifted with from God. Everything else I have was somebody else's. You've had the only thing I have to give, as I now am. Anything else must wait.'

'Yet you've shown me your secret places. You've let me use those secret places, to my heart's content.'

He remembered the first showing to him of her wounds.

She smiled at him, a radiance that lit up the bed. 'I've shown you the secret places of my body, and willingly so.'

She turned over in the bed, her back towards him. As if from a far continent, her last words came. 'As for the secret places of my soul, for that you will have to wait.'

Gresham knew of no more final goodnight.

And now he was lying in his vast bed in 1605, years on from that first meeting and years on from the night when he had taken her virginity. He was satiated, yet as mystified by this woman he loved as he had been by the side of the pond in that filthy village all those years ago. Perched on the very edge of sleep, the knowable world of Cambridge, the dangerous world of Robert Cecil and the imponderable world of Jane raced round in his head until they blended into a wild half-dream. Cecil was screaming at him, blaming him that his mistress was soon to be elected as Master of King's College. He recoiled in the face of Cecil's spitting anger, yet thinking it would not be the first time a bastard had been involved in the governance of that College.

In his dreams, the bloated face of Will Shadwell rose up from the deep.

'Beware! Beware!' it moaned at him. 'You are in waters too deep for your soul!'

'My soul, poor tattered thing, was lost a long while ago,' whispered Gresham. 'And I have been in waters too deep all my life!'

At that the ghost of Will Shadwell vanished, and Henry Gresham slept in peace. Just before he did so, the name of the man stooped over his tankard in the tavern came to him.

'Wintour. Robert Wintour . . .' What did he know about Robert Wintour? It would come to him. It always did.

CHAPTER 3

Father Garnet was in prison. As prisons went it was pleasant enough. The half-timbered house had been sheltering Jesuits safely for years, its walls peppered with hiding places. The fire burnt cheerfully in the grate, the oak panels mellowed in the evening sun and there was wine at hand. Yet it was still prison.

A curlew sounded in the meadows outside the house, its forlorn, mewing cry echoing the priest's mood. Father Garnet was tired, more tired than he had ever been in his whole life. It was no crisis of faith. When he summoned the image of Our Saviour into his mind the rushing well of tenderness, the biting pain of love were the same as ever, undiminished and unrelenting. Rather, it was simple exhaustion.

How long had he been in England, fighting for the faith that was his life? Fighting for it *with* his life?

He had forgotten how many years, years of being continually shunted from one secret house to another, years of disguise, of whispered Masses in shuttered rooms. The Jesuit priest was a hunted animal in England, yet at least the real animal was given a quick death by the hounds. If the priest was found he would be stripped and trussed to a wooden hurdle, dragged through the streets behind a horse, to be reviled and spat at by the worst sort of scum. Hauled on to a scaffold, he would be dropped and hung until the choking edge of suffocation had plunged him near into unconsciousness, and hurriedly cut down whilst still aware. Rough-handled over to the nearby block, the executioner would then hack off his testicles, to show that he should never have been born, and thrust them before the priest's agonised face. Then the crude blade would strike into the chest, and the heart be torn out, the bleeding, pathetic flesh held up for the baying crowd to see, to the cry, 'Here lies the heart of a traitor!'

Father Garnet's dreams were haunted by the first, coarse feel of that rope around his neck, the gasping panic of strangulation, the sharp, shrieking cut of the metal. Was it weakness to be so scared? Could he pray to be spared this pain, or should he pray to have it inflicted on him, thus becoming a glorious martyr for the Faith? A good man, he prayed for neither. The first was unfair and a coward's way, the second was untrue. He prayed instead simply for the wisdom to understand.

O my God. *Why hast Thou forsaken me?*

Garnet tensed. Horse's hooves sounded outside his window. He looked expectantly at the bell over the fireplace in his room. Were it to ring, tugged frantically by a loyal servant, Garnet would hastily grab his bottle and glass so as to hide his presence, run outside into the passageway and back into the adjoining room. The fireplace there was kept deliberately blackened, ash in the basket, as if used every day. Behind it lay a priest-hole, activated by a hidden lever. Within lay a rosary and a crucifix, scraps of dried-out food and a single, thin and emaciated turd. This was evidence enough that a priest had once lain, eaten and shat therein. The stench of urine, added to every three days by loyal Catholic servants ordered to piss there, gave force to the message.

The real priest-hole lay behind. Two men might crouch in it, but not stand or sit. A thousand men might seek how to enter it, but never find the means of entry unless they were told. Even the

56

fiercest fire built in the first fireplace would not singe the occupants of the second priest-hole, for all the damage it could have done to occupants of the first.

A cheerful call wafted up from the gatehouse, greeting the rider. Father Garnet relaxed again in his chair.

He felt a dread terror as he contemplated that young fool Catesby and his hellish plot. Catesby had told his servant what was planned, then sought to calm the servant's disquiet by sending him to confess to Father Tesimond. The servant, thought Garnet, had a deal more common sense than the master, but then that was usually the way. As for Tesimond, he had received the confession and run straight to Garnet, in turn confessing all to him.

It was a nightmare. Garnet could no more break the secrecy of the confessional than he could sell his soul to the Devil. He could not disclose what Father Tesimond had told him to any person upon earth on pain of the loss of his immortal soul.

It would not just kill the Lords and Government of England, Garnet realised, a single tear forming in his eye and cooling as it found release and trekked down his cheek. It would kill the cause of Catholicism in England for years, perhaps for ever, uniting the country in a frenzy of hatred against the Popish impostors. It was the most awful, the most terrible thing that any young madcap rebel could conceive and carry out. And he, Father Garnet, was bound by the most awful vow of all not to reveal his knowledge. He had to persuade Catesby to give it all up. An emissary to the Pope had to be the answer. Surely if the Pope condemned the plot, even so overweening a vanity as Catesby's would have to recognise its folly?

A sharp cramp cut across his stomach. Too much food and wine, and not nearly enough exercise, he knew. Or an omen of the executioner's knife cutting into his most sensitive flesh in front of the howling crowd . . . He stumbled to his feet, and vomited up most of his day's food into the flames of the fire.

Gresham stood bolt-upright in the rough iron tub, as naked as the day he was born, scrubbing with satisfaction at the few suspicions of dirt left on his reddened flesh. It was before dawn, two guttering candles piercing the gloom, and Mannion stood silent in a corner as the early morning ritual took its course. He held a huge towel over his arm, with the rest of his master's clothing waiting draped over two stools.

It was still a good body, Mannion thought with quiet satisfaction, though God knows why Gresham insisted on spoiling it with water. He knew every one of the wounds that criss-crossed his master's body, could probably name and date the cause of each one. Yet they were superficial, healed. The hips were narrow and muscled, the shoulders broad and strong and the dusting of hair across the manly chest so much more satisfying than the blanket of dead seaweed so many sported there. There was no self-consciousness in Mannion's frank appraisal, any more than there would have been embarrassment in Gresham's receipt of it, had he even realised it was taking place. Mannion knew every inch of that body, had carried it on his shoulders as a child, whooping through the apple orchards. He had thrashed it once, and only once, when its seven-year-old owner had stood up imperiously and demanded that Mannion do its bidding as he was a mere servant. Years later he had washed it when its owner could only whimper, half-conscious, with the searing pain of wounds that seemed never to heal. He had fed it by hand for months, never speaking, holding the sustenance in front of the mouth for hours, sometimes forcing it down the throat when all else failed.

With no obvious signal Mannion stepped forward. Gresham held out his arms, back towards Mannion, to receive the towel he knew would be draped across his shoulders. Without turning, he spoke. 'God, man. Your breath stinks. What on God's earth were you up to last night?'

Gresham stepped out of the tub, turning to grasp the towel round his cold frame.

'My duty, young master,' replied an impassive Mannion.

58

'And what duty might that be?' enquired Gresham shortly, irritated that his own conversational gambit required him to speak at this time in the morning.

'Why, sir, I'm a man. And the world must be peopled.'

And that, thought Gresham, showed why one should not engage in conversation with the servants.

He allowed Mannion to dress him. He could not remember when Jane had first started to sleep the night with him, regardless of his carnal needs. He knew it was shortly after their first, frantic lovemaking. He had resented the presence in his bed, the last citadel of his private person, when instead of leaving after their coupling she had turned over and lain gently on the far side of the bed, back towards him. Her young and muscled body lay there, its curves as relaxed and bored as a seasoned choirboy's arm swinging the censor. He had willed it to move, and gone to sleep so doing, waking up to find it gone and about its business.

He did not understand how in entering her body he had let her enter his mind.

Jane had never interfered with his silent routine of early morning washing, and Mannion's attendance on it as his body-servant. The relationship between Mannion and Jane was one of life's great secrets as far as Gresham was concerned. After that first day, when she had screamed to be taken off Mannion's horse, he had not discerned so much as a flicker of disagreement between them. In his presence they were formal, even brisk, in their conversations. At times Gresham thought they used a shorthand between each other, a language he could not understand. It never crossed Gresham's mind that what united them was their love of him.

His breakfast was milk warm from the cow, brought from the fields near Islington. The bread was fresh-baked in the House's own ovens, and smelt divine. There was cheese, and strips of bacon burnt to the black as if on a campaign fire, a taste he had never lost. There was a concoction of eggs beaten up with milk and then heated over the fire until it bubbled a gentle yellow, a half-eaten beef pie. Dr Perse in Cambridge had advised him to eat a hearty breakfast above all other meals, and it suited Gresham's constitution. There were many who ate no breakfast at all.

Gresham finished his breakfast. Mannion left the room briefly and returned with one of the kitchen maids, who cleared the wooden table. There was a rustle, and the briefest sense of a fine perfume. Without turning round he sensed that Jane had entered the room. He waved a hand, motioning both to be seated.

Gresham nodded to the small beer and Mannion poured himself a tankard. He drank like a sewer, with a vast, slurping contentment that only just stopped short of the belch he clearly needed to deliver after devouring the whole tankard.

'For God's sake, man, let it go before you explode.' Mannion let loose a torrent of wind that started at his feet and came out finally from his mouth like the blast of the trumpet on Judgement Day. Jane looked at him as he rocked with the force of the expulsion, the tiniest flicker visible at the corner of her mouth. Gresham looked on with distaste, his lip curling.

'You are disgusting!' he said.

'Aye, sir. Disgusting.' Mannion poured himself another tankard and placed it cheerfully in front of him. 'Truly disgusting. But no longer thirsty, for which I thank you.'

It did not occur to Gresham to ask how many other gentlemen of his wealth and standing discussed the most important matters of the day after breakfast with their body-servant and their mistress. As for how many gentlemen were blessed with a body-servant who won both the morning's opening conversational gambits, he preferred not to think. The girl had made it clear from early on that she had a brain to match her body, one source of her capacity to irritate him more than any other person on earth. It was so much simpler to have the body as one container, and the brain in another, and far more convenient for the latter to be contained in a man. He had said so to Jane once. She had considered the proposition thoughtfully, and then hit him with the bedpan.

The upper room in which they sat was one of Gresham's favourites. Dressed with dark oak panelling that had been young in the Wars of the Roses, it had a large window and balcony overlooking the street. Already the hubbub of London was audible despite the lavish expenditure on glass in the window. As with most houses, the introduction of glass had not caused Gresham to remove the old, unwieldy shutters, which were an excellent defence. They had been thrown back as he had entered the room, revealing a watery, smoke-stained dawn.

Gresham gave a brief résumé of where he thought things stood, speaking as if to himself but knowing his silent, attentive audience. He listed the death of Will Shadwell, the meeting with Cecil, the strange task of Bacon. For Jane's sake he went over the story of the informer, the lack of any incriminating evidence on Bacon. They knew his ways, knew that in some way this careful repetition of the facts, this thinking aloud, enabled him to order things in his mind, to speed up thought. The fingers of his left hand began to drum gently on the rough wood of the table. It was a rare gesture for a man who held himself always in fierce physical control.

'I'm uneasy. There's something in the air. Unrest, trouble. I don't know. Yet the feeling is there. As it was before Essex, the same feeling. What gossip is there in the markets and the fine shops, Jane? What are they talking of in St Paul's?'

The old cathedral of St Paul's was the crumbling centre of London. Even though it had lost its steeple to lightning some years before, it still dominated London in its centre. Occupying over twelve acres at the western end of Cheapside, it would have taken Jesus two lifetimes to clear it of its moneylenders. It was here that those caught by the new plant tobacco came to buy, here where every servant in London looked for vacancies on the *siquis* door. It was here that the *gallant* casually threw back his fine cloak to reveal the satin lining, and the younger son skulked in the doorway to hide his ragged doublet. It was here that the scaffold would be erected, the men twitching their last moments in earshot of the sermon being preached from St Paul's Cross. Puritan and Papist, gentleman and cutthroat, fine lady and bawd met, mingled and, not infrequently, came to blows or copulated. The country bumpkins who increasingly flocked to London were drawn to St Paul's and drew with them the lowlife who preyed on their naivety. It was the best centre for gossip in London, exceeded only by the Court itself.

Jane went there nearly every day to visit the booksellers. She had more or less taught herself to read and had devoured the library built up by Gresham's father. The only time she had badgered him for money was to add to the library, to which he had willingly agreed. The House now had one of the finest collections of books in London. As a child she had become almost a talisman among the booksellers, the men vying with each other to attract her to their stalls. They knew her as the foundling of the fabulously wealthy and strangely reclusive Henry Gresham, and latterly his 'niece'. Yet when she made her purchase solemnly every Friday, always from a different stall, she got the best price in London, as well as the best gossip.

'Those who talk of books are full of Jonson's *Sejanus*, of course – it was played some two years ago at the Globe. It's not very good, actually, very loud and long. Martha and I went. Thorp first took it on and entered it in November last, but refused to print it, and Blount's now taken it over. Jonson's friends say it's good to his face but damn it behind his back, and he's very vexed indeed with the world!'

Jane's face lit up as she relayed the tittle-tattle of the booksellers.

'When has Ben Jonson *not* been vexed with the world?' asked Gresham with a laugh, trying to imagine a world where his friend Jonson would be at peace with anything. 'Who wouldn't be vexed, with the ghost of Kit Marlowe grinning up at you from Hell and that clever brat Shakespeare taking the crowds at the Globe? But there must be other gossip?'

'There's always gossip in the places I visit, though none concerning Bacon. Except the normal, that is,' she replied, her brow furrowed in thought.

'So what *is* the normal?' asked Gresham gently.

'The normal is that he's a man of great ambition, a man of law and a man of Parliament, who'll sell his soul to the King for preferment. His fiancée's a shrew, and he prefers the company of young men.' She giggled. 'As, so it's said, does his intended. There's no noise abroad that any of the young men are unwilling.' She looked him straight in the eye. 'It's become fashionable these days to try what's new. A courtier who wishes to be in the light of fashion will say that he needs his women, but that he loves only his young man or his boy.'

'Will they now? How very daring,' mused Gresham. 'Does this gossip talk of sedition, of treason, of plotting?'

'It talks of the King,' said Jane. 'They say the new King screams if he sights cold steel.'

It was rumoured that James's mother, Mary Queen of Scots, had witnessed her Italian lover Rizzio murdered in front of her, in some Godforsaken frozen Scottish palace, while the child that was to become James I was live in her belly. A drawn sword or dagger had ever since sent him into a fit either of madness or of swooning.

'They still talk of Raleigh, of course. Aren't people strange and fickle? The mob used to hate him when Essex was alive, but now they say Raleigh was the first Englishman to be tried and sentenced before the charge was heard.' Raleigh's trial, conducted by the irascible and lickspittle Attorney-General, Sir Edward Coke, had been a farce.

Gresham growled his response. 'Do they talk of how Raleigh was betrayed by the man who protested to be his deepest friend? By the man whose son Raleigh helped to bring up? Do they talk of Cecil so?'

'They talk more of the numbers in the King's service at Whitehall,' said Jane truthfully, 'and how they grow by the day. It's the talk of town that soon every gentleman in the country will be paid a pension to be in His Majesty's Chamber, and every working man in the whole country employed in the King's palaces. The

Scots Lords offend everyone. It's said that they stink, that to sit next to them is to get their fleas, that they've no breeding and that they rut like stags when they're not too drunk to know what they're doing.'

Gresham knew that over a thousand men worked to serve the King in his palace at Whitehall. It was a far cry from the days of Old Bess, for whom each coin she parted with was like a drop of blood.

'The merchants see what the King spends, and worry about their profits and yet more taxes.'

'There's more, though – talk of a Popish plot, now the treaty with Spain is signed. The Catholics are angry. They had high words of promise from the King, and had great hopes of his Catholic wife. It all seems to have turned sour, and the fines are bleeding some of the great families to death, they say.'

'It's not just talk, the first bit,' said Mannion. 'It's true.' He spoke with an air of total finality. 'The girls in the stews hear the pillow talk. The young merchants are full of the Government costing too much and doing too little. And they say the Papists are restless.'

'Well,' said Gresham with heavy irony, 'that has to be it, then. If the girls in the stews say it's true who can deny it?'

Jane carried on, ignoring Gresham. 'Any Papists who heard my Lord Archbishop preach his sermon at St Paul's Cross on Tuesday last will be more than restless. They'll be scared. He damned all Papists to Hell. He said the King would pour out the last drop of blood in his body to defend the Protestant faith.'

So, thought Gresham, there is anger in the country. Three angers, in fact. The anger of the Catholics, the anger of a disappointed people in their profligate King and the increasing anger of the King against the Pope's followers. Yet when had there not been anger in the country? And none of what he had heard explained Will Shadwell's death, or his intuitive sense of unease.

Jane and Mannion were waiting expectantly. He looked at Jane, his expression unfathomable. She wondered what thoughts were hidden by those dark eyes. For all that she believed she knew Gresham better than anyone except Mannion, there were times when she was frightened by her inability to read his mind and his soul. Had she known the image in his mind she would have been saddened and horrified in equal measure.

Gresham was thinking of blood. Its smell and its look. There is no smell like fresh human blood, as there is no smell like rotting human flesh. The first is warm, salty yet strangely thin, the latter so vile as to make a man retch into his boots. Gresham had seen so much blood shed, smelt so much dead flesh. It was so bad at times that even as he looked at Jane, flushed with all the fires of youth and excitement at the joy of living, he saw the blood pumping beneath her fair skin, saw her raped and mutilated by a troop of soldiers as he had seen so many young girls, smelt the rank odour of her death. Gresham saw the skull beneath the skin.

Would there be rebellion so soon again? Had people learnt nothing from the waste, the torment and the agony of the Essex rebellion, so short past? Were fine young men to be butchered on the pikes of mercenaries, their reeking guts to be torn out and shown to their wives? Were the Catholics to launch yet another blood bath in the vain hope that the country would join their rising?

'May I speak?' It was Jane, reluctant to interrupt his reverie.

'Madam,' replied Gresham with a short bow, 'the Four Furies have left for their supper after a hard night riding people down and I am temporarily without my wand of power, or a standing army, so I fear I lack the means to stop you talking.'

Jane waved her hand dismissively, as she would to a rather silly child. 'My Lord, I'm worried that you should become involved between Bacon and Cecil. There's danger in going on to any ground where there's no map. How do we know what argument might exist between the two of them? How can we know that you're not simply being used in some way to gain advantage for Cecil, perhaps at great cost to you?'

'She's right,' said Mannion. 'I'm as good a swimmer as anyone, but even I wouldn't swim certain stretches of the river, where I don't know what the current's doing.'

Gresham thought for a moment. He stood suddenly. Something had sealed in his mind as he listened. He felt a fear and an uncertainty, but now he knew where it sprang from and what he intended to do about it.

'I agree, it almost certainly is dangerous. But I won't know how dangerous until I find out more. Cecil rarely tells the whole truth when he briefs one of his men. He likes to keep his spies in the dark, just as much as he likes to keep everyone else in the dark. Men like him distrust the light.'

He walked over to Jane, pulled her up gently by her wrists and stood gazing at her.

'I see my lawyers this morning.' The vast fortune left to Gresham by his father carried title to thousands of acres of land and numerous properties, and with it continual detail of tenancies and rents. When in London Gresham's lawyer was always desperate to see him, the pile of documents that needed signing stretching from St Paul's to the river.

'After that, I visit Moll Cutpurse this evening. If there's knowledge to be had, Moll will have it. And tomorrow, we see the King.'

Jane gave a squeal of excitement, clapping her hands together.

'Have you no shame, girl, to be so carried away from your wits by an evening of over-bred drunkards and whores cavorting at the expense of the nation?'

'But, sir – I've so little chance to meet either! My life here is quite matronly and respectable. And how can a girl resist drunkenness and envy and pride and greed and gluttony and lechery and sloth and all those other *terrible* things unless she can learn to recognise them? And this is not *ordinary* sin. This is *royal* sin. It's positively my duty as a loyal subject to witness it! Where are we going? What is it His Majesty celebrates?'

Mannion grunted. 'His *Majesty* celebrates a cow farting in a field, as long as he can drink to it.' He took a swig of beer.

Jane appeared perfectly content without a social life in Gresham's absence. Such a life was hers for the asking. Money and fame mattered more than morality in the London of King James I, and the beautiful 'niece' of the wealthy and mysterious Henry Gresham would be a catch for any hostess, and a fine chase for any man in town. She never appeared tempted, but it did not mean that the young woman in her failed to enjoy hugely the opportunities when they arose.

'His Majesty, for once, is being economical. He kills two birds with one stone. The masque is both to welcome the ambassador from the Emperor, one Prince George Lodovic, and to bid farewell to the Spanish Ambassador,' announced Gresham.

Mannion had grabbed a crust which the maid had missed from the table, and was chewing on it with his few remaining teeth. 'They do say as the noble Prince' – no-one could put more loathing into the word *Prince* than Mannion – 'comes with his baggage over-stuffed.'

'He brings three Earls,' piped up Jane, eagerly, 'one Baron, twenty-four gentlemen, twelve musketeers and one hundred servants. It's the talk of St Paul's,' she said, with great authority.

'Pigs feeding at the trough!' exclaimed Mannion, stuffing a remnant of Gresham's meal into his cavernous mouth, and spitting out a bit of bacon gristle. Something seemed to have got stuck in what was left of his molars. Gresham's eyes were drawn reluctantly and with extreme distaste to the sight, as Mannion dug for the stuck strand of meat with the enthusiasm of a miner sure he was on to a major seam of pure gold ore.

King James would be displeased at having to break off from his hunting. It was necessary for his health that he should hunt, he had told the Privy Council, and his health was, after all, the health of the nation. He had demanded they help take some of the burden of State affairs off his bending back. Cecil would have rubbed his hands with glee, thought Gresham, at being left to rule over the very fabric of government in the absence of the King. However, there was so much money from Spanish bribes sloshing around the Court that the departure of the Ambassador needs must require the King's return from hunting, and probably provoke the whole Court to go into mourning.

'What's the entertainment?' asked Jane.

'The entertainment will be provided by several fat Aldermen whose health will be put to great strain by the weight of jewels they and their even fatter wives will don for the evening, and a race between most members of the Houses of Lords and Commons to see who can place his face closest to the buttocks of His Royal Highness.' Gresham warmed to his theme. He started to mince round the chamber, bowing to various walls and doors with an inane smile on his face. 'The winner gets a pension, a title and the right to take first shot at Cecil, Earl of Salisbury. The loser has to try and extract an intelligent comment from Her Royal Highness the Queen Anne, but may opt to be hung, drawn and quartered instead, on the grounds that this is a sentence that at least leads to a relatively quick death.'

'My Lord!' said Jane, genuinely shocked. 'You shouldn't speak so about the King and His Queen!' She adopted the cool calm of the enigmatic beauty when at Court, but would talk for hours afterwards when she returned home about who had been wearing what and been seen speaking to whom. Gresham had once taxed her with her love of everything royal, pointing out some of the less savoury features of King James I of All England.

'It's perfectly possible, my Lord,' she had replied primly, 'for the institution to be divine whilst its agents on earth are merely human.'

Gresham looked at the eager sparkle in her eyes, and relented. At least she was not being distant, aloof and dignified, which he hated.

'I'm given to understand that His Majesty has commanded a masque from your good friends Ben Jonson and Inigo Jones, in which the virtues of Faith, Hope and Charity will appear to welcome Prince

Lodovic, and bid farewell to the Spanish Ambassador. We go because Sir Francis Bacon will be a guest – a guest of honour, in fact, reading a pretty speech of welcome from the House of Commons. It's at Whitehall, of course. I remember you told me you had a most commanding book of sermons to read, and so informed the Lord Chamberlain that I'd be going alone . . .'

'Sir!' Jane shrieked in anguish, before the lights dancing behind his eyes told her the truth.

Gresham had obtained details of all Bacon's engagements by bribing his clerk. A word to one of the Gentlemen of the Bedchamber and an invitation to Gresham had been immediately forthcoming. It gave Gresham a grim satisfaction that he had no need to beg an invitation from Cecil. As a major landowner and the patron of what many considered to be Cambridge's leading College, and as a known servant of the Crown for many years past, Gresham had no need of such help.

'Do I do gracious, or do I do alluring?' asked Jane.

'You "do" whatever will preserve and protect *my* honour,' said Gresham, 'which is a far more important thing than *your* female vanity. However, I'll gracefully accept as my due any information you might come across in the course of the evening.'

He had taken Jane with him as his niece to a levée some years earlier and been incensed by her flirting with a young nobleman. He had been about to box her ears when she had poured out to him a torrent of secrets so damaging to the young nobleman's father that twenty full purses would not have bought the information.

'Weren't you ashamed?' he asked, part in horror, part in amazement at the skill with which the little vixen had stripped the fool of his secrets.

'Why?' she had asked, with total sincerity. 'I'm more worried about conceiving a baby than I am about being bedded by one, and anyway I do it for you.' She did, Gresham had realised. This was a woman who far preferred pitting herself against a man in the search for secrets to preparing a fine capon for supper, or supervising the making of the season's preserves. Her *bête noire* was sewing.

Since then he had used her whenever it could be safely done.

Gresham stood up and paced the room. 'Tell me, who goes out with you on your errands to St Paul's?'

'It's usually young Will. He secretly hopes to marry me and he defends my honour . . .'

'No jesting.' The swooping, instant change of mood – like a hawk coming out from behind the sun, Mannion had commented – was upon him, and it froze the air. 'From now onwards you'll take three men with you, two in company, one a way behind. Make one of them Harry.'

Harry had seen service abroad, and been a gunner on one of the ships that had fired so many shots with so very few hits against the vast galleons of the Spanish. He was tough, very strong and totally ruthless.

'As you wish.' Jane curtseyed to Gresham, a troubled look on her face. 'Am I permitted to know why these extra precautions are necessary?'

Because, thought Gresham, *I have let happen what I vowed would never take place. I have fallen in love with you. You are wanton, and then you are saintly, you are strong and hard and then the softest voice I know, you are fierce in one moment and vulnerable in the next, you fight to the bitter end yet you are defenceless. I do not understand you, though I know you in bed, and I know that when I am with you my heart beats faster and my life has an extra colour in its palette. You have become precious to me, and that gives power over me to any person who decides to take you and hold you and hurt you. You could be held and used against me, young miss.*

'Whatever trail it is that Cecil's setting me on it'll carry danger. I can't believe other than that Will Shadwell was on his way to see me in Cambridge, and someone cared enough to kill him. Does that damned bead mean anything? Maybe Will had come across something the Catholics want hidden, or perhaps even Bacon is

70

considering a public return to Rome. I must assume there's a link, even if I don't know what it is.'

'Well,' said Jane, 'Will Shadwell certainly wasn't the type to be coming to Cambridge to sign up for a degree.'

'Cease your nonsense,' said Gresham, caught unawares by her flippancy and the image of Will Shadwell in undergraduate gown and cap. He felt himself starting to sound pompous, and so switched tone, knowing it would annoy her. 'You, mistress, are an additional lure of great value to an enemy. My honour wouldn't permit your being taken and held by an enemy. Were I to be sidetracked by having to extract you from some den of thieves I would lose what little scent I might have followed. It would be most inconvenient.'

Jane stood up. 'Thank you, my Lord. It is good to know.' Her tone would have frozen the River Thames in midsummer. 'A poor thing such as me must never be an *inconvenience*.' She left most of the hinges still on the door.

Gresham grinned at Mannion. 'Call her back, will you, if the stairway's still standing.'

It took her longer than was necessary to reappear.

'I hadn't realised that it was *convenient* for me to appear before you, my Lord. Is it *convenient* that I stand, or would it be more *convenient* for me to kneel at your feet?' No arrow about to be released from the bow quivered with more hidden tension, or stood up straighter and more tall.

My God, thought Gresham, *you would fight God and Lucifer together if they made friends again and joined forces against you!*

Gresham, enjoying his rudeness, pointed a finger at her. 'Will you sit down, you stupid wench, and be silent?'

Jane planted her arms akimbo, looked him full in the face with a fire that beat the burning of Gwent. 'Yes, *sir*, I will sit down, if that be your will. No, *sir*, I am not stupid, nor am I a wench, and no, sir, *I will not be silent!*'

'God's blood!' barked Gresham. 'Am I to be served by an old man who thinks of nothing but beer and young whores, and a young wanton with a voice like a fishwife and a temper to match, who throws a fit every time she is challenged by her master?'

Mannion lacked the education to recognise a rhetorical question, so answered it, thoughtfully. 'Aye, sir. I reckon you are.'

There was a moment of frozen silence, then Gresham, Mannion and Jane burst out into peals of laughter.

Thomas Percy was sulking. It was nothing new.

'I swear the man was using loaded dice. Three sixes in a row, would you believe? I challenged him, but the fool of a landlord came between us and made us go outside.'

Percy was a brilliant swordsman, not perhaps the match of Jack Wright, but nearly so. The difference was that Jack Wright fought to win, with a dark intensity that was as terrifying as his swift movements. Percy enjoyed winging his man, cutting him here and there, taunting him, before moving in for the kill.

'When we got through the crowd, the bastard made a run for it! Coward! Who would believe it?'

'He must have heard of your prowess, cousin. Few men would stand against Thomas Percy with a blade in his hand!' It was Catesby, silky-smooth in voice, sitting at the head of the table where the plotters had dined.

Percy glanced suspiciously at Catesby, looking for mockery. He found none in the bland assurance of Catesby's eyes, and brought out a stained cloth with which he wiped the dripping sweat off his brow. Percy sweated like a pig, or like the inside of glass on a drenching rainy day.

Jack Wright, seated as always at the rear of the room, made one of his rare contributions. He spoke slowly, as if measuring every word: 'What of your peasants and their lawsuit?'

'Animals! Animals!' Percy spluttered into renewed anger, grabbing his tankard and spilling half its contents as he rammed the ale down his throat. Wright glanced at Catesby, the merest hint of a grin on his dour features. Catesby raised an eyebrow. Stirring Percy

72

into anger was so easy that it had almost ceased to be amusing. Men's hair had turned white with fear. Had a lifetime of anger turned Percy's hair so white?

'Am I to let them lie in their hovels all hours of the day and night and pay no rent? How much trust would my Earl of Northumberland have in such a member of his family were I to leave them to stink and rot and pay no rent?'

'Dead men pay no rent . . .' It was Tom Wintour who spoke, Tom who had been in on the conspiracy from the start. A small, dark, wiry man, his restless wit was at odds with the glum pessimism of his elder brother. Robert Wintour had been recruited only recently, following again his younger brother but doing so with markedly little enthusiasm. Well, thought Tom, that was nothing new. He had long ago accepted that of the Wintour brothers he would have to generate the energy for both of them.

'Dead be damned!' Percy was warming to his theme, and never failed to rise to Tom Wintour's wit. 'There was no chance of that! We tickled them a little, that was all. There was a time when men would have taken it as their due, stout men who could take their punishment and not go whining to the law!'

And Percy's men had tickled their wives and daughters, by all accounts, with thirty of the tenants complaining direct to the Earl of Northumberland that his Constable and land agent had attacked them for rent they had already paid.

'And what of it, Robin?' Percy dropped into the familiar name, the one Catesby's friends used. 'Why must I go at my tenants like a dog after a hare? You know why! I need their miserable money! Must I be banker to this conspiracy, as well as its only link to the Court and all else?' Percy flung the question out like a spear, and already the thick sheen of sweat had formed over his whole face. Dark stains were visible under the arms of his shirt, his doublet cast carelessly over a nearby chair, and the same dark stains were on his hose over the cleft of his buttocks, and up his shirt along the line of his back.

Catesby took the angry question with a smile, waving his hand as if to say thank you. Far less of Thomas Percy's money had gone to swell the coffers of the plotters than Percy liked people to think, but he had been asked for, and had given, good coin. If this angry, self-serving torrent of words was the price Catesby had to pay for Percy's money then it was a price he was willing to pay.

'You've done well,' said Catesby placatingly, 'and all of us know it. We're grateful, truly grateful . . .'

The Duck and Drake in the Strand was rapidly becoming one of London's most fashionable taverns, and had long been a favoured ground for the conspirators to meet. It was convenient for Catesby, who had lodgings only a few doors away. Percy subsided into a grumble. It would flare up again soon, Catesby knew. He could write the speech.

Was Thomas Percy not kinsman to the mighty Earl of Northumberland, the patron who had appointed him Constable of Alnwick Castle, the Percy stronghold in Northumberland? Had not the great Catholic Earl entrusted Thomas Percy above all others to act as his emissary to the upstart James VI of Scotland, offering the support of English Catholics to the Scottish King in exchange for simple tolerance of their faith? Had not Percy won the support of the King for the Catholic cause, only to have it wrenched away from him by that Anti-Christ Robert Cecil, the poison in the ear of the new monarch? Had not a month past that same Thomas Percy been made Gentleman Pensioner to King James I, allowing that same Thomas Percy access to the King of All England? Was it not Thomas Percy who had negotiated the rent of the house adjacent to the House of Lords from John Whynniard and Henry Ferrers, the house from whence a tunnel could be dug to undermine the very fabric of England's Government? Catesby's own house in Lambeth was almost opposite, for all the use he had been. It was Percy's power, influence and charm that had closed the deal, Percy would point out, causing Whynniard and the Catholic Ferrers to look the other way.

Thomas Percy was a powerful man, thought Catesby, and a useful one, but flawed to his very centre. The anger that seemed to flare continually at the core of his being, anger against his tenants, against the invidious Cecil, against his lot in life, fuelled him but at the same time clouded his judgement. Was he noble-born? Percy's claim to be a member of Northumberland's family was at best tenuous. Yet the real problem was that of all the five original conspirators, Percy was the only one fighting for himself.

Catesby knew he was not fighting for himself. He was fighting for God. From as early as he could remember he had fallen in love with the Mass. The flickering candlelight, the language that resounded to the pit of one's brain, the transcendental union with a spirit higher and greater than that of man – even as a child his soul had risen to the Mass as a flower reaches towards the sun. He had recognised the joy of that faith, but seen the savage surgery it had caused on the body and mind of his father and mother. When he was a mere eight years of age he had seen his father tried in the Star Chamber for housing a Jesuit Father. Robert had known that Father, a foul-smelling man who had smiled all over the young Robert until the evening when he had plunged his hand down the boy's front and fondled his private parts. We do this for Jesus, the Father had said, his thumb and fingers working away. And there is more we can do for Jesus. And for this man my father is facing imprisonment and execution, thought the young Robert. He screamed and punched, even then strong for his age, and bloodied the priest's nose.

The priest had gone soon thereafter, spirited away as they always were. The humiliation, the fierce and burning bitterness, had lasted for years. Catesby had been driven to be the best at everything he had done, driven by the memory of a lost father whose suffering had soured his soul, a father whose suffering was betrayed by those for whom he suffered. Yet the meeting with his Catherine had shown him his true course. He had worshipped her from the first moment they met. When on his wedding night he had joined with her, her

75

giggling turning first to a panting and then to a gasping and then to a scream of pleasure, he had known true salvation. She was the most beautiful, the most lovely, the most heavenly thing that had ever happened to him. Despite his dashing good looks and his charm, it was his virginity that he lost to Catherine on that night. As did so many men, he gave his soul as well to the first woman who opened her legs for him.

He had been lulled by the love of the flesh, human flesh, not the flesh of Christ Our Lord. He had gone as far as to flout the true religion, seduced by his new, human love into denying Divine love. True, he had continued to hide and to host a succession of Jesuit priests, part in honour of his parents, part in honour of many of those priests who truly placed the souls of their parishioners above all worldly concerns. He appeared less and less at Mass, and had his first son Robert baptised as an Anglican, to the scandal of the Catholic community and his father's friends.

'And do I have to settle the score for this as for everything else?'

Percy was being truculent over the bill, and his tone penetrated Catesby's inward pattern of thought.

'No fear of that, Thomas,' said Catesby. 'Here – take it from my purse, and my thanks for your company along with it.' He tossed the smaller of the two purses he carried so that it landed with a solid thump on the trestle. Percy could have picked it up, but he sniffed and turned away, returning to talk at Jack Wright, who nodded every few sentences but said nothing. It was left to Tom Wintour, reliable and ever-restless, to take it, unbar the door and go to find the landlord.

Then his world had collapsed, Catesby remembered, only half deflected by Percy's intrusion. Robert his son, on whom he and his wife doted, died suddenly, to be followed by Catesby's father and then by his lovely, his adorable Catherine herself. He had worn mourning on his body, yet it was his soul that was truly black in shock. It was a punishment from God, retribution for his turning away from the True Faith.

They did not realise it, any of the others, but in seeking to destroy the Government of England, the dashing and charismatic Robert Catesby was saying sorry to God and the True Faith.

Percy was droning on still, petulant, like a spoilt child denied a sweetmeat. In a month or two he would probably be dead, as they all would be dead. Yet by their death they would have become martyrs to the Faith, opening the floodgates that would allow Christ to reign again in England. A faint smile played on the face of Robert Catesby as he contemplated the thought. Christ had died so that all of humankind could be saved. What did a few lives matter if by their death England was allowed to live again?

They were in the library of the House, the room where Gresham knew he was most likely to find Jane once her domestic duties were over.

'What new people have you taken on in these past three months?' Gresham asked.

'Two, I think – a kitchen maid and a porter. Why do you ask, sir?'

'Someone must have been watching Will Shadwell. There must be a chance, therefore, that someone is watching his master. The best place to keep watch on a man is from inside his own house . . . Walsingham had a bribed servant in every nobleman's house in London.'

'Sir!' Jane exploded. 'I'd trust every man and woman of them with my life!'

'Jane, they worship you, God knows why – *but there's never any servant on God's earth who's free from sin!* You must learn. I'm truly sorry. It's a hard lesson. *Trust no-one.* Wasn't Judas Jesus's most favoured disciple, and what's a disciple but a servant? In any event, they probably risk too much by trying for someone already in employment. No, the easiest way would be to plant a rotten flower in this garden of rest. What of the two new people?'

'One's a distant cousin of Martha's. She's a lovely girl, about

77

whom I've had to have strong words with your body-servant.' She gazed darkly at Mannion, who shrugged his shoulders as if to ask what a venerable innocent such as he should have to do with a young girl. 'He may pay his dues to your body, my Lord, but he'll keep away from those bodies over which I've charge and care. In any event, she's no spy. She lacks the brains, poor thing, apart from anything else.

'The other's a Northumbrian. He says he's seen service at sea. He comes with an excellent testimonial from my Earl of Northumberland's houses. He's a strong worker. I hired him above the others because he plays the lute.'

Gresham had the extravagant number of five musicians in his permanent employ, who played for him every evening he was in the House. Though Gresham hated public entertaining it was politic for him to drag himself to lay on five or six events a year, the taste and expense of which made them highlights of London's social calendar. For such events his band would be augmented by other musicians. It made for better music if there were such already in the employ of the House, if only through it allowing more of the practice which Gresham knew was essential for any good musician. The Cook played a merry flute, if a little too merry for Gresham's private ear of an evening, but more than good enough for a raucous evening where the finer points of intonation would never be heard by the guests.

'Was he with us when my room was gone through?' The room Gresham used as a study had been carefully searched one night some months ago. Only someone with an intimate knowledge of his papers would have spotted that a search had ever taken place.

'It happened on the first night he was with us,' Jane responded, with a frown.

'Didn't that make you suspicious?'

'Three houses had windows broken that night, on top storeys, including our own. There was a roofwalker about that night, for certain. It never crossed my mind to think that your intruder was anything other than such a man, on the look-out for whatever he might find.'

The houses crowding in on each other in London's streets meant that the roofs of even the finest properties often nearly touched each other. For the brave and the foolhardy, and for many thieves, there were roads across the roofs and into the houses more clearly laid out than the roadways beneath.

Gresham turned to Mannion.

'Bring this new man to me, in a half-hour. Send him to the dressing room, off the back balcony.'

'Do you want me there?' Jane asked.

'I think we're best left to do the business alone,' said Gresham. This time Jane took no offence.

They moved to the rear of the house, facing the river. Gresham's father had built a second great Hall at the back, with one of the finest balconies in London overlooking the Thames. A 'cut' from the main river allowed boats to dock at the House's own jetty. The room they chose to interview the new servant was just off the balcony, small and framed in brick and timber.

There was a clumping up the stairs, and Mannion ushered in the new man. He was tall, well-built and powerful, some thirty-five years old with a mop of reddish hair. There was no change in Gresham's expression as he greeted him.

'Good morning. Welcome to the House. You're pleased with your new post?'

If the man, Sam Fogarty as he had given his name, felt any surprise at this affable expression of interest from his master, he did not show it. He spoke confidently, looking Gresham in the eye. The accent was thick as sewage, but comprehensible.

'I'm well pleased, sir, to be in your Worship's service. It's the envy of London among servingmen to work in such a place.'

Gresham nodded to Mannion, who drew silently closer.

'Tell me, Sam, how long have you worked for my Lord Cecil?'

'Cecil, sir?' To his credit, Sam's face hardly blanched. 'I've never worked for Lord Cecil. I came here from the north . . .'

He did not hear the blow coming from Mannion, but merely saw his world explode into stars and an instantaneous moment of blinding pain.

When he came to, minutes later, his feet were tightly trussed with stout cord, and his arms loosely tied behind his back. The top half of his body was extended over the opened trap door, a black hole from which a foul smell blew into the room.

'One push from Mannion,' said Gresham carefully, coming round from behind the table at which he had sat with a goblet of wine in his hand, 'and you'll descend that chute head-first. It's brick-lined. It descends the height of the House, with enough curves in it to break your head to pulp. At the bottom is an old well. It's been spoilt by foul water from the river creeping in. We no longer use it for water. As far as we know there's no exit to the river. Or to anywhere else. Those who survive the descent splash around for as long as they have breath and then drown. We've heard them for a day or more, but they always fall silent. Now tell me, how long have you worked for Lord Cecil?'

Sam's head was aflame, his gut sick with the foul stench of rotting flesh that swept up from the black depths of the trap door.

'I know of no work for Lord Cecil . . .'

Mannion pushed his body an inch or two closer to the drop.

Sam screamed.

'You see,' Gresham responded conversationally, 'I remember faces. I remember being ushered out through the servants' hall of his Lordship's house some two . . . or was it three? . . . years ago. And you were there, Master Sam, with your red mop, holding court to most of the kitchen wenches. I recognised you as you walked through the door. Your voice, as much as your hair and face. You were shouting to the wenches, back then, telling them a bad joke as I recollect . . .'

Gresham grabbed the man's hair and pulled his head back,

looking into his fear-crazed eyes. 'Now tell me, Sam Redmop, for the last time. *How long have you worked for Lord Cecil?*'

'Sir . . . my Lord . . .' Suddenly, the man's whole body sagged. 'Spare me. Spare me. Four years. No more. Four years only.'

'Break his leg. The left one.'

The body writhed in protest. The crack was sickening as Mannion's club smashed the bone into a clean break. Sam screamed again.

Mannion pulled the body back from the abyss and flung the trap door shut, bolting it securely. He turned then to the writhing and gasping body, cut loose the cord around its legs and with a practised efficiency set splints around the twisted limb.

Sam's body could only flutter now, on the edge of unconsciousness. Gresham yanked his head round, more gently this time.

'We'll pay for a surgeon to look to your wound. You'll walk again, and walk as good as ever you did if you're careful. The pain you'll suffer is your payment for daring to seek to spy on Henry Gresham. No one spies on Henry Gresham. No one enters his household as a spy.

'You'll be held, in a secret place, until you can walk. You'll be given money, enough to get you back to Northumberland, and a little more. After that, it's up to you. Your Lord Cecil will be told that you came to visit the House, and that you suffered an accident in which you were most unfortunately drowned. As far as Cecil is concerned you'll be dead. If he hears of your existence, he'll assume you've deceived him and turned to my service, and he'll kill you. I suggest a new name and a new livelihood. The old one is truly dead.'

Gresham let the head drop, and turned away. He stopped by the door. 'It's not good to seek to betray Henry Gresham. Remember my mercy in sparing your life and sending you on your way.'

He left, closing the door quietly behind him. Two porters entered and carried out the groaning, semi-conscious figure. Mannion growled a sentence of instruction at them. They nodded.

Mannion found Gresham in the Minstrels' Gallery of the Great Hall.

'Is it wise to declare war on Cecil?' he asked bluntly. 'Do you intend to send such a message to him?'

'Old friend, do you think I'm a fool?'

'Sometimes.'

'Well, rest assured. Master Sam believes his death has been announced to Cecil. That makes him truly a dead man if he seeks to return to Cecil's service. As for me, I'll send no message to Lord Cecil. Far better that he should wait and wonder what's happened to his spy, see his man vanish into silence. Let's keep his Lordship guessing, old man. And whilst we're so doing, let's find out what's truly happening out there. And why Lord Cecil wants a spy in my house. He keeps me guessing about Bacon. Now I shall keep him guessing about his spy.'

Mannion pondered this for a moment. 'Who'll tell your mistress that we hired a Judas?'

'I'll tell her. It wasn't her fault. It's only by chance I was able to spot him as what he was. Just as important, will you help me to tell Cook and your mistress why I ordered two rotting sides of beef?'

The trap door over which Sam had been suspended led to no well. It was a service chute, a straight drop to the ground floor where goods delivered from the river could be hoisted up to the top storeys of the House. A shutter at the bottom deprived it of light when closed. Two decaying sides of beef suspended on a shelf feet below the trap door provided the stench of the charnel house that so fixed the minds of those suspended above it.

A short distance away down the Strand, Robert Catesby's party was also breaking up, Thomas Percy still bleating to whoever would listen how hard done by he was.

Catesby marvelled at his own sense of relaxation, seeing and almost tasting the fear on the skin of the others. Even the delay in convening Parliament – it would not assemble now until

November 5th – could be handled. The cursed powder would be subject to its interminable decay. The risk of a chance discovery in the cellar, or drink or pillow talk from one of the conspirators revealing more than was wise, was ever-present and grew with each extra day. Yet they had come this far. They would prepare as well for November 5th as they had for October 3rd. God would protect them.

He began to hum the words from his favourite song of the moment:

> 'Thou art my King, O God . . .'

It had a springy, firm rhythm and a quick tempo, one of Tom Campion's best, he thought.

> 'Through Thee will we
> Overthrow our enemies
> And in Thy Name
> I will tread them down.
> I will tread them down . . .'

Tom Wintour paused as he left the tavern. It had been a week or more since he had had a woman. The whores at The Duck and Drake were of the best kind, aimed at the fashionable clientele of the tavern. Even at this hour a handful were on duty, dressed like Court ladies. Why not, he thought, as his roving eye caught the glance of a particularly fine girl dressed in deep red. Why not? She was one of Moll Cutpurse's girls, he knew, and Moll's girls were the best there were.

CHAPTER 4

Gresham slipped out of the side gate of the House in the early evening. His doublet was worn and stitched in two areas, his hose washed out and his cloak threadbare at the edges. It was more and more difficult for him to act as an unknown in the city, or in Cambridge, but his change into the clothing of a gentleman fallen on hard times was not disguise, but caution. Where he was going, fine clothes were a call to robbery as well as a call to attention, and Gresham wished for neither. His sword hid its fine steel under a plain hilt and a weather-beaten scabbard. Behind him came Mannion, dressed in a rough jerkin.

'We walk,' he announced firmly to his rather sour-looking body-servant. 'You're getting too fat, and you need the exercise.' If Mannion muttered something under his breath, Gresham chose not to hear it.

It would have been far easier by boat, using the House's own vessels, the single bank manned by the vast-chested George, or even the magnificent four-bank of semi-regal splendour. Yet Gresham preferred to walk, despite the filth of the streets and the appalling press of the crowds. A restlessness came over him at times which could only be released by exercise, and in this instance there was the extra dimension of a need to feel in touch with the life and blood of the sprawling and corrupt city. And, of course, it allowed him to be rude to Mannion.

London was at its noisiest. The lawyers flushed out from Westminster were there in force, heading back into the City along the Strand, soberly dressed and bent forward to hear the muttered protestations of their clients. It was a long walk, from the Strand to Fleet Street, entering the City at Ludgate and skirting St Paul's. From Watling Street and Candlewick Street they turned right to cross London Bridge, joining the throng of citizens heading to Southwark for the playhouses.

They passed the stalls of the puppeteers in Fleet Street, each trying to shout above the din of the colliers, the chimney sweeps and the incessant din of the barrel-makers and every other worker who seemed to need a hammer above all other tools. The fresh-water carriers with their yokes and double wooden buckets, the strangely brownish water giving more than a hint of the River, the oyster sellers and the orange sellers all yelled their wares into the summer day.

They crossed London Bridge, its ancient piers supporting the half-timbered shops and residences that made it one of the talking points of Europe. Gresham eyed the pitted and mouldering stone, feeling the bridge shudder beneath his feet, wondering as he always did how much longer it could survive the neglect of its foundations and the thundering torrent of the Thames.

The Dagger in Southwark was Moll's place of business, before the magistrates or her creditors forced a change to another den. A significant portion of London's underworld was gathered there, nursing their sore heads. The assembled mass was one of the most unattractive sights he had ever seen, thought Gresham, a collection of rats and wolves in human form. He gave the merest nod to several with whom he had worked in the past. Gresham was ushered into the inner den of Moll, past three of the burliest men in London, all nursing vast cudgels.

'Hello, Mary Frith,' said Gresham, his face alight with mirth at the figure before him.

At first sight, it was not a woman at all who met their gaze. Dressed in doublet and hose, with hair cut short, Moll Cutpurse looked for all the world like a man, ensconced on a stool, legs set fairly apart and a brimming tankard of ale in her hand. The smoking pipe clenched firmly between her teeth added to the impression of a lad-about-town, determined to enjoy the day and the night as if it were his last. Only on closer examination did the smoothness of her skin and the twin bulges beneath her doublet become apparent.

'Mary Frith! You insolent vagabond, you spittle of Bedlam!' The figure wreathed in smoke put her stool forward on to three legs, where previously it had been resting back on two, and grinned in equal measure at Henry Gresham. 'Mary Frith died years ago, as any true bastard knows full well.'

Henry Gresham, a true bastard, accepted Moll's greeting with a low bow.

'Bastard as I am,' he replied, 'I salute an even greater bitch, be it Mary Frith or Moll Cutpurse!'

'You whoremonger!' she said joyfully, rising up from her stool and moving round the table to greet him. 'You come to me now for news, when you used to come within me! Am I so worn out as no longer to excite your fancy?'

'Madam,' said Gresham, bowing even lower, 'I'm old and weary, starved in my bones, a mere dried-out husk of the man I used to be. I can admire your beauty from afar . . .' he stepped back and looked with admiration at the trim figure hidden beneath the man's clothes, '. . . but, alas, it needs a young man to sire a beauty with so much youth still in her!'

Moll sat down on the table edge, stuck out her feet and took a huge draught of ale. Licking her red lips, she eyed Gresham up and down appreciatively.

'You always were a liar, Henry Gresham, and I like that in a man. You're none of your penny-pinching, arse-grabbing kind of liar. You,' she said as she poked him with the end of her clay pipe, 'you lie like the Devil himself, and take delight in it. For that, I'll even forgive you the bruises! And you always did have a body from Heaven, even if your mind was from Hell.'

Moll was fun enough to deal with and to lie with, but her evil temper was infamous, her mood swings greater than the tide on Dover beach, and she had had men, and women, murdered for a twopenny debt. She was one of the most dangerous people Gresham had ever known. She ran more brothels and stews than anyone except the Bishop of London, offered more watered-down wine and beer to tavern-goers and fenced for half the vagabonds in London. She defied authority, even to the extent of appearing on stage in front of a cheering full house at The Swan to recite bawdy ballads and sing songs that a sailor would blanch at. She had been arrested more times than she had eaten dinners, always bribing herself out of trouble with the seemingly endless money at her disposal.

'Enough of this babbling.' Moll bored very easily. 'You've no more need of poor Moll and her like in the old way, even if I hadn't become a respectable businessman, which I have. And I hear you have someone to keep your bed warm at night, so what is it you intend to rob a maid of instead?'

'I've never robbed you of anything you weren't hot to give, Moll Cutpurse,' said Gresham firmly, 'and for anything else I've taken you've received good coin in exchange. Enough of this babbling, indeed – yours and my own. The business is simple. What do you know that I should know?'

Moll slumped down behind the table, signalled Mannion to take a seat and took another vast gulp from her flagon, motioning irritably for it to be replenished by one of the villains standing guard over the door. He took it in his huge paw, filled it from a nearby barrel and gave it back to her. She looked moodily at Gresham.

'You're the fine one, Henry Gresham, aren't you? The others, they come to me with threats or with flattery, and they come to ask me a question. Where's the purse with seven angels in it stolen from my friend in St Paul's gone to, Moll?' With each question she adopted a different, whining tone. 'Find me a girl, Moll, a nice clean girl. Find me a boy, Moll, a nice clean boy. Oh Moll, my cousin's inherited a pretty penny in plate and keeps it in his house, and it should be mine, Moll, it should be mine . . . I need to throw the dice for high stakes, Moll, or play the cards, and where are the best games to be had, Moll . . . I need a woman who'll do it *this* way, I need a woman who'll do it *that* way, I need a woman who'll do it in ways I haven't imagined . . . so many questions, so many crimes, so many deceivers. Yet you . . . you Devil incarnate . . . *you* ask the one question to which I've to give all the answers.'

Moll got up suddenly, stuck her thumbs in her belt and walked over to the window.

'I know you might as well stick your fine head up a cow's arse as gain any joy from the man Bacon. Neither you, nor the Privy Council nor God in his Heaven will ever prove anything against him that matters a fart.'

It was pointless to ask Moll where her information came from, or which of the many men Gresham had tasked with news of Bacon had reported back to her. There was hardly a major household in London where one or more of the servants was not in her employ, information being as valuable a commodity as gold or women. Gresham knew that on occasions in the past Cecil had used her as an informant – it had been the cause of their first meeting.

'So what else do you know that I should know?'

'Had you come before tonight, I would've had little more to answer. I don't know why you've been set on a goose chase. Maybe there are those who want you set on a far road. But there's some-thing brewing nearer to home, I reckon. Something more in your line of business . . . how much will you pay, for other news, Henry Gresham?'

'A fair price.'

'Then you'd better meet a girl.' Moll gestured to one of the human tree trunks on guard. 'Wake up Nell from her groanings and bring her here – fast!'

A red-cheeked young girl with the look of being fresh up from the country was brought into the room. She had been crying, and there was a livid bruise down most of one side of her face and stains on the extravagant red dress she wore, all crumpled now. She limped, clutching her left hip with every faltering step she took.

'Yes, mistress, what is it, mistress?' the girl said, with fear in her eyes.

'See this man?' said Moll, gesturing to Gresham.

'Yes, ma'am.'

'Well, forget you ever saw him. Before you do, tell him the story of last night. Go on, girl. Do it.'

'It were . . . I was . . . I was downstairs when this man cum in. I know'd him from before, two, mebbe three times. He were quiet, but a swaggerer at the same time, if ye takes my meanin'. We went upstairs, and we did it, and after, as he was coming out of the room and before I was proper dressed or anything, this other man comes out of the other room and knocks into my man, sort of . . . it were an accident, I know for sure, there's no light up there hardly at all and . . .'

'Get on with it, you stupid slut!' growled Moll.

'Well, before you can say a word my man, the one I been with, he has his sword out and he's fightin' this other man. This other man, he run back into my room and I start screamin' an' my man he turns an' clouts me one on the side of the head with the handy bit of his sword an' I goes down screamin' an' he kicks at me to shut me up an' then this other man he trips on his sword . . .' The girl started to blubber and to wail again, dabbing at her eyes. '. . . an' the point of his bloody sword goes in the side o' my arse, it does, real hard and deep, an' it hurts and hurts an' there's a mark there now for life, it be, for life . . .'

'It'll be a short life, that's for sure, girl, if you carry on like that,' said Moll. 'Tell the gentleman here what your man said while he was riding you.'

'Well, sir,' said the tearful Nell, 'he were rough with me, very rough indeed, an' I says, "Now, sir, can you not get as much pleasure by being a little more gentle with a poor girl?" and he says, goin' at it even 'arder, "If I bain't be gentle with that damn'd King and his rotten crew I bain't be gentle with you, girl!"'

Gresham tossed a coin to the girl, which she caught with practised ease, even though he knew it would be taken from her as soon as she left the room. She gave a faint smile to Gresham, and a pleading look towards Moll. She ignored it, motioning the girl to leave.

'That's all?' said Gresham.

'No, not all,' said Moll. 'The man's name is Tom Wintour.'

The name triggered the memory of the miserable-looking man in the tavern. Robert Wintour, Tom Wintour's brother.

'He nearly killed the other man and lost me a good girl for a while, so I was less than well pleased. I had him cornered by three of the lads and taken out round the back, to teach him a lesson, as you do. He caught one of the lads with a dagger he'd hidden on him, and it got serious. He was screaming at my lads something about this not happening to him, he'd God's business to do. It was so bad I came running myself. Before I could get there this Wintour catches one of my men in the neck, dives between the other two and gets clean away. It's bad for business, all round. One of my men might die. There should be no man who beats my ruffians. It's not good for my honour, you understand. The other man he went for on the night has a bad wound and won't walk straight again. And that's bad for custom. Keep it clean, keep it quiet.'

Robert Wintour. Tom Wintour. Wintour of Huddington Court. Gresham remembered now, as it all fell into place. The western Marches were a terrible area for the old religion, defying London to take its Catholicism away from it. He had been sent to enquire into one particularly crusty old Catholic, a Sir John Talbot, heir to the Earldom of Shrewsbury. It was feared he was plotting a rebellion. He was harmless, as it had happened, a fact which had not stopped the Government from locking him up on and off for over twenty years. Gresham had become fascinated by the network of blood relations, marriages and alliances which criss-crossed the great Catholic families of the area, binding them tight together like the finest cloth. Talbot's daughter had married Robert Wintour, Gresham now remembered. Tom Wintour was the younger brother, but the brains of the family. Their house of Huddington Court was rumoured to be riddled with more priest-holes than the Vatican.

'So a swaggerer beats a whore and wounds some men, and damns the King and talks about God's business . . . it's not much, Moll.'

'Not much for you, Henry Gresham, who has his inheritance, and no need to earn a daily crust by the sweat of his brow. Moll here has to work for his living.'

Gresham noted Moll's use of the word 'his' to describe herself. It was a trick she only fell into when she was at her most serious, or her most dangerous.

'Yet there is more,' she carried on. 'Does the name Catesby mean anything to you? Jack Wright? Kit Wright?'

The names echoed somewhere in the channels of Gresham's brain. Catesby . . . a handsome young man on the ill-fated march through London of Essex's supporters, fighting with useless courage as the supporters of the Crown closed in on him . . .

'Minnows that once swam in the great pond of the Earl of Essex?'

'Fools enough to march through the streets of London trying to rouse support for the Prince of Fools, when every girl in town could've told them it would fail!' replied Moll.

'What have these small fry to do with Tom Wintour?'

'A lot to do with Tom Wintour, judging by the number of times they all of them hire a private room a stone's throw away from you in the Strand.'

'And what is to stop a group of friends meeting for a good supper to reminisce over old times and how they nearly overthrew good Queen Bess?' said Gresham, playing Devil's advocate.

'With a priest in the next room to say Mass, and locked doors, and much swearing of oaths? And with young Thomas Percy as thick as a thief with the whole sorry crew?'

The Earl of Northumberland, leader of a significant portion of English Catholics, had recommended himself to Gresham by setting himself up as a firm opponent of Cecil and vilifying the stunted creature, decorously, at every opportunity. As ever, Northumberland's action revealed the capacity of the English Catholics to always back a loser. Thomas Percy Gresham remembered as a runt of a man who claimed more blood links with Northumberland than most thought he was heir to, and who for some inconsiderable reason Northumberland had apparently made steward of Alnwick Castle, the dripping pile of masonry hung on the bleak Northumbrian coast.

'Does Cecil know of this?'

Moll turned to her tankard, discomfited. 'I doubt it. And certainly not from me, if he does. Cecil and I are . . . not dealing with each other, as things stand.'

'Why, Moll,' said Gresham, the half-smile lighting his face, 'what did we do to his Lordship?'

Moll scowled, and then let a half-grin cross her face. 'Why, it was a good song. They loved it at The Swan. Here, it was so good I bought this in the street three hours after I had first sung it.'

Gresham looked at the crudely printed ballad sheet Moll thrust into his hands. He read the words with increasing astonishment and good humour.

'I would believe almost anything of Cecil,' he said, struggling to keep even half a straight face, 'but surely not with a three-legg'd goat *and* a candlestick?'

'Aye, well, we poets must give free rein to our imagination, mustn't we? Careful – that cost all of a penny!' she exclaimed as Gresham pocketed the paper.

'Include it in the bill,' he said lightly.

'There's more,' she said. 'Will Shadwell was a man of yours, wasn't he?'

'He's no man's man now, except the Devil's, I suspect,' said Gresham, interested again. 'What of him?'

'I heard today of his death. He dined here a week before, in the Norfolk room.' Private rooms in the inn were named after the English counties, or so Moll said. Gresham believed they were named after noble lords who had bedded their whores there. 'He dined with Thomas Percy.'

'Did he now.' Gresham's face was stony, impenetrable. Did Thomas Percy have a string of rosary beads around his neck? wondered Gresham.

'Had you considered he might have been on his way with news for you?'

'I'd considered it,' said Gresham.

'Percy got drunk that night. Very drunk. Will was playing drunk, but I swear he was plain cold sober. He was on to something, I'll swear to that too. Will never refused a drink unless he was on to something. Did you know Will was a sentimental old fool?'

'It wasn't my most obvious conclusion, as far as character judgements go.'

'Well, he had a ring, a gold ring, he used to wear round his neck. No-one would know, unless you saw him with his clothes off. He bought it for the first girl he lost his cherry to. She died young – some story or other, I don't recollect the details and who cares? – but he kept the ring about him, always. It was his charm. Never took it off, even in bed.'

'Does this romantic story of young love actually have a point?' said Gresham, rudely.

Moll gazed at him levelly. 'It's always a wonder to me how you've managed to live so long. Yes, it's got a point. The point of a great ruffian in here a couple of nights ago, wearing Will Shadwell's ring on his great hairy finger!'

Gresham was very still for a few moments. 'And this ruffian? His name?'

'Sam Fogarty, or so he said. Great lump of a man with red hair.'

'And a Northumbrian accent as thick as cake?'

Moll looked startled. 'You know him?'

'I think we've met,' said Gresham. It was clear he was going to say no more.

'Well, you great ox,' said Moll, in one of the sudden mood swings that affected her, and turning on Mannion, 'does your master know what bills you run up in my houses?'

Mannion stood up with the lazy ease of a man half his age and delivered a mock bow to Moll. 'I go where my master sends me, Mistress Moll. If I'm to go undetected I can't stand out now, can I, and must blend into the background. Don't the learned say that when in Rome a man must do as the Romans do?'

'By that argument I wonder what you'd do if you found yourself in Sodom,' Moll replied tartly. 'I wonder a man such as you stands for such insolence,' she said, turning to Gresham.

'He has a very small brain,' said Gresham airily, 'which means he thinks with his rod, which is unfortunately much larger. I'll reprimand him, and no doubt he'll weep for his insolence.'

He pulled a purse out from under his cloak and tossed it on the table, where it landed heavily.

'Generous as ever, Sir Henry. Why do you who have so much play these dangerous games? You've no need, surely? Why play Lord Cecil's games?'

'Who's to say it's not Cecil playing my game? I play because I have to,' said Gresham, which was at least true. 'And because of all the things I might die from, I fear boredom more than any other. You above all others know that feeling, old Moll. We're two of a kind.'

She looked at him for a moment. 'That we are – and both likely to die on the gallows or on the rack.'

There was a brief, companionable silence.

'WHAT'S THIS DAMNED POISON THESE OAFS KEEP SERVING ME?'

Without warning she hurled the tankard at the head of the man nearest the door. It smashed against his forehead, leaving a deep cut. A second later a knife flashed out and caught the sleeve of his jerkin as he raised it towards his wounded head, pinning his arm by the cloth to the door.

'*That's* how to fight,' she said with satisfaction, as blood dripped on to the boards from the man's head. 'Quick. Unexpected. Sharp. That's how a man should fight.'

There was no debate about travelling to the Palace of Whitehall for the King's masque. The finery worn by both Gresham and Jane would have died on the streets and suffered a seizure on horseback. Jane's gown was not as diaphanous as the fashion now worn by many of the Court ladies, but was of the deepest emerald green, trimmed with pearls. The necklace she wore had belonged to Lady Gresham, and had at its centre a diamond as perfect as any the King owned. Gresham wore a doublet of black, as was his custom, but of such fine satin that it seemed to breathe with a life of its own, flowing with his body as he moved and accentuating rather than hiding the muscularity of his body. On his finger was the one ring, at its centre the Gresham emerald, another stone to make King James, who was obsessed with jewels, turn as green as the gem with envy.

Four men manned the barge, the edge of each oar tipped in gold. A small house hung on the stern of the barge, with the richest of hangings that could be drawn back to allow a view of the passing river, or closed to give privacy to the occupants of the two gilded seats, almost like thrones in the finery of their embellishment. The larger vessel required eight crew, but Gresham hated the ostentation that would have shown in his use of it for so public an arrival.

A string of vessels was making its way upriver to Whitehall, having to beat against tide and current. The feasting and merry-making had been going on all day, but most guests who were not actually resident at Court would come simply for the climax of the revels, the grand dinner and the masque written by Ben Jonson.

Gresham gazed out over the river, oblivious to the excitement of Jane by his side. A heavy, ornate boat with an inexperienced crew had lurched out of line as an oarsman missed his stroke, and slewed round into a plain wherry, splintering part of its bow. The two boats lay dead in the water, being swept downstream, the boat-man's grapple firmly embedded in the hull of the rich barge. A shouting match was underway between the boatman and the lead-ing servant in the fine barge, the fat alderman in the barge trying to retain his dignity and pretend he was above the demeaning spectacle.

Limitless wine had been available all day at court – Spanish wine, French wine, the sweet white wine so beloved of the King, Alicante, Rhenish, Muscatel, sack, Madeira, fine sherries and even ale and beer – and would continue to flow all night. Every creature that walked, flew or swam God's earth would be skinned, plucked or scraped, roasted, boiled, tossed in oils, pickled or jellied and served up to the throng. Every matter that grew in or on the ground would be harvested, peeled and diced or sliced, placed into pastries or set into jellies, covered in creams and decked with spices, to go along-side the honeyed sweetmeats and the cakes. On the last such event Gresham had attended, a groaning trestle table had given way under the mountain of food, and collapsed with such weight as to break both the legs of the servingman who had placed the last huge side of beef upon it. As darkness came on, torches, lamps and candles would seek to turn the night into day, and the light would glitter on the vast jewels that the men and the women wore to show their wealth and their status. The plate on the King's table would be all gold, and nothing less than silver would grace even the furthest table. Meanwhile in the sweated, smoking kitchens greasy cooks slipped, slithered and yelled for the attention of their underlings and aimed swipes at the kitchen boys with their ladles and heavy spoons. Even by the time they made their landing, Gresham knew that men and women would be spewing in the corners of the court-yards, and sometimes even in the rooms. Increasingly drunken men would piss where they stood, and even some of the women would hardly wait to walk into a shadow before pulling up their skirts and doing likewise, the more brazen shrieking with hilarity at their party as they did so.

Meanwhile, as the torches lit the sweating faces and threw shadows into the corners of the beautiful building, as the light glanced off the jewels and the silver and the gold, just beyond the reach of the light, there lay the ordinary men and women of England. Most would be lying on a pallet if they were lucky, on an earth floor with a leaking roof and walls little more than mud. Their meal would have been some portion of a rough-baked loaf, with more sand than flour in it if the miller was up to his trade, some scraps of filthy meat, a fresh-caught fish if Fortune had smiled on them. Their children would be bare-footed, and if the family had a poor animal it would be there in the room with them, its stink just another stench to go with that of the bodies for which soap was a ludicrous luxury.

Contrasts, clashes; the peace of the Church and the violence it caused among men; the beauty of the music echoed by the retching of the drunk and pampered guests; the wildest perfumes alongside the stink of piss. It was all summed up by the person of the King, thought Gresham. The jewels bedecking his body would be worth hundreds of thousand of pounds, never mind those on his wife's flesh, his clothes worth an Emperor's ransom, yet the man himself was unkempt, unwashed and stank to high heaven. What matter the show, if the inside was rotten?

As the four men pulled strongly towards Whitehall and the King's Landing, Gresham asked, not for the first time, how a just God could let such a world exist. The answer was obvious. There was no justice. There was no logic in creation. There was no God.

There was simply survival. The measure of a man was not how he seemed before his maker, but how he seemed before himself. To live long was to succeed; to die young was normal; to die was to cease to exist, and so life was to be lived to the fullest and to the utmost while it was there to be savoured. It was a joke, a joke so vast that no one human could ever properly understand the cosmic scale of its laughter.

He gazed fondly at Jane, her girlish excitement palpable. She had spent the last stages of the voyage excitedly demolishing the dress sense of the other guests as they hove into sight. Immediately they came in earshot she became a haughty and silent presence, stepping daintily from the boat and causing all eyes to turn in her direction.

It did not take him long to find out that he had missed Bacon's speech of welcome – only one of many, Gresham heard, and rather too intellectual and rambling for the taste of most of the early revellers and the Court. Gresham felt a momentary pang of annoyance.

Already casting around and looking for Sir Francis Bacon, his eyes lit on Cecil. He was huddled in a corner with a small *entourage* of cronies. Or perhaps he was standing straight, but just looked huddled. The air seemed to darken around Cecil and his cronies wherever they stood, as they moved through the quadrangle, and become more chill. Cecil's eye caught Gresham's. He raised an eyebrow by the tiniest height, and gave the slightest possible nod of his head, before returning his gaze to his own company.

'Bastard!' muttered Gresham, cheerfully, and sought about him for someone important to torment. Then he remembered Jane, feeling a conscience pang that he must see to her amusement, and was rescued by the sight of Inigo Jones and John Donne with his wife. Jones was a bag of nerves on this night, as his design for the 'machinery' of the masques which Queen Anne loved so much was to receive its first test after the banquet. As for poor Donne, banished from Court for marrying his patron's wife and sent for a time to the Fleet prison, he was allowed back occasionally so the King could pester him into accepting high office in the Church. He could not give up the wife he loved, which stopped him from one area of preferment, and he was at heart a Catholic, which barred him from accepting the preferment offered by the King. Donne was threadbare, but surprisingly cheerful, and the love he showed for his wife was pathetic.

There was a tap on Gresham's shoulder. A servant, plainly dressed, spoke softly in his ear.

'My master requests a brief interview with you, sir. Would you be so kind as to spare a few moments of your time?'

'Your master's name?'

'He would prefer to announce himself.'

Gresham flicked a finger at Jane, muttered a few words in her ear, and left her with Donne who was rewriting the opening of Genesis to suggest how the new King came to be created, to the credit of neither the Holy Book nor King James. He motioned to Mannion, who emerged from out of the shadows where he had ensured a plentiful supply of food and drink.

The servant led them to a small room on the first floor of a nearby quadrangle. He opened it, and invited Gresham to enter. A figure sat in a tall chair, back to the door, in front of a small table and a blazing fire. There were no hangings for a man to hide behind that Gresham could see. He smiled at the servant, who was holding the door half open, bowed down low, and kicked the door back out of the man's hand with all his might. It flew back on its hinges, banging off the wall with a magnificent crash, and rebounding with sufficient force to knock the shocked servant forward on his heels. The figure in the chair started sufficiently to knock over his wine glass, and leapt to his feet, turning in alarm to view the cause of the upheaval.

It was Sir Francis Bacon.

'My apologies, Sir Francis,' said Gresham, albeit with his infuriating careless grin on his face. 'Doors are good places for men to hide behind with a knife, particularly so when one does not know who it is one is being invited to meet.'

That, thought Gresham, will teach you not to give me your name.

Bacon looked as if his heartbeat had returned to merely twice its normal rate by now, and some colour had come back into his cheeks. He nodded to Gresham and invited him to sit down.

'My apologies, sir. I'd forgotten what it is to be a man of action – particularly as it wasn't in that role that I asked to see you.'

There was well-cooked meat on the table, and what looked like a delicate dish of fish. It too was cooked through, unlike much of the food Gresham had seen outside. A fire blazed in the hearth. A man who could command good food, a fire and a private room at one of His Majesty's gatherings was no fool, Gresham thought.

Bacon was a relatively small figure, his most notable feature what his friends described as deep hazel eyes, which his enemies (who outnumbered the friends) described as snake-like. He motioned to his servant, who was muttering words by the door among which could be heard 'oaf', 'ruffian' and even a hint of 'call yourself a gentleman . . .' He was rubbing his hand, which had near been wrenched from the arm when Gresham had hurled the door out of its grip. The servant, with marked unwillingness, brought a bundle tied in tape to Gresham, and surlily plonked it down on the table before him. It was a bundle of books, six in all, identical.

'I call it *The Advancement of Learning*. I've been working on it for many years. In it I ask for the cobwebs to be blown off our vision of learning. I ask that we seek anew to experiment, and to learn from that experimentation, as the only way that true learning will advance.'

'I'm honoured, Sir Francis. But why should I be so honoured, the mere bastard son of a merchant and an occasional supplicant at the altar of learning?'

'I was more inclined to make a present of six copies of my book to the Patron of Granville College, Cambridge, and the man who more than any other is responsible for the rising star of the College.'

Gresham looked at Bacon impassively, inclining his head slightly forward as if Bacon had spoken to him in a foreign language he did not quite understand.

'Forgive me, Sir Henry. I know your wish to be anonymous, and whilst I don't understand it I can be capable of respecting it. Yet I too have my spies – or, rather, I have those in Cambridge who will respect me for my mind, and trust me as such, rather than see me as a lawyer, a Parliamentarian or a candidate for high office. Your secret is safe with me, and with old Thomas here – who is, by the way, the only one of my feckless crew of servants who I'd trust with such a secret.'

A muttered 'young vagabond' could be heard from the doorway. Gresham hoped Mannion would not kick old Thomas to silence him.

Gresham picked on one phrase of Bacon's statement. 'Are you a candidate for high office, Sir Francis?'

'I'm worse, sir. I'm a *failed* candidate for high office. With superb judgement,' he said with heavy irony, 'I backed Essex, who lost, and so I lost the support of the Queen. That was the first disaster. I opposed Cecil, who won, so now I have an enemy in the most powerful man in the land. That was the second disaster. I then prosecuted Essex – who, by the way, ignored all and every piece of the excellent advice I gave him – and in so doing lost the support of any poor fool who had not already left my party. That was the third disaster. I am a mediocre lawyer with an excellent brain, and lawyers don't need a brain. That is the fourth disaster. I am troubled with occasional pangs of morality, and lawyers need that even less, which is the fifth disaster. I am also ruthlessly ambitious, and thereby offend even my few friends, which is the sixth disaster. I am not so much sinking, Henry Gresham, as vanished beyond sight of mortal man!'

Gresham burst out laughing. 'Yet some who appear to sink deepest rise upwards again fastest! You were knighted only two years ago, Sir Francis. Not a disaster, surely?'

'No. Merely a consolation and a leaving prize, earned more by my dear Brother Anthony than by myself.'

101

'I can only conclude,' Gresham replied, 'that given your own ranking of your good judgement, any regard you have for me is also a doomed misjudgement. Am I then the leading contender for the post of seventh disaster?'

Bacon joined in the laughter. 'Just as those who cook with the Devil need a long spoon, so you'd be as well advised to try and fly without wings as to nail your colours to any part of me. But no, what I want from you, if you're willing to grant it, is simple enough. I wish you to read my book. Then, if you think there's any sense in it at all, I wish you to give five copies to the five people in Cambridge for whose learning and judgement you have the most respect.'

'Just as you say it's not a good thing for a lawyer to have brains or morals, so these commodities aren't always in the most supply at the High Tables of Cambridge or Oxford. You trust me, a bastard and an ex-soldier, to make such a judgement?'

'As for the bastard, the ex-soldier or the many other things I hear you might be, I've no knowledge except what you tell me. Yet I've some feeling for another creature who bears your name.'

'And who might that be, Sir Francis?' enquired Gresham lightly.

'The author of *Machiavelli's Choice*, and also the author of *Sonnets on the Source of Power*.'

To the best of Gresham's knowledge his pamphlet on Machiavelli had been circulated secretly in Cambridge to the tune of only a hundred copies, with no way of tracing the authorship back to Gresham. He had been new on the scene at Cambridge in those days, and wished to test the water of the town before making his commitment to it, to Oxford or even to Wittenburg. Seemingly within days it had been the talk of every High Table, generating considerable excitement and a surprising measure of agreement and approbation. The *Sonnets* had been even more privately circulated, in manuscript and never printed. John Donne had sniffed and said nothing when he read them, so Gresham had known they were good. Bacon was very well informed, or capable of inspired guesswork.

So Bacon knew. So it was done. Leave the past behind. Do not fight what cannot be changed. Gresham rarely spent time making decisions. Life was for living, for deciding, and not for thinking. Showing no shock at Bacon's knowledge, he simply said, 'I'll take the books, Sir Francis, with gratitude, and will do as you wish, provided I like what I read.' He smiled broadly at Bacon. 'If not, I fear I will cast the books as deep as you think your reputation has sunk!'

'Worry not,' said Bacon, 'reputations are shallow, meaningless things, but like all things insubstantial they can rise as easily as they can sink.'

Gresham took another decision. 'Sir Francis, while we're here you might perhaps answer one question that is concerning me at the present time . . .'

Bacon looked up, pleased with the outcome of the exchange, invigorated by the dialogue. 'Of course,' he said.

'Why has my Lord Cecil tasked me with finding damning evidence of unnatural practices on your part?'

The colour drained from Bacon's face, and his mouth snapped open. There was presumably a tongue inside it, but it was finding it the Devil's own work to make a noise. 'He . . . I . . .'

The surly servant bumbled up to the table, looked witheringly at Gresham, and heaved a goblet of wine at his master. Bacon drank deeply, coughed only slightly, and returned to earth.

'As I think I've made clear, I wasn't aware that Cecil had any such designs – and, indeed, can think of no reason why he should do so. I pose no threat to him at present.'

Ruthless? Ambitious? Capable of deceiving? Almost certainly all three, Gresham thought, but somehow not *corrupt*, and, to Gresham at least, not dangerous. Gresham took another decision.

'Sir Francis, I don't know what you do between your sheets, or between the sheets of others, and frankly I don't care, provided you keep out from under my sheets. Tell me, if I were to pursue this chase Cecil has set me on, would I find a truth that would rock

Church and State on its heels, and see you in a court not as a lawyer but as a criminal?'

The eyes of the two men locked together for what seemed a very long time. Bacon spoke first.

'You would find an impending marriage the heat of which wouldn't raise the temperature of a drop of Thames water by a single degree – and might even freeze it. You would find a man for whom talk with women has never been easy. You would find a lonely man, Henry Gresham, more lonely than you might imagine, who surrounds himself with young male servants who cheat him and run him riot and drink and eat him dry, but who fill the air with laughter, excitement and energy. And if some of those young men keep him company at times, then there's no force to it, no violence, and there's comfort for a lonely man and I think something not without a certain value for the young men, if they so choose. I don't mean money, Sir Henry, but something softer. Is that hard for you to understand, with your fine strong girl by your side?'

'No, Sir Francis,' spoke Gresham, softly, his gaze still locked into Bacon's, 'it's easy to understand, for I have been there also, albeit only once.' Bacon's eyebrows rose. Gresham broke the look, and got to his feet.

'You'll hear no more of this from me. I'll tell Cecil you were left in a cornfield as a child by mistake and had an unfortunate meeting with a reaper and a very sharp scythe.' Gresham applied his most serious expression to his face. Bacon, whose hazel eyes had twinkled at the thought of the reaper, assumed an equally serious expression. 'But, Sir Francis, will I get six more of your volumes if I forbear to tell Cecil about the sheep?'

Bacon's laughter followed him out of the room. A man in need of laughter, thought Gresham, and a man starved of it for too often and for too long.

A couple of young nobles had joined the supper party when Gresham returned, of families whose fathers had not gained the pox from their horses, and Jane was at the centre of a crowd of admirers. Her dark eyes sparkled more brilliantly than the jewels that adorned her, the rise of her breasts and the flick of her head to remove a ringlet from out of vision accentuating the raw sensuality she carried almost, but not quite, unconsciously. Beautiful women are so often spoilt, mused Gresham. They know their beauty, they are flattered by it and they use it, as they are made to feel superior by it. But you, my Jane, simply accept your beauty and take no credit for it. You believe in yourself, girl, but not so that others must suffer for your belief. She glanced at Gresham to gain his approval. He grinned at her, pathetically pleased that his opinion mattered to this creature who had him in her thrall.

'What, drunk again, my lady?' he riposted, and she laughed full out loud at the nonsense and the heady excitement of it all, forgetting in the face of him the icy detachment she favoured at Court.

No-one paid any attention to the King, who was following his usual practice of seeming to woo the ladies sat near to him at the same time as veering frequently into appalling rudeness and acid attacks on their kind. The Spanish Ambassador was nowhere to be seen.

Clouds of wet smoke began to drift out over the courtyards and artificial lake created by the workmen, sign that the masque was about to begin. Not all the musicians were drunk, and in the light evening air they made quite a passable noise, Gresham thought. Sufficient wisps of smoke were persuaded on to the lake for at least a suggestion of mystery to be created. A huge gate at the far end of the lake opened silently, and with no visible sign of propulsion the gilded boat drew out from the gate with the flimsily clad figure of Faith in the prow. Large towers rose up from the lake as the ship passed by – Inigo had excelled himself, as every one actually worked – and a choir joined in with the musicians to herald the progress of the boat. It was all rather jolly, thought Gresham to his surprise, as lights sprang up around and on the lake, and he found himself admiring both the ingenuity of his friend and the music, whose composer he did not know.

James, without his Queen, awaited the arrival of the first boat in a gilded palace erected at the other end of the lake. He was drunk, but not embarrassingly so, taking short but frequent sips from his jewel-encrusted goblet. There was spittle on his mouth: some said his tongue was over-large, causing him to dribble.

Inigo Jones had come to stand by Gresham.

'Not bad, eh?' he nudged, and then his face sagged. 'Oh no. Dear Christ, no . . .'

A whoosh of flame came from the barriers between the lake and the bonfires. Something like two dying snakes curled up and flopped over, smoking at the edges. They were the ropes destined to haul back the first boat as it sped towards the King, slowing it down and finally drawing it to a decorous halt by the landing stage under the King's viewing platform where Faith could descend and deliver a beautiful, if over-lengthy, speech to the King. Instead of slowing down it sped on with seemingly ever-increasing speed. Faith began visibly to lose faith, at least in things worldly, lost her lines and began to look round in anguish for someone to do something to stop Faith turning into Despair. This did gain the attention not only of many more of the assembled throng, but also of increasing numbers of the musicians who lost the beat and increasingly played their piece as if its finish was a race where there might be five minutes' difference between first and last.

A peasant girl would have shown more mettle in a crisis, but Lady Broadway had been slapped into playing the role of Faith by her husband, who desperately needed the King's favour. She started to scream and flap her hands, reducing most of the audience to fits of laughter. The boat crunched into the landing stage and she was flung forward through the air, landing tumbling head-first almost into the King's lap, head over heels, her masque dress over her head and showing clearly that my Lady wore no undergarments. The King, who looked fuddled, seemed hardly to notice. There was a cheer from a group of drunken courtiers as Lady Broadway, like her vessel battered but not yet sinking, somehow rose to her feet and tried to deliver a garbled version of her speech.

> *'To thou, Great Guardian of Our Faith,*
> *Preserver of our country's peace . . .'*

Gresham looked down at Jane, who was laughing with such violent physical force that she looked like to burst out of her own dress.

'Well,' said Gresham, 'that was good. I wonder what comes next?'

The remainder of the masque went without interruption, the climax being the delivery of the empty-headed Queen Anne as Charity to her husband. The King clearly believed charity began at home, and left his rostrum almost as soon as his Queen had landed and delivered him an extravagant kiss.

There was a tap on Gresham's wrist. He turned, half expecting to see old Thomas. Instead it was one of the young Scots Lords, half drunk, who through an accent thick as alcohol-soaked ship's timber intimated that His Majesty wished to see Henry Gresham and his niece.

The King was in the Great Hall, rather than the Presence Chamber, a blazing fire sending most of its heat up the chimney and the chill of a foggy summer night beginning to creep into the room.

'Good evening to you, Sir Henry Gresham. I hope you and your . . . niece . . .' his gimlet eyes flickered over Jane, 'have supped and dined well?' He spoke the 'Sir' as if it were 'Sair', the accent thickening the more he spoke.

The words were slurred, but only slightly so. The man had a strange mix of muscularity – no-one who rode to hounds as often as he did could fail to be fit – and the same sense of a warped body that came from Cecil.

Gresham bowed low, to match Jane's deep curtsey.

'Your Majesty, we are humbled and inspired in equal measure by your Highness's generosity and benevolence to your humble subjects. Your Majesty affords us great honour by your hospitality.'

Well, I managed to say 'humble' twice, 'Majesty' twice and Highness once, thought Gresham. *Not bad.*

'I hear you have been of good service to Our State in times past, Sir Henry.'

Ears around the Hall pricked at this. Many of the time-servers were either unconscious of spewing their guts up in their favoured location, or banging at their whores, but the professional power-brokers would neither have drunk too much nor expect to go to bed before His Majesty. There was no sign of Cecil, Gresham noted, but those who reported to him would be sprinkled throughout the Hall.

'What little I have done can never be enough, Your Majesty. Those of us who can offer some small service only regret it is not more.'

Will Shadwell really regrets he could not do more. Like stay alive. Do you know how many die to keep you informed, you Scottish runt?

'Aye,' replied the King, belching delicately into an ornately ruffed sleeve. 'Yet tell me, Sir Henry, why are you alone of my subjects not beating a path to my door requesting favour? We do not see you at court, Henry Gresham. I see no letters from you pleading for advancement.'

The King was rumoured to despise those who did not come to him begging. The endless requests he received – and granted – for largesse were flattering to his soul, confirmation of his power.

Oh God, why I do get into these conversations!

'Sire, it is true I have done work for your State and Kingdom . . .'

Well, everyone's State, if the truth be known – but truth and Kingship ne'er did sit easily side by side.

'. . . which work has been its own reward.'

Well, that was true enough. It had to be, of necessity, for the likes of

Gresham. *The miserable bastards Walsingham, Burghley and Cecil had not paid for so much as a horseshoe.*

'It is also work that has needed little advertisement, and perhaps been best done quietly and discreetly. As for advancement, Fate has been kind to me. I have what I need to be content.'

'Would that the rest of my subjects felt so!' exclaimed James, sipping at the wine in the jewel-encrusted goblet he held in his hand. It was difficult to know if his enthusiasm was genuine or counterfeit. His hand was fine, white, delicate, Gresham noticed.

'May I say more, Your Majesty?'

'Aye,' replied the King, gazing at Gresham from under hooded lids, 'you may indeed, man.' The Scottish accent had become more marked. The Scottish Court was rumoured to be far more informal than the English Court, and James exchanged words with his servants as well as his courtiers at mealtimes.

'It is in the nature of Kingship for the servant to ask of the master. Yet the good servant knows that the master who gives without being asked gives with twice the heart he might otherwise have done.'

And take that up your tight Scottish arse and do with it what you will.

King James I of All England, the first man in history to have had actual sovereignty over the two nations of Scotland and England, gazed speculatively at Gresham. *This man is not drunk,* thought Gresham, *merely liberated by alcohol. Nor is he stupid. No, very far from stupid.*

'I go shortly to Oxford. I must not offend by seeming to neglect the great University of Cambridge. Does Granville College have rooms fit for a King?'

'There is no room in the land fit for Your Majesty,' said Gresham, bowing low again.

You creeping little toad. When in Whitehall, do as the sycophants do . . . Yet Gresham was surprised to see a glint of humour in the King's eyes, recognising the ironic flattery for what it was.

'But certain, Your Highness, if such rooms do not exist now they

109

will do so by the time Your Majesty grants us the honour of Your presence.'

'So be it.' The interview was ended, not impolitely. 'I shall visit you, Henry Gresham. You are near to my hunting lodge at Royston, are you not, in Cambridge? I bid you and your beautiful . . . niece God speed and a safe journey home to your fine house on the Strand.'

Gresham let out a long breath as they emerged from the Great Hall.

'What was all that about?' asked a bemused Jane.

'I think he wants you as his mistress, and was just looking to see if you fitted the bill, so to speak,' said Gresham, and received a poke in the ribs for his pains. 'Mind you, looking at you now, it's probably the House he wants, as being more beautiful and certainly more valuable . . .'

'I didn't like the sound of "your fine house on the Strand",' said Jane. 'It's ten to one he wants it for one of his stinking Lords.'

They mounted their barge and set off back to the House. The four men had drunk but were not drunk, Gresham was pleased to see. The river was a dangerous place at best of times, and in pitch dark with a fog it was more dangerous than ever. The torches set all round their boat gave each of the men a halo as the flickering light caught the moisture in the night air.

Jane curled up on to his shoulder, wrapped in a vast boat cloak. He looked fondly down on her dark head, and softly began to sing to her, a song by Tom Campion.

> 'Come you pretty false-eyed wanton
> Leave your pretty smiling
> Think you to escape me now
> With slippery words beguiling . . .'

She turned her head to look up at him.

'I've no desire to escape, my Lord,' she said solemnly, 'unless you have truly novel plans for the remainder of this night.'

Gresham laughed softly, and then suddenly stopped.

The sound of fierce rowing came to them from somewhere very near on the river, regular, hard splashes in the water, even the sound of men exhaling hard, grunting with effort. Six, possibly eight men, rowing hard in the fog and yet with some skill, and showing no light – there was no missed stroke there, but a hard, regular and practised rhythm. Coming nearer, as far as the fog would allow noise and location to be identified.

Gresham stood and exchanged glances with Mannion. He nodded.

'Douse and arm! Douse and arm!' he hissed to his four men. He turned to Jane. 'Down, down! Into the middle of the boat. Crouch as low as you can, and cover yourself with the cloak.'

Other women would have screamed or asked fool questions. Jane merely nodded, and crouched down low in the boat's centre.

The boat moved gently, rocking in the swell.

Gresham's boat crew were well trained. A rich man's boat at night on the river was fair game to the river pirates, and Gresham's men had often needed to row him into situations where good manners mattered less than sharp blades and a stout heart. The torches at the prow, stern and sides were doused. The men set their oars at the rest position, and scrabbled in the central locker for the crossbows that were kept there, passing one apiece to Mannion and to Gresham. The crossbow was a good, one-shot weapon for the sort of engagement they might face. Once wound there was no need to draw the arm back to fire, merely a trigger to pull and release the short, lethal bolt. The trajectory was flat, ideal for short-range work, release was instant if the weapon was pre-wound, and it could then be discarded for the short boat axe that the lockers also carried. A sword was too long for the close work that fighting on a small deck required, a dagger too short. A heavy, double-sided short axe was ideal, allowing the fighter to carve his way through an enemy and knock aside, with a long knife in his other hand for really close work.

The men shipped the oars, silently, only a rustle of cloth and foot on board betraying their presence. The crossbows were well maintained, and wound without the infuriating screech that would have given them away. They drifted in silence, the fog and the darkness blinding them, the only sound the lapping of the water on the boat's hull. Both shores were too far away for what dim light might be showing there to penetrate the mist. If they kept this drifting up for too long they would be swept through, or more like smashed on to, the arches of London Bridge.

The enemy had given themselves away by stopping as soon as the torches had been doused. A nobleman hurrying home would have continued on his way. A large, expertly rowed craft showing no light and coming up from behind, and presumably marking them on their torches, that stopped when they did? It was after one thing: them.

Gresham motioned silently to Mannion to put over the tiller, sending them towards the Southwark bank and away from home. In the dark the other boat would have to move in one direction or another if it was to find its prey. Gresham guessed the other boat would assume he would steer towards the left bank, not towards the darker and more uninhabited right bank.

He guessed wrongly. There was a sudden explosion of water and noise of rowers starting up. A large wooden prow appeared from nowhere out of the mist, smashing into their hull. Perhaps a sudden break in the mist had given their position away. Gresham would never know. A grapnel was flung over and stuck into their hull, and the eight men on the other boat made a mad rush to board.

He exults in this, Jane thought, as the boats crashed together with a splintering blow. The deck lurched up beneath them. Gresham's head was flung back, and he swept up the crossbow with a roar almost of glee. Loosing its bolt, he flung it downwards and hurled himself with maniac force towards the enemy, sword upraised.

The attackers were at a disadvantage in that first moment. The torches had been doused long enough for Gresham's men to gain some night vision. The enemy had made a mistake by hitting them bow-on and not drawing up alongside. The bow of the other boat only allowed two men to stand and jump from their vessel on to the other craft. The crazy movement of both boats affected the attackers, who had to jump, more than it did Gresham's men. The enemy were silhouetted for a brief instant. One of Gresham's men, the youngest, fired high and wildly, but the other three bolts stung home in the flesh and bone of the first two attackers, sending one screaming backwards into the well of his own boat and the other into the river.

Six remaining.

Gresham and Mannion held their fire for the briefest instant. The man who had fallen back into his boat caused the others coming behind to stumble momentarily while they found their feet in the rocking vessel. Gresham shot to the left, Mannion to the right. It was an old routine. One man died instantly, with the bolt through his neck. The other twisted at the last second and the bolt went through his right arm. Weakened, then, but not to be ignored.

Four remaining, with one wounded.

A blow from one of the boarders, who seemed to be wielding a mixture of clubs, swords and daggers, felled the youngest of Gresham's crewmen instantly, yet the unexpected crossbow fire had reversed the odds. A scything blow from Harry, who captained the barge, sent one of the boarders off into the river, another from young Will opened up another's face from left to right, slicing through the left eye and releasing a fountain of blood that appeared black against the white skin of the man's face.

Two left, with one wounded. The fight was over.

Mannion had not left his position in the stern. Gresham had moved down into the well of the boat, behind his men, standing over Jane. He felt rather than saw the slight tugging behind him, the deck moving in a different way beneath his feet. He swung round to see three bedraggled men hauling themselves out of the water from the side opposite the battle. Two of them were stumbling to their feet on the narrow deck, dripping water over the planks. The enemy had been cleverer than Gresham thought, and sent men round to the undefended side of the boat to catch them by surprise. The man with the bolt through his arm took courage when he saw his compatriots, and with a huge bellow lurched upright and hurled himself into Gresham's boat. It leaned viciously, dangerously under his weight.

Six boarders now to five defenders.

Gresham felt the battle lust come upon him. A red haze covered his vision. He lunged at one of the boarders who had not quite made it on to the deck. He twisted away, Gresham's axe landing where his wrists had been an instant before, but still held on. In making his move Gresham exposed himself to the man on his right, whose face suddenly took on the shape of a cross as a crossbow bolt penetrated his head from one side to another. His eyes crossed and an expression of total confusion came across his pock-marked face. 'Oh!' he said quietly, and sank to the deck. The man who Gresham had missed flipped over the hull and on to the deck, jumping to his feet.

Five boarders to five defenders.

Harry looked to have taken a broken arm, but was still swinging gamely with his left hand. Will and the other man were forcing their two remaining boarders back towards the bow. Mannion jumped down to join his master, throwing the crossbow he had reloaded to one side. Gresham made as to pull back for a mighty swing with his axe, saw the man opposite him start to lunge and bent aside, plunging his axe into the back of his head with a sickening thud as he fell past him.

Four attackers to five defenders.

Half turned, he saw a sight from Hell. The boat was bobbing erratically up and down, caught in the waves the battle had generated.

The enemy with the crossbow bolt in his arm was standing over the huddled bundle that was Jane, the boarding axe he had grabbed from the deck raised high above his head, a killing lust in his eyes. Blood from his wounded arm was falling, dripping into Jane's hair.

Slowly, so slowly, the arms went back over the man's head, as slowly, so slowly, Jane appeared to be bowing her head and scuffling about in her skirts. Slowly, so slowly, she flung up her beautiful head, and in her hands was a long, thin dagger of Spanish steel. Like a nun praying for an offering she clutched the dagger in both her hands and in supplication raised it to the man bending over her, thrusting it hard into his groin. His scream of dying agony ripped through the fog, brought even the fighting at the bow to a momentary halt with the animal scream of pure pain. The axe dropped to the deck, and the man toppled backwards, the dagger still inserted in his middle. Jane was clutching at the hilt like a drowning woman, sobbing with her own agony. She seemed unable to let go, and she toppled over with the man, ending lying on top of him in an awful parody of the beast with two backs.

Three attackers to five defenders, all forced now to the bow of the boat, all desperately fighting for their lives against Gresham, Mannion, Will, Jack and the wounded Harry.

In one fluid movement Gresham turned and hurled his axe forward into the forehead of the man in front of him. It clove his head near in half.

The remaining two men looked at their struck companion and dropped their weapons, raising their hands, looking beseechingly into the eyes of Gresham.

'Kill them,' said Gresham.

More screams rang out above the water.

Gresham turned to Jane. Very gently he rolled her off the corpse of the man she had killed, ignoring the frantic sobs that were shaking her whole body. Very gently he prised her fingers from off the hilt of the blood-soaked dagger, the blood already drying and sticking to both their hands. As she let go of the dagger, the man's head lolled back, mouth gaping, revealing his bare neck.

A string of beads, rosary beads, lay on the sweated hair between shoulder and neck.

Gresham placed an arm under her shoulder and picked her up in his arms, carrying her to the rear platform where only a short while earlier they had sat in so much state. The other boat still clung to them, the grapnel holding. It had splintered a V-shape in their side, above the water line, and the boats screeched as if in pain as the broken and exposed wood of both vessels rubbed against each other.

Jane was shivering as well as shaking, great racking sobs heaving through her whole body. He said nothing, as yet. He knew what was to come. Her eyes were wide, startled, endlessly moving in her head. They rested for a brief moment on the man she had killed, his head flung back in the agonised rictus of a shrieking death, the hilt of the dagger still sticking up into the night air like some awful erection.

He held her as she vomited over the side, her meal floating away silently downstream. The vomiting noises continued long after she had emptied her stomach.

'Why?' She turned to him, finally. 'Why?'

He did not answer, merely held her closer as Mannion and the others set about finding where they were and towing the other boat home.

Why, indeed.

Why was he being hunted on the river? Why was life a string of so many squalid little agonies, always ending in death, the smell of fresh blood?

He had the answer to neither question. As for the last question, it had been asked of humankind for all eternity, with no answer that he could believe.

He held Jane in his arms, mourning the death of innocence.

CHAPTER 5

Gresham had lain awake during the night, his whole body tensed with anger. There were few tears left in him, and he shed none that anyone could have seen.

He knew what life was. Two thirds of a woman's children could be swept off from life before they were months old, whilst ague, palsy and the plague could bite into the wealthiest and poorest households alike with no warning. There was only one answer. Live, whilst there was life. Fight the powers that condemned men and women to know the truth of their prison yet have no means of escape. Laugh in the face of the fragility of existence.

Yet the tide of despair had swung down on him, as he had known it would, and engulfed him. The dark of the night flowed into his mind and extinguished all light. The mood came on him rarely, but when it did it threatened all that he was. He felt the pulse beating through his body, felt how frail was a human's hold on life, knew how easily the pressure of that pulse could be let out from its prison by the deftest and gentlest wielding of the knife or dagger. As the blood pounded through his head, causing an agonising pain to throb behind his eyes, the temptation to release the pressure with the sharp cleansing point of metal became almost unbearable. It was as if his blood was prisoner inside his body, screaming and pummelling to get out, as the sailors trapped between decks on the *Maria* had screamed and punched at the unyielding timbers in their frenzy to escape. No more pressure, no more pounding, no more pain. Release. Yet he was a coward, he told himself as he stared sightless into the dark. 'Conscience doth make cowards of us all . . .' That man Shakespeare had it right, damn him.

His own innocence had died long since, and his survival was a matter of pride rather than of necessity. He had known in his heart that a new dawning and a first sight of the night would come to Jane, as it came to all thinking people, and that the black edge of despair would tear at her soul. The knowledge that it would come did not lessen the pain of its arrival. She had killed a man, and such a thing killed a part of the person who did the act. There was no other way. It was the way of life to demand death. So at least he would meet Jane in Hell. Yet he had reluctantly decided before the events of the previous night that any Heaven without Jane might as well be Hell for him.

He had put Jane to bed, and then gone to an old, battered chest that nowadays he rarely had cause to open. Among its contents was a bottle of a reddish fluid. The smell of it hit him as he opened it, and in a second he was back in his cot in the Lowlands, crying for the blessed liquid that would ease his pain and send him back into the numbed, drowsy state that was his only escape from suffering. The physik had been supplied by an ancient orderly. Gresham knew neither its origins nor its contents, but years later he had gone to one of the most secret and successful apothecaries in all London and described the colour, smell and taste of the physik, as well as its effect on a ravaged body and mind. The apothecary had nodded, gone to a back room and emerged with a small vial.

'What you were given was in all probability a much diminished potion than this you see here now,' he had lectured. 'Be warned. What is here is five, ten times the strength of what you had before. Taken in small measure, and only in time of strictest need, it will

118

offer release from pain both of the body and of the mind. Yet be warned. Taken too often, it will imprison the taker whilst appearing to release him.'

So the mixture, whatever it was, was dangerous to know, should only be taken sparingly and if the dangers were ignored would destroy you. Not a bad emblem for his dealings with Cecil, thought Gresham. He forced a minimal dose down Jane's barely resisting throat, and left her. He knew that her drug-induced sleep would fade into a more natural slumber, and that the twin healers of time and sleep would allow her not to forget what had happened, but to accept it and still live on. In time. For the pain in that time he could do little, except help her over the first hurdle.

That done and Jane settled, he posted Martha by her bedside and took himself off to think.

Someone had tried to kill them on the river, that much was clear. Simple robbery? Gresham doubted it. There were easier pickings on the river that night, far easier than a boat manned by six sturdy men. The attacking boat had gone straight for them. It had been well-manned, heavy-built, expensive. This was not an attempted robbery. It was an attempted assassination.

There were too many men, and some women, who might want Henry Gresham dead. There had been a rosary bead on Shadwell's corpse, and Shadwell's final meeting had been with the Catholic Percy. There was a rosary round the neck of the ruffian who had tried to kill Jane. Had Gresham come too close to a new Catholic plot, first through Will Shadwell and then by means of Moll, and made himself their target? Or had he offended Bacon? Did Cecil want him dead, despite the papers that Gresham's death would release? Had someone found out his role in the Essex rebellion, and sought to take revenge in the name of the dead leader? Or had one of the Spaniards flooding the Court after the peace treaty found out about his involvement in the Armada, and decided that to exact vengeance on water would be sweet revenge for the loss of so many Spaniards and so much prestige? The Spaniards were the most

Catholic nation in Europe, with rosary beads enough to fill the Thames. Had King James discovered the role Gresham had played in the execution of his mother, Mary Queen of Scots, so many years ago, an execution which had acted to blood the young Henry Gresham into the world of espionage and intrigue? Mary had been a Catholic . . .

There were simply too many options. Once, hiding in a ditch in Norfolk in pouring rain, a young rabbit had emerged from its burrow on the side of a dried-up stream and gambolled on the bed of the old watercourse, below Gresham. He had welcomed the animal, feeling in it an unspoken companion and noting that his cover must be good if the rabbit had not realised his presence. Then, swollen with the torrential rain, a dyke had burst and a small, rumbling wall of water torn down the old path of the stream. There were four, five, perhaps even six ways up from the bed, and Gresham willed the rabbit to run up one of them to safety. Yet the number of choices seemed to confuse the animal, which was still looking, stopping and starting when the water hit it and tumbled it along in its path, sucking it against one too many boulders. Its broken, twisted body lay there until the crows had plucked half its flesh off through the wet fur. Too many choices confused a man, as they had confused the rabbit. It was not movement that killed, but staying still. Someone was forcing an issue with Gresham. Someone wanted him dead. He must decide who it was.

Concentrate! Will Shadwell's murder had started it all, and a supper with a drunken Thomas Percy. Whatever he had heard there sent him running pell-mell off to Cambridge, and triggered his killing. Percy had command over men, was ruthless and would murder in an instant if he thought it would serve his own ends or ensure his survival. Had Percy ordered Shadwell's murder, regretting what he had told him, and Gresham's murder, fearing what he might find out? Percy was newly and surprisingly appointed to the King's bedchamber. He could have wished to kill Gresham as a

Catholic fearful of the exposure of some plot, or perhaps even on the orders of the King.

Shadwell's ring linked Sam Fogarty to the murder, and because he was Cecil's creature linked it directly to Cecil himself. Yet it could be dangerous to draw too many conclusions from that. Gresham knew at least two nobles who were taking money from both the Spanish Catholics and the Lowland Protestants, and a rogue such as Sam could have two, three or four masters. Sam Fogarty was a Northumbrian. Was he in the pay of the arch-Catholic, the Earl of Northumberland, as well as in Cecil's pay? Or was Sam Fogarty's true master the Catholic faith, and was he a spy in Cecil's household for that faith, as well as a spy for Cecil in Gresham's household? If Fogarty was a religious fanatic then the chances of Gresham getting the truth out of him were slim indeed. Men who were prepared to die on a bonfire for their faith, and who feared the fires of Hell if they betrayed it, often could not be broken even by torture.

If Cecil wanted Gresham dead he would have been better off leaving him in Cambridge, where his only servant was Mannion and where a drunken student could climb into College under cover of dark, never mind an assassin. Yet Cecil had called him to London, to live in the well-guarded House, and where even on the river he was guarded by sturdy and loyal men. Cecil had much to lose by Gresham's death and too many secrets that risked exposure, but how much did he have to lose if the King his master had ordered Gresham's death? Now there would be a conundrum for his Lordship! Ordered to kill Gresham and out of favour if he failed, but very much out of favour if he succeeded and Gresham's papers became public knowledge. Cecil was devious enough to try and satisfy his master and keep Gresham alive by arranging a murder attempt, but ensuring that it failed. Yet if his assailants on the river had been in any way uncommitted to their task, Gresham had seen no sign of it.

One coincidence struck Gresham as too obvious to be dismissed.

Shadwell and Percy had dined in The Dagger. Shortly afterwards, Shadwell had been murdered. And where had Gresham chosen to go almost as soon as he could after seeing Cecil? To The Dagger, to meet the most notorious purveyor of information in London. Shortly afterwards, someone had tried to murder him. Visits to The Dagger were clearly very unhealthy propositions at present, and not only because of the quality of the ale. If Thomas Percy was behind the murder of Shadwell, Gresham's visit to The Dagger must have sounded every alarum bell in the man's head. What if Percy believed Shadwell had left a message for Gresham, writing down secretly whatever it was as insurance in case he never reached Gresham? What if Shadwell had told Moll whatever it was he had learnt, knowing it was only a matter of time before she met Gresham? It was time Moll left town, even if only as a precaution. She and The Dagger were too close to this fire for it not to burn her sooner or later, and he had too much affection and need for Moll to want to see her share Shadwell's fate.

Gresham roused Mannion, who slept on an old army mattress by Gresham's bedroom door. Hastily he scribbled a note by the flickering light of the candle.

'Here, take this to The Dagger, to Moll. Don't leave before you see it in her hands. Go armed, and wake three men to go with you.'

It was two o'clock, with not even the bakers nor the milkmaids stirring, but Mannion did not question his orders. He gave a simple nod, and left. If Moll Cutpurse had any sense she would be gone from London by dawn, or hidden in some rat-infested warren in the City where even the King or a Catholic God could not find her. She would know when to emerge. Her kind always did. Would whoever the murderer was have gone for her already? He doubted it. A killing on the river, shrouded in fog, was one thing. It would take longer to flush Moll out of her den, cunning vixen that she was, and longer even than that to mount an assault on The Dagger, with Moll's private army of ruffians around her.

He was no nearer an answer, though if Moll took his advice he might at least have stopped another murder.

Should he have kept one of his attackers alive? In terms of Gresham's code of conduct the answer was clearly no. Life was the cheapest of all commodities. There was a simple rule for such piracy, as there was for the footpads who preyed in gangs on many roads: kill, or be killed. From the moment that prow had appeared out of the fog every person on board both boats, except poor Jane, knew that no quarter would be given. He killed only those who sought to kill him. It was life and the nature of death. In terms of information, would preserving one have helped? Probably not, he mused. Of course one of them could have been persuaded to talk. Any man could be persuaded to talk, given time. Yet torture could easily make men talk not the truth, but what they thought their interrogator wanted to hear. Under torture truth became less important than the release from pain. Gresham doubted any of the men even knew who their employer was. The boat would have been picked up from an anonymous wharf, the leader of the men recruited by a nameless nonentity in a back room in some ordinary or cheap tavern, and the leader then left to recruit his crew. Whoever had planned this attack was no amateur.

The key was a series of names, the names provided by Moll: Thomas Percy had in some way to be the key, and his name led to the others: Tom Wintour, Robert Catesby, Kit and Jack Wright. They were all Catholics, all members of the ill-fated Essex rebellion. Something one of them knew had caused someone, possibly one of them, to mount one murder and try another. What was the cause on which they were meeting? What did they know that had to be kept at all costs from Henry Gresham?

He needed a way in to that group. He needed a lever, a way of prising open the door to this group and letting his ears and eyes into their dealings. He waited in silence, allowing the candle to gutter and die, until the first flush of dawn streaked the sky and he heard Mannion return.

'She's not a woman that likes to be woken up, master, that's for sure!' Mannion seemed undisturbed by being awakened in the small hours, and sent halfway across London with no breakfast.

'If she takes my warning she won't be going back to bed tonight. She's at the root of all this, or at least The Dagger is . . .' Gresham explained briefly his thinking and the conclusions it had led him to.

'This pack of Catholics is the key, the names she gave us. I must find out what they know. Every cutpurse and vagabond, every spy and traitor, every whoremonger we know – I want them all on the trail of these names. I want to know when they launder their linen and where they throw the piss from their chamber pots . . . and work through those few we know we can trust. We mustn't be linked to these enquiries. *And we must move fast!*'

Mannion nodded. This vast trawling for information looked as if it might be the biggest they had undertaken, but its principles and its urgency were not new. Yet despite that urgency, he did not move immediately.

'Master?' Mannion was unusually hesitant. Gresham turned to him, expectantly. Mannion spoke slowly, as if he had given the matter much thought.

'She's young. She's strong. She's more than in love. She's given herself to you. She'll survive anything. Except your despair.'

Gresham thought for a moment.

Must I forever hide, he thought for a brief moment. Then the moment passed.

'Thank you,' he said, simply. The two men, divided by age and by breeding, locked eyes with each other. Words and thoughts for which no language had been invented passed between them in an instant. It was all that was needed.

Gresham became brisk, businesslike. He gazed at Mannion thoughtfully, and spoke with a light-heartedness he did not feel.

'I've no doubt you'll have been bragging about the twenty men you killed on the river?'

For once, Mannion did not respond with a grin. 'Too serious for that, master. I've been in fights enough, you know as well as I. But it was a close-run thing last night, too close. Someone wants us dead, and they don't mind who else they kill in doing it. It was different, seeing her involved.'

'Who wants us dead? Who is it this time?'

Mannion did let a grin light his face, then. 'Why, there's no shortage, is there? It's a fine job you've done of offending just about everybody, in this country and half of Europe, and you not halfway through your natural life as yet.'

'Be serious, old man. You must have your thoughts, as I've mine.'

'I don't think,' said Mannion firmly. 'I just do. That's what I'm best at. I leave the thinking to you.'

'But you have a nose on you, don't you? Who do you smell in all this? Percy and his Catholic brood? The King? Cecil? Spaniards?' Gresham issued the names as if he was punching the air with them.

'My nose tell me this one stinks to high heaven. And there's only one person I know who stinks that much. Cecil. He's in it somewhere, I'll warrant.'

'If Cecil's the one who wants me dead, he must think he can bear exposure from the papers I have lodged in Rome. Does that bring any of our recent visitors to mind?'

'Tom Barnes?' responded Mannion.

Tom Barnes was a devious, sideways-looking rat of a man, servant to one of the greatest villains in London, Tom Phelippes. Phelippes was a forger, code-breaker and general villain to the Government, who had tried one intrigue too far against his masters, and was now residing in less than comfort in the Tower of London. He had been betrayed by his servant Barnes, who had a disturbing habit of turning up on his master's business at midnight and banging on the downstairs shutters of the house he was visiting, instead of the door. Gresham had received just such a visit shortly before his departure to Cambridge, and shortly before Barnes had betrayed his master. Barnes had brought with him, and demanded a pretty price for, one letter in particular which he had stolen from his master's desk. That same letter was still under the boards in Gresham's Cambridge rooms. Gresham had been about to take the matter up with Phelippes himself when the man had suddenly been removed to the Tower.

'Well now,' mused Gresham, 'I think Mr Barnes and his papers are suddenly explained to me, in a way that was not clear before.'

'Are we going to the Tower?' asked Mannion.

'Yes,' said Gresham simply. 'We must.'

'Can we have breakfast first?' asked Mannion.

The Tower of London stood guard grimly over the eastern section of the City walls, where they joined with the Thames. They went by boat, the only sensible way to travel such a distance. Gresham had four armed men come with him. He had not won a pitched battle on the river to be wiped out in some street skirmish. Rather than using one of the House's own vessels, with no Harry fit to take command, Mannion stood by the House's jetty and cried, 'Eastward Ho!' Knowing Gresham's mind, he dismissed several boats, vying for the rich trade of the great houses on the Strand, until one with a young head came in sight.

'Do you land, or do you shoot the arches?' enquired the young man, grinning at his passengers. The hundreds, thousands of men who plied their trade on the river were as filthy with their mouths as they were with their clothes and bodies. This one looked almost healthy. Most people landed before the bridge, picking the boat up again if needs be after it had leapt through the narrow stone arches of London Bridge.

'We go the *fast* way,' said Gresham firmly. Young as he was, the boatman was both strong and skilled. There were feet on either side of them as they shot through one of the narrow arches of London Bridge, the speed and the danger as exhilarating to Gresham as it always was.

They smelt the Tower before they saw it. A permanent dispute existed between the Lord Mayor and the Lieutenant of the Tower over the City's draining of the town ditch into the Tower ditch. The dispute had been raised to a new level when the City had opened the sluices that let all the sewage from the Minories into the town ditch and so into the Tower ditch. The stink was vile, and even the hardened inhabitants of the Tower were gagging for sweet water. He left the four men to await his return by the postern gate, and took Mannion in with him.

He remembered the first time he had gone to see Raleigh after his farcical, trumped-up trial. Here was the man who had taken on the might of Spain and defeated it, a man with the mind of a scholar, the tongue of a poet and the heart of a lion. A lesser person would have been in tears, and Gresham knew that Raleigh had already tried to take his life. Yet there was no sign of that in the man sitting quietly at his writing desk in the Bloody Tower where he was lodged, still dressed in Court finery. He had raised an eyebrow as Gresham had entered the room.

'Well, my friend, how goes the world with you?'

'I'd thought rather to ask the question of you,' Gresham had replied.

'With me? Why, as you can see, all is well. The thickest walls in England protect me from my enemies . . .' he motioned to the environs of the Tower around them, 'and I have my wife and son at my side.'

He called out and Bess, the early cause of his troubles with Queen Elizabeth, came into the low-ceilinged room, wiping her hands. She was pale and hollow-eyed, but her face lit up as she saw and greeted Gresham. Bess Raleigh had mothered many more men than her own son, and saw Gresham as a favoured, albeit wayward, stepson.

'My Lord,' said Gresham, 'how can this be?'

Raleigh gave a dry, gentle laugh.

'How can it be that I'm accused of being a traitor in league with Spain after having spent all my life fighting that country? How

127

can it be that I'm convicted in a trial where the only evidence is retracted and I'm never allowed to confront my accuser? How can it be that one of my oldest allies and friends seems to be my chief accuser, the man whose sickly child my own dear wife helped to nurture and feed?'

Bess smiled at the mention of the boy she had treated as her own. Cecil's sickly son had been welcomed into the warmth of Bess Raleigh's household and brought up alongside her own bawling bundle of extreme good health.

'Why, my friend, the answer is simple. I'm a mortal being, and I live in the world God has created. And I have pride.'

He was not standing, Gresham realised, because he could not stand. The strain upon him, recent illness and his attempt on his own life had left him too weak to stand. The body had come near to being broken. The spirit, Gresham realised with an upsurge in his heart, was very much alive.

Raleigh's pride and arrogance had made him many enemies, but the wits at Court were saying that he was now the only man whose guilty verdict at trial had proved him innocent in the eyes of the great mass of people. The numbers queuing up in the hope of seeing him, on the narrow walk by the Bloody Tower that fronted the river, had swelled, until it seemed that every person of note in London was lining up hoping to see the great man, the last of the Elizabethans. The Bloody Tower itself still smelt of the new building work and fresh timber brought in to accommodate such a distinguished prisoner. A prison, thought Gresham, needs no bars.

Two years now into his imprisonment, Raleigh welcomed Gresham warmly. Mannion he clapt on the shoulder, thrusting a bottle and a fine silver drinking goblet into his hand.

'Here, you great Goliath, take this out on to the river walk and shout out that you're the great Sir Walter Raleigh!'

Mannion grinned and left, closing the door behind him.

'And as for you,' he continued, turning to Gresham, 'drink this.' Raleigh offered a beaker to Gresham.

'Water?' asked Gresham.

'Drink it and see.'

Gresham took a reluctant sip, tasting the fluid on his lips and mouth. There was a slightly brackish, unpleasant tang to it, but it seemed wholesome enough.

'Don't worry!' roared Raleigh in laughter, seeing the expression of distaste on Gresham's face. 'It won't kill you, or at least it hasn't killed me this week past. It's nectar, young fellow Do you know what it is?'

'Is that a question in rhetoric, or one I'm expected to answer?' said Gresham dryly.

'That fine fluid you're guzzling was once sea water. Sea water, mind! The water that taunts mariners on their longest voyages, those mariners who're dying of thirst but yet can't partake of the water that surrounds them. Imagine what it could mean for exploration not to have to take casks of water aboard, to take your very drinking water from the sea itself . . .'

'Is your concern the health of the mariners, or the extra looted Spanish treasure you could cram on board in place of the water casks?' asked Gresham innocently.

'Both!' roared Raleigh, rocking back on his heels with an explosion of mirth. 'It's my ability to combine the practical and the spiritual that marks me out as a great seaman!'

'It's my ability to agree with my master that makes me such a good servant,' replied Gresham. 'Even if it means lying like the Devil.'

Raleigh was in the best of moods, his huge energy refusing to be constrained. As well as writing a *History of the World* he had a chemistry laboratory in a room a short way off from the Bloody Tower, where he had concocted the brackish water from a sample of sea water.

'Time,' he told Gresham, 'time is what I need. The process for the distillation is not right yet – it works only one in five, six times – and the machinery is too cumbersome and yet too fragile

129

ever to set to sea. No point in having fresh water only until the first blow lays the ship on its side. And time, time is what my Lord Cecil and His Majesty the King have given me in plenty!'

'Time is what someone is trying to take away from me . . .' Gresham revealed to Raleigh what he knew, and what his fears were.

A sombre expression fell over Raleigh's face.

'You're right, there are too many names,' he said. 'And Sir Walter Raleigh is hardly the person to ask for advice in evading an enemy's clutches,' he said ruefully. 'One thing's clear, you need to get inside this Papist crew. But that'll take time. The man Fogarty – Sam, was it? – will be of no use to you. He's either Cecil's man, in which case he'll be more frightened of Cecil than you, or a Catholic, in which case he'll be more frightened of Northumberland or God. Tom Phelippes, now, he might be an answer. You say this man Barnes, this servant of his, brought you letters? Incriminating letters? Then Phelippes is your man. Try not to kill him, will you? It does seem to be getting something of a habit with you.'

'Is he a friend of yours?' asked Gresham, startled.

'Not a friend, but a new face, and one with some interesting tales to tell. The social circle within the Tower may be very select, but it's also somewhat restricted. Prison's worst punishment isn't loss of liberty. It's the onset of boredom. Phelippes had the look of someone who might liven up more than one evening's dinner.'

'On that basis I'll try and take off only bits that aren't life-threatening. Remember it as just another sacrifice I make for my lord and master.'

'Take care, Henry Gresham.' Raleigh was suddenly serious. 'They have me in their clutches. One free spirit is enough for them. Take care not to give them, or your Maker, another one into their power.'

This time Gresham did not make straight for the gates when he had finished with Raleigh. The guards were as slack as ever, and a small bribe allowed Gresham and Mannion into the room occupied by Thomas Phelippes. Getting out of the Tower was always much harder than getting in, but for prisoners in the Tower with their own money life was akin to that in a reasonable inn with a fractious and bad-tempered landlord. The door to Phelippes' room – or was it a cell? – was unlocked, the turnkey needing only to unlock the door that blocked the end of the dank corridor.

Phelippes' accommodation was not the best, Gresham noted. The famous prisoners in the Tower, including Walter Raleigh and his accuser and friend Lord Cobham, were kept in lodgings that had some style, and could use the Warden's garden. Phelippes was incarcerated in one of the poorer towers. The window in his cell was high in the wall and heavily barred, and there was no view out on to the garden area that the best class of prisoners could use and the next best class at least gaze out on. There seemed to be little furniture in the room.

Thomas Phelippes was a small, physically unprepossessing figure with a stoop and a pockmarked face. His origins were obscure, and he had been despised by the Court for his lack of breeding, but he had risen to be one of Walsingham's espionage chiefs by virtue of his intelligence, his ability with languages and most of all his ability to create and penetrate the most obscure ciphers.

'Good morning, Tom,' said Gresham, as cheerfully as the setting allowed. He of all people had no reason to feel cheerful in the confines of the Tower, given the various humiliations and pains he had had inflicted on his person whilst within its boundaries. Yet even without his own memories it was a dreadful place. It stank from its own ditch, and the central block of the White Tower, dating back to King William, was as blunt and as cruel a statement of power as Gresham had witnessed, a building with no concessions to form or beauty and a record of cruelty within its walls second to none. The outer walls, though representing a huge span of English history, were similarly uncompromising. The Tower was a fortress, pure and simple, a blunt instrument in the wielding of total power.

It was an evil place, a place where even music would be sucked into the darkness and silenced as so many souls had screamed soundlessly within its space.

Phelippes had risen to his feet when Gresham and Mannion entered, his features lightening for a brief instant. Then his face fell back into a worried frown, though his pleasure at his visit was still clear. Gresham noted, but did not comment on, the frown.

'Henry Gresham, by God! And that walking tree trunk of a manservant who always hangs about you! How are you, sirrah? How goes the real world about its business?'

When Walsingham had died, the empire of espionage he had built up had slowly decayed without the power at its centre. Tom Phelippes had been left in the comfortable position of Collector of Subsidy, with easy bribes at hand and a comfortable house that gave him the chance to witness all those who set sail to France, and report on them to Cecil, his new master. He lived in apparent amity with Arthur Gregory, a Dorset man whose greatest ability was to open sealed letters and reseal them without the final recipient being any the wiser, and that disreputable little runt of a spy by the name of Tom Barnes. It had all seemed very happy, until of a sudden Phelippes had been whisked off to the Tower, apparently at Cecil's command, and left there.

'The world changes little, Tom,' said Gresham easily, 'and the people in it are as corrupt as ever.'

'Well, then,' laughed Phelippes, 'things don't change at all.'

He busied himself with the contents of the basket Mannion had brought with them – the best the kitchen of the House could provide, with three bottles of very speakable wine from its cellar, the best laid on top. Gresham noted the hunger with which Phelippes attacked the food.

Phelippes finished his mouthful, took a swig of wine from the cheap wooden beaker on the bare table and looked at Gresham.

'Others would talk. Ask questions. You just wait. And bring me food and wine. Why?'

'Why wait? Or why bring you food and wine?' Gresham asked. He eased himself forward on the three-legged stool on which he sat, one of the few pieces of furniture in the cell. 'I wait because you're a crafty old fox who'll tell me what you wish to tell me when you wish to tell me, and not before. I bring you food and wine because it costs me little, and because that crafty old fox helped me once in the past, and, who knows, may help me again now.'

'And what help do you need, Sir Henry, with your fine fortune, your fine house and your fine lady? What use can a crafty old fox be, if he's been locked in his lair and looks likely never to leave?'

Gresham spoke softly, without self-pity, as if relating a simple matter of fact: 'They are trying to kill me, Tom.'

A sudden silence descended in the dark, damp room. Was there just too little surprise on Phelippes' face?

'Not for my fine house, I think, nor my fortune, not even for my fine lady. I don't know why, and I don't know who. And you will know that for us, knowledge is all.'

'Aye, I know well enough,' replied Tom, his first hunger assuaged and the lure of the wine taking over. 'Or at least, I used to know. They've tried to kill you before, and will no doubt do so again. And one day, Sir Henry Gresham, they'll succeed, as they will with all of us.'

'Why, Tom,' exclaimed Gresham cheerfully, 'if they don't succeed, God or the Devil certainly will. But before that I'd like to think I'll give them a run for their money.'

'How many have died so far?' asked Phelippes glumly, looking at Gresham with eyes that had not lost their shrewd cutting edge.

'On my side, just the one. Poor Will Shadwell. Remember Will – the plague in human form, with more illnesses than a trugging house, but loyal in his own way, and worthy of a better death than drinking too much river water. As for the others, hired men, on the river, at night. They won't be the last, on present form.'

'I remember Will Shadwell. He would have died happy if he

drank himself to death, but not on water. So what can this poor prisoner do for you?'

'First, tell me how you come to be here in this pit. I thought things were going well for you, before this business. Why has the wheel of fortune cast you down so readily?'

'I became idle, too comfortable. I relaxed – the one thing *you* have never done. I'd wind of a Papist storm brewing abroad. Too many comings and goings, from the wrong sort of people. I wrote to that damned villain Hugh Owen, calling myself Vincent, pledging myself to whatever cause he was espousing, hoping he'd reveal himself to me, and write back with something I could show to Cecil. There was no reply.'

Phelippes took another swig of wine. The bottle was already half gone.

'So I replied to my letter myself.'

'You wrote to that traitor Owen abroad . . . and then replied to your own letter yourself?' asked an incredulous Gresham.

A wide grin split Phelippes' ravaged face. 'Why not?' He spread his arms wide. 'A man must live, after all. Cecil wouldn't know a proper spy if one came at him and bit his arse. I put the reply in my best cipher, and called myself Benson. Benson wrote a good letter, hinting at many dark plots against Crown and Country. So I sold his letters to Cecil.'

There was an explosive laugh from Mannion, and an equal snort from Gresham.

'So you forged a letter to Owen, forged his replies and sold them to Cecil? A most economic use of material, Tom. Didn't the Lord Cecil smell a rat?'

'A rat? He smelt nothing except the sweet smell of conspiracy, and loved every second of it. And then that fucking bastard, that . . . *slave* Tom Barnes stole a copy of a letter in Vincent's hand and a letter in Benson's hand – Cecil had only seen Benson's hand, you understand – and showed them to Cecil. I hadn't bothered to use a different hand. It wasn't at all part of the plan for Cecil to see

Vincent's letters. How was I to know Cecil would see samples of both handwritings, which were, of course, identical?'

'Whereupon his Lordship became . . . cross?' mused Gresham.

'Cross! He pissed his fine linen and sent for me straightaway, pissed all over me and with a fair dose of shite as well and sent me here, the warped devil that he is. He's no sense of humour, that man. After all I've done for him and his scurvy State!'

'Is he more cross with you by the minute? Your quality of accommodation is hardly the best the Tower can offer.'

'No, that's not Cecil. I do believe he's forgotten I'm here. It's that walking fart Waad – Sir William Waad to you – that walking fart with *lumps* in it. You know his Fartship is now Lieutenant of the Tower, sworn in only days ago. I could do some swearing. Raleigh and some of the important prisoners put him in a terrible mood when he inspected his new fiefdom. He's too scared to touch them, except with words, but I'm easy meat. I was moved two days ago.'

Phelippes settled back on his stool.

'Enough of me. I accept your charity with good grace, yet there must be a price. Speak. What is it you want of me?'

Gresham gazed calmly at Phelippes. They had known each other for years, and if not friends had at least been comrades in the dark, shadowy world of spies and double-dealing intrigue.

'An explanation, Tom, just an explanation.'

A film of sweat was on Phelippes' brow. It was a warm day, but the cell was dank and chill despite the heat of late summer.

'An explanation? Explanation of what?'

'Of why when your servant Tom Barnes stole letters to show to Cecil, letters you most certainly did not wish Cecil to see, he found a packet of letters which most definitely were for Cecil, one of which appeared to be in the hand of one Henry Gresham. Letters written by you, forging my handwriting and appearing in every regard to come from me. Why, you old devil, you'd even used the same paper as I use myself! Well, Tom Barnes decided to show that packet to me, instead of obeying your orders and delivering it to

Cecil. He knew I paid well. You write a fine hand, Tom, particularly so when you seek to make it my hand.'

'I know nothing of . . .' spluttered Phelippes, real fear showing now in his eyes.

'They are interesting, these letters I seem to have written, Tom. I didn't know I was a Catholic, though my plea to the Pope to support an invasion of England to throw King James off his throne is as powerful a piece of writing as I've never put pen to.'

Not only was the letter a superb forgery. It would have discredited Gresham for ever in the eyes of the masses, showing him a mere lackey of the Spaniards and an enemy of England. With that reputation Cecil's chance of ducking whatever furore the letters in the Papal archive created would have been vastly increased. Who would believe accusations written by a traitor? And, thought Gresham, it was even cleverer than that. The very provenance of the letters giving the dirt on Cecil – letters lodged in the Papal archive – would in itself suggest that Gresham was in league with the Papacy, and therefore a traitor.

'Why, Tom?' asked Gresham, gently. 'Why help to spread false tales about me?'

'I . . .'

A dagger had appeared in Gresham's hand, and Mannion had moved to be in front of the iron-bound door.

'I'll kill you, Tom Phelippes, if I have to. You do know that, don't you?' said Gresham conversationally, the fine point of the dagger resting gently on top of the table's rough planking, held vertically there by the tip of Gresham's finger.

'I know it,' said Phelippes, whose face had gone a deathly colour, the pockmarks standing out lividly on the flesh of his face, 'yet if he who gave me the orders to forge your writing kills me for telling, as he surely will, why should I not choose an easy death now?'

'Because you can never know for certain that he will kill you, or find out what you told me, but you know you are surely dead by my hand if you don't tell me.' The level gaze of Gresham's eyes held and locked Phelippes' vision. He started to blink rapidly, like as rabbit caught in the light of a flaring torch. He shook his head, a tone of defiance beginning to underpin his fear.

'You can't kill me here, Henry Gresham!' he announced. 'I've no knife, I'm searched for weapons. Only you are with me. They'll accuse you of my murder as surely as Herod was accused of the slaughter of the innocents.'

'Perhaps they would, Tom, if I were to kill you with my knife,' mused Gresham. 'But you see, you've already drunk your death in that wine I so kindly supplied, and which you were so kind to drink in such quantity. My good friend Dr Simon Forman assures me of the potency of the mixture. You've drunk your death, Thomas Phelippes – unless, that is, I care to let you drink this antidote I happen to have in my purse, within the hour.'

Gresham withdrew a thin, stoppered bottle from his purse, containing a clear fluid. Phelippes' eyes followed it, as they would a vision from Heaven or Hell. Simon Forman was rumoured to have concocted more poisons than the Borgias.

'So do you want your next drink, Tom Phelippes? Or will you have done and be content with your last drink? Your last drink ever, that is . . .'

'You wouldn't do this to me!' spluttered Phelippes.

'I wouldn't *have* done it to you, before you betrayed me. Those letters you forged in my hand are my arrest, my trial and my hanging, drawing and quartering on the block, Tom Phelippes, as you full well know. Your death would seem a fair exchange. Enough of this chatter. Do you talk, or do I leave you to die?'

'I talk. The antidote . . .'

'Comes when you've finished speaking. First the letters. Why?'

'Because Cecil commanded – why else do you think? And because he paid. You know the loyalties in our game. To money and to preservation. Friendship comes a long way third.'

'Your honesty does you credit. A pity it didn't come earlier. Here, you may drink from the one bottle.' Gresham tossed the glass towards him. Phelippes grasped at it convulsively, ripped the stopper out and crammed the fluid down his throat. 'It takes two bottles to stop the work of the poison. The second is there when you finish. These names. Tell me what you know. All that you know.'

Gresham tossed a piece of paper to Phelippes. On it were the names given him by Moll Cutpurse.

Tom Wintour, Robert Catesby, Kit and Jack Wright and Thomas Percy.

Phelippes looked up, startled, his professionalism temporarily overcoming his fear. 'Catholics, one and all. A set of brothers. All related, by birth or by marriage. Catesby and the Wrights were held in the Tower together in '96.'

'Tell me about each one.'

'Why, do you think I've a clerk to hand?' Gresham held the glass bottle over the flagged stone floor. 'This has to come from my head, you know! Peace, peace, I'll try.'

Phelippes rocked back and closed his eyes.

'Catesby . . . old Catholic family, handsome devil of a man. Good swordsman too, by all accounts. Caught up with Essex, wasn't he? You would know better than I . . .' He gazed slyly at Gresham, who returned his look unmoved. 'Wife died, so I believe; thick with the priests. House in Lambeth, or used to have one there. Also lodgings in the Strand . . . A hothead, powerful, many friends. One to watch, definitely, one to watch . . .

'The Wright brothers . . . Catholics to the core, good swordsmen both . . . reckoned some of the best in the country. Up to their necks with Essex and his song and dance, with their friend Catesby. Travellers to Europe, both of them, up to no good. It was me who tipped off Walsingham about them . . .

'Tom Wintour . . . Wintours of Huddington Court, sitting on a fortune with the saltpans at Droitwich – God knows what they have to rebel about with their money. Another known Catholic, younger brother. Restless, fiery, witty, fond of the women and the wine . . . another traveller, up to no good I would guess . . .

'Percy . . . now there's a man of piss and wind. Does Northumberland's dirty work for him, went to negotiate with good King James for Northumberland, angry, vainglorious . . . King seems to like him . . . hates Cecil . . . nettles in his arse and an ambition that burns him dry. Wild, wild, to be steered clear of . . . master of no-one yet servant to none in his heart as well . . . For God's sake, man, *will you give me that bottle!*'

'Eventually,' said Gresham calmly. 'One more thing. You're a professional traitor, Tom, aren't you? So who's my lever into opening the lid of this affair?' Gresham's eyes could have pierced through the timbers on a ship's side as they looked at Phelippes. 'Who can be bribed into betraying their friends from this group? Who is there of your kind amidst these men?'

Phelippes looked longingly at the bottle. Gresham made no move.

'Tresham,' he croaked. 'Francis Tresham. I know he's not on your list, but he's been in bed all his life with those who are. He's a thieving, violent, angry little runt, and if his friends and relatives are up to mischief you can bet Francis Tresham won't be far away.'

'More,' said Gresham. 'I want more.'

'Big Catholic family.' The sweat was now running in small beads across the cavities on Phelippes' face. 'Father a patriarch, big builder, big spender. Had to bail the boy out endless times. Had to bribe him out of here, the Tower, after the Essex rebellion. Young Tresham's lucky still to have his head. He's a wild one, out of control – *for God's sake give me that bottle!*'

'Here.' He tossed the second bottle to Phelippes, who fell upon it and managed nearly to swallow the bottle as well as its contents.

'Don't betray me again, Tom,' said Gresham as he took his leave of the miserable cell and its occupant. 'In an hour or so you'll start to feel ill, and then your body will seek to expel the poison you fed it, by venting your bowels and your stomach. It'll be forcible, and it'll hurt, I'm pleased to say. A lot. You'll be able to take no food for three, four days, perhaps even a week, and your gut will hurt all that time as if it had been fed molten lead. But you'll recover, unless you catch the plague in the meantime. And by the way, the other wine is pure.'

It took them an interminable time to move through the various gates that let them out to the Thames, twice as long as it had taken them to enter.

'You've not used poison before, master,' said Mannion. There was no accusation in his carefully guarded tone.

'I haven't this time,' said Gresham.

But I was sorely tempted. Forman gave me the bottle of poison that is here still in my purse. I was ready to pour the wine into the goblets we brought in the basket, and slip the poison in by sleight of hand. I wanted him to die, to suffer for what he had done. And I don't know why I stopped in time.

'There was no poison?' asked Mannion incredulously. Gresham's act had clearly convinced him.

'No poison in the wine. The last bottle contained a potion that Forman assures me will give Thomas Phelippes a gut-ache that he'll remember for the rest of his misbegotten life.'

Mannion started to laugh, his hilarity causing his whole body to shake so that he had to grasp one of the rotting wooden stakes by the jetty.

'In dosing him I did no more than my civic duty. A change gives as much peace as a rest, and those who tend Phelippes will soon have a new stench as a change from that of the ditch!'

Gresham laughed alongside Mannion. In his laughter was a sense of release. Without conscious thought on his behalf, he now knew who his enemy was.

Jane had awoken when they returned to the House. Traces of the drug were still in her. She was sitting in a back room overlooking the river, thin and drawn, with a blanket over her shoulders despite the summer's day.

Gresham was brusque with her. 'I think I know why someone tried to murder us on the river last night.'

140

She turned to look at him, the fire in her eyes dead.

'Wake up,' he said to her, more gently. 'Wake up, or give in. You never let that stinking village kill your spirit. You never let me kill your spirit. Now choose. Are you going to let a ruffian who wanted your life take it from you, even though you killed him?'

Something like a tiny flicker of fire, as if from a grate where the embers had been left overnight, came into her gaze.

'It was . . .' She was about to collapse into sobs again, Gresham could see. He spoke, sharply, unkindly.

'It was indeed. It happened. You can't change that. Either let it destroy you, or conquer it. There's no halfway house.'

Instead of shouting at herself she did what Gresham had hoped, and shouted at him.

'How can you stand there so calmly? How can you let the blood wash off your hands so easily? How can you forget? These were men last night, not animals. We were so happy, and then from nowhere . . . this *awfulness* came and hit us and I . . . I had to . . .'

'You had to kill!' He was shouting now. 'Do you hear? You had to kill! Do you think you alone of God's creatures have a special existence? Do you think in this Godforsaken world God would come back to give you a special exemption from reality. Wake up, woman!' He moved close to her, kneeling down to breathe in her ear. 'And never tell me that I forget. You don't have that right. I remember, all of the times, all of them. *And I do not forget.* I learn to hide the memories.'

He knew then he had won, and he knew then why he loved her for her courage, for her independence and for her strength. She sat for a moment head bowed, then looked up at him. There was no extra line on her face, no extra wrinkle or grey hair, yet she had aged in a way that no physical mark would ever show. She would never be the same again, but she would be stronger, more able to survive. What she had lost to gain that victory he did not know. It was the price for survival.

'I'm sorry,' she said, with a slight sniffle still in her voice that

141

made her pathetic, still vulnerable. 'I was rapt in my own grief. It's as you say. Do you remember it, on that horse all those years ago, me with your cloak over my village filth?'

'Remember what?' Gresham was confused.

'What you said then. I don't think you knew much about little girls. You spoke to me very solemnly, as you might your bride taking her home in splendour on their wedding day. You said, "Your life starts here. We wipe out the history of every day as we live it, and if we're brave we can start it all over again with every new day. This is your new day." I thought you were mad, and very, very handsome and dashing. No-one had ever spoken to me like that before.'

'Was I really that pompous?' If the truth be known, he did remember it.

'And still are. But I'll forgive you. I'll try very hard to make it a new day. But you must be kind to me. There'll be times when it's hard, and when I'll need loving, and not shouting at, to keep me from falling into the abyss.'

In the imperceptible way that it is with people, something in them had meshed again, and moved forward with an unspoken, unseen power.

'So why was I turned into a murderess last night?'

There was a flippant edge to her voice, as well as a dark undertone. Gresham sensed that the use of the word 'murderess' was deliberate, part of her feeling her way to an acceptance of what had taken place. He did not challenge her description of herself. Let her feel her own way to her own form of salvation. There was no simple rule.

He told about the forged letter that Tom Barnes had brought to him.

'Why didn't you tell me about the letter?'

'I wanted to tell you when I had an answer, not just the question.'

'Is that wise? To share the information with me as it comes isn't to admit weakness, it's simply to recognise that two minds can sometimes do more than one.'

'On that basis,' said Gresham, 'I should share all my information with Mary the maid, Martha the Housekeeper and Harry the boatman. Oh, and there's young Will, Cook of course, and . . .'

She cut him short. 'The difference is that none of them have a mind like mine. And they may love you in their fashion, but I love you in mine. And mine is stronger.'

That shut him up, for a moment. She carried on.

'The forging of the letter was a long-term plan, anyway. Who tried to kill us? What triggered . . . last night?'

'I think I know now. I've been confused, ever since Will Shadwell's murder. At one time I had Percy killing Shadwell, and organising the business on the river in case Shadwell had left a message for me. Then I thought even the King might be involved, or Bacon, or even the Spaniards. But I was wrong.'

'So who is it?'

'Cecil. It has to be Cecil who tried to kill us. I think Cecil was trying to outflank me anyway, probably before all this started. He knew I had papers that would damn him. He must have hated my having that hold over him, wracked his brains to get himself out of the trap. Letters apparently in my handwriting pleading for a Catholic overthrow of England was an idea of brilliance. It not only makes me a wholly unreliable witness, but it makes my papers coming from the Papal archive an admission of guilt.'

'All you've said is that Cecil wanted to be able to counter what you had that threatened him. Why did he suddenly decide to have us killed?'

'Will Shadwell, I'm sure. He's at the heart of it. Will must have heard something that sent the poor fool scurrying to me, and the evidence is that he was murdered by one of *Cecil's* men, not by Percy or anyone else. I've been too clever for my own good. I invented all sorts of reasons why Sam Fogarty could have been working for Northumberland, or perhaps for Rome and the

Catholic cause. The only two things we know for certain are that Fogarty works for Cecil, and he was involved in Shadwell's murder closely enough to have taken Will's ring. That links it back to Cecil.'

As Gresham had hoped, the chance of explaining why her horror had happened gripped Jane, drew her mind out from the depths of her depression, forced it to work.

'But Cecil didn't try to kill you after Will Shadwell. He called you back to London and sent you off after Bacon.'

'Cecil must have feared something Shadwell knew enough to have him killed. Then he must have wondered if Shadwell had got the news to me. Whatever it was, it must have been of such great importance that I couldn't be allowed to know it and to live. Cecil wouldn't want to alarm me unnecessarily in case I knew nothing, so he must have called me back to London on a wild-goose chase after Bacon to sound me out. I didn't give him any cause for suspicion when we met because I knew nothing then that linked Will's death to him. Truth is always the best defence. Cecil read me right that day. I didn't suspect him of Shadwell's murder, or of anything other than being the slimy rat I know he is. So Cecil must have felt really pleased with himself, and sent me off after a red herring in the hope it'd keep me out of trouble and off the scent of whatever it is he wants to hide from me.'

'Then why did he then suddenly want to kill you?'

'It has to be my trip to see Moll. Cecil must have thought I'd gone to pick up a message from The Dagger. It was stupid of me to go so openly. There must have been endless numbers of Cecil's spies in that place, seeing me walk through and reporting back. Shadwell met Percy in The Dagger, and Moll puts out that she knows everything, even if she doesn't. What was to stop Shadwell leaving papers for me back at The Dagger, as insurance in case something happened to him? It's what I would have done. Poor Cecil. He must have congratulated himself that he's stopped the trail and sent me off on a wild-goose chase, and then I turn up bold as brass at The Dagger. He must have had a seizure. I sent Mannion to warn Moll. She'll go into hiding. Cecil is bound to be after her, to find out what she did know.'

'And I suppose once he'd commissioned one set of letters to prove you a traitor, he felt he could simply commission another to cover for your death. One other thing points to him,' said Jane. 'The boat that attacked us, it was new, well-found, expensive. The men on it . . . may have been thugs, but they were trained, after a fashion, and many of them. All that signals money, resources, the power to gather a crew and a boat at short notice. There are few people in London outside of Cecil who could call on resources to that level. But why the rosary beads?'

'Who knows? Even Cecil can't have that many thugs at his disposal. The man whose beads Shadwell broke could have been the same man you killed on the boat.'

'Do you really believe that?' said Jane. 'Or are you trying to make me feel better? I didn't kill a man, you're trying to tell me. I simply executed Will Shadwell's murderer?'

She was too clever by half, thought Gresham, too astute for his tricks even in the immediate aftermath of her grief.

'It's possible. Or it's Cecil setting a false trail, suggesting Catholics are behind the murders, putting up a smoke screen behind which he can hide. Rosary beads are cheap enough, after all.'

'We may have got closer to *what* happened,' said Jane, 'but we still don't know *why*.'

'True,' replied Gresham. 'Well, Tom Phelippes may have given us our key into these Papists. Francis Tresham, he said. A pleasant piece of work by all counts, but I'd back Phelippes to know a traitor any day. He looks at one in the glass every morning, so he should know.'

Jane rose. Her gait was tired, the movement an effort. 'I'm going to bathe and to change, and shout at a few servants to stop them sympathising with me and treating me like a sick woman.' The

House knew what had happened on the river, of course. Gresham doubted if his own boat crew had stopped telling the story even now downstairs in the kitchen. It was a good story. Let them tell it. It bred a pride in his servants and it made sure that the crossbows in the boat would be well oiled. 'But just one thing more. You've warned Moll. Yet won't Cecil be suspicious of Tom Phelippes, if you walk up to him as you walked up to Moll? Won't you have signed Tom Phelippes's death warrant, as you nearly signed Moll's?'

'Will I?' said Gresham carelessly. 'Well, now, there's a thought.'

'Is that all you care?' said Jane.

'Yes,' said Gresham, 'it probably is. He betrayed me. And it'll be interesting to see if someone tries to take his life, won't it? If they do, it will prove Cecil's involvement. No-one else has the key to let an assassin into the Tower, do they?'

Raleigh hated most of all the time when the bell tolled and the Tower was emptied of all its visitors. In the day he could lose himself in the bustle of the King's prison, in his laboratory and in his writing. At night too he could turn, in the silence, to his books. Yet in the late afternoon, when the people hurried to leave the Tower, then it came upon him that he could not leave, that he was truly a prisoner.

He had freedom to walk in the inner ward, though a warder would trail him quietly if he did so. The image of Robert Cecil haunted his mind. Cecil's power had destroyed Essex, and was now set to destroy Raleigh himself. In a strange way, it was probably not personal at all, Raleigh mused. He believed that Cecil had been, probably still was, genuinely fond of him. Affection had never stopped Robert Cecil ordering a man's death. Why would he do it?

Because Raleigh had the two things that Cecil most dreaded in a rival; the capacity to hold a crowd, to be a popular leader, and the capacity on occasion to act on principle, and not simply through self-interest. Cecil would never make a crowd eat out of his hand, and he had always feared those who could cut direct through to the hearts and minds of the common people. Nor could he predict which way a man might jump if ever he stepped off the predictable path of self-interest, and on to the more dangerous road of principle, and Cecil hated those whose moves he could not predict. It needed only the tiniest push to separate Raleigh's head from his body, he knew. He had become a threat to Robert Cecil, a potential rival for the heart and mind of the King and the heart and mind of the people. Already with no charge to answer he was locked inside the strongest prison in the land. One slip, and Cecil would have him in his shirt on Tower Green, ready to kiss an axe in place of Bess.

Henry Gresham was a man's man as well, thought Raleigh, a born leader and someone men would die for. Yes, and women too. He too had caught Raleigh's habit of not only having principles, but occasionally letting them command his actions. Was that why Gresham now seemed to be Cecil's target? Perhaps in part, but it could not be the whole answer. It was Raleigh's potential to sit in Cecil's chair by the side of the King that made Cecil want him dead, and Gresham would never aspire to sit next to any throne, though he might condescend to underpin it. Was the long battle between Gresham and Cecil finally coming to an end, in Cecil's favour as it would have to be? Anger at the power the man Cecil was able to wield fought with black despair at his powerlessness to make things change.

He turned towards the Tower which lodged Phelippes, expecting to find the door locked for a less privileged prisoner. It was ajar, he saw, to his surprise. He quickened his pace. As he reached the ancient, heavy wood and iron door he heard a crash as of an object being hurled across a room.

He had no sword or weapon, but the old warhorse needed no second notice. He pushed through the door, ran to the cell, crashed through that half-open door. A tableau met his eyes, as if cast in wax.

A tall, powerfully built man in a rough jerkin with a hood pulled over his head was standing in the middle of the small room, a dagger in his hand. Tom Phelippes, his eyes wide-staring in terror, was hunched behind the trestle he had grabbed and was using as a shield, on his knees, his face pleading. Such scant furniture as the room offered was thrown around the room. Raleigh guessed the attacker had come in silently, perhaps behind Phelippes, whose animal instinct had alerted him in some way. He must have hurled the stool at his attacker, and then grabbed the trestle as his only defence.

'Halt!' Raleigh's roar of command had cut across the decks of Spanish galleons, brought drunken crews to order and quelled mutiny. In that small room it had the force of a cannon blast. Yet Raleigh was unarmed.

The attacker swung round, face half-hidden by the hood. There was silence, a triangle of people – Raleigh by the door, Phelippes crouched on his knees in the far corner, the attacker in the middle. Slowly, carefully, never taking his eyes off those of the attacker, Raleigh raised both his hands in front of him, and moved, one gentle pace at a time, to clear the way to the door. He could take the man on, but the dagger put the odds firmly in the attacker's favour. Yet if he tried to kill Phelippes and beat off Raleigh then he might be overcome, the dagger won from him and used against him. Raleigh moved aside two more paces. The path to the door for the attacker was clear. Raleigh nodded towards it, raising an eyebrow quizzically. Leave, it said, with your job undone but your body intact. Or stay, and fight two men, and run the risk of killing the Tower's most famous prisoner. The attacker returned Raleigh's gaze, glanced briefly towards Phelippes. Was there a hint of a smile on the half-hidden, unshaven face? The attacker drew himself up to his full height, gave a short, almost formal bow to Raleigh, and backed out towards the door. He was out through in an instant, the soft pad of his feet vanishing up the passageway. There was no shout of alarm, Raleigh noted, even though the warder trailing Raleigh could not help but be outside the tower.

'Well, well,' said Raleigh, stooping to help Phelippes to his feet.

The man was gibbering with fear. 'I had thought it was my misfortune to be tried and killed in public, but it appears we guests of His Majesty have more to fear from a private reckoning . . .'

'Can I get you out of here?' Gresham asked. He had obeyed Raleigh's summons to come to the Tower. 'You know it can be done, has been done . . .'

'No, I think not,' said Raleigh. 'I'm not at risk from a vagabond murderer. Even Cecil wouldn't dare have me murdered here, though I don't doubt even now he's thinking how to achieve the same end within what passes for the law. No, this was all about our friend Tom. He had one chance at Phelippes, and if it had been done silently and quickly it would have been a three-day wonder. He daren't try it again, and I'm safe enough.'

'But that's not why you refuse to escape?' queried Gresham.

'No, I suppose not. You know me too well. If I escape, where do I go? To Spain, and prove that I was a traitor all along? All I do by running is prove my accusers were right. My battle is here. As you have reason to know, I'm not a man who runs away from battles.'

'Yet you're suggesting that I should do just that?'

'Not run away, no. Hide, yes. Go to Cambridge and lie low there, perhaps? It's such a small place you'd be bound to hear of any outsiders coming to the town who might pose a threat. Go abroad? You've enough hiding places there, haven't you? Cecil is all-powerful. He wants you dead, for what you might know, just as he wants me dead for what I might become. You can swear until Doomsday that you know nothing and he won't believe you. My advice is to take a leaf out of that girl Moll's book. Lie low, go away.'

'I accept half the advice,' said Gresham. 'Hide and lie low, yes. But not in Cambridge, nor in Europe. Here, in London, in Cecil's back yard, where I can still do my work, turn the tables on him. I have my battles, like you. Like you, I don't run away. I stay and fight.'

CHAPTER 6

Robert Catesby was riding through the gently rolling, lush-green pastures of Worcestershire. He had made good time on his journey to meet Ambrose Rookwood and enlist him into the conspiracy. He had cultivated the friendship of Rookwood for years, waiting for just such a moment. He needed Rookwood's wealth, and the horses that wealth would buy. No-one understood his genius, he mused. There was no-one else who could have had the vision he had, conceived of the plot and welded so many different individuals to it. Well, history would know.

They had abandoned the tunnel. It had come near to killing them, not their victims. It had to be God's will that just as the tunnel had proved impossible the lease on a house with cellars directly under the House of Lords had become available. It was stacked now with powder, hidden under piles of faggots and firewood. With one blasting roar of flame that would light up London and burn for years he would destroy all semblance of government in Britain. Into that vacuum of power he would ride with three hundred men. Horsed, armed and ready, they would first of all sweep up the Princess Elizabeth from her thinly guarded home at Coombe Abbey and offer her as the heir apparent. The same three hundred men, swelled by then with other Catholic supporters, would race through the Midlands and along the Welsh borders where Catholic support was at its strongest, gathering strength all the time. Meanwhile the 1,500 Spanish troops idling at Dover would throw off their pretended stupor and race in turn to Rochester. With no army to oppose them, they would sit astride the Thames and starve London into submission if it failed to support the uprising. Fawkes had promised it would be so, returning from Europe with secret assurances. Catesby and every Catholic who could ride a horse would by that time be streaming in their thousands to the gates of London, whilst Sir William Stanley would be bringing his English Regiment over from Europe, land them at Southampton to underpin the new regime, regardless of Spain's support. Again, Fawkes had confirmed that all they were waiting for was the excuse to move. With Percy acting as intermediary to the Earl of Northumberland, and the threat of all his power sweeping down from the north seemingly assured, God had to be on their side.

Robert Catesby would change the world. He smiled to himself as he urged his horse onwards.

The countryside he rode through was dressed in shades of green, with the increasingly darker and richer colours showing the first heaviness of autumn. The thick woodlands on the tops of the gentle hills contrasted in their untamed wildness with the neat rows of the tilled land in the valleys and the strips of pasture. Seen from the inside of a healthy young body, astride a fine horse and with a thick cloak to hand to keep out the chill of evening when it came, it was truly God's green and pleasant land. One could almost forget the rising tide of persecution that was first of all choking and then surely killing off the great families of England, who for years had asked nothing but peace to worship God in the one and true way of the Faith.

Catesby reined in, and gazed out over the pastoral landscape, with a few wisps of smoke showing the whereabouts of peasant cottages, and a fine stone manor on the hillside exuding calm and authority over the scattered holdings. He imagined his own men pounding through and over the harvest-bare fields, the glinting helmets of the Spanish troops catching the sun as they struck fear and trembling into the hearts of the ignorant peasants in the fields.

If the grand vision was simple, and the grand players in place, it was the detail, as ever, that caused the problems. The men had kept their mouths shut, Catesby knew, but there was talk among the women, and of course among the servants. It could hardly be otherwise. The stockpiling they had already done, under the guidance of John Grant and Robert Wintour, could hardly have gone unnoticed by the womenfolk. The stables were fuller by the minute. There would have to be more horses, more weapons. Most of all, he was desperately short of money, and in particular money for horses.

Well, Catesby had an answer to all those problems, he thought as he rode on his way to Huddington Court, the home of Robert Wintour. You could not defeat gossip, but you could block it by spreading other stories and simply overloading the capacity of the tongues to wag. As for money and horses, there were three names he was prepared to risk as new conspirators now there was so little time left to go for them to get it wrong – Ambrose Rookwood, Sir Everard Digby and Francis Tresham. Three young and moneyed men were about to be persuaded to give God, and Robert Catesby, some of their wealth.

His horse shied as some loose stones dislodged by its passage rattled down the steep embankment upon which he rode. It was a nervous creature, but strong and powerful, and he instinctively leant forward to soothe its nervousness.

Horses were the key. Catesby had timed his visit carefully. Ambrose Rookwood had one of the finest stables of any man in England, and his love of horses was legendary, as was his love of fine clothes. That same love of fine horses meant he would never stay with the women and the others on the recent pilgrimage some forty of them had taken to Winifred's Well at Holt. He would ride on ahead, stopping over at Huddington on the way to his own ancestral home at Coldham Hall. It was a woman's thing, this pil-grimage, thought Catesby, but Rookwood's love of his wife had sent him on it and his desire to drive a good horse hard meant that he would ride ahead on its return. That in turn meant that Catesby would see him without the presence of Elizabeth, his wife. Rookwood was a dandy and a showman, but he listened to his wife, who had a great deal more sense than he did. The last thing Catesby wanted was pillow talk the night after he had enlisted Rookwood.

He rode into the courtyard and handed his horse over to the groom who came rushing up to him. Other men might take their mount to the stables themselves, and see it in its stall, fed and rubbed down. Catesby saw no reason why he should do what a ser-vant could do just as well. He had more important fish to fry, as the small, dark and elegant figure of Rookwood did him the honour of coming down the steps, almost dancing with joy, and caught him in a warm embrace, as if it were his house and not Robert Wintour's.

Yes, thought Catesby, as they went arm in arm into the house. You have two things I stand most in need of. You have horses and you have wealth.

Catesby felt a growing excitement as he agreed to a warming cup of wine, even before taking his boots and riding cloak off. The dour Robert Wintour had appeared, radiating as much warmth as if Catesby were Anti-Christ come to visit. Rookwood was chattering on about a new Hungarian riding coat he had just acquired, with its velvet lining. You have a fine fortune and a fine wife, Catesby thought, and enough brats scampering about your home to fill a farmyard. Your days are filled with your fine horses, your fine wife, your fine sons, your hawks and your hounds.

Rookwood brushed aside the servant hovering to take Catesby to his room, as if it was he and not Robert Wintour who was master of Huddington, and strode up the stairs himself in his eagerness to show his friend where he would be resting his head.

Catesby followed his friend up the stairs to his chamber. Once

Catesby had held a loving wife, had the fine son and the fine house warmed with love and happiness, before they were cruelly dragged away from him. Rookwood's family faced destruction and execution from the involvement Catesby brought, the friend with the viper in his pack.

That, thought Catesby, is their problem, not mine. Life dealt cruel blows. Why should Rookwood, Digby or any other body on earth have the happiness that Catesby had been denied? If there was a hint of pleasure in Catesby's damnation of his friend and all that his friend loved and cared for it was a very private emotion, one he chose not to let see the light of day.

Gresham had gone to the cellar where Cecil's spy, Sam Fogarty, was being held until he had strength enough to be carted out of London. The man had cried out in fear as Gresham had entered.

They had been ordered to kill Shadwell, he had said. He did not have to say whose orders these were. He was Cecil's man. They had cornered him finally on the outskirts of Cambridge, stalked him through the night, hurled the body into the river. No, he did not know why the death had been ordered. Why should he and the others be told? Their business was to kill, not to ask why.

By the time he had finished, the man was speaking almost confidently, believing he was useful to Gresham. Gresham looked calmly down at him.

'This is for Will Shadwell,' he said. In one swift movement he lunged with the dagger in his hand, penetrating the eye exactly in the centre of the pupil and driving upwards until the splintering sound of bone told him he had carved through the soft brain to the skull. It was the blow that had killed Will Shadwell. As the man fell he flung his arms out, hands facing up to the ceiling as if in supplication. They were still trembling. Gresham pulled the dagger away, and stood up.

Jane had woken in the night, as he had known she would. He had held her as the truth had returned, bringing on wracking sobs, imagining it to be like holding a woman through the pangs of birth. Yet it was not a child that had been born from her, but knowledge. Later, at night, they had made love, gently, in the way that she had taught him for the times when the edge was gone from their violent, urgent need for each other's bodies. It had seemed as if his whole body had poured its passion and its intensity into that one focal moment of release, met by her soft cry. For a few seconds after that moment, even sometimes for a few minutes, Gresham felt at peace, the demons inside him stilled. So it was with Jane, he suspected. A new demon was in her, a shared demon. How it would fit with the others inside her head, the restless spirits whose nature he could only guess at, only Jane would know. There would be no more tears for others to see, Gresham knew. She had killed a man. She would learn, like him, to cry inside her head .

He needed to hide, to take cover, to go to ground. Yet at the same time he needed London and the access it gave to his network of spies.

He woke with his mind clear. Breakfast over, he spoke with Jane and Mannion, his tone clipped and definite.

'Raleigh was right. We have to lie low, to hide ourselves until we can find out what all this is about. We're moving, to Alsatia,' he announced. 'Or rather, I am moving. Jane, you can stay here. If you do, you'll be well protected, as protected as money and men can make you. Even then, we can't guarantee there won't be an assault on the House, or more likely a fire to drive you out and into the arms of whoever wants purchase against me. In Alsatia we'll be on our own. Safer, for a while, until our identity leaks out. Yet more in danger, from those we'll be surrounded by. Not to mention plague and pestilence.'

He looked at her, noting her chin jut out just that little bit further as he spoke, sensing as much as seeing the head tilt upwards.

'I come with you, my Lord, if you'll have me.'

'So be it.'

Alsatia lay between Whitefriars and Carmelite Street. No

155

constable or night watchman ever troubled the narrow streets of Alsatia, no law enforcement agency ever lightened its paths. It was a haven for any criminal escaping the hue and cry. Authority in Alsatia lay in a man's brute force and cunning. A force of order, but never law, was more or less enforced by whatever criminal warlord had dominance at any given time, but mastery could change hands three or four times in a year as rival groups and gangs fought their silent and bitter wars out of sight of any judge or jury. Unlike other areas such as Southwark, where the brothels and gambling dens could flourish until the law took notice of them, Alsatia offered little or no entertainment, merely a kennel where wild dogs could hide and lick their wounds, if they were not first killed by their own kind also in hiding. It ranked with the brick kilns of Islington and the Savoy, its distinction being that of all the human cesspits in London Alsatia was the most foul and the most extreme, talked about with bated breath by the good citizens of London, and with the reddest flush of embarrassment if ever mentioned by a woman.

'But first I have another shorter journey. To my Lord Cecil.'

There was a gasp of breath from Jane. Mannion looked glum, and sucked at his tooth with the hole in it. Whenever Gresham took a decision Mannion thought was ill-advised, a piece of flesh or bread always seemed magically to reappear in that tooth.

'Surely not!' said Jane, emboldened by shock and fear. 'He must be behind all this! What madness is it to walk into his parlour!'

'It *is* madness, which is why he won't consider it, because it's something he would never do himself. That's why he's not his father's son. Oh, he'll plot and scheme and poison and murder, but he's cautious, always cautious. He thinks all men are lesser versions of himself. He's at his weakest when dealing with someone totally unlike him, someone who's never thought like him in all his life.'

Gresham took Mannion and four men with him to see Cecil. Unusually, he rode the cumbersome great coach that his father had ordered. It was a monstrous machine, and made every rut and canyon in the roadway seem three times deeper than it was. It was fit only for old men tottering their way from one visit to another, or fine ladies too fat or too well-bred to walk or mount a horse, and Gresham hated it. Yet it had solid walls and was defensible, with its very cumbersome nature turning it into a fortress on wheels when under attack.

It was fitting that a man with Imperial ambitions lived in a palace. Gresham barged his way through to the ante-chamber. With the King returned from Oxford, and happily killing as many wild animals as he could find in Royston, Gresham knew Cecil would be sitting at the centre of his web. A crowd of hopefuls were waiting kicking their heels, desperate for an audience.

Gresham approached the Clerk sitting like a little God at his desk.

'The King's Chief Secretary is far too busy to see those who come without prior arrangement,' announced the Clerk, sniffing through an elongated nose whilst looking down it at Gresham. 'If you insist I will take details of your petition,' he added in a tone that made it clear the petition was doomed never to meet his Lordship's eyes. A host of other eyes focused on Gresham, from the threadbare old man with a tattered bundle of papers clutched in his hand to the *gallant* in fine silk and satin but with a haunted look in his restless eyes. The place stank of fear, of despair and of lost hopes.

Gresham leant over and whispered something in the Clerk's ear. His eyebrows rose until they were entangled in his hair. The Chief Clerk to the King's Chief Secretary scuttled off to knock hesitantly on the guarded door. He emerged a short while later, looking even more flustered, and bowed to Gresham, ushering him in. Mannion remained outside, impassive.

Cecil was alone. It was possible that he might have had a hurriedly dismissed floozy with him, more likely one of the wild Irish harpers whose music he had so taken to. The expensive hangings could have concealed any numbers of doors. How could a man with so much ugliness in his soul have so much love of fine art and music? thought Gresham. Yet somehow Gresham doubted Cecil had been with anyone. Cecil simply liked to keep people waiting, and he fed on the anxiety and desperation of those parked outside his door, almost as if the power to deny them his presence confirmed the very power that he held.

The setting was different from the room where Cecil met his spies. It was opulent, with the hangings alone worth a small fortune. It was vast, the mullioned windows letting in bars of strong sunlight that glowed on the richly polished table in the centre of the room. Cecil sat in a huge, ornately carved chair at the head of the table. The usual mass of papers was spread before him. Why so many papers, thought Gresham, for a man with the most ruthless memory he had ever known? Ten perfectly carved matching oak chairs were ranged each side of the table, with a single, simpler chair at the end of the table. Ordered around the room were twenty or so other chairs, each worth a yeoman's ransom. The message was clear. This was a room that dwarfed the individual. It spoke of meetings of powerful men, of decisions taken by rulers.

It was also a room where clearly the petitioner was meant to sit at the end of the table with a vast lump of gleaming wood between him and the Chief Secretary. Gresham, who was never good at obeying orders spoken or unspoken, simply stepped round and marched up the side of the table.

Was there a flicker of fear in Cecil's gimlet eyes? It was difficult to say, the damned table was so long and Cecil so far away from the door.

Gresham walked the length of the table, remembering to drag his feet a little. He stopped by the side of Cecil, pulled out an adjacent chair and casually seated himself, as if drawing up a chair to his oldest friend. As he did so he pulled his sword scabbard aside with just a touch more force than was strictly necessary.

'Do sit down,' Cecil said softly, making a vague motion with his hand, long after Gresham had done so. There was no sign of anger that the man he had tried to kill was here, alive, seated in front of him.

'Thank you, my Lord,' said Gresham, gracefully.

There was a silence. It stretched into an uncomfortably long time. Gresham sat calmly, a quizzical smile on his face, his eyes never leaving Cecil's impenetrable black gaze.

Cecil broke first. 'You did ask to see me, I believe?'

'Did I?' said Gresham, in a surprised tone. 'My apologies, my Lord. A number of your servants have attempted to *make contact* with me, and so I assumed the invitation was yours. I wondered perhaps if you wished news of Sir Walter Raleigh, your Lordship's old friend?'

'My servants?' said Cecil, apparently equally surprised, and ignoring the gibe about Raleigh. He knew Gresham's relationship with the most distinguished prisoner in the Tower. 'You surprise me, Sir Henry. I was not aware of sending any servants to speak with you.'

No, thought Gresham, *you just sent a group of ruffians to murder me. I suppose you could call them your servants.*

'That is certainly true, my Lord,' replied Gresham, 'as the servants in question did not have the holding of speech with me as their first priority.'

'I am surprised, therefore, that these speechless creatures were able to identify themselves as my servants. Are you sure in your surmise? I would be angered indeed if there were those seeking to impersonate servants of His Majesty the King's Chief Secretary.'

Mistake, Gresham thought. *Your first mistake. You should not need to use your rank to boost your credibility.*

'I would not worry overmuch, my Lord.'

'And why should that be, sir?' enquired Cecil, raising one thin eyebrow and feigning boredom despite the patronising impertinence of Gresham's tone.

'The scoundrels in question were an unhealthy lot. Indeed, I believe all but two of them died of a sudden, one is near to death and another broke a limb.'

Let Cecil think one of the murderers lived on. All the bodies could not have been washed up yet, and even Cecil could not keep a count of every body in the Thames.

'How very unfortunate,' mused Cecil.

'Not at all, my Lord,' replied Gresham. 'Rather I view it now as God's justice on any soul impertinent enough to pretend to be in your Lordship's employ. Thanks be to God.'

'Well, well,' said Cecil, flatly. 'This has been most interesting. Most interesting.' His tone suggested it had been as interesting as an examination of his master's scrotum. 'But do tell me, *as you are here*, how things go with the investigation of . . . Sir Francis Bacon.'

Gresham leant forward, suddenly, conspiratorially. Even the icy control of Cecil could not stop him from a sudden, sharp movement back in his seat.

'I have it on the firmest evidence,' said Gresham with total sincerity, 'that he is the Fiend incarnate.'

'How so?' said Cecil, revealing more interest than he intended.

'It is said that he possesses the Philosopher's Stone, the alchemist's secret, the magic stone that turns all it touches to gold. There is one problem, and one problem alone.'

Cecil's avarice overcame his intelligence. 'Problem?' he said, his eyebrows knitted together in concentration. 'What problem?'

'In its present refinement Sir Francis's stone will turn to gold only the turds of members of the true aristocracy. He has tried it on all manner of substances, and on all manner of turds, but it will only work with those produced from men of the highest breeding.'

Gresham stared hard at Cecil. Cecil's family was of low birth, brought to ascendancy by the mind and not the breeding of Cecil's father, old Lord Burghley.

'This is a problem indeed, my Lord, because as my Lord knows better than I, there are many *cheap and imitation Lords* about the place nowadays, my Lord, Lords who claim, my Lord, high birth and breeding but who are only lately come into their Lordships, my Lord, and have no more breeding than a turd. My Lord.'

If ever hate could burn a hole in a man's eye sockets there is smoke in your eyes now, thought Gresham.

'Clearly,' Gresham continued, relaxing against the hard back of the chair, 'this matter is of equal importance to the enquiry into Sir Francis Bacon's sodomite tendencies, a matter which I know carries the highest importance to the welfare of the nation. Indeed, one part of the anatomy seems to turn up wherever one looks in the case of Sir Francis. I shall enlarge the scope of my enquiries to cover both areas, so to speak.'

Cecil was stock-still, as if frozen. Gresham could see the tick, tick of the pulse in his neck. It was double Gresham's pulse.

I think you do not have a very great sense of humour, Chief Secretary to the King, particularly where the butt of the humour is yourself.

'On less serious matters, I must report, my Lord, that I have been experiencing minor difficulties in the conduct of my investigation.'

Cecil's eyes had gone on a brief journey to Hell, noted the suffering that could be inflicted on a human body, and returned to the land of the living with renewed enthusiasm, particularly as they looked at Gresham.

'Do tell me,' he said, in a voice of coach wheels on gravel.

'I suspect the wicked *Sir Francis* has detected my enquiries.'

Let's play you at your own game, thought Gresham, *bluff and double bluff. Let Sir Francis be my code for Robert Cecil. Let's see your mind race to break that code.*

'*Sir Francis* has set men to spy upon me and scoundrels to murder me. I believe he has also forged letters in my hand, purporting to show me as a Papist.'

'Good heavens!' said Cecil softly. 'Such wickedness!'

'I know, my Lord,' said Gresham, shaking his head in sadness, 'such wickedness is almost beyond the imagining of men of good conscience such as you and me. However, I am reassured in my heart. You see, I have weapons against such villainy.'

'You do?' enquired Cecil, his voice caressing Gresham.

'I do, my Lord. You see,' he leant forward to whisper the information near to Cecil's ear, 'I have letters from *Sir Francis* to the Infanta of Spain offering his support to her claim to succeed Her Majesty the Queen upon Her Majesty's most untimely death – whilst at the same time he was expressing his total loyal service to His Majesty King James when His Majesty was King of Scotland! Can you imagine such infamous double-dealing from a servant of the Crown! And what is more, these letters have *Sir Francis's* very own personal seal on them, the seal he never lets off his hand. They are potent proof, beyond the wit of even the best forger.'

'And how,' said Cecil in a voice that was almost also a whisper, 'did you acquire these letters?'

'I murdered the messenger that was taking them to Spain, as he sought to board a ship in Dover,' said Gresham flatly. 'You will understand, I am sure, my Lord. We servants of the King have sometimes to take drastic action to preserve the peace. They are good letters, remember. The hand and the style are unmistakable, and, as I said, they are sealed with . . . *Sir Francis's* seal. His special signet. I believe he uses it still.'

Gresham did not glance at the signet ring on Cecil's finger, the ring containing his personal seal. Nor did Cecil.

'Yet *Sir Francis* could still do you great harm, Sir Henry. The Papist threat is ever with us. You would do well not to be implicated.'

It had taken very little time for Cecil to pick up the code.

'That is true, my Lord. But were you ever familiar with the work of that great rogue, Kit Marlowe? The lines are from his *Doctor Faustus*. I believe it is Mephistopheles who speaks them. "It is great consolation to the damned to have companions in distress." If *Sir Francis* succeeds in implicating me, I know of course I would have your Lordship's support in any charges brought against me. Your Lordship has always supported his friends.'

Take that in Raleigh's name, and for his sake!

162

'Not to mention the support of several Bishops in the House of Lords who know my fervent Anglicanism. Even were that mighty support to fail, I would at least have the comfort of knowing that I would drag my accuser down to Hell alongside of me.'

'So many secrets, Sir Henry. So many secrets,' mused Cecil. His eyes swivelled back from the window where they had rested their gaze, and fixed on Gresham. There was no change in the tone of his voice, or the posture of his body. 'Tell me, does *Sir Francis* know that you once sodomised a young man in the Low Countries, and that the young man in question was executed in a most gruesome manner when you refused to acknowledge your crime? I am sure that your . . . niece knows what happened. I understand you are very close to her. And that servant of yours . . . and the students in the fine College you have endowed in Cambridge, and its Fellows. It is in the nature of academics to be forgiving, of course, and they and students never gossip or laugh at a man . . . how could they, when their studies bring them so close to God? No, I am sure those who have cause to love you will find forgiveness in their hearts, should this thing become known . . .'

The sinking feeling, as if given a sudden blow to the stomach. He had known it would come. This was what had been in the papers Cecil had stolen from Walsingham, in the paper that Cecil had produced in order to blackmail him into going on that stupid mission overseas so long ago. He had steeled himself for it, knew that Cecil would not be able to resist playing his final card. It was a victory over Cecil, after all. It was Cecil declaring his hand, when he, Gresham, had cards in hiding still. Victory; yet it hurt still like the pains of Hell.

No-one looking at Gresham's neck would have seen the tick of his pulse increase. There was no film of sweat on his brow. Knowing that the human eye could sense the tiniest tightening of muscle – it was the sense that had kept him alive on several occasions – he forced his muscles to relax, kept himself draped nonchalantly over his chair.

'You are kind in your concern for my past, my Lord, and for my future. As it is, I told Sir Francis Bacon of the incident to which you refer.'

The tiniest, tiniest flicker of a muscle in Cecil's eye . . . Always start a lie with a truth . . .

'And my niece and servant know everything I know and everything I have been . . .'

Which if I have knocked you off your guard you will not realise does not include everything I have done . . . Now. Now was the time. Now he signed his death warrant, or arranged a little longer life for himself, for Jane and for Mannion . . .

'Yet you are correct, my Lord. I know my secrets are safe with such as your Lordship, yet it would cause me grief if some were to know of what you speak. There is a further matter.'

It was vital that Gresham injected the right blend of bitterness, near-shame and worry into his voice if he was to be believed.

'I am . . . ill, my Lord.'

'You are?' said Cecil, coming to life, and with a gleam of hope in his voice. 'I am saddened to hear it.'

For only the briefest moment Gresham was tempted to confess to the plague, if only to see how fast Cecil could run.

'It is . . . a growth, my Lord, here in my side.' It was actually a penny loaf, strapped to his side whilst still warm from the kitchens, but producing a suitable lump just under his ribcage, bulging under his satin doublet. Thank God Cecil did not keep hounds in his hall. They would have sniffed at the doublet and in all probability tried to drag the bread from under his shirt.

'I am told it is serious. It would have been most interesting to pursue *Sir Francis*, to enact revenge for his assaults on my person, but unless I obtain total rest I am assured that I will do to myself what *Sir Francis's* men tried to do to me. I am leaving London, my Lord, with those closest to me. It will be difficult for *Sir Francis* to find me out. I am practised in hiding. Should I be pursued or harried any more I have made arrangements for the letters I mentioned

164

to be delivered to someone who hates him, and who will guarantee sight of them to the King.'

That would set Cecil thinking. The list of men with good cause to hate him would stretch three times round Whitehall and still reach all the way to the Tower. And they did say the King liked younger men, men with straight bodies and golden hair . . .

'I wish you a full and speedy recovery, Sir Henry. You are master of your own affairs. But if indeed you propose to "vanish", as you put it, I am sure *Sir Francis* would not over-exert himself in finding you. He will feel, I am sure, that his point has been made. Men such as he hate meddlers, do they not?'

'It would appear that men such as *Sir Francis Bacon* do not just hate meddlers, my Lord. It would appear they try to murder them.' Gresham drew a deep breath. 'Which leads on to my final question, my Lord.

'Why was Will Shadwell killed?'

Gresham put the ragged edge on his voice, forced the sweat to coat his forehead. A man required to control too much, a man for whom serious illness and the ordeal of a growth being hacked from his side was pushing him over the edge, a man desperate to clear his affairs in the knowledge that he might not be of this earth for too much longer – all these Gresham tried to cram into his question.

'Shadwell?' said Cecil. 'Shadwell? I do not think I . . .'

'My Lord!' Gresham interrupted him, made his breathing heavy, short, let his hand creep to his side as to contain pain. 'Enough of this play-acting! It was a game I played once. I am not the person I hope to be at this time. I lack patience. Time is not my friend. Will Shadwell was murdered, on your orders. The murderer has sworn this is so. Will Shadwell was my man. Foul thing he may have been, but he was bound to me as my servant. He who kills my servant stains my honour. I have redeemed that honour by killing the man who killed Shadwell. Can we for this once speak plain? *Why did my man have to die?*'

There was a long, long silence. Would the fencing cease? Would

165

he ever get a straight statement from Cecil? Cecil moved his gaze away from Gresham, the eyes seeming almost sightless, resting somewhere beyond even this room. What is passing through his mind? thought Gresham. What certainties, what agonies of decision? What happens inside the mind of such a man as Robert Cecil?

'Imagine a land,' said Cecil, getting to his feet, 'a troubled land. A very troubled land.' His voice was soft, whispering almost, a tone Gresham had never heard. Cecil walked slowly, almost limping, to a portrait hanging on the wall opposite the window. He is in pain, thought Gresham. He finds it hard to walk. He hides this pain, but now for a moment he has forgotten to hide. The portrait was of a young woman. The old Queen, Queen Elizabeth, Gresham saw.

'Imagine a land,' said Cecil, looking up at the portrait, 'that deludes itself into a sense of its greatness. A poor land with powerful neighbours, threatened always from without and from within. A land with no obvious ruler to take over. Let us imagine that a ruler is found, at last. An experienced ruler, a ruler who has survived in a colder and even bleaker land, a ruler who offers some hope of peace and stability. Such a ruler is a treasure, to be guarded and preserved. Yet all things come at a price. In this imaginary land this imaginary ruler is . . . troubled by women. His upbringing has not left him at peace with women. He prefers the company of men. And it is rumoured, in the vile way that such rumours will grow, the company of boys.'

'And Will Shadwell?' Gresham's voice had also dropped almost to a whisper.

'Scum. The scum who for countless ages have greased and oiled the wheels of power with their rank sweat, and their blood. And let us imagine that one of these scum, a perverted, evil creature, a creature who lies with women and yet who lies with boys and men, believes he has found a boy . . . hurt by this ruler. Found him, lain with him, and now wants money to silence him.'

Cecil moved back to the table, and sat down, heavily. His

166

hooded eyes looked at Gresham, with the nearest thing to passion in them Gresham had seen in him.

'A Minister to a King may be threatened, and he may fence, parry and lunge, may battle with his wits against his enemies. But a King, a King is different. No man, be he scum or be he noble, can challenge a King. No man who threatens a King can live. The King's health is the nation's health. Whatever threatens that health must itself die.'

Gresham spoke softly. 'There is no threat to a King from me. Nor ever has been.' He paused. 'There would have been no threat even had Will spoken with me. Will never spoke. He had no time. And you were worried about a note, or some secret letter from Will to me? Was that why my rooms were ransacked in the House?'

Cecil was silent. Both men took the silence as meaning yes.

'Well now, there's an irony would have appealed to Will. You see, I know my men. I know those who work for me. *And I know that Will Shadwell could neither read nor write to save his life.*'

He stood up, remembering to make it look painful, and left without ceremony given or received. Cecil was standing by the window, motionless, as the great door closed.

He had told the truth about Will Shadwell to Cecil, at any rate. If Cecil had bothered to check, instead of simply ordering Shadwell and Gresham murdered, he would have found Shadwell could neither read nor write. As for Cecil's tale, it could be true, or it could be another lie. Thomas Percy was a newly appointed Gentleman of the Bedchamber, better able than most to supply details of who entered the King's inner chamber. Cecil probably did think he was protecting the realm from its enemies by all he did, that he was the saviour of the nation.

Mannion was waiting for him. The crowd of hopefuls had not diminished.

'Now for Alsatia?' enquired Mannion, expressionless.

'Now for Alsatia,' confirmed Gresham, remembering to limp slightly as if in pain from the load strapped to his belly until they were well away from Cecil's lair, and sure they were not being followed.

There was no Watch to call out the hour in Alsatia. No constable or serjeant-at-arms entered Alsatia to serve his warrant. There were no walls around Alsatia, yet its boundaries excluded friends of the state just as the iron walls of the Tower excluded its enemies. If London was a fine ship, Alsatia was its bilges, the lowest sump where all that was foul-smelling gathered and stank. Gresham's spies, his scum, came to the various meeting places in ones and twos, draped and cloaked not against the cold but against discovery and recognition. No-one walked straight in Alsatia. All skulked along in the shade of the leaning, stinking buildings, all sought to walk in shadow.

The House lay shuttered, many of the servants sent home to the country to help with the harvest. The dust gathered in Gresham's rooms at Granville College, his place on High Table empty.

Gresham had set up camp on the first floor of a foul-looking three-storey house with mildew rotting the outer timbers. Inside it was a different story. Stout new doors blocked the way into the first-floor rooms, which were newly floored. The shutters of seasoned timber had had paint loosely splashed on them to make them look old, but underneath the mess were also clearly new.

'You've had these rooms prepared?' asked Jane. She looked thinner, and there was still a slightly haunted look to her eyes, but her spirit was returning.

'Of course,' said Gresham, genuinely startled. 'This isn't the first time I've had to vanish.'

The pile of books in the corner was one antidote to boredom. Disguise was the other. Mannion adorned himself in the rough jerkin and cowl of the stonemason, tools strapped to his belt. Gresham wrapped himself in a poorer version of Mannion's costume, setting himself up as apprentice to the older man. Jane they put in a filthy smock. She could be a common-law wife, a whore or even a sister to Gresham. In Alsatia no-one cared, and in the wider streets of London no-one had time to notice.

Slowly, excruciatingly slowly, the information dribbled in, often as tattered and piecemeal as those who brought it. It was three weeks of boredom, of trudging through the filthy streets, of keeping two eyes in the back of their heads, of disturbed nights when a scream or a howl sent Gresham and Mannion grasping for their swords. Three weeks before a real picture began to emerge. Most of it came from servants, of course. There was no house where the servants did not know more than their Lord and mistress about what was going on.

Sharpy Sam was one of Gresham's most valuable sources. An elderly, grandfatherly figure, he was a wandering tinker who would sell you an occasional pot or pan and sharpen your knives, or sing you the latest ballad over supper, and was tolerated by the authorities in his illegal wandering life simply because he was useful. Many an unsuspecting scullery maid had taken pity on Sharpy Sam and invited him for a morsel of food and a warm by the fire, to find herself left a short while later with a memory of pleasure and a bastard in her belly.

Gresham knew Sam's annual progress. The Midlands and the west in high summer, London in late autumn and the south coast for the winter months. He had sent one of his own men, a young, lusty recruit with a love of horseflesh and women, to ride hard after Sam and brief him with the same names Moll had given him. Catesby. Kit Wright. Jack Wright. Tom Wintour. Thomas Percy. And Francis Tresham, of course. Even before Sam presented himself to talk to Gresham there was news enough, so much news indeed that Gresham marvelled at even Cecil's not finding it out. The men had been meeting regularly. They were all Catholics, all linked by blood or by marriage, and frequently by both. Then, out of the blue, a greasy John at one of the taverns in the Strand reported another name. Guido or Guy Fawkes, an armourer and mercenary.

The name and his profession clinched it for Gresham.

Why did a group of Catholics, many of whom had a history of rebellion only a few years earlier with the ill-fated Essex, want to meet with a soldier and armourer? Such men knew about weapons, armour and powder. The presence of one of Northumberland's relatives and henchmen had to be crucial. So did the servant gossip of great stocks of weaponry and horses over and above any conceivable need being laid in.

A group of dissident men in regular conclave. A professional soldier. A potential leader drawn from one of the oldest aristocratic families in the kingdom. Weapons and war supplies being bought in.

It had to be an uprising.

With the Spanish troops quartered in Dover? Possibly. Was Northumberland involved? He was the only Catholic with the breeding and the standing to act as Protector if King James was done away with. If Gresham were in Northumberland's rich shoes, he would not bother with the Spanish troops in Dover, except as perhaps a distant threat to divert Cecil's attention. Rather he would turn not only to all the young English Catholic men blooding themselves and defining their manhood in the European wars, but to all the disaffected soldiers in Europe who might smell easy meat in knocking a new Scottish King off an English throne. After all, had not a Catholic ambassador described James in the hearing of his court as 'a scabbard without a sword'? Europe was more scared of Queen Bess than they were of James. Scottish Kings were brought up to defend themselves by a knife in the back, not a cavalry charge to the front. There was nothing approaching an army in England, and the only man left to build and lead a fleet was Sir Walter Raleigh, languishing in the Tower on a trumped-up charge of treason.

Gresham paced up and down the small room, spilling his thoughts to Jane and Mannion.

'It must be an uprising!' he exclaimed. 'These men aren't

170

courtiers, men who wish to rule! They're gentry, foolish idealists, men who think because they've held a sword and fought off a drunken ploughboy in a market-town brawl that they're soldiers. I don't believe the Earl of Northumberland could stir himself to be King if he was asked by Jesus himself! No, their plot must be to kidnap the King. He makes it easy. The man's besotted with hunting. Where easier to grab a monarch than in a forest where his men are bound to be split up? Take him, hold him in some stronghold with two or three hundred well-armed men. Move your mercenaries and your missionaries over from the Lowlands before a navy or an army can be mustered. The King's a coward. Show him some cold steel, prick him a little, make him sign what you will. Make him call a Parliament, make him promise God on earth to the people. Ride him in state back to London . . . they will have to kill Cecil, of course . . .'

Gresham's mind was racing ahead, as it always did, plotting the moves he himself would have undertaken in order to turn the uprising into a new government.

'Would it work?' The question was Mannion's.

'It could be *made* to work. I must meet these men, this Catesby and this Tresham above all. Then I will know.'

Then, almost at the end of September, Sharpy Sam had sent a message to the House for Gresham to meet him, in a Deptford tavern a stone's throw away from where Kit Marlowe's murder was meant to have taken place.

Sam was a Devon man with a deep burr in his voice. Like most of his kind he was a pirate at heart, but for some reason had turned from the sea twenty years past to take up his wandering trade.

'They were on a pilgrimage,' he had told Gresham over their third flagon of ale. He spoke slowly, measuring every word as if it had a value. 'Would you believe it? As bold as brass they were, some forty of them, paradin' through the marches as if they owned the land, priests in tow. Not as some of them looked like priests, as I remember,' he said disapprovingly. He took a pull of his ale, rolling the taste around his tongue before swallowing it. 'I made for Huddington, thinkin' I'd let them come to me instead of my chasin' all over the countryside, and got myself taken indoors. There's no doubt the servants and womenfolk are all a-twitter – more horses in the stable than the Duke of Parma, more swords than the Armada. They says it's for the young folk to go an' fight with the Archduke. Archpiss, if you ask me. More like that lot want the Archduke over here, rapin', lootin' and pillagin'.' The phrase obviously rang a bell with Sharpy, who repeated it, rolling it around his mouth like the ale. 'Rapin', lootin' and pillagin'.'

'Disgraceful,' said Gresham, 'all this rapin', lootin' and pillagin'.' There was a sniff that could have been a splutter from Jane, but which turned into a loudly blown nose. She was parked behind Gresham, dirt all over her face, and training herself to look longingly at the beer the men were drinking. 'Noisy girl, isn't she?' enquired Sharpy. 'Nice tits, though,' he added approvingly, and grinned at her. If Sharpy realised that Gresham had suddenly acquired an inability to put a 'g' on the end of his words, he did not show it.

'Well, there's two bits of news as might interest you. The first is that man Catesby. Handsome bugger, fancies himself. Pure luck, as it happens. I was down at Huddington – that cook they 'ave, she's special in the kitchen and special up against an apple tree – when this Catesby rides in to see his friend, Rookwood. He'd come ahead, seein' as he likes fine horseflesh, and likes to ride them hard. Lovely boy, Rookwood. Dressed like a paint shop. Talk is among his servants, Catesby gets going with Rookwood, he comes over all miserable, spends the night on his knees in a tiny room there, one candle. He's mumblin' a prayer, and they tries to listen. Can't hear much, except somethin' about "God's vengeance" and a "great enterprise" and "preserve my family". That put the fear of God into the servants' hall, I can tell you. Well, anyhow, next mornin' Rookwood takes a great mass o' money out of his chest and gives it to this Catesby. Catesby's up to somethin', that's sure.

172

An' it's somethin' that needs a ton of money, that's sure as well. I bin there with Essex and his bunch, I were there with Babington and *his* bunch, I seen it and I smelt it before. It's rebellion, I tell you, the stupid buggers. Some people don't deserve to be born with heads on their bodies. Should be taken off at birth, to save the hangman the trouble later on!'

'There was other news, Sharpy?'

'Right enough. Another tankard of this would be welcome . . . thanks. That boy Tresham you asked after? News is, his father's dead. Not before time, by the sound of it. Pompous old bugger, they says as know. Left a ton of debt, but young Francis got a pretty penny still. Not before time. They say as how he's up to his young neck in debt. 'E's a bastard, that one. Tried to do in a pregnant girl, fiddled his father out of land.'

'I don't think I'm going to like this Francis Tresham,' said Jane.

'I think you'd better pray to God you never meet him!' answered Gresham.

The house in Alsatia was starting to feel like home, Gresham thought ruefully as they finally made it back there from Deptford. It was not the house that depressed him, he knew, as he mounted the stairs and slumped down on a chair, the black mood mounting in him.

Mannion went downstairs, to bring them wine.

'Does it matter, this uprising?' Jane had tuned in to his mood, was trying to tease the melancholy out of him without seeming to do so. 'All Kings and Queens are rotten,' she said calmly, in a sweeping generalisation that Gresham noted as disposing of humanity's favoured form of government for several thousand years past. 'Look at our King. His legs can't hold up his body, his tongue's too big for his mouth so he slobbers like a baby and his clothes are as ragged as the jewels he places on them are bright. He stinks and he's lousy. He learnt his statecraft in a small nation that's only learned to survive by alliance with France and by murdering its rulers, and so he negotiates a treaty with Spain instead of realising that we're victors over Spain and a great power now in our own right. His wife has no brains and his favourites no balls . . . excuse my language . . . are we worse off if he's knocked off his throne?'

'You know Machiavelli? The books I gave you?'

'I've read them, yes.'

'And?' enquired Gresham.

'He's like most men. He thinks he's talking about everyone but he's actually only talking about himself. He's arrogant, so he spoils a good idea by claiming too much for it.'

Gresham thought for a moment. 'Machiavelli was captured and tortured when his Prince failed to be ruthless and strong. We don't need leaders who are good, or beautiful, or kind, or generous. We need leaders who're effective. Most of all we need peace. Stability.'

'You sound like Cecil, if what you told me about your little chat with him was true. How can you say that, who was brought up to war? You, who've lived your whole life as if it were a war? You, who of all people I know seem to exult in a fight?'

'Because I know for what I fight.'

'And what might that be?'

He sat in silence for a moment, reflective.

'I fight to survive. It's all I can do. It's all I know. You, me, Cecil, we think we're in control, but really we're all actors in a play written by a madman, a play with no meaning and no sense. I know we can't win that fight, I know death is more powerful than any of us – but at least if I fight to survive I haven't given in. That way, death at least takes me on my terms. None of us can make the sun stand still. Yet we can make it run.'

'Is that why you fight Cecil?'

'I'm fighting him firstly because if I don't, I die. We've a truce at present, while he thinks I'm ill, but what he tried once he could well try again. The more I can find out about what he doesn't want me to know, the better armed I am against him.'

'Yet you could destroy him.' Jane said it as a simple matter of fact.

'I could destroy Cecil, I think, rather than merely keep him at bay. I *choose* not to. This isn't just about his life, or my life. For all his evil and his double-dealing, for all that he sums up everything I hold in contempt in a man's lust for power and wealth, his very evil helps hold the country together. It is as Machiavelli says. A man doesn't have to be pure to be a good ruler. He merely has to rule, and if in so doing he consigns his soul to Hell, then that's the price he pays for his worldly power. I fight Cecil only when he fights me, and when he ceases to rule well and with power. If there's an uprising planned and he can't see what's brewing, then I'll fight his ignorance only.'

'Is that all?' asked Jane. 'Would you fight for me?'

'I'd do more than fight for you,' he said simply. 'I'd die for you.' It was a simple statement of fact, uttered with no sense of drama. 'But I fight for someone else as well.'

'I'd rather hoped I was the only one . . .' said Jane, who to her obvious irritation had managed to get something in her eye that was making it water.

'I fight for John Plowman, thin-wrapped in the bitter cold, pissing in the field in which he works and coming home with his hands bitten and scarred by the very plough that feeds him and his family and his Lord. For Meg Milkmaid, who's there waiting for John Plowman as he comes home. He may growl at her, or he may kiss her, or he may have her against her will, but that's in the way of things, that's how we were made, that's how we were meant to be. I know there are few freedoms in their lives – no freedom from hunger, from pain, from illness or from a corrupt and vengeful master. Yet they've some choice, and they make some choices. There's a freedom in the air they breathe, in the sight of cold blue light on a frosty morning, in the first leap of a fish in Spring. There's something good in their children, ragged-arsed though they be, some good in the work they do.'

'Well,' said Jane, pragmatically, 'this particular Meg Milkmaid remembers something a little different from her upbringing in this wonderful countryside you talk so lovingly of.'

'At least you were there for me to find you. You hadn't been trampled under a warhorse's hooves, stuck as a bleeding trophy on the end of a pike and ridden through the lanes with soldiers whooping for joy.'

He turned on Jane, not seeing her, but seeing instead the horrors that haunted him still at night.

'I've seen such things . . . such things as make me despair of God or Heaven. You remember Marlowe? "Why this is hell, nor am I out of it . . ." Well, I've seen no God, not here on earth, but I've heard God in music and in words, seen something of a God in the sunset or in a light-filled stone chapel in Cambridge as a song rises to Heaven. Yet I too think we live in Hell, and like Marlowe I despair of God, and from that despair comes my anger. And what have we, when all is left? John and Meg, living a life of hard toil, lit only by their need, their lust to survive, to see things through, to feed and clothe themselves and pass on that bare sustenance to their children. There's dignity enough in their mere survival, in their struggle to have and to hold a little human happiness to themselves in their short time here. They have enough to cope with, without we inflict rebellion and war on them. They need our help to survive. What difference to Meg and John and their growing horde if it's a James, an Elizabeth, a Henry or a Richard on the throne? What means it to them if it's a Plantagenet, a Tudor or a Stuart? What matter, as long as the soldiers stay in their barracks and their whorehouses, the enemy dare not invade and their Lord stands in some fear of London if he takes too many liberties with his tenants?

'We gentry, we nobles, we fight for the glitter, Jane. We fight for our power, our jewels and our wealth. Most of all we fight to gain power, because in wielding that power we give some meaning to our pathetic, flimsy little lives, before they are snuffed out by illness, by bad luck or simply by time.

'*We fight for the wrong things*. We shouldn't fight for our own power, our own lusts. We should fight to preserve a life for those

176

who have no power except their power to survive. We should fight for those who have no power to fight for themselves.'

There was a silence.

'My knight in shining armour,' said Jane, part teasing and part heart-torn, 'mounted on his pure white charger. Hasn't your charger gained a little dirt during the fight? How many men have you killed, Henry Gresham? How many of them do you remember, when you lie awake at night, thinking that no-one knows, or when you dream, and mumble restless names in your sleep? Do you really know what you fight? And is it so John and Meg can have peace in their mud hut of a home?'

There was a strangely flat tone in Gresham's response. 'So John and Meg can be left with some vestige of choice for their own lives. So they can survive too, with a shred of their dignity left to them as well.'

'He's right, mistress.'

They both jumped. Neither had heard Mannion enter the room. For one so large he could move like a cat when he chose.

'You take your pleasures where you can. You fight when you must. It's not about winning. It's about survival.' He handed them both a chalice of wine. 'See that there? Drink it. Enjoy it. It won't taste at all when you're dead meat. Nothing tastes when you're dead. So the whole game is to stay alive. Just that. There's no living at all for the dead.'

Jane levelled a dark look at Mannion, and then at Gresham. 'So by the men's philosophy, if you've to kill a whole nation to stay alive yourself then it's justified? What about Meg and John and their brats then?'

'It don't come to that, hardly ever,' said Mannion easily, sitting down and slurping from the tankard of ale he had brought for himself. 'Only Kings think that the whole country dies if they die, and so kill all their folk in the name of their reigning! No, and that's why they need men like Sir Henry here, to work for them and do their dirty work. It's what he does. He puts them right. His job is to see that only enough men die. Bastards like that Essex, bastards like this Catesby, they reckon their glory is in how many people they take with them. Forget how many Sir Henry's killed. Ask how many he's saved.'

'Women think differently,' mused Jane. The fire was crackling in the grate, and throwing shards of red and yellow light over their faces as they sat in an unconscious circle, framed by darkness. 'We carry a future in our wombs. We don't see life as stopping with ourselves. Rather we see ourselves as the means of carrying it on.'

There was an awkward pause, as the childless Gresham looked into the burning heart of the fire.

'Well,' he said finally, 'one of us here is redeemed. With the number of bastards you've fathered, old man, we must have a future. Though God help us in it if the bastards take after their misbegotten father.'

It was an old joke, and as with many such it was not the sense of it that drew them together, but simply that it had been spoken at all.

Jane spoke at last, after a long pause. 'You realise the danger if you infiltrate this group of Papists? Cecil will kill you if he finds you're active. The Papists will kill you if they find you're in on whatever their stupid secret is. The Government will kill you first and ask questions later if there's even a hint you're implicated in the plot. You're already tainted with being one of Raleigh's few remaining allies.'

'I always liked being popular,' replied Gresham calmly.

'I'm serious,' said Jane. 'If you walk into this plot, if you somehow get hold of this man Phelippes put you on to, it'll be a gate that slams shut behind you. There'll be no going back, and no knowing what lies in front of you.'

'Humans were designed to go forward, not look back,' Gresham said. 'That's why our eyes are in the front of our head.'

'So is this man going to be your gateway in? This Tresham?'

'Francis Tresham is the man. I feel it. He's our way in, our only way in.'

Gresham curbed the impatience that was threatening to tear him apart. His informants told him that Catesby was still off on his travels. Whatever it was that Catesby planned, he would need to be at the centre of things in London to organise the final planning and co-ordinate his uprising, even if the main action was subsequently to take place in a Hertfordshire forest where His Highness hunted the stag. They had some time, he told himself, though how much only God and Catesby knew.

Then the news came in. Francis Tresham had been seen in London.

All that remained now was to kidnap Tresham.

Syon House, London home of the Earl of Percy, was on alert. The Earl, often a quiet and studious man, was in one of his tempers. Henry Percy, ninth Earl of Northumberland, noted the hesitancy in the step of the servant who came in answer to his furious ringing of the bell. Increasingly deaf, and slow in his ways, Henry Percy had shown from his earliest days an ability to conjure up a temper out of nothing. They used to call him the Wizard Earl, though not because of his ability to conjure up a rage. Rather it was their ignorance, their seeing black magic in his simple experiments and refusing to accept that knowledge could be advanced by such means without recourse to God or the Devil. Raleigh had been an ally, and his reward had been a farcical trial for treason and a judgement that left him rotting in the Tower. Others of the so-called 'School of Night' had died scandalous deaths, like Kit Marlowe, or simply faded away. Now only he was left. His power in the north – that dreadful land of rain, mist and pickpockets – was unchallenged, even reinforced by the accession to the English throne of a Scottish King. True, neither King James VI of Scotland nor King James I of England could stop the reivers and the incessant border raids, and no-one ever would. Yet at least the Earl of Northumberland knew that he would not have to be the vanguard against an invading Scottish army in the lifetime of the present

King. No, the threat to him no longer came from the north. It came from London. Yet precisely from where in London it came was more difficult to answer. From the carcass of James I, leader of the nation the Percys had been in bitter conflict with for centuries? Or from the twisted body of Robert Cecil?

Percy shuffled across the room. There were no rushes nor fine carpet on the stone flags of the floor, and the fire in the vast hearth was unlit despite the chill the stonework inflicted. He had inherited Syon House from his wife Dorothy, who held the leasehold on it. He was well rid of her, and in keeping the house and losing the woman he had kept the better part of the bargain. Autumn would have come early to the north, as if the harsh countryside resented the warmth of summer and could not wait to return to the cold. The noise of the grey sea crashing against rock the colour of the castle walls was one of his most vivid memories of the north.

He stood by an open window, letting the taste of London wash against his face and skin. His so-called relative, the young Thomas Percy, would be busy telling the City how he had the confidence and the assurances of the ninth Earl of Northumberland, his relative and patron. So much to the good. Young Thomas would learn as many had before him why the senior branch of the Percys had survived the savagery of the north and all the politics of London could bring to bear, and why there had always been a third person present at their meetings. A flicker of something that might have been the start of a savage smile lifted the corner of the Earl's mouth. He would learn, would Thomas Percy, as would all enemies of the Percy clan and the Catholic faith. They thought him easily led, as if he could not see through their pathetic flattery. They joked about his inability to keep a secret, not realising how carefully he had cultivated that image. Well, Robert Cecil, jumped-up Earl of Salisbury, would find soon enough whether Henry Percy, ninth Earl of Northumberland, could keep a secret, a secret that when revealed would destroy Robert Cecil for ever.

CHAPTER 7

'Istill don't think I like the sound of this man Francis Tresham,' said Jane, working through the pile of papers on which Gresham had scribbled notes and records of interviews.

Mannion's proposal for securing the undivided attention of Francis Tresham was simple. Waylay him in a street, knock him on the head and drag him off to Alsatia. Even in London's anarchic streets it struck Gresham that this direct action might draw unnecessary attention to those involved. Jane had the simplest and best idea. Send Tresham a note in his lodgings, a note promising that he would hear something to his advantage if he came to their address in Alsatia, with a time scrawled on it.

'Spiders don't go chasing flies,' said Jane. 'Flies come to spiders.'

Jane had read her man correctly. A sensible young man, newly come into his inheritance, would not have risked the trip into Alsatia on what might have been a wild-goose chase. But Francis Tresham was not sensible, not once during his whole life.

'So he comes here, knocks on the door – and then we knock him over?' suggested Mannion hopefully.

'He'll be on his own, if we tell him to,' said Gresham. 'If he's come this far, we're hardly going to need to drag him in through the

181

door unconscious, are we? Do you only have four ways of responding to anything?'

'As many as that?' enquired Jane innocently.

'Eat it, drink it, bed it or hit it. Has it ever entered your mind to *think* about something?'

'No,' said Mannion, 'takes too much time.' He gathered up the breakfast dishes. 'And whatever it is I do, it's kept me alive all these years.' He clumped down the stairs, clearly feeling himself fully justified.

Tresham's servant gloried in the name William Vavasour. He looked down his nose at the hefty bribe Mannion put with the note to his master, but did not refuse it. Tresham's greed triumphed over any discretion he might have had, and he turned up on cue at the door of the ill-favoured house as night was falling. A huge rat was feeding off something that might once have been flesh. It looked haughtily up at Tresham, and scuttled off only when it had delayed long enough to show who held the real command. The grumpy and ill-looking couple Gresham had installed on the ground floor of the house let Tresham in, and the man motioned with his head for him to go upstairs. As he did so, the door clanged shut behind him, and Tresham turned to see the doorway blocked out by the figure of Mannion.

'Upstairs . . .' Mannion breathed at him, and he fled up the thin wooden treads like a bolting rabbit.

Gresham sat at the table. The shutters had been closed, and the room was full of lamps. He was dressed in black, with a small, neat white ruff the only contrast on his dress. Several of the Gresham jewels sparkled on his fingers and his clothes. There was a chilling stillness to him. He flicked a hand, inviting Tresham to be seated.

Tresham was a wiry, unkempt figure in his late thirties, Gresham knew. He would have guessed him some years short of that, his boyish face showing few wrinkles. At first glance he was quite handsome, but the effect was reduced by a set of thin lips and eyes that flickered all the time like a snake's tongue. His shirt was filthy, the doublet over it richly slashed and pointed but crumpled and dirty. He wore muddy riding boots over a fine hose that would not have shamed an audience at court.

'Who are you? What do you want?' Tresham barked out the words, his hand fingering the fine sword hanging by his waist.

'I'm your avenging angel,' said Gresham mildly, 'and I can send you to Heaven or to Hell. What I want is to decide which one it will be.'

'You have no hold over me, you . . .'

Gresham cut Tresham short with one simple motion, holding up the palm of his hand.

'Francis Tresham, born 1567, first child and only son of Sir Thomas Tresham of Rushton and Muriel Throckmorton of Coughton. Educated at St John's College and Gloucester Hall.

'First arrested in June 1591. You altered a Privy Council warrant, didn't you? Instead of some Godforsaken tailor who owed you money you substituted the name of a troublesome tenant. Then you beat him up and his pregnant daughter.'

'That's not true! The man was a rogue, he . . .'

'Shut up,' said Gresham, quietly, and for some reason Francis Tresham did so.

'Bailed out by your father this time, and countless times thereafter. Married Anne Tufton of Hothfield, and soon one of the wild band who gathers in Essex House giving promises as rashly as they spend money they do not have. Arrested again in 1596 for possible involvement in a Catholic conspiracy, and arrested in 1601 for involvement in the Essex uprising. Bribed out of the Tower, to the near ruin of his father. The father who is now dead, of course. The loving father who spent thousands of pounds on rescuing his son, despite the fact that the son in question, allowed to live in the manor of Hoxton, tried to cheat his father out of lands he owned there . . .'

Tresham had sat with head bowed. Suddenly he placed both his hands under the table and heaved it up at Gresham, following it

183

with a mad rush, his sword half out of his scabbard. It had worked for him in countless taverns and brawls.

He could not remember properly what happened next. The strange, dark man was suddenly not behind the table, but standing to one side. Tresham felt a huge blow to the side of his head, and then a searing, roaring pain. The dark man's toe connected with vicious power between his legs, the flat of his foot sending him flying through the air. He flew into the wall, cracking his head on a timber, and blackness descended.

'I knew you'd have to hit him,' said Mannion contentedly, dragging up the prostrate figure and propping him upright against the wall. 'Shall I tie him up?'

'No,' said Gresham. 'Let him try again, if he needs to. He must know who his new master is. He won't learn tied up.'

When Tresham came round he was aflame with pain. The most beautiful girl he had ever seen was sponging the blood off what felt like a large hole in his head. He felt sick with the agony in his groin.

The girl spoke calmly, as she took the sponge away. 'I think I'll not try to ease the pain down there,' she said. 'Look at me.'

He did so. Her eyes were the most startling dark pools he had ever seen, burning with an intensity he had only seen before on the coldest and clearest star-lit night.

'Take my advice. Don't fight him. Here, or elsewhere. He'll win, and you'll die. Listen, do what he says, and you might live.'

She placed the bloodied cloth in a rough wooden bucket, and moved out of the light. Was he in Heaven, or in Hell? And was this stunning creature an angel or a devil?

'What do you want?' asked Tresham, muzzily.

'Shall we start again?' It was the same figure, dressed in black, seated behind the same table that had been returned to exactly the same place. Yet this time there was a silver jug and two goblets on the table, and a delicious smell of fruity wine. The wild thought crossed Tresham's mind that the man had known he would hurl the

184

table back, had not placed the wine on it until the first, annoying little trial of strength was over and they could get down to business. A different type of fear began to flood through his veins, a fear so sharp that it started to soften the physical pain and make it less important.

'Guido or Guy Fawkes. Robert, or Robin as he is sometimes called, Catesby. Thomas Percy. Thomas Wintour. Robert Wintour. John Grant. Kit Wright. John Wright. Robert Keyes.'

Suddenly the pain returned.

'Do you want to come and sit at the table? To take some wine with me? You're not bound.'

The confidence, the sheer arrogance of the man. As far as Tresham could see there was only the woman in the room, seated in a corner. They had not even taken his sword or dagger away. An overwhelming sense of defeat came to Tresham. He crawled to his feet, sucking in his breath as the blood flowed through his broken head and sent needles into his brain and groin.

'What do you want? Who are you?'

Tresham knew the questions were sounding like an increasingly pathetic litany.

'I want you.' Gresham spoke as if it were the simplest thing in the world. 'I know that something evil is being planned by a group of men who number you among their friends. I believe you either know of it, or are in a position to find out. And I know that you face ruin and prosecution already, because you've been in trouble too many times, and you'll be associated with whatever these your friends are up to regardless of whether or not you're involved. You're a very lonely man, Francis Tresham.'

He paused for a moment.

'And you're a fool. You've chased every fashion and innovation the world could offer, without thought, without sensitivity and without feeling. You've lived your life as if life itself was created only for you, and for your enjoyment.'

Tresham looked up, startled.

185

'Granted, you seem to love your wife as much as you love anyone except yourself, but even that's not much. I believe you're one of nature's traitors. A spy. A double agent . . .'

'My father was a pompous old fool.' There was defiance, a cruel arrogance in Tresham's eyes. As well as a capacity for a very quick recovery. 'He spent thousands on vainglorious buildings. What matter if some of that money was diverted to my vainglory? At least I was a living thing, not a thing of cold brick and stone! For him I feel no guilt.'

'I'm sure you don't,' said Gresham. 'But now you'll turn traitor for me.'

'And why should I do that?'

'For self-interest, as you've done everything in your life. Because if I know that your friends are about to behave most dangerously, so will others know, and you're too selfish to wish to be dragged down with them. Because I'll give you a great deal of money. And because I'll kill you if you don't.'

'How much money?'

Gresham told him. His eyes opened wide.

'Can you prove to me you have that much money?'

Gresham tossed a purse on to the table. It shivered under the weight. Tresham pulled it open, let the gold coins run through his fingers. Gresham felt rather than heard Jane's disapproval from behind him.

'Do you have to give good money to such a . . . *stench* of a man?' Jane had asked. She had never quite got used to, and never quite brought herself to believe, how much Gresham was worth. He saw money as a tool. She saw it as security.

Tresham's mind had been focussed by the gold. Perhaps here there was real profit, as well as mere survival.

'If my . . . friends are as indiscreet as you say, what if their ship breaks up and they're cast on the shore while I'm still inside it?'

'If needs be, you'll be spirited out of the Tower and sent off to France.'

'You can do that?' Disbelief mingled with wonder caught Tresham's voice. The sheer weight of gold had shocked him.

'Yes. Enough bargaining. How much do you already know of what your friends are planning?'

There are moments in life when huge crossroads come to bear in one time and in one place, not just on the life of one human, but on the life of countless thousands. A decision taken one way, and history spins instantly down one road, making that road seem the inevitable, the only choice. Yet there are countless other roads, and but for one decision, one moment frozen in time, the inevitable might never have happened. Without realisation, without seeing a tiny fraction of all the roads that might have been, in a filthy hovel, Francis Tresham chose his road, and in so doing chose the road for countless other souls. There was no priest there to sanctify or bless the act, no ritual to clothe and comfort the deed, no scribe ready to record a laundered version for later generations. There was only a man dressed in black with a neat white ruff and piercing eyes.

Tresham sat back, reached forward for wine as if daring Gresham to deny him.

'I know Robin Catesby has some idea to remove the Government and to bring in Catholic rule to England. He and the others have been talking for years. We've all been talking. Yet we've done nothing. Until now. Those names you mentioned. They've been meeting, all of them, more even than normal. There's talk, gossip. Whatever this plan is, it has the women all a-twitter, and the priests looking like a woman had been elected Pope. I know no details. Catesby's sworn me to secrecy. He told me it was safer if I knew nothing that could be tortured out of me, but that my time would come. He told me that he must keep me warm for the fire that would break out later. I think he's nervous of me.'

'You mean your friends don't think you're trustworthy?'

Tresham shrugged, carelessly.

An interesting young man, Gresham thought. Not without

courage – the trick with the table would have worked with someone of less experience and speed. The crack on the head and the kick to the prospects of the next Tresham heir must still be causing him considerable pain, as would the shock of realising that his secret was in the hands of a potential enemy, yet he had recovered quickly, was thinking on his feet. He was offering no emotional pleading, no excuses. He was scum, thought Gresham. Will Shadwell with money and some breeding. An adventurer, a wanton.

'How do I know you'll pay me the rest?'

'I will,' said Gresham. 'It's as certain that I'll pay you if you spy for me as it's certain I'll kill you if you don't. Anyway, in the gospel, even Judas was paid.'

How would he take that hit?

Tresham blinked, but recovered. 'Without Judas, Christ might have lived. And if that had been true, we would have been deprived of all the bishops and prelates the world has ever seen. How could we have lived deprived of such comfort? Perhaps even Judas was sent from Heaven.'

Witty, too, thought Gresham, in a clumsy sort of way. His victim was speaking again.

'Who are you? For whom or for what do you work? Are you one of Cecil's men?'

'Be careful,' said Jane from her corner, 'unless you want the other side of your head broken, and more besides!'

'No,' said Gresham, 'I'm not one of Cecil's men. I'm someone who sees a torrent of blood falling on the heads of innocent and guilty alike. I can't stop that blood. I can, perhaps, limit it.'

'How can I know that? You're asking me to trust my life to you, without even a name I can call out should I die doing your will.'

'Then best make sure you don't die. And best make sure not to betray me. It's not good for those who seek to do so.'

'That I do believe. What do you want from me, if I'm asked to join whatever is planned? Just to betray my friends? Or to kill someone?' Neither prospect seemed to alarm Francis Tresham.

'Your friends have betrayed themselves already. I suspect they're like you, dead men merely waiting the fall of the executioner's axe. As for the rest of it, I want information.' Gresham felt like adding that whatever he asked for and received, its aim would be to get as few killed as possible. That might make it less attractive for Tresham. He kept silent.

'There's something I've not told you,' Tresham said, reaching another decision. He had adapted to the new circumstances with ferocious speed, thought Gresham. 'I'm bidden to dinner with Robin Catesby next week. At William Patrick's ordinary, The Irish Boy, on the Strand.'

'Who else goes?'

Tresham reeled off some names. One of them was Ben Jonson, the playwright, another the Catholic peer Lord Mordaunt.

'There'll be another guest. Myself.'

'How so? Do you want me to ask for another invitation?'

'No. How I get there is my concern. All that's required of you is to give no sign of recognition at the dinner. This Catesby,' said Gresham, 'describe him to me.'

Mannion escorted Tresham back to his lodgings, following a few paces behind. Francis Tresham had suddenly become a very valuable commodity. Gresham stayed with his other valuable commodity.

'I was right,' said Jane, 'I didn't like him at all.' He had leered at Jane as he left. 'I'd hate to be a woman in his power.'

Gresham needed to meet Catesby face to face. The man described by the informers and the man described by Francis Tresham was a larger-than-life figure, a maniac preacher with the capacity to lift people off their seats and brand them to his cause. Yet Gresham had known such people who were pure charlatans, whose bravado vanished at the first hint of reality. Was Catesby such a person, weaving a huge web of intrigue to feed a massive pride, a vessel of much noise and no substance? Or did he have the power to mount an uprising, to knock settled government off its perch and into the raging seas of rebellion and unrest?

Gresham had to see this Catesby, had to meet him, had to taste the flavour of the man in the flesh.

So it was that there was an extra guest at dinner in The Irish Boy.

Robert Catesby waited outside Harrowden, his horse restless, shaking its head and pawing the ground. It was as if the animal picked up the unease of its master. Tom Bates looked questioningly at his master, to ask if he wished Bates to take the horse walking round the yard. Catesby shook his head.

Everard Digby was taking an unconscionably long time to say farewell to his wife and children, he thought. It was not as if they were riding to the ends of the world. It was only some fifteen miles from Harrowden to Gayhurst. They had all gathered at Harrowden, both the Vaux women, the new Lord Vaux, the other women and the priests and all the other band of wittering folk. They thought him hot-headed and rash, but he had the sense to realise how dangerous these gatherings were so soon after the pilgrimage to Flintshire had wound its very public way through the marches.

Digby – Sir Everard Digby – had also been one of the company at Harrowden, which was why Catesby had invited himself to attend. Yet the moment to get Digby on his own, to broach the plot and the vital part Digby had to play in it, never seemed to present itself. In desperation, Catesby had hinted at how much the party would enjoy a stay at Gayhurst, Digby's home, after the dilapidated state of Harrowden. When the ever-innocent Digby had agreed with his usual enthusiasm, it had been easy for Catesby to suggest that the two old friends might ride on ahead, to check that all was ready to receive the new guests at Gayhurst, or Gothurst as it was sometimes known.

Catesby saw all people through the mirror of his own soul. He had seen for years how the power and the charm he could direct on to his fellow men and women would eat away at their reserve and caution, however hard they tried to resist it, and make them as clay in his hands. For most of his life luring people into the web of his personality had been a game, a pleasure to put alongside hunting, gambling and, latterly, bedding a pretty woman.

Yet he felt uneasy over his final recruits. Francis Tresham was a wild and an angry thing, a man with no real belief that Catesby could anchor on to. Yet Catesby had always known that Tresham would also acquire a great deal of wealth on the death of his father, something which all along had made him an attractive proposition. Well, he would clinch it in London and then at Clerkenwell. The need for money was too pressing to allow for any delay, and once sworn in Tresham, like all the others, would have too much to lose by betrayal.

Everard Digby was a different proposition. Catesby needed him not only for his money, but for his personality as well. One of Digby's attractions was his innocence. Another was his staunch Protestant background. He had been converted by the priest Gerard, who not only behaved and dressed like a gentleman but, thought Catesby, actually believed he was one. Father Gerard had caught Digby somehow when he was ill, and used his panic to show him the true path. Amusingly, he had converted Mary, Digby's wife, entirely separately, with neither of the pair knowing of the other's conversion. It was typical of Gerard to keep the news from them and enjoy their consternation at the discovery.

It was that radiant innocence, that wholesomeness that Catesby needed. Everard was not only known at Court. He was feted as one of its rising stars. He looked like a God, and he rode a horse as if he had been sewn to it in the womb. He was an excellent swordsman and, by all accounts, a brilliant musician, though the latter was something Catesby had never acquired the taste for. Someone had to invest Coombe Abbey and take away the Princess Elizabeth. If it was a rat-arsed Tom Wintour, John Grant with a face that looked like it had come from Hell or a drunken Thomas Percy who broke in to Coombe House to take the Princess Elizabeth, the servants would as like fight to the death as do the decent thing and surrender before anyone got hurt, reckoning they were dead already. The Princess Elizabeth was only a girl after all, and too much fear could cause God knew what complications with her. Didn't girls who thought their virtue was threatened throw themselves off high walls? Any girl with half her wits about her seeing Wintour, Grant or Percy coming towards her would know she was going to get more than a handshake. Yet if Digby was the attacker there might well be no fight at all. He was a Court favourite, a knight and one of the new King's Gentlemen Pensioners, known as a family man through and through, and with a visage that could calm a raging bull. Princess Elizabeth was no use to Catesby or to Catholicism skewered on a blade or cast down into a ditch. Why, Digby's charm might even keep the truth away from her about what had happened to her mother and father for some crucial hours. All the more likely if Digby himself did not know the truth – or at least, not the whole truth.

Why should Digby throw away a beautiful wife, a beautiful family and some of the best prospects in the country to join a wild plot? Catesby smiled to himself as Digby came pelting down the steps to his waiting horse, full of apologies and orders to his men. Beneath the sweet innocence the world saw in Sir Everard Digby, Catesby saw a mulish determination and stubbornness where it came to religion.

They set off along the deserted road, Tom Bates riding behind and carefully out of earshot. For a while they let the horses have their heads. It was as if they could not wait to shed the inactivity of the night in the stables, the pounding of their hooves driving the stable dust out of their bones and the remnants of the night out of their riders' bodies.

'Digby, old friend, will you do something to please me?'

They had reined in by the side of a brook that was almost a trickle, but which in a month would be roaring like a mini-torrent.

'I'd give my life to please you, Robin. You know that.'

'Will you swear an oath of secrecy to me? An oath that on all that's holy, and on all that you hold holy, you'll never reveal what I say to any living soul on earth?'

The ever-present smile on the youthful face of Everard Digby had gone now. There was still the flush of outrageous good health to his face, a face that had been full of happiness and contentment at his fine mount, the fine October morning and the excitement of riding with his friend. A frown of uncertainty caused little-used lines to crinkle in his face.

'I do so swear. You have my word as a gentleman. But why . . .'

'I've asked you to swear a simple corporal oath, old friend. The others, the others who're sworn to secrecy, they've had to swear and seal the oath with the blessed sacrament. It's a measure of the faith I have in you, you who've always been special to me, that I need no more than your word as a gentleman. Here . . .' Catesby produced his dagger from his belt. A fine silver inlay, its hilt formed the sign of the Cross, 'swear, here on this dagger. Swear you'll be secret. Swear you'll be silent.'

They made a strange tableau that fine October morning, two finely horsed gentlemen etched against the skyline, the luxury of their lives a mystery to any peasant who might have seen them, imagining some joke or jest to be passing between them as they rested their horses by water.

'I swear,' said Digby, nervous now, but laying hand on the hilt. How cold it felt.

The pair moved on, the ever-present Bates behind them.

'Do you believe in me? Do you believe that I see things others don't see, understand things others don't understand? Do you?'

'Why, yes, of course . . .' Digby was nervous, unsettled. 'You know I've always looked up to you above all others, Robin. Wasn't I one of the first to recognise and tell you that you were special?'

Catesby put out a hand and stopped Digby's horse. It snorted, pushing its head up and down, irritated to be halted.

'Digby, I'm God's messenger. I have known it for years. God is working through me. Do you understand? Do you believe in me?'

193

He had stopped so the sun was directly behind him, and perhaps the threatening summer shower and the humidity was responsible for the faint aura that seemed to glow round Catesby's head and shoulders.

Everard Digby felt the hot tears scorch his eyelids, and a mixture of embarrassment, fear and awe caused him to stumble in his words.

'I . . . I do believe in you, Robin. You've always been so certain, always known best . . . yes, perhaps it is God I hear speaking through your mouth . . . I . . . I . . .' The hot tears broke their confine and flooded down his face.

'Sssh,' said Catesby, taking his hand and laying it gently across Digby's mouth, as if he were a kind father soothing a baby. 'And listen to me. We plan to destroy the King and his minions. We've powder stacked beneath the Lords, primed and ready. On the day when Parliament is opened, when the King and his heir, when Cecil and his crew, when all those who've oppressed the True Faith are gathered under the one roof, we'll light a fire that won't be extinguished until God's rule is again dominant in England. We'll blow them all to Hell. Even as the blast is happening we'll seize the Princess Elizabeth, and ride through the Midlands and west, raising thousands to add to the three hundred we've assembled. Percy will bring his men down from the north, the Spanish troops in Dover will throw off their idleness and march to Rochester, strangling the Thames and London's life blood. From the south will come the Catholics of Europe . . .'

It is doubtful if Digby heard beyond the first half of Catesby's words. The colour drained from his face. His hands clutched at the horse's reins so hard as to make the animal jump and slither in protest. It was not the movement of his horse that made him put a hand on his pommel, but the sudden wave of sickness and fear that came over him. He stumbled into words.

'This is . . . strange beyond belief. It's a terrible thing, a terrible thing. You ask for my support . . .'

'I *demand* your support.' Catesby leant over to his friend, driving hard with his voice as his chin jutted forward and his voice rose. 'This is no fancy, no boy's play. This is God's work, I know it, a blast that will echo up to Heaven and down to Hell! There can be no-one on the sidelines in this. You're in, or you're a coward. Are you a coward?'

Digby was too young and too spoilt to see that he was being goaded by the accusation of cowardice, goaded into not thinking.

'I'm no coward!' The cry was drawn out of him, as if from a drowning man at the bottom of a deep well. Catesby gave him no time to relent.

'You'll join us then? You'll risk your life for your faith? The faith you've so newly found? Or will you give it up as easily as it came to you? Are you a Christian, or do you simply worship at the altar of ease and comfort, saying the words but denying the duty of faith? Is your belief real, or is it false coin?'

A small tear formed in Everard Digby's right eye, and rolled gently down his cheek. The wind whittled away at it, making it tremble as it hung on his flesh.

'Must I join, Robin? Must I do this?'

'If you're a Christian, you must. If you're a coward, do nothing, except remain secret. Let the men risk all for justice and for their faith, while the children stay at home.'

If the barbs hit home there was no reaction on Digby's face, as round, as innocent and as woebegone as a boy who has been told that Christmas will not happen after all. It was a face that would have melted the heart of a devil, but not the devil sent to accompany Sir Everard Digby on his lonely road to damnation, the devil who went by the name of Catesby.

'I'm no coward, nor no boy. If I must join, I will join your hellish plan, God help me and my loved ones.' There was a pathetic dignity in his tone.

But you have not yet said that you *will* join, Catesby thought. And I need you. I need your wealth, I need your horses, and I need your chivalry and your access to the Court so that the Princess

Elizabeth will come sweetly and there will be no second blood bath. They rode on in silence. Catesby's skill lay in knowing when to talk, but also in when to stay silent.

'What of our friends, Robin? What of the Catholic Lords? Are they to be blown to perdition, as well as our enemies? How could God forgive such a crime?'

'Rest assured, it's taken care of. Those who're worth saving will be preserved, without knowing how or why they were saved. We've thought long on this, and we need you.'

'What of the priests? What do they say? How can a priest sanctify murder?'

'The priests know. They've approved the matter,' Catesby lied. Perhaps a priest knew under the secret of the confessional, but that was not to approve the act, merely to recognise that nothing could break that secret and the bond it established between a man, his priest and his God. How could he head off the young fool going to Father Garnet to confess? Garnet would not reveal the confession directly, but he could take steps in Europe to deny Catesby the help on which his rebellion would depend.

'When we reach your home, I'll show you the texts that make what we do a necessary evil. The Scriptures have always allowed acts of violence against the heathen – were the innocents on the walls of Jericho to be spared before the anger of the Lord? Were the Philistines to be allowed to triumph over God's people and his armies? Didn't the Pope sanctify the death of that whore Elizabeth when she declared herself against God's people?'

Catesby leant over again, and reined in his friend's horse. Gayhurst was visible in the distance, a wisp of smoke and nestling buildings.

'You know what threats we face. Do you want your children to inherit from their father? Do you wish our cause to be ruined, our people cast into penury, our faith trampled into the dust and mud? Then do nothing. Or rise up against the tide of fortune, and fight. *Fight like a man.*'

Sir Everard Digby gazed out on to the home of his wife and his children, the scene of his idyllic marriage and a life as near perfect, in his opinion, as the age could offer. There in the brick and stone of Gayhurst was a future to bring redemption to Hell, a smile on the face of the universe. Was he to risk it all in one fateful throw? Was it his duty? Was it his lot to suffer now, having been blessed so much in his early life?

He turned to his friend.

'You say the priests know of this? They've agreed to it? You'll show me these passages?'

I have you now, exulted Catesby. I have you, and your fine horses, your money and your manners. I have you.

'I will, Everard. Upon my life and upon my soul, I will.'

He set his face into a hard frown, as befitted a man set on serious business, hiding his exultation. Was there a particular pleasure in wrenching a man away from his beautiful wife and fine sons, in placing that wife and her brood in the way of risk and total loss? Digby had been too happy, thought Catesby. No mortal deserved that happiness, it was not the way of the world. Pain, suffering and sacrifice, those were the way of the world. Pain, suffering and sacrifice that all the world had to experience before they could gain entrance to God's kingdom. He was doing Everard Digby a favour by plunging him into Hell on earth. It would guarantee him his place in Heaven.

Ben Jonson's Court was The Mermaid tavern, his Presence Chamber its tap room and his courtiers a huge and adoring crowd of actors and writers, and an equal crowd of would-be actors and writers. However, The Mermaid was far too public a place for a man to be seen who was not meant to be in London at all. The next best bet was Jonson's lodgings.

Jonson had money, now that his liaison with Inigo Jones was producing a torrent of Court income. Gresham doubted that his friend's incomings would ever exceed his outgoings. His lodgings were in a back street a long way away from any fashionable area, but gratifyingly near Alsatia. It was not early in the morning when Gresham, in a workman's uniform, arrived at Jonson's chamber door. He had brought Mannion with him, feeling threat in the very air he breathed. Jane he had brought partly because of the feeling that she was only safe when with him, and partly through the realisation that it was folly to leave a young and beautiful woman on her own in Alsatia. She was also becoming very bored, a sulphurous cloud of tedium hanging over her in the tiny environs of their bolt hole.

The landlord knew Gresham, and let him in with a grin. Jonson had been too drunk to bolt the door when he had fallen into his bed. He lay fully clothed, his snores shaking dust off the ashes of the dead fire. Gresham crept up to him from behind, placed a dagger gently against his throat and hissed loudly in his ear, 'Pay me the money you owe me now, or die!'

Jonson leapt up as if a charge of powder had been set off beneath him, and landed back on the bed, feeling the steel against his throat, eyes as staring wide as a dead fish, unable to see his assailant. He started to gargle, white froth coming from his mouth.

Jane spoke. 'Or he might let you off if you give him a mention in your next play. Ugh! Do you *ever* wash a shirt?'

Jonson's whole body subsided back on to the bed, hearing the familiar voice, as if the life had drained out of it. Jane was wandering round the room, which looked as if an exceedingly dirty garrison of troops had been stationed in it for months. She picked up various bits of linen, wrinkling her nose as she threw them into a pile.

Jonson rolled over on the bed. 'You bastard!' he grunted at Gresham.

'True. But at least *my* poetry's good,' responded Gresham with a grin.

'"Calumnies are answered best with silence",' responded Jonson. When he quoted from his own works he always stuck his chest out.

'*Please* don't quote from your own work, Ben,' asked Gresham. 'Only someone of exceptional arrogance would even remember what they had written, never mind spout it to an unsuspecting public at every opportunity.'

'I am exceptional in everything I do,' grunted Jonson, rubbing his head and heaving himself upright.

'Exceptional as a sycophant, I believe. What were those lines you wrote to celebrate Robert Cecil's sudden uplifting to be Earl of Salisbury? Do I remember . . .

> "*What need hast thou of me, or of my Muse*
> *Whose actions do themselves so celebrate?*"'

'Aye, well,' Jonson responded, pulling on a pair of boots, 'a man has to live.'

'"I do honour the very flea of his dog"?' asked Gresham, quoting from *Every Man In His Humour*.

'Please don't quote from my works, Sir Henry,' said Jonson solemnly. 'I find it degrades the beauty of my lines.'

Jane was an avid playgoer, and Gresham had become converted during his time with Kit Marlowe. They had known Jonson for years. He traced his roots back to Scotland, and had done so when it was not fashionable to be so linked, and was a Catholic, when it had never been fashionable. He was also an entirely self-taught classical scholar of awesome knowledge, a brawler who had killed a man, a poet of huge genius and a boor, a man of great intuition who at times showed the sensitivity of a stone privy in the Tower. Ben Jonson's body could be and had been caged. His spirit was uncontainable. That at least he shared with Walter Raleigh.

Without expression, Jane picked up the overflowing yellow chamber pot from beside the bed, opened the shuttered window and hurled out the contents into the street below. A fierce yell and a squeal suggested it had found a target. Jonson stopped rubbing his head and feasted his eyes on Jane's trim figure, a beatific smile on his lips. He recovered quickly from shocks. His life had produced enough of them for him to have had to learn quickly.

'Avert your gaze, old lecher, and listen to me. You dine with Lord Mordaunt and Robert Catesby soon enough, I hear?'

Jonson struck a dramatic pose on the bed, the effect somewhat ruined by a button popping off as he raised both his arms. He launched into verse:

> '"Come, my Celia, let us prove,
> While we can, the sport of love!"'

'My name's Jane,' replied the object of his attention, poking with her foot at the remnants of what could have been last week's meal on the floor. 'As for your kind proposition, "all the adulteries of art/They strike mine eyes, but not my heart".'

'Spoken beautifully!' exclaimed Jonson, gallantly. 'Almost as well as I could do it myself!'

'Lord Mordaunt? Catesby?' interjected Gresham.

'You're well informed, as ever. What of them?'

He got up clumsily from the bed and walked over to a low, rough-carved table with some bottles on it. Jane stood before it and glowered at him. He veered in mid-course, changing direction to the jug and ewer with something like fresh water in them. He bent over it, motioning to Gresham, who came and poured the contents slowly over his head. He stood up and shook his wet mane like a dog coming out of the river.

'I'm growing thin. I stand in need of a good dinner,' Gresham said, replacing the empty ewer. 'I will be your Scottish cousin who's arrived from the north, in the hope of rich pickings in this city which has newly learned to love a Scotsman so much. Under the circumstances, young Catesby will be delighted to add an extra place to the table, so your kinsman can taste the delights of life with the nobility.'

'Hmmph!' grunted Jonson. 'I trust you've a good Scots accent?'

He looked enquiringly at Jane, and when she stepped aside went to the table and poured two beakers of cheap sack. He offered one to Gresham, who declined it, sipped appreciatively at his own life-saver and offered Gresham's to Mannion. 'You're invisible, I see . . .' It was the phrase he used when Gresham did not wish to be recognised. 'Why this sudden interest in my friends?'

'Is Robert – Robin – Catesby a friend of yours?'

Jonson sat down heavily on a stool. He tossed some written sheets to Jane with an inquisitorial raised eyebrow. She caught them, nodded and settled in a corner to read the scribblings that were Jonson's next play.

'It's most unfair and unusual that someone so beautiful should have intelligence as well,' grumbled Jonson, changing the subject. '"Blind Fortune still/Bestows her gifts on such as cannot use them."'

'Is Catesby that beautiful?' asked Gresham, pretending not to notice.

'Not him, you fool. Her. That angel who has mistakenly taken to living with an old satyr such as yourself. Perhaps she's hoping to reform you. Beautiful women like to reform lost men,' he added hopefully, watching her as she became instantly lost and totally absorbed in the manuscript.

'I thought it was her honesty you most liked?' There had been a massive row between Jonson and Jane when she had last criticised a piece of his writing. He had called her a lying slut and broken a perfectly good stool by hurling it against a wall, following which Gresham had broken his head. He had rewritten the piece though, Gresham had noticed. 'But you haven't answered my question. Is Catesby a friend of yours?'

'I know him. Everyone of my faith knows him. A friend? Hardly. I refuse to acknowledge the sun shines out of his arse, which is a prerequisite of anyone wanting friendship with him. Young Catesby sometimes has difficulty distinguishing between worshipping our Saviour, and his being our Saviour. He's not a good . . . influence, I think, on our younger people. But he has a good table. And I'm a good guest.' He gazed sadly down at the remnants of liquid in the now-empty beaker. 'They'll all be Catholics there. Are you after Catholics? Will your presence at our table bring harm to our faith?'

Gresham thought for a moment. If he was to expose a plot to kidnap the King, harm would come to the plotters. But to Catholicism? More harm would come if the plot were allowed to go ahead than if it were destroyed.

'To your faith, no. To some people of your faith, in all probability, yes. To you, too, Ben, if you plan to be in rebellion against the State, as well as against every person of culture and taste . . .'

The bantering tone did not hide the seriousness of Gresham's answer.

There was a bellow of laughter. 'Me? A rebel! God help me! Don't you think trouble enough comes looking for me, without me sending out invitations for more of it to come visiting?'

Ben Jonson had a mouth as big as his capacity for drink, and a wild reputation, but Gresham had never known him betray a secret. Or, at least, never betray one of Gresham's secrets. Gresham had rescued Jonson from the bailiffs and debtors' prison. The old secrets between them stood custodian over the new ones. Jane gave instructions for the bulging bag of washing to be sent off by servant to the laundress at the House. His manuscript she took away with her. The boredom of Alsatia was due to be lessened at least a little.

'There's risk in this dinner,' said Mannion flatly on their return. He was right. For all its huge size, London was a small town where those at the top of its society were concerned. The other guests seemed unlikely enough on the surface to recognise Gresham for who he was, but disguise would be prudent, and Gresham worked on two principles. Either one altered the original hardly at all, or one went for something outrageously different. He opted for the latter.

'Hold still, will you!' said a cross Jane as she applied the last of the dye to his hair and beard. It had been turned from the darkest black to something reddish, if not verging on positive ginger. A

202

salve applied to his face, neck and hands (and, on Jane's insistence and in the face of his firm opposition, to the whole of the rest of his body) turned his skin dark, almost like that of a Moor. He had not trimmed his beard since they moved out of the House, with the result that it now straggled and looked, as Mannion said, 'Like a badly blown cornfield.' From his extensive wardrobe Gresham had chosen a suit of clothes that a country bumpkin might have been offered by the worst country tailor as being the height of fashion in London. The whole dreadful mess was topped off by a vast bonnet that clashed with his hair and beard and his suit of clothes, and a large eyepatch.

'For the first time in my life, I fear death,' he said to Jane as she finished the last patting on of paste to his beard.

He saw her face fall, and immediately regretted his teasing of her.

'Why so? If you feel that way, you must . . .'

He raised his hand to stop her. 'Can you imagine what my tailor will say if I go to my coffin dressed like this?' he asked, aghast. The swinging blow to his head was arrested only just in time as she realised it might disturb the newly applied colour.

Dressed like a country bumpkin, and a Scots one at that, Gresham was near besieged by every criminal on duty in London, who saw him coming and could not believe their luck. After he had been pestered with offers of women, card games, bowling alleys and dice halls where only yesterday a fortune had been made to rival Lord Salisbury's, couplings of such power achieved to rival Samson's, and various places where both had been achieved simultaneously, it was a relief to arrive at William Patrick's ordinary. Jonson always arrived at dinner as early as possible, to maximise the amount of time spent troughing at someone else's expense. He met Gresham, held back a brief explosion of apoplexy with commendable restraint, and brought him in to the company.

It was a lively affair. The Irish Boy served excellent food, with wine that was certainly drinkable. Gresham, who had a nose for these things, noticed that Catesby did not stint himself either with the room he had taken or the food and wine served. The room was fresh-painted and had clean rushes strewn on the floor, with hangings of some expense on the walls. A large window let some of the noise of the Strand through, as the cracks in the floorboards and door let some of the noise of the thriving, bustling ordinary up to assail their ears, but not enough to impede conversation.

'It's guid tae meet yae al, guid, guid . . .' Gresham, who had decided to be called Alexander Selkirk, slurred his words and let them tail off incoherently, a man middlingly drunk but also bemused with new sights and sounds.

He need hardly have bothered. Catesby barely glanced at him before he was dismissed. Jonson was the man, the star brought in to show how well-connected Catesby was, and all eyes were on him. A major playwright, a talking point at Court who was also a Catholic: Ben Jonson was a superb social catch.

'Well met, sir, well met.' It was Tom Wintour, shaking hands with the company, clapping those he knew well on the back. So this was the man for whose sake a whore's bottom would be sore for weeks to come, thought Gresham.

'Here, this is Selkirk, Alex Selkirk, a cousin of mine from Scotland . . . Cousin Alex, meet Tom Wintour . . .' Jonson was barely remembering to introduce Gresham. There was a crowd of people, there was good food, there was wine, and Jonson was expanding with almost every minute that passed by. Tom Wintour had come with Catesby. He was a short, stocky figure, with a round face and a cannon-fire way of speech. He was quick, agile, keeping his wit under control but showing a pushy argumentativeness that Gresham imagined could be explosive in more confined or tense situations.

'Have you brought a lot of your friends with you down from the north?' asked Tom Wintour with outward innocence. The reference to King James's horde of hangers-on drawing a guffaw from another member of the company.

'No, no,' replied Gresham, 'but I may hope tae do so if the pickin's are reet guid enough!'

A man to be watched, thought Gresham, someone with the power of the hothead but also the determination and intelligence to be a dangerous enemy. He had the body of a fighter too, Gresham noted, for all that he lacked height.

'My, and you must tell me who your tailor is, Mr Selkirk!' It was Tresham. He had given no flicker of recognition. 'Clothes like that will make a stir anywhere you go!' Another guffaw from the company, except Lord Mordaunt, who thought himself too refined to laugh. Tresham seemed to delight in wearing clothes that had clearly cost good money, but which were crumpled as if tossed carelessly aside at the end of the day. He played his part well, making several scurrilous jokes about the Scots that would have perplexed the real person Gresham was pretending to be, yet got home to other town guests.

Jonson talked endlessly, largely about himself, but he did so with such power, force and good humour that there was a dance in the eyes of all those who listened. The appalling rule of the Lord Chancellor and his power over the plays, the sheer vagabond criminality of all printers and the complete lack of any resemblance to a civilised race of theatre managers and actors, the wonder of Latin, the plan for the next masque, the plan for the next play, the belief that a grateful city should afford its greatest living playwright a theatre of his own, the dreadful affair between Sir Robert Dudley and the mistress he wished to marry . . . fuelled by greater and greater quantities of alcohol, Jonson's genius and his buffoonery climbed towards the stars in harness.

And what of Catesby? Was this a man full of piss and wind, or a man capable of kidnapping a King? As Gresham observed him it seemed as if the room became darker and darker, the sense of an evil presence almost unbearable. As even Jonson grew tired, and the stories thinner and more unbelievable, so quietly, with hardly a ripple, Robert Catesby began to dominate the conversation, the room and all the people within it.

'We're all victims to the printers!' Jonson was almost shouting now. 'They buy the work, they print the work, they bind the work and they sell the work – and, if they so please, they put another man's name on the cover! And they get the profit, whilst the poor man who produces the work, whose brain sweats it out over weeks and months – he gets the leavings after the cursed printer has done! Why, these men are nothing more than vultures!'

Catesby broke in. The very quietness of his voice commanded attention.

'Why,' he said to a perspiring Jonson, 'you revile the printers, yet they're as the lice upon your body. They lie still and wait for you to come to them. They backbite and they infect, yet you've no remedy. They feed off you, yet you stop them not. If they grow fat on your blood, isn't it your fault? Throw off your old clothes, man. Scrub your skin. Take the louse between your thumb and finger . . .' he picked up a nut from the table, 'and crack it . . . thus!' The nut shattered over the table. 'Blood for blood; take back your blood, man, or cease your complaining.' It was said gently, conversationally, yet it had the menace of steel slithering out of a smooth scabbard.

There was a pause, and conversation resumed along with the bringing of two fine, freshly baked pies. Later, another of the guests, Lord Mordaunt, raised an obscure theological point, on whether to equivocate or withhold the truth was the same as to tell a lie. Catesby fixed Mordaunt with his eyes and led him down a theological line that had the man tangled in his own arguments as badly as a young ostler caught in the reins of a train of horses.

Catesby knew his Bible, Gresham had to give him that. Textual evidence dropped from him like other men oozed sweat. Gresham had mimed becoming progressively more drunk as the evening wore. He decided to speak.

'I dinnae like the Bible.' That brought a hush, as Gresham knew it would. He had spoken in his thick Scots accent, as a drunk would when suddenly brought back to awareness for an instant. 'There's tae much blood, tae much killin'. Tae many of ma friends have deed . . .' Gresham started to sob, in the maudlin way that drunks did when they had uttered a profound alcoholic truth.

Catesby did not even look at him as he replied. 'Too much killing, Mr Selkirk? No, surely not. There can be no life without death. Christ wasn't our Saviour until he died in agony.'

'But ma poor wifie! Ma lovely Agnes! An innocent wee lass, taken awa' before she had time to say her prayers . . .' Was Gresham pushing it too far, would the reference to the dead and innocent wife draw forth a response? It did, but not of the type Gresham expected. Catesby smashed his tankard down on the table with such force that three wooden platters jumped off and rolled along the floor. No-one moved to stop them.

'Innocent? Innocent! We're alive now because we feed on the dead flesh of animals, *innocent* animals! Like the lamb in the Old Testament, the innocent must be sacrificed so the higher order may triumph. Their squealing over their death does them no credit. Rather they should praise those who sacrifice them, praise those who make something meaningful come from their paltry death. Did Joshua ask for the innocent to leave the walls of Jericho? When the walls fell, do you imagine the soldiers asked who was innocent and who was guilty before they raped and pillaged in the name of God? Innocence is not a virtue. It is a handicap.'

On that note the party ended. Gresham had met many men in his life, some good, some bad, most merely human with all the frailty and weakness humanity brought along as their natural baggage. Pure goodness he had met, surprisingly, far more often than pure evil. Indeed the number in that latter group he could count on the fingers of one hand.

Tonight, Gresham knew he was in the presence of evil. It was in the eyes. It was always in the eyes. Catesby's had a fierce, fixed gleam, an inner light that did not come and go with the moment, with the rising fumes of wine to the head, the excitement of sex or even the lust of battle. The intensity of that madman's gleam did not waver or flicker. Yet it was so gentle, a flash of yellow deep in the pupils, deep and intense burning, that it was almost buried in the proud and handsome tilt of the chin. Gresham had seen that light in the eyes of a judge, in the eyes of a hangman. It was the evil of a man who could not conceive he could be wrong, but whose self-belief could only be satisfied, like a dread hunger, by feeding it with the belief of others. All men, and all beliefs, were simply fuel for Robert Catesby's vanity. In the handsome, dashing figure of Robert Catesby, for a brief and terrible moment, Henry Gresham saw the pride of Lucifer, walking on earth.

'Normal men suspend their feelings,' said Jane, trying to wash as much as possible of the dye off his body, and trying to understand what Gresham, still shaken, had told her. 'When they kill, or when they rape and mutilate, they lock away their feelings behind a great iron door, only opening it when the business is done. Because they didn't feel it when it happened, they tell themselves it never happened. This man, it seems, has no door to shut. Perhaps it was ripped off its hinges when his wife died?'

'Or perhaps it was never truly there.' Gresham shivered and not only with the cold. 'Here, your hands are cold. Let me take over.'

'When I've finished the bits you can't reach. Be still.'

'Why do I doubt so much? Do you doubt? Everything?'

She had hardly ever seen him like this, reverting almost to a child-like questioning and simplicity, the veneer of cynical amusement and wit broken through and shattered. It was not that his body was naked before her. For a brief moment, it was his mind. She was careful not to interrupt the measured sweep of her hand, or reveal her feelings in her voice.

'Sometimes I doubt. Who isn't prey to doubt?'

'Catesby. Catesby isn't prey to doubt. He takes the fear, the worry, the doubt we humans have and he forces it out, drives it from him somehow in a way he doesn't and I don't understand. And then he turns it into something evil, a fire that draws other people to it like a moth to a candle, and burns them up before they've realised what's happening. Or perhaps makes them so they don't care, makes them so they want to be destroyed.'

They made love in the tiny bed, little more than a mattress cast on the floor, and Gresham felt the warmth creep back into his soul.

Well, his question was answered. Not so much piss and wind, Master Robert Catesby. More an avenging, fallen angel, willing to unleash the winds of Hell on earth.

CHAPTER 8

It was dark outside, the first wind of winter dashing against the houses, and bringing with it a fine rain that first put a layer of watery, tiny jewels on a woollen cloak, and then soaked it through.

'I saw him as if for the first time last night,' said Francis Tresham. He was sitting at the table with which he had tried to knock the brains out of Henry Gresham only a few days previously, sipping morosely at the fine wine Gresham had placed in his hand. 'He's a vulture, isn't he? I suppose I've been under his spell most of my life. I think it was your being there that let me take a step back almost, to see him as he really is. He doesn't care about God, does he? Or perhaps he thinks he *is* God? Either way, I realised last night, for all his talk, who Robin Catesby does care about. Himself.'

Which is perhaps why you would recognise it more easily than others, thought Gresham, as it describes the pair of you equally well. Gresham's hair and beard had returned to their normal black intensity, apart from an occasional flash of orange when the light caught it from a certain angle.

'I could ask Jonson who you are,' said Tresham. He frequently changed the tack of a conversation, without warning. It followed the restless, ever-changing direction of his eyes, as if anything he gazed at for more than a few seconds became too hot for them to rest on. Perhaps it was a trick to catch the listener unawares, perhaps it was just his nature.

'You could ask,' said Gresham calmly. He knew Jonson was safe. If Tresham did not know that fact, he would find out easily enough without need of words from Henry Gresham.

'Tell me again what it is you offer me.'

'When we've amassed enough information to deal with this plotting, you'll receive travel documents to France, a thousand pounds in your purse and secret passage to a ship, out of the way of your friends or Cecil, whichever one is most hot to kill you.'

'How can you do that?'

Because, young man, I have had a plan waiting these years past to release Sir Walter Raleigh and get him to sanctuary in Europe, a plan he has refused to use, believing it would be taken as confession of his guilt were he so to escape.

'I can do it. That's all you need to know. You'll be taken to the south coast and there put on a boat, and delivered to France. The thousand pounds is in addition to any money you can raise yourself. You'll want to tidy your affairs, won't you, and leave as much as possible to your wife and family? You'll be given another name, and papers in that name that will pass any muster.'

'What about my family?'

'That's up to you. They can come later, when the hue and cry's died down, or you can leave them. You can tell me later.'

If Tresham had decided whether he would desert his family or not, he was not going to let Gresham see it.

'I think I'm to be inducted on Monday. I'm bid to another dinner, at Lord Stourton's, in Clerkenwell. The invitation came from Robin. Stourton's my kinsman.'

'I know,' said Gresham, whose mind by now carried an encyclopaedic list of the inter-relations between England's Catholic families. 'So is Lord Monteagle. It's no secret.'

'It's strange the invitation comes from Catesby, not from my relative. It makes me think there's a reason other than the pleasure of my company for my being invited.'

'Then you must go.'

'What freedom do I have?'

'Freedom to do what?'

'Can I speak as myself, or do I have to speak from a script that you've written?'

'There are only two conditions. Firstly, you must speak as keeps you on the inside of whatever is happening. If by staying there you can bring it to an end, then so much the better – *but you must under no circumstances be so dismissive that you're excluded.* You're no use to me in ignorance. The second is that you must report back to me immediately, and tell me everything that took place.'

'Here?'

'Usually, yes. On Monday, no. There's an inn, the sign of The Mermaid, at Clerkenwell. Ask to be shown to the room taken by Mr Cecil.' Tresham's eyes widened. 'Mr *Robin* Cecil. I'll meet you there.'

'Can he be trusted?' The question was Jane's. She had read Jonson's manuscript, liked it, and was now descending into restless boredom again. It was going to be called *Volpone, Or The Fox*, his play. It had made her yearn to go to the playhouse again.

'We'll find out soon enough. While we're under this threat I don't want you out of my sight.'

'I know,' she said simply. 'But if we're found out then I'll be the least of your troubles. I can be secret, too, you know. When it really matters.'

A number of those Tresham had been at school with, and some of his adult friends, were now dead. Several had died of the plague, one thrown from a horse, others of illnesses that seemed to have no name and no cure. Another had been knifed in a brawl, and spoken gaily to Tresham as the life blood had ebbed from him. The death of his father had shattered him more than his so-called friends knew. Enemy that he had been, his father had offered a strange security and comfort. Sir Thomas Tresham had been an anchor point in his life. And now even that great certainty was gone.

He had felt so brave, when he was young. Now all he felt was fear.

Clerkenwell lay outside the City walls. Until recently a village to the north of the City, bounded by the Fleet on one side and Charterhouse on the other, the relentless march of London had swallowed it up, its residents claiming that the country winds blowing over it from Islington kept the plague at bay.

Stourton had married Frances, Tresham's sister, and though there was a twenty-year age gap between them he had become close friends with Catesby. Lady Frances Stourton had a permanently world-weary look to her, and conducted all her business distractedly, as if something terribly important was happening elsewhere.

'Francis, you're very welcome here, as ever.' She used the same tone of tired affection, as ever. She was in mourning, of course, and Lord Stourton all commiseration at the loss of his father-in-law. At the same time, he seemed distracted, removed from his usual self. Catesby was no different, seeking first to charm Frances and then turning his attention on to Stourton. Yet dinner was ended early, and Catesby asked leave to hold a few words with Tresham. Tresham felt his heart tighten.

Winter was drawing in, and a steady fire in the new hearth lapped at the edges of the cold. The room was square, with latticed glass looking out over the garden. The panelling was light, almost irritatingly so, being so new as to not have darkened or weathered properly. Family portraits glowered at Tresham. They were a proud crew, the Stourtons.

Catesby looked at Tresham, and felt, not for the first time, the stirrings of unease. For long simply a plaything, a stringed instrument on whose neck Catesby could play whatever tune he pleased, Francis Tresham would always be a risk. A risk of a different kind, Thomas Percy, had failed to deliver the rent money due on the

213

Westminster house whose cellar hid such a terrible secret. Fawkes had had to be sent to pay Henry Ferrers and Whynniard what they were owed, masquerading as 'John Johnson', Percy's servant. Just as pressingly, Fawkes was insisting on the money needed to hire the ship from Greenwich that would take him abroad after the explosion. Fawkes had been hired for his skill with powder. It was not expected that he would remain on after the explosion, but nor had Catesby expected him to be quite so pressing with the money for his escape route. That great baby Everard Digby had provided some coin, but Tresham was now heir to a rent roll of £3,000 a year. Tresham was rich, was from one of the great Catholic families, wasn't he? Then it was time for him to be called on.

Francis Tresham could feel the blood leaving his face and hands as Catesby told him the bare bones of his plan. Rarely had he heard anything so mad. Could a man's heart stop and he still live on? How could he report this to the man in dark clothes? He drew a deep breath. He recognised the tactic from lesser conversations. Catesby had first of all delivered the shock, and now was winding up into full justification, a passionate torrent of words starting to flow from him, in contrast to the almost jerky rhythms with which he had described his plan to take most of England's nobility to Hell. Tresham stood up, held up his hand.

'Stop this, cousin, stop this. Will you be silent?' No-one told Robert Catesby to be silent. A flicker of yellow covered Catesby's eyes, and vanished as quickly. 'Are you mad? Would you damn us all?' Tresham started to pace the room, unconsciously wringing his hands together as if to squeeze the correct words out of them.

'This isn't damnation – it's salvation,' Catesby answered, urgent to make a speech.

'Forgive me. I hadn't realised God had taken a simple little word out of "Thou shalt *not* murder". How can it not be damnation to kill so many, guilty and innocent alike? Why, to kill some of our greatest friends? Of a sudden you have a monopoly on Divine judgement, do you, cousin?'

'I don't, but those who do have sanctified and approved the plan. You've heard Father Garnet speak of how a smaller evil is permissible in the pursuit of a greater good. Of how if the innocent in an evil city are besieged then they must take their chance with the rest? I can show you the texts that . . .'

'Faith! Damn your stupid texts! And damn the stupid priests who read them! Hold off that, will you? I'm no scholar of theology. Yet if you really do believe that the Bible sanctifies such an act, let Francis Tresham for the first time take on the robes of a saint. The Bible be damned. *I* tell you this act is an act of madness, as well as an act of murder! It'll kill us all!'

'Are you then willing to be the only Catholic in England too much of a coward to take up the cause? Are you willing . . .'

'Hold off again!' Tresham had never before interrupted Catesby, never mind doing it twice in quick succession. Few had, when he was in full force, or seeking to get there. A force of nature, his father had once described him, not entirely approvingly as he had seen every servant girl go weak at the knees in his presence. 'You can forget the old cowardice trick. It's been used once before, and it doesn't work. Remember poor Tom in the orchard?'

Years ago at Harrowden three of them had planned a raid on a neighbour's orchard, seeking the sweet apples that were his pride and joy. When they had seen the neighbour working in a far corner of the orchard the other two, one of whom was Tresham, had argued for strategic retreat. Catesby had roundly accused them of being cowards, at which the other boy, Tom, had leapt the wall and crept towards the trees. His howls as the neighbour had laid a springy branch with far more force than was necessary across his buttocks had kept Catesby and Tresham company as they huddled on the other side of the wall. 'I hear Tom speaking to me,' an angry Tresham had whispered harshly to Catesby, 'telling me how much pleasure he takes in being a hero!'

Back in the present, Tresham was too angry to be diverted from his point. 'This isn't about cowardice. Have you thought, man, that the nation will be appalled to think such an act could be undertaken in the name of religion – a religion that preaches peace to one's neighbour! Every act of repression, every crippling penalty, will be justified by reference to this act of evil. Common folk will rise up against us! More than common folk! Every decent person in the kingdom will want our blood in revenge! This won't save Catholicism! It'll ruin it for ever! Are you mad?'

If any of Tresham's passion was penetrating Catesby's self-belief, it was not clear to Tresham.

'It must needs be done,' he said, calmly. 'It's the necessity for all Catholics. We're forced to dangerous measures. We've no choice.'

'And what support will you get? Where are your troops, your invading armies? Do you think Spain has signed a treaty so we can go to war again?'

'The Spanish troops in Dover will march to Rochester and strangle London at the neck of the Thames. Percy's hordes from the north will march, and Catholics from Europe will flock to our support!'

'And on whose word will these mighty offers march? Has the King of Spain told you in person that his troops will be at your beck and call? Has mighty Percy told you his peasants will march in winter to uphold your glorious act, those peasants he hasn't seen for most of his life! Have the commanders in Europe given you their word in writing they'll make that perilous voyage to put out a fire in London that'll never cease burning! You're mad, cousin, mad!'

Catesby seemed unmoved. There was a strange light in his eyes, an almost unnatural calm in his manner. 'Fawkes is a soldier, a man of tried and tested mettle. He's been in Europe. He brings us word from the most high sources that the Spanish troops will act in our favour. He also brings word that Sir William Stanley will bring the English Regiment over to aid us. As for the Earl of Northumberland, he speaks through Thomas Percy, in whom his actions show complete trust.'

'Fiddle-faddle! This Guy Fawkes, who is he? I guarantee you he's as close to the King of Spain as my nose is to my arse! Stanley is a clapped-out old man looking for a pardon and a safe return home, and God help us all if Percy's on your side. Why, that sweating idiot would betray his own mother for a farthing and a pint of piss!'

'Calm down, cousin. Here, take a drink.' Tresham noted for the first time the jug of wine placed in advance in the room, and the exquisite goblets, new like everything else in the house. 'This is new to you. To others of us, those who've lived with it a long time, the shock isn't so great. Give it time. Give *us*, your friends of long standing, some of that time. Surely we're owed that much.'

'But what of our friends? Of Montague? Mordaunt? Of my relatives? Monteagle? Stourton? You can't kill every Catholic noble in all England!'

Tresham's heart was racing, his whole body pounding. He sat down heavily, drank deeply.

'We can try and warn some of them,' said Catesby. 'In dangerous times all men face grave dangers.'

'Money. I'll give you money.'

Catesby got to his feet, ready to embrace Tresham.

'No, not money to further this idiocy. Money to go away.' Catesby frowned. 'At least let this Parliament sit itself out, let's see what it does, what acts it passes. Who knows if the rumours are nothing but noise? Take a hundred pounds, take more. Take yourself and your hot-headed friends off to the Spanish Netherlands. Take time to think, and watch.'

'And leave thirty or more barrels of powder sitting under the Lords' chamber? Risk removing it, being discovered? To be hung, drawn and quartered on a public scaffold for *not* having blown our enemies to Hell? Surely not, cousin, surely not.'

Catesby was chiding him, as he might a child who had made a wrong translation.

'So, are you on our side, or a traitor to it?'

The irony of being called a traitor by a man who was about to blow up England's Government was not lost on Tresham. The heart of him

217

wanted to cut and run, to leave the whole damned business behind him. Yet his head told him it was of no use. He had been so close to these men that he would be swept up and hung when news of it leaked out, as it surely would. This meeting with Catesby had sealed his fate, he realised. If they could condemn Walter Raleigh, what chance had he? Besides, he thought as caution tugged at the heels of his flying imagination, his only way out might be his interrogator, the gentleman with the piercing eyes and beautiful . . . whore? Consort? Even wife? From now on, whatever he did, he would be seen as one of the conspirators. He looked into Catesby's eyes, and realised that he had never truly known him. If he denied the conspiracy he could not even be certain that Catesby would not kill him. His calm was more terrifying than his anger would ever have been.

'You've made me a part of your confounded plot. I supped with you last week, and now I'm dined here. Laying a trail, are you, one even the stupidest hound could follow? I've known you all my life. If your plot fails, do you think any of us will escape? You've hooked me to your line, cousin, without me even knowing there was metal in the water.'

'So are you on our side, or a traitor to it?' Catesby's tone was mild, but relentless.

'I'm a coward in your cause, Robin. Nothing but a bad cause can make me a coward.'

It was starting to get dark when he flung out of Lord Stourton's house and struggled through the streets of Clerkenwell. The summer's dust and two-foot-deep iron ruts had been replaced with clinging mud and filth that threatened to go over the top of even long boots, or suck them off the feet that wore them. He found the sign of The Mermaid and doing as he had been bidden asked for the room kept by Mr Robin Cecil. The innkeeper, a surly figure, called out a tap boy and sent him to guide Tresham. He left him outside a first-floor room. Tresham knocked. There was silence. He looked around him. The wooden balcony which ran round the three sides of the inn, facing inwards into the yard, was empty. The inn seemed near deserted. Those who had colonised Clerkenwell had enough money to keep a full table at home, without need of the inn. He knocked again. Silence. He tried the door. It was open. The room inside was bare, cold. No lights, no sign of anyone having been there in days. Leaving the door swinging on its hinges, he went down the rickety steps, and out into the increasingly gloomy late afternoon.

'Your news?'

He jumped and had his sword half out of the scabbard before he recognised the figure in black.

'Not here, surely?' Tresham stuttered. Something like a grin flickered across the face of his interrogator. He led Tresham to another room on the other side of the yard. Inside there were the remnants of a meal, a good meal as far as Tresham could see. And the woman, together with the huge man Tresham had seen before. Without a word the ox of a servant began to clear, assisted by the woman. There was an extraordinary relationship between the three of them. Master, servant and whore? Man, wife and servant? Friends? Co-conspirators themselves in some plot he could only imagine? There was an ease between them that dismissed hierarchy, an intuitive understanding so at times they hardly needed to speak to each other to understand.

Tresham sat down on a stool, took the offered wine.

'I know what it is they plan.'

Without a word being spoken Tresham heard the other two draw near.

'Speak,' the dark man said.

Tresham took a deep breath. 'My cousin has stacked thirty-six barrels of prime gunpowder beneath the Lords' Chamber at Westminster. It's in a cellar, hired by Thomas Percy, hidden under firewood. They plan to blow up Parliament, at the State opening, killing the King, the Prince, Lords, Commons and all. Three weeks. Three weeks from now. November the fifth.'

There was a gasp from Jane, and even from the normally stalwart Mannion. Gresham sat like stone in his chair.

'Is this . . . serious? Will they do this thing?' he asked, after a long pause.

'It's serious. They'll do it.' Tresham was warming to his theme, feeling strangely more at home with this man and his woman and his servant than he had with his brother-in-law and with Catesby. 'The powder's there, placed by a man they brought over from Europe on Stanley's recommendation, one Guido or Guy Fawkes. My cousin Percy's a Gentleman of the Bedchamber. The house is hired in his name, with this Fawkes masquerading as his servant. John or Jack Johnson, I think they call him. They mean to do it. The plan is to kidnap the Princess Elizabeth from Coombe House, and put her on the throne.'

'They're mad!' Gresham spoke almost in a whisper.

'I said as much, but to no avail. There's no reason in my cousin.'

'Who else is involved?'

'Those you know of. Some others you don't know. Is it necessary I give their names?'

'I doubt very much that I'm the one who will do them the greatest harm.'

'Over and above the ones you know? Ambrose Rookwood. Everard Digby. Tom Bates, Catesby's servant. That's all I know.'

'No nobility?' Gresham asked, with sudden interest. 'Who is to be the Protector if this succeeds? Who's driving it? What about Northumberland?'

'He was mentioned through Thomas Percy. Apparently Tom has given Robin his word that Northumberland's hordes will come streaming down once the Parliament is blown to Hell and backwards. Yet it could be bombast, from that man of all men. None others of true quality were mentioned by Robin. For God's sake, man, Stourton's married to one of my sisters, as is Monteagle! These are my *family*!'

Family has never meant very much to you before, thought Gresham.

'May I speak?' It was Jane. Gresham nodded.

220

'What good will come of it? Why can they think your religion will be helped by this . . . this slaughter?'

In a tired voice Tresham explained the Spanish troops, the English Regiment and again the hoped-for involvement of the Earl of Northumberland.

Gresham got up and paced the room. His tension was clear.

'It makes no sense. Northumberland hardly knows his northern lands, never mind commanding enough loyalty from his minions up there to let them come down and put their heads on a block.'

'It don't always need blue blood to shed plenty of the red kind. Commoners can kill as well.' Mannion spoke, and Gresham swung round to him.

'But commoners need a leader. Even the Peasants had Wat Tyler,' responded Gresham.

'Is Catesby such a leader?' It was Jane who spoke the words. They hung in the air.

'Could it be so? That Robin sees himself hailed as Protector? Surely no . . .' Tresham was aghast, unwilling to be convinced of what his heart told him.

'Lucifer thought he could defeat God and be hailed in Heaven,' said Jane. 'Why should his works on earth have any less pride to them?'

It was pure accident that brought Catesby into direct contact with Viscount Montagu. He had been walking through the Savoy, on his way back to the Strand, when he turned a corner to find himself face to face with the young Catholic Lord. A brave young man, Montagu had spent five days in the Fleet prison as his reward for speaking out in Parliament against the acts of recusancy. Just the sort of man to make Francis Tresham snivel in pity at the thought of his death, thought Catesby. Did they not realise, he and his kind, that if Christ had to die to save the world then a few men dying to save Christ was no price at all to pay?

Catesby could not afford to ignore Montagu. He had been seen

221

and recognised. The great Catholic families of England not only knew each other; they had frequently been brought up with each other.

'Good morning, my Lord,' he said, bowing low. 'Are you well?' It was verging on the impertinent to speak so directly to one so well born, but Catesby was increasingly fed by a fire of risk. If Montagu was offended, he did not show it, asking after Catesby's health in turn with every show of sincerity.

'Is it the Parliament that brings your Lordship to town?' enquired Catesby. Montagu's home was in Sussex. He offered to Catesby the fact that he was visiting his aunt, and hoped to gain the King's permission to be absent from Parliament. He did not need to specify his reasons to Catesby. Both knew that the devout young man would baulk at being present if any more laws against Catholics were passed, and might land himself in prison for an even longer term if he spoke his mind.

'I'm sure your Lordship takes no pleasure to be there,' offered Catesby sympathetically. Well, if Montagu was already chasing the King for leave of absence, there was nothing Catesby needed to do more, except offer Montagu's likely absence as his doing to Tresham and the others.

A storm was brewing, Catesby knew. His plot had been based on the Catholic family of England, the blood links between them that formed a mutual bond of huge strength, despite their bickering. Yet families protected their own. The death of some members of that family – leading members, the nobility who had held sway for years – was proving a sticking point. Catesby needed to stiffen their resolve, in this most crucial of all times.

He knew that Fawkes, the Wright brothers and Tom Wintour and a servant were due to meet that day at The Bell in Daventry. He had sent his own servant, Tom Bates, to keep an eye on them. It was time to start drawing them all to London now. Whatever the risk, they had to meet with each other more and more. Only with them under his eye would he be assured that they would keep to his path. He had seen dissent in plots before, seen how disunity tore a plan of action apart. He was their leader. Only with him would they haul together on the one line, bring the strength they needed to the great project.

'I need a Bishop, and a College of Theologians.'

'What's a theologian?' asked Mannion, unhelpfully. He had been let off the leash for half a day, and had returned to the house in Alsatia looking smugly self-satisfied. Gresham and Jane had pointedly not asked him what he had been up to. Despite the length of their time in the bolt hole, Gresham had seen no sign that they were being watched. His scalp had not itched. He wished he could give Jane the same freedom, albeit she would not choose the same destination as Mannion. Perhaps another disguise and a trip to the playhouse was an answer.

'Why would they help?' asked Jane.

It was late evening, and the house should have been in bed. It was Gresham who kept them up, feeling forced to take pen and paper, and to try and sketch out the problems that lay before him.

'Why, I'd listen to what the Bishops said, and know that the opposite answer was the right one. Or I'd listen to the theologians argue, and become so angry that I'd choose a path, even if only to silence them and their ramblings.'

'Will it help to speak the problem out again?'

'Perhaps. Who knows? It's all a question of what we do now. I believe the story of this powder. It's fanciful, even farcical, too much so to be an invention. No, the powder is there, right enough. Why it's there, and what to do about it, that's much harder.'

'Surely we know why it's there?'

'We know why Catesby and the others think it's there. We know how they intend to use it a bare few weeks from now. But such a monstrous evil . . . I can't believe there isn't blue blood at the heart of this, somewhere.'

'Well, you have three Catholic Lords in Cecil's pocket – Suffolk,

Northampton and Worcester. Between them they run over half of the country.'

'That's the problem. What've they to gain by a plot to overthrow the King and his Chief Secretary? They're well in bed with both of them, sitting very prettily on top of their own particular dung heap. They'd be mad to rock the boat, never mind blow it to pieces.'

'Northumberland then?'

'Possibly, but if so, only at a distance. The old Earl is no archplotter. He prefers his study and his experiments, and brooding in silence on how harshly the world has treated him. He's deaf, you know. Deaf people live in fear, fear of things going on that they don't know about. Northumberland is more frightened than most. He knows his family history. He knows no-one in London trusts a Percy. If he's in this, then he's pulling strings, like a puppeteer.'

'Surely all this is irrelevant? What they plan is obscene. It's an evil to end all evils. It must be stopped. Can't you simply swallow your pride, go to Cecil and reveal everything you know?'

'Cecil wants me dead, remember? I daren't go to him, not without threatening one other person I care for greatly.'

'Raleigh? Surely Sir Walter would never be involved in something such as this?'

'Sir Walter involved? Never in a thousand lifetimes! Raleigh has never had to hide his powder, and I would have been the first to know if this was his hatching. But Raleigh's life hangs by a thread, and Cecil needs only the flimsiest of excuses to cut that thread. One hint of a plot and Raleigh is dead. Raleigh doesn't need to be involved in reality. All Cecil needs to pin the plot on to Raleigh is the slenderest of leads. You see, Raleigh is a real threat to Cecil. While he rots in the Tower, and the people line the riverbank to cheer him on his daily walk on the walls and a King who has had him condemned can't run the risk of executing him – now there's a threat not just to a King, but to the Chief Secretary who betrayed his friend! Popularity, Jane. Popularity. Raleigh has become *popular*.'

Gresham was on his feet now, pacing the room.

'It's the one thing Cecil can never have, the one thing he fears! Cecil has intellect in plenty. He has wealth, he has power and he has cunning, and he's cautious beyond belief. Yet the one thing that threatens him is a popular uprising. He's no feel for the common man, no, nor any love for them. He can sit in his palace and scheme and manipulate and plot and plan, but he can't reach out like Sir Walter can reach out and make people's hearts sing and their spirits rise just by the sight of him. So he fears Raleigh above all others, my poor captain in his captive tower, and he fears that Raleigh might win over the King. Raleigh's the symbol of the popularity Cecil will never have, and a power he'll never have, the power to move people's hearts and minds. Cecil knows it's a power that could be used to knock him off his perch, so he fears it as well as envies it.'

'But what's the link between this and this powder plot?' asked Jane, genuinely bemused.

'What if Cecil knows something is brewing? The details can't be clear to him. No man like him would knowingly leave a ton of powder beneath his seat of power. But say he's caught the rumours, and sees in this plot a way to prove Raleigh a traitor at last? Say he bides his time and then seizes as many of the plotters as he can find. How many under torture wouldn't confess to Raleigh's being the ringleader? It would explain so much. Why Cecil is desperate to keep me out of the way, why he feared me so and set me off on a false trail. I've made no secret of my allegiance to Sir Walter. For God's sake, I visit the man in his prison openly! There are few men who could unstitch a plot to make Raleigh appear a traitor, and few who would want to do so as much as I. I'm one such. Perhaps the only such.'

'Did it kill Will Shadwell?' asked Jane.

'Of course,' said Gresham. 'Percy must have blurted something out to Shadwell when he was drunk. I wonder if Will took the story to Cecil first of all? That would be a fine joke. Cecil watching this lovely little plot bubbling away, his marvellous excuse to get rid of Raleigh once and for all, and along comes Will Shadwell ready to spoil it all with an early disclosure. I flattered myself thinking Will Shadwell was running with a story to me. I bet he was running *away* from Sam Fogarty and his crew; he must have picked up he was being followed, and seen me as the only person who could protect him against Cecil.'

Jane was looking perplexed. 'But I still don't see why you can't just go to Cecil? Expose the plot and you stop a slaughter . . .'

'And I give Cecil myself as well as Raleigh, served up nice and hot on a plate! Think what happens if I appear in front of Cecil with the details of this fantastical plot. One of Raleigh's fiercest supporters, and a spymaster to boot? I'm clapped into jail the minute I open my mouth, and instead of saving my master I become an agent for his death! How easy to have me not as the *discoverer* of the plot, but as one of its *leaders*? There's a forged letter to prove me a Catholic. What was done once can be done again! I've supped with the plotters, haven't I? And I have a direct link to Raleigh. They can have me backwards and forwards between the plotters and the Tower quicker than a pair of oars in the flood tide. They can rack me until I say what they wish, never even need to bring me out in open court. Look at Raleigh's trial – his chief accuser was never even presented!'

'You would never testify against Raleigh!' exclaimed Jane.

'I would never *willingly* or knowingly testify against him, while I was in possession of my own senses. But courage and fortitude have nothing to do with torture, Jane. Christ himself on the Cross denied his father. It's not just their bodies men lose on the rack. It's their minds. Anyone can be broken, in time.'

'So you can't speak out, and you can't remain silent. Aren't there others you could reveal the details to?'

'That must be the answer. Young Tresham's a complicating factor. He's to be stopped from cutting and running, by the way. He's impulsive by nature. Before too long he'll weigh the odds –

God knows, I would if I struck a deal where I could be arrested and taken to the Tower as a traitor if my mad cousin spoke one word to the wrong people – and work out that it might be better for him just to vanish off to France on his own.'

'So who do you tell, and how?'

'There're enough pompous fools in the employ of the Crown who'd leap at the chance to discover a plot, but the mere discovery isn't enough. If the powder is simply found, it could still be proven as Raleigh's as much as anyone else's. No, however it's done, it has to be by some route or other that keeps it within the Catholics, identifies the whole awful business as driven by religion.'

'Well,' said Jane, 'you'd better get that pen and paper ready. How many Catholic sympathisers do we know?'

Someone was crying, not too far away in the house. The noise could be heard even above the noise of a great house being shut up and closed down, a keening wail that seemed to have no start and no ending. It would be one of the servants, Tresham thought. He was still not recovered from his madcap ride from London to Northamptonshire. Many of the servants had worked their whole lives for the Tresham family. They were wailing, as servants always did, yet little they knew how much better for them it would be to be dispersed before the avenging angels of Cecil descended on the house crying treason. He had done with Rushton, whatever happened. Already the house felt as if it belonged to someone else.

Tresham believed he could still stop the plot. If that was the case, Rushton could be opened up again easily enough. The death of so many Catholic nobles was the key, he was sure. It might not work as an argument for postponement on Catesby, but it could work on the others. He had laboured the point with his dark angel. The man showed so little resemblance to Alexander Selkirk, the semi-drunk Scot who had accompanied Jonson, that Tresham had to pinch himself to know they were one and the same. 'Selkirk' had not disagreed with him, but gazed levelly into his eyes and said resignedly,

'You must try, as best you can. It's best you don't know of the other plan to destroy this plot before it happens. You'll be all the more surprised when you do hear of it. Remember when you're challenged to stick with the truth.' Tresham had pondered on that, not really understanding, and pleaded to be allowed to ride north and close up his home, bringing his family down to London.

'Why should you wish that?' the man had asked.

'I leave this country for a while, whatever happens. I need to put my affairs in order, gather my money and bring my family together so that when I vanish they can help and support each other. I must also consider being arrested.'

'Why so?'

Tresham had had the same thoughts as Gresham. 'One loose word from any one of the plotters and they could be betrayed. I'm implicated now, regardless. If I'm arrested I can plead that I tried to stop the plot – which is quite true – and stayed with Catesby simply to act from the inside to further act against it. If I move my family to London it will confirm my innocence. A man who fears the fire doesn't move nearer the furnace.'

'No,' said Gresham, 'but a man who wants to light it most certainly does.'

You are, thought Gresham, very optimistic indeed about your likely fate if this plot is discovered. Live in hope, though. It does no harm.

'A lesser brain than yours,' he continued, 'might think to strip his house and gather his wealth, then return to London and vanish quietly before anyone knew what was happening.'

Was this man a mind-reader? Just such thoughts had been gaining increasing strength in Tresham's mind.

'Such thoughts wouldn't merit serious attention, from a sensible man, for two reasons. Firstly, a man who vanishes is still alive, and can still be found. Secondly, there is a watch on you at all times. It's an experienced watch, by people who make their living out of it, and would as soon as kill you as keep tail on you. We'll decide when you leave, together. Let this be our own private little con-spiracy.'

So it had ended, and Tresham taken the mad ride to Rushton. Dust was rising everywhere, as hangings were taken down and the few precious carpets taken up, clothes and bed linen assaulted to rid them of dust before being packed tight into the chests that littered the halls and stairways. What few fires there were blew smoke throughout the house, as doors were banged open and shut to the carts and horses waiting outside.

There was one final thing to be done, apart from face the anger and incomprehension of his mother, wife and sisters. The family papers, so carefully tended and preserved by his father, had been sealed three times over, and placed in the house where no unfriendly eyes would ever gaze on them. It felt like a burial.

Tresham headed for White Webbs, the Enfield home of Anne Vaux. He knew that Father Garnet would be there, together with Catesby, Fawkes and Tom Wintour. Catesby had assured him that Anne knew nothing of the detail of the plot, yet he felt a deep unease. White Webbs had become the gathering centre for the conspirators. It was riddled with priest-holes, and conveniently close to London. He could not believe Anne Vaux would agree to mass slaughter in Parliament. Yet he could not see how she would not know, given the iron hand of control she and the other Catholic women exercised over the Faith in England. Father Garnet was a garrulous fool, and to be trusted as much as any Jesuit, yet how had he supported this murderous plan? Catesby was insistent that Garnet knew about the plot and endorsed it.

Tresham felt a deep, inner exhaustion as he entered the familiar doors, doors that once had been comforting to him. Catesby, Fawkes and Tom Wintour were there, with Robert Keyes. He had not liked Fawkes on their one previous meeting, feeling in him a contempt for the civilians with whom he was temporarily involved. His dislike had increased now he realised that this was the man who had planted the powder, and the man who was prepared to light the fuse to it. To Hell with the Lords in Parliament, who probably deserved to go there anyway. The powder could blow up whoever it pleased, but there was a terrible danger of Francis Tresham being caught in the blast.

From the start Tresham sensed a difference in Catesby. They were seated together in a room of dark oak panelling, bare of portraits but with mullioned windows overlooking the tended garden. By it a kitchen maid was poking at a mass of green in the kitchen garden, seeking the best plants to take back inside to Cook. Tresham looked enviously down on her bent back, noting her complete absorption in her task. Could his life ever be that simple?

'We're bound to blow up several of our own kind. Not just common people – the people whose leadership we depend on! Are we Catholics, or are we cannibals, feeding off our own kind?' Tresham was pushing at the point.

There was a sardonic grin on Fawkes's face. He rarely spoke, and when he did it was with a strange tang of Yorkshire and Spain in his accent.

'People die in wars,' he said now. 'Innocent people, as well as guilty people and soldiers.'

'For too long,' said Catesby, 'we've seen our battle as being about ideas and faith. Those things aren't what we fight *with*. They're what we fight *for*. And fight we must. Do you think those who might die in the Lords would think their lives ill-lost if by their death we bring God's rule back into England?'

'They won't be able to tell us, will they?' grunted Tresham. 'They'll be dead.'

'Some, not all. Many won't come, because they know they'll have to pass legislation against our kind. Others we can warn.'

They ran through the list. It was far too long. There was young Thomas Howard, recently appointed Earl of Arundel and restored to that ancient title. How could the young Lord Vaux be allowed into the massacre, given what the Vaux women had done for the Faith over the years? Tresham argued, as he had to, for his two brothers-in-law, Monteagle and Stourton. Then there was Lord Montagu . . . why, Catesby had dined with two of them hardly a week past. Had he taken their supper whilst looking at them and knowing he was signing their death warrants? . . . Tresham had an unexpected ally in Robert Keyes, when he spoke in defence of Lord Mordaunt. Keyes was Tresham's age, a large man with a flowing red beard, but a generous soul, for all that he was a poor man. He had been one of the first to join the conspiracy. Perhaps it was the pair of them speaking out in favour of Mordaunt that provoked Catesby to show his fangs.

'Mordaunt!' he sneered. 'Why, I wouldn't tell that man a secret for a room full of jewels! It's precisely because of men such as him that we can't tell all and sundry what's to happen. They'd destroy us as readily as if we marched to tell the King ourselves.'

'But the young Arundel,' said Tresham. 'Surely if we kill such as him we're killing our hope for the future?'

'Why, then, stop him from coming by other means. Isn't there a man here who could give the boy a wound that'll keep him in bed for a week or two?'

A splutter of conversation broke out around the table. Catesby let it run.

'Hold!' he announced firmly, after fully quarter of an hour of pointless debate with no conclusion. 'I myself have warned Montagu.' He glared round the table, daring any there present to deny him his right. 'One or two of the others, possibly, I might tell hours before, if I so decide. You will leave it with me.'

There was total silence around the table.

'This is no petty squabble,' he carried on, in a low voice that carried as if it had been sharpened. 'This is the battle for the soul of England. Didn't Christ die to redeem us all? Wasn't Christ innocent of all evil? Didn't his mother, and his father, have long hours to mourn his death? Sometimes the innocent must perish with the guilty, sooner than lose the battle.'

They arranged to meet again on October 23rd, at The Irish Boy.

A wider gathering was planned for the day after at The Mitre tavern in Bread Street, between Cheapside and the river, though not for the conspirators. Catesby was cheerful enough to muster a smile when he told his devilish company not to meet him there. He was due to meet ambassadors for the archdukes. He had spread the word that he and Charles Percy, Thomas Percy's brother, were forming a troop to go and fight in Europe, partly to lure away any Government spies in the taverns, partly to reassure Anne Vaux and Father Garnet. For those who did not probe too deeply, the expedition was good enough cover for their purchase of horses and weapons.

From Bread Street, mused Francis Tresham, you could see both the Tower of London, its White Tower with its four new pepper-pot cupolas, and St Paul's, still without its steeple after a lightning blast in Elizabeth's reign. Prime executions spots, the Tower and St Paul's. He felt a clawing in his stomach, and wondered if the crowds would be gathering in one of those spots to see his disembowelment before November 5th.

It had to be stopped, this madness. It had to cease.

CHAPTER 9

The miners were thin, wiry creatures with an aversion to washing their backs and muscles made of corded steel. If they were to avoid discovery, it was essential that their work was done at break-neck speed, and in silence. The men could be housed easily enough, shutters kept tight and a single candle the only light. Food and drink were brought in after midnight, with those bringing it carting the waste away at the same time, usually choosing to dump it in the river where it was sluiced away. The men had been well briefed. Any curiosity they might have had was torn out of them by the sheer physical pressure of the work. The armed guards placed there to ensure that none of the bumpkins went sightseeing had an easy job.

'Silence!' Their overseer barked a whispered command and the men froze, those still in the tunnel slinking back. A rattle of hooves and wheels outside had stopped. There was a shouted command, the cart started up again. The men relaxed, the remainder climbing their way out through the hole in the floor, dripping sweat on to the newly sanded boards.

The men worked naked in the tunnel, though a few made a rough pouch for their testicles, to protect them from cuts, or placed a sweatband round their head. By their standards it was not difficult work, the main opening having been cut, but the scenes underground still looked like a vision of Hell. The feeble yellow light flickered over the naked bodies, glinting off the sweat that caked them, and seeming to emphasise the dark patches where muck and earth had become embedded in the miners' flesh. The air was foetid, stinking of sweat, piss and decay, and the light cast huge shadows on the rough wall as the miners hewed away at the subsoil and rock. The shadow dancers seemed like huge mythical creatures, beating punishment into an unyielding earth to the tune of the picks' out-of-tempo clink and thud. The job would soon be done, the miners sent back home richer but none the wiser.

Above the ground, London went about its normal business. The bankers and moneylenders bowed low and opened the doors of their fine timbered houses in Goldsmiths' Row, whilst yards away, hidden from sight and mind, the rat-infested rookeries held families of eight or ten souls, crammed into the one room. The prosperous shop owners took their over-dressed wives to sit on the benches by St Paul's and to hear the sermon, watching all the time to see which Privy Council member and which wife of which famous Lord was sitting in the privileged north gallery of the Cathedral wall. Meantime hungry-eyed men waited for the gawping sailors and country bumpkins come to see the great Cathedral, knowing that a false dash at a purse would mean the gallows only a few yards away from where the word of God was being preached. God was a strange master in this greatest of all cities. A wretch was being whipped through the street at the tail of a cart, for having denied God, whilst the moneylenders thronged the aisles of London's Cathedral. The bright-painted two- and four-oar wherries cried out for trade on the riverbank, peaking as the time came for the afternoon performances in the playhouses across the river in Southwark. Sitting on one of their plush-covered cushions was a young girl, dressed as if for Court. She ran her hands through the water, the same water on which swans were floating a short way away. She had been told not to, but the pattern of the water and the sensuality of its cold across her hand were too great to resist. Later, she sucked her hand without thinking, watching as they neared their landing jetty and gazing in wonder at so many fine ships on the river. In seven days she would be dead, the incessant bleeding to which her surgeons submitted her sapping her body's resistance to the flux which raged through her thin, under-developed body. It is London, and in the playhouse Hotspur is about to proclaim:

> 'O gentlemen! The time of life is short;
> To spend that time basely were too long.'

When the play is finished, many of the same audience who listened to Shakespeare's poetry will stay on and pay to watch wild dogs tear a bear to pieces, the bear being tied to a stake.

'The one who worries me most,' said Gresham, 'is Monteagle.'

'Why more so than the others?' asked Jane. They had filled pages of paper with their scrawlings, gathering together all they could reach on the Catholic Lords.

'He hunts with the hounds and runs with the hare, I think,' said Gresham. 'If you were to pick someone more likely to be in this foul business, it must be him. His family are Catholic through and through. He's connected to the Howards and the Stanleys, through his mother. He fought with Essex in Ireland, even mounted a madcap rescue of him. He was at the siege in Essex House, and managed a pardon somehow. Tom Wintour acts as his secretary. He's married to Tresham's sister Elizabeth. He must have dined with every Catholic sympathiser in the country this past year or so . . .' Gresham's hand swept over the papers where they had tried to record the whisperings and reports of the spies they had sent out. 'And, to cap it all, he's a bosom friend of Catesby, so much so that he declares in public that when Catesby goes from him a light goes out in his life. Good God. If someone said that of me, I'd vomit.'

'Sir Henry,' said Jane, fluttering her eyelashes, 'when you leave my presence the sun goes out of my day, the moon goes out of my night and the liquid goes out from my . . .'

'Shut up!' said Gresham. 'You're a disgrace to your sex.'

'Surely Monteagle must be a conspirator, then?' said Jane, unabashed. 'Isn't he a prime contender for your blue blood, waiting behind the scenes and pulling all the strings? Catesby might have his own good reasons for not letting Tresham know Monteagle is involved. If you ask me, it's Tresham's money Catesby needs more than anything else. If Catesby had really wanted Tresham in he'd have recruited him much earlier. If he's suspicious of Tresham, wouldn't he hide Monteagle's involvement from him?'

'It works as a theory, but only to a degree. Why hold back on Monteagle, when he's told Tresham that the Earl of Northumberland is involved through Thomas Percy? Northumberland's a far bigger fish than Monteagle. And then there's the other side . . . look at all this. Monteagle gets given a massive fine after the Essex business – but there's no sign it was ever paid. Then look what happens. No sooner is he let out of jail and a new King on the throne than he gets his estates in Essex restored, and his right to sit in the House of Lords. Suddenly, everyone wants to know Lord Monteagle. James asks the French King to let his brother out of jail, he's made the Lord Commissioner who pro-rogues Parliament, wins a nice job in Queen Anne's court, gets his name on the charter when Prince Henry gets made Duke of York. My, my! Our Lord Monteagle is very popular all of a sudden, don't you think?'

'Everyone knows James favours those in the Essex rebellion,' said Jane, 'not just you.'

'I'm one of the few who knows James helped organise it,' said Gresham, 'however much others might suspect it. But there's more in it than that. This man's had good fortune positively poured all over him.'

'Good spy,' said Mannion.

He had seated himself on a stool, gazing out on the narrow, foetid street as night closed in. He had given the appearance of not listening, but it was always a mistake to assume that Mannion was not listening.

'Explain,' said Gresham.

'Monteagle. He'd make a good spy. He's an insider with the Papists, isn't he? An insider by birth, what's more, something you can't just buy. So if I'm Cecil, what do I do? Pay off his fine, or even simpler, write it off, provided he keeps me informed about what's happening with the Papists. That fine would've ruined Monteagle, ruined anybody. I'd be a bloody good spy with that fine hanging over me. Fits all round. Cecil hates common people. He'd far rather work with one of Monteagle's kind, all velvet-arsed and coach and horses.'

'That would explain why Catesby hasn't trusted Monteagle with the plot!' said Gresham. 'What a fool I am! Mannion – you're a genius. Of course Catesby must wonder why Monteagle wasn't ruined by an £8,000 fine! Of course he must look at all this preferment, and reach his own conclusions!'

'Well now,' said Mannion, 'I'm a genius now, am I? That's not a description I've had from you before. It's the tobacco, I believe, it grows the brain.'

'Grows the vomit, more like,' muttered Jane, who had banished Mannion from smoking his reeking pipe anywhere inside, but could not banish the smell of burnt sewage he carried on his clothes, his breath, his beard and seemingly his very skin.

'Monteagle has to be the man,' said Gresham, as if relieved of a great weight. 'He must already be one of Cecil's informers. If he's told of the plot, he'll have to run like a rabbit to Cecil. That fine won't be suspended for very long if one of Cecil's supposedly best inside men with the Papists doesn't know about something like this until too late. It'd be death for Monteagle.'

'So how are you going to tell Lord Monteagle?' said Jane. She was out of sorts, her playful mood suddenly changed, sulking. 'Get me to dress up as a milkmaid and walk up to him in the street . . . "Forgive me, my Lord, but do you know that your Papist friends have put a ton of powder under the House of Lords and are planning to blow you to Heaven or to Hell when it's opened by the King?" Or write to him with a list of names? "*Item*: one raving idiot, named Robert Catesby. Talks a lot. Thinks he's God. *Item*: a second raving idiot, named Thomas Percy. White hair, sweats a lot. *Item*: various other conspirators, assorted. *Item*: one stack of gunpowder, fuse inserted . . . "'

'You're rarely boring,' said Gresham. 'Infuriating, yes, but boring, no. You're in danger of becoming *really* boring. Will I write him a letter, yes. Do I need your help with it, yes I most certainly do. And if it's the wrong letter, then hundreds of people might die unnecessarily and a civil war decimate this country.'

Jane's mood changed instantly. 'I'm sorry,' she said. 'It's an explanation, not an excuse, but I've found these past few weeks here some of the worst weeks in my life – or, at least, my life after I met you. I'll try.'

'Thank you,' said Gresham. The women he had known before Jane were strange, inward, mysterious creatures. Jane had that quality of mystery, of being a book with most of the pages still withheld from his eyes and understanding. Yet in her also there was a simplicity. He would not need to secure her apology with gifts, with cooing words, or be blackmailed later by her because she had given in to him. She had said. It was done. It was also a change of mood that would test the patience of a saint.

'So what form must this letter take?'

'It must seem to come from a Catholic, to stop this business spreading out to affect Raleigh or any other innocents for that matter. Bad enough if it's seen as the Pope's business, but better that than it becomes all England's. It can't be seen to come from any one man, or woman for that matter, because it must make them mount a general search for powder, not a single search for one man.'

'You're missing the important thing,' said Jane.

'Which is?'

'*The letter must seem to come from a plotter*. One of their own. An insider. They must hear the letter's been delivered and read. They must know one of their own has written it. Only that way will they not know which way to turn. They'll feel betrayed. Their insecurity will make them break, and flee for cover.'

'You realise,' said Gresham, 'that if I do that I throw suspicion on to Tresham? He's the last to join, the least committed. Monteagle's his brother-in-law. He's the one with the most to gain, as far as they can see, from the plot fizzling out. Won't they kill him?'

'He has to take his chance, doesn't he, as we all do?' There was no venom in Jane's voice. She had been on the river that night, she had read Machiavelli. She knew now that power and survival were not easy bedfellows with any simple morality. And she had taken a strong dislike to Tresham. 'Anyway, it's not that simple. Rookwood and Digby have even more to lose than Tresham. Anyone who knows Percy seems to understand why people associate treason with the family. And Tresham won't know about the letter. He'll be genuinely surprised. And if he feels the pressure building up too much, we ship him abroad. In fact, why don't we do it now? We've no further need of him.'

Gresham shook his head as if to clear it of debris. He was not thinking tonight. He knew the plot. The date was decided by Parliament, not Catesby, so he could not argue that he needed Tresham in with the plotters. Indeed, if Tresham fled it might work up an even greater panic among the plotters, force them to cancel their plans even more readily.

Yet that could wait. The important thing was the letter.

It took them two days. Firstly, the text had to be worked on and devised, a task that burnt the candles down to the base of the candlesticks. Then Mannion had to be sent, in disguise, to St Paul's to buy clean, fresh paper. One seller had a consignment fresh delivered from the Spanish Netherlands. It amused Mannion to think of the letter written on Papist paper, so he purchased it. The letter itself was written by Jane. When she had been learning to write, Gresham had come across scraps of paper in various hands, all of which he learned were Jane's cast-offs. From very early on she had shown the natural forger's instinct. She had an inventory of writing styles she could call up from memory, as Gresham had a library of accents he could use at will. The hand she chose was clear, flowing, large. It was the old-fashioned hand of a lawyer who had drawn up a draft will for Sir Thomas Gresham, years ago. In a house where paper was never thrown away, Jane had come upon it and practised her writing on its back, deciding to copy the hand on the reverse side halfway through.

When they drew back from the table it was with almost total exhaustion. The letter lay before them, a rectangle of new paper with the clear lines marching across the page. There was a word scratched out on the first line. Jane in her tiredness had written in 'your' too early and made to throw the paper away, but Gresham had stopped her. In some way the scratched-out word made the letter look authentic, as if written in some haste. The text read:

'My Lord, the love I have for some of your friends breeds in me a care for your preservation. Therefore I advise you, as you care for your life, to think of some excuse to be absent from this Parliament. God and man have come together to punish the wickedness of our times. Do not dismiss what is written here, but take yourself off to the country where you may await events in safety. Even though it appears no trouble threatens I tell you this Parliament shall receive a terrible blow, and yet they shall not see who hurts them. Do not condemn this warning. It can do you no harm, and it may do you some good. The danger is passed once you burn this letter, and I hope God will give you the grace to make good use of it. I commend you to His holy protection.'

It was perfect, thought Gresham. It would hand Monteagle a God-given opportunity to do a service to the State which would see

240

him set up for life. If Cecil and the King had any sense they would check and clear the cellars in ample time, and another plot would have been dismembered before it could do harm.

'Will it do?' said Jane anxiously, rubbing at her aching wrist.

Yes, thought Gresham, it will do. It has the certainty of a man convinced he is right, and just the right element of lip-smacking at the thought of evil being punished. It flatters Monteagle by singling him out. Is 'a terrible blow' explicit enough? Not for a man wanting to warn the Government, but explicit enough for a man simply wanting to warn off Monteagle. Would it work when it was shown to the King, as it had to be? Yes, thought Gresham. It would appeal to King James's sense of his own cleverness. It was a riddle a child could solve, but which a King would think had required Divine intelligence to work out. If it got to the King, and to Cecil.

If it did, and it was believed, there would be no explosion, no tangle of twisted limbs, stone and beams at Westminster, no smell of fresh blood on the morning air, no weeping and mourning, no terrifying purges and counter-purges, no executions and trials. A Catholic Lord would have exposed a plot by Catholic madmen well in time for it to be defused, literally and figuratively. In doing so the essential loyalty of the Catholics of England would have been proven, Catholic families would rally round to condemn the planned act of madness and many who would otherwise die would live on, to do with their lives as they wished.

If it failed to reach Cecil and the King, if its message was not deciphered, then that was another story.

'It's magnificent. When I tire of you, you can work as a lawyer's clerk, and make eyes at all the handsome men of law.'

The eyes that glared back at him looked as if they would put to best use a barrel of powder under Gresham. She was not to be teased out of her worry.

'This is no joke!'

'What's no joke is that the job's only half done,' said Gresham. 'What if Monteagle is the man behind the plot? What if he's the puppeteer? I don't believe it, but I can't discount it. If he is, he'll read it and burn it. He might not even tell the other plotters. We must make sure as well it's placed in his hand. What if Tom Wintour as his secretary opens it, and decides to mount a witch-hunt and still keep the plot alive?'

'Is nothing ever simple, in this world in which you live?' asked Jane.

'Tom Ward,' said Mannion. 'He's your answer. He runs Monteagle's house for him.'

Lord Monteagle was dining at his house in Hoxton, north of London. It was originally a Tresham house, and it had come to him when he had married Tresham's daughter. Tom Ward had just seen his master in to supper, and was checking to see that the main courses – salt beef and mustard, a leg of mutton stuffed with garlic, a capon boiled with leeks and a pike in a rich sauce – were ready to serve. It was unusual to eat so well at seven o' clock in the evening, but Lord Monteagle had been at Court, and asked for a fine supper to be served in place of the dinner he had missed. Ward felt a tugging at his sleeve.

'There's a genl'man outside says he has a most urgent message for you, sir, 'bout your sister.'

Then why the Devil can't the man come inside and give it, cursed Ward. Yet a lifetime of being a Catholic, of never knowing when he might have to hide his faith, of a religion conducted in secret, made an assignation in a dark street just another fact of life, and no rarity. He went out into the street, lit only by the light spilling over from the still unshuttered windows of the house. A man in a long riding cloak, with hood drawn about his head, was waiting in the shadows. He stepped forward, not enough to reveal his face, and proffered Ward a letter.

'This is from Robert Catesby to your master. It's a matter of life and death – true life and death, your own, your master's and those of your faith. Your master must see it *now*, read it *now*. If there's delay in this, you'll have more blood on your hands than Pontius Pilate!'

The figure turned and moved away, leaving a stunned Ward holding the letter in his hand.

He went back into the house, his mind made up. His master fawned over Catesby, and if this letter was from him then there was no reason for Ward to deny it his master, nor reason to think its origins were suspect. Ward knew, as all the Catholic servants knew, there was a stir about, wild talk everywhere. All the more reason to get the letter to his master.

Monteagle was in good form. His table was groaning with the best of food and wine, his company gathered around him, his future secure. What man would not be happy who only a few years before had been banished from London, and now found himself done honour in Parliament and made a favourite of the King? The wheel of fortune had indeed turned in his favour, from his being cast down to his heading for the topmost heights.

Ward leant over and whispered in his ear.

'What? What?' he asked, irritated at the interruption. Ward was still trying to keep his voice low. Monteagle was near to bellowing back at him. 'A letter? What letter? Oh, away with you, man, give it to me here.'

He took the letter without looking to see if there was a decipherable seal on the wax, and broke it open with a grin to the others that bespoke a man so burdened with office that he could not keep importunate messengers away even at a time when all decent men were in their house and home. His eyes were blurring with the smoke that had blown back from the fire, and he only dimly saw the large, almost child-like handwriting, beginning, 'My Lord, the love I have for some of your friends . . .' Oh God, he thought, another begging letter for money or preferment. What it was to have influence in the Court! There was food on his fingers, and in any event it was impolite to read letters in company at table.

243

'Here, Tom, read it out, will you? My eyes are furred with this damned smoke. Whoever swept that chimney deserves a thrashing, not my good coin!' It would be amusing for his family and friends to hear the type of letter famous men such as he received.

Ward stepped up, took the letter, and squeezed his eyes as if to help him concentrate. He was not a fluent reader. Nor, he was thinking, am I an actor in the playhouse, to be set up in front of all the company to give a public reading. He stumbled as he tried to come to terms with the unfamiliar handwriting.

'My Lord, the love I have for some of your . . . friends breeds in me a care for your . . .'

'Enough, enough!' cried Monteagle, laughing and making the company laugh. 'We don't have all evening, Tom. Here, you, you can read. Take it and enlighten us.'

Bad enough to be asked to stand up and perform, thought Tom Ward, but worse to be humiliated by having the task removed. He gritted his teeth. Another footman, unusually able to read, took the letter nervously and began to speak it out.

'My Lord, the . . . love I have for some of your . . . friends breeds in me a care for your preservation. Therefore I advise you, as you care for your life, to think of some excuse to be absent from this Parliament.'

The laughter and the small talk faded into silence.

'God and man have come together to punish the wickedness of our times. Do not . . . dismiss what is written here, but take yourself off to the country where you may await events in safety. Even though it appears no trouble threatens I tell you this . . . Parliament shall receive a terrible blow, and yet they shall not see who hurts them.'

244

There was total silence now, the noise of clattering pans in the kitchen coming through into the room. The faces of Monteagle's family and guests were upturned and glistening in the light of the candles, looking towards the footman. The servant looked down at Monteagle, seeking his permission to carry on or to stop, his throat dry, his heart pounding through his head. Monteagle gazed like a stone ahead of him, eyes fixed on something invisible on the wall. The servant waited, then carried on.

'Do not condemn this warning. It can do you no harm, and it may do you some good. The . . . danger is passed once you burn this letter, and I hope God will give you the grace to make good use of it. I . . . commend you to His holy protection.'

There was total silence.

'Is this some joke?' Monteagle demanded of the company. 'Some idiotic *pasquil* to stop me from my duty?' There was no-one who felt able to answer. The silence lengthened.

'Saddle my horse,' said Monteagle, quietly. 'I ride to Whitehall. Now.'

Without a further word, he swept out of the room. Behind him his company for supper looked and waited for who would say the first word. It was a long time in coming.

Gresham watched from the alleyway a short distance up from Monteagle's house. He heard the yelling and the stirring in the stables, saw the lights move back and forth in the darkened yard, heard the rasping sound of rough bolts being drawn back on stable doors. With a spurt of mud Lord Monteagle and two other horsemen sped out of the house, and down the street in the direction of Whitehall.

The cold had taken all feeling out of Gresham's feet, and his hands were little better. The old serjeant who had coached him in the Netherlands would be chiding him now, were he alive. 'Yer have to keep the blood flowing inside yer limbs if yer want to stay alive,' he would have said, 'and stop someone shedding it outside yer body!'

Well, the business was under way. It had a power and a force of its own. Gresham saw history like a great river, with estuaries beyond number flowing in intricate patterns away from the main course and then, after interminable rambling, back in again. He did not have the arrogance to think that he could stem that river, unlike many men. He knew that at times he had placed a dam across one of the estuaries, blocked the course it would otherwise have run. So the water would not take the course it would otherwise have done. Perhaps it would go where he willed it to go. Yet water, and rivers, had minds of their own. No man could determine Fortune. All one could do was try.

Gresham did not see Tom Ward retire to his own small chamber, produce a pen and paper and write a hasty note, which he then sealed with a copy of his master's seal. The various marriages between the Ward and the Wright families had cemented a relationship which had gone back decades. God only knew what the letter Ward had given to his master meant for Kit and Jack Wright, but if there was devilment afoot Tom Ward guessed they would be in it to the hilt. The man who had given him the letter had mentioned Catesby. Well, Tom Ward knew Catesby was at White Webbs, most likely with one or both of the Wright brothers, from what he had heard. Ward scribbled down the barest details of the letter and its disclosure, and sealed what he had written. Within minutes of his master's riding forth, one of the strongest riders in Monteagle's employment was similarly pounding through the mud, this time on Ward's orders to head for Enfield. Within hours Catesby would know of the letter.

It was a shaken and dishevelled Monteagle who loudly demanded entry to the Chief Secretary's private apartments at Whitehall. Yet he was not as dishevelled as on a previous appearance, not far from this very spot. To his shame and chagrin he had fallen into the Thames and nearly drowned during the Essex rebellion, being dragged out looking little better than a corpse. Even now as he was rowed up the Thames the cry would come across the river from an anonymous wherry, 'I thought that's one as preferred to swim the river!', followed by a guffaw of laughter.

These were not the rooms to which he had been taken, several years before, in fear of his life. His reception there had been as icy-cold in tone as he had expected, but very different in content. Cecil had recruited him as an informer with the clinical certainty of a surgeon sawing off a leg. What choice did he have? The deal allowed him to retain his religion and its observance, and acquire the state he thought had been lost for ever. In return he only had to keep Cecil informed – and as Cecil had said, that information was more likely to preserve both the peace of the nation and peace for Catholics than it was to disrupt. Well, if ever he was to prove that true it was now.

The door swung open into the brightly lit room. A supper such as he had just left was about to be served on a sumptuously carved table. At its head sat Robert Cecil, Earl of Salisbury, Chief Secretary to King James I. It was not the sight of Cecil that took Monteagle aback. It was his guests. Edward Somerset, Earl of Worcester. Henry Howard, Earl of Northampton. Thomas Howard, Earl of Suffolk. Four of the most powerful men in all England, and three of them known as either Catholic or Catholic sympathisers.

The irony of it would have struck Monteagle less forcibly had he noticed the letter on the table between the four noble Lords, a letter written on paper from the Spanish Netherlands, in a broad, large and almost child-like hand. Cecil had turned it over, face down, smoothly as Monteagle had burst into the room. It read:

'My Lord, were you and my Lords of Northampton, Suffolk and Worcester to meet for supper on Saturday evening at your palace in Whitehall you will find a message come to you there that will preserve your souls as good food preserves the flesh, and do much to preserve the nation and your self.'

'Will it work?' Jane had asked.

'Who knows?' said Gresham. Jane's hand was stained with ink, crooked with the time she had spent crouched over the paper. He leant over and placed his hand over her own. His hand was cold, hers warm. 'The presence of the three great Catholic Lords when the letter's delivered will serve two purposes, if it can be engineered. It'll force Cecil into action even if he's biding his time to implicate Raleigh in some way. It'll clear the Catholic Lords of any involvement.'

'If I was Cecil,' said Jane, 'I'd think some madman wanted all four of us together to assassinate us.'

'You'd need an uprising to do that, and an army to go with it. The request's for them to gather in the heart of Cecil's stronghold, not for him to come unarmed to a field in Islington at midnight. No, there are two key words in it for Cecil – "souls" will tell him it's to do with Catholics. I'm sure he doesn't know details of the plot, but if all London is buzzing with rumours that there's a plot of some sort he must have heard something, and he'd be madder than he is to ignore anything linked to those rumours. And we've mentioned *his* "preservation". There's nothing closer to his heart than that. It might work. We're not lost if it doesn't. The presence of the Catholic Lords is a bonus, not the main prize. The main prize is to get that powder removed and the plotters dispersed.'

Monteagle knew nothing of this. He had steeled himself to present before the Chief Secretary, and now found himself facing a court consisting not just of one but four of the people in the strongest position to influence his life, career and prospects.

The slippery element in Monteagle that had let him survive as long as he had came to his rescue. He bowed low to all four men. Collecting himself, he asked if it were possible for him to have a private word with his Lordship, with no disrespect, of course, intended to the other three noble Lords.

Cecil glanced at the other three, nodded briefly to them, and motioned Monteagle over to a side room. The servants had laid the wine there, before bringing it in to the supper, and one of them scuttled out as if branded as Cecil swept into the room.

Give me your damned message, Cecil was tempted to say, so that I can at least know where I stand in a business that is becoming too complicated for its own good. But, of course, he said nothing, merely enquiring politely about Lord Monteagle's health.

Lord Monteagle's health, he mused, would not stand many more rides such as he had clearly just made. He was having trouble catching his breath, the mud was caked up his waist and sweat dripping down his cheeks on to his beard. Monteagle was pouring out the story, offering Cecil the letter finally, after he had given a highly embossed version of its contents.

A slight shudder passed through Cecil as he saw the hand on Monteagle's letter, matching that on the paper turned over on his table.

'Thank you, my Lord,' said Cecil carefully, refolding the letter. 'It is good that you have brought this to my attention, whatever the consequences might be.' He nodded to Monteagle, ushering him out and back into the main chamber. The three Lords waited like gargoyles on a Cathedral wall, only their flickering eyes betraying their tension.

Without a word, Cecil handed the letter to Northampton. Northampton's ferocious ambition was widely known at Court, being born out of so many years in the wilderness during Elizabeth's reign. As a convert will cram a lifetime of passion into whatever years remain him, so Northampton was determined to make the best of what time remained to him by the political fireside. The letter was passed round to the other two, who read it in silence. Unknown to Monteagle, Northampton glanced down at the earlier letter, lying in the centre of the table, eyebrows raised. No, Cecil's eyes signalled, let that remain between us, not between ourselves and this young Lord.

'Government receives many such letters, my Lord Monteagle, as you may well know,' said Cecil finally, breaking the long silence.

Monteagle was visibly deflating in front of the harsh glare of power. His shoulders slumped. Had he made a complete fool of himself?

'Yet I have had word for some months past of scheming abroad, scheming, I fear, from those of your faith. We will show this to His Majesty, expose it to his wisdom and invite his view. Plots are as fruit, my Lord. They need time to ripen.'

Show it to His Majesty? Tonight? Tomorrow? Had he done the right thing to ride through the night and interrupt this supper? Or would his letter be placed in a pile of submissions or petitions, to be dealt with in due time and in due order?

'His Majesty . . .' stumbled Monteagle.

'Is in Royston,' answered Cecil, calmly, 'hunting. He remains there until the thirtieth, when he stays at Ware, returning to London and Whitehall the next day. There is no invisible blow waiting in the forest, I am sure,' said Cecil condescendingly, turning to the other three Lords. He was rewarded by thin smiles from them.

'We are grateful to you for your care in this matter, my Lord. Be assured, it will not harm your credit with His Majesty. You may return to your supper with a heart and mind at rest.'

He was being dismissed. He bowed low and backed out, even as servants began to bring in the delayed meal to the chamber. It was a perplexed young Lord who rode more slowly than he had come through the dark streets, to a supper by now hopelessly spoilt.

'You didn't need to put me so close,' said Mannion, rubbing his hands by the fire. 'With the noise he made you'd have thought it was an army coming to Whitehall, not just three men.'

Gresham had stationed Mannion by the main gate of Whitehall, to check that Monteagle had gone where it was intended he go.

'What do we do now?' asked Jane.

Gresham gazed at her for a moment, then moving so quickly that she could not react he grasped her round the waist, pulled her towards him and placed a long and lingering kiss on her full lips.

250

'I'm not a meal to be picked up off the table when it pleases!' she exclaimed, pulling away. She had returned the kiss, though, he noticed.

'Don your serving-girl clothes!' cried Gresham. 'We go to the playhouse!'

'Can we afford to? What if we're seen?'

'After all this time in this hovel, I think we can't afford not to. We'll dress as servants and stand at the back of the Pit. And after that, we're back to the House and civilisation, I think.'

'Are we out of danger, then?'

'I'll limp back into town as if a growth has been carved out of my side and I'm only recently recovered. Wherever I go people will look at me and feel ill, though I shall of course keep to my bed for weeks on end. An invalid will present no threat to Cecil. And anyway, the plot is out – what has Cecil to fear from me?'

Robert Catesby had spent the morning trying to ease the worries of Anne Vaux at White Webbs. It did not matter if he succeeded in demolishing her fears. All that mattered was that he allayed them. Hardly a week to go, and then he could throw off this continual need to hide behind fabrication and deceit. A week from now, and the world would know the truth.

The letter arrived at midday, brought to table by Tom Bates. The messenger, a simple serving lad, had become hopelessly lost, as a result of riding through the night, and had nearly killed his mount. Catesby read the hasty scribble, expressionless, and carefully folded it before slipping it into the large pocket sewn into his breeches. He finished his meal quietly, allowing Anne to chatter about the fate of various neighbours' experiences of childbirth and children in general. He rose from the table, thanked Anne politely and nodded to the others round the table. Tom Wintour needed no hint or secret signals to rise shortly afterwards, and join him. Not long after, the Wright brothers followed suit.

'We appear to have a slight problem,' said Catesby dryly, handing the note to Wintour, and on to the Wrights. The colour rose in Wintour's face as he read it. 'We owe a debt to your kinsman, Tom Ward, I think,' added Catesby, as first Kit and then Jack Wright took the letter. Both the Wrights had been in on the plot from its earliest days, and neither Kit nor Jack Wright would utter three words where none would do. Two strong, taciturn men, they grunted as the import of the letter sank in, and looked to Catesby.

'We're discovered!' For a brief moment, the hatred that drove Wintour to contemplate an act of mass murder showed clearly on his face. Stupidly, he turned to look over his shoulder, as if even then the troops of the King would be trampling across the lawns of Enfield to arrest them both.

'Peace, cousin,' said Catesby. 'We're safe as yet. Think. Think what it means.'

'It means Cecil and the King know about our plot!' Wintour's face was grotesque, distorted with the mix of anger and fear that coloured it dark red.

'It means no such thing!' Catesby's words were like a slap across Wintour's face. 'True, the letter sounds a warning over Parliament, but they'll look for an army to be the agent of harm, not one man in a cellar!'

'We're not named. Not any of us.' It was Kit Wright, who often spoke both for himself and for his brother.

In his haste to warn Catesby and the Wrights, Tom Ward had written only that Monteagle's letter had advised him not to attend Parliament and had warned him of a strike against Parliament. Would Catesby's relative calm have been shattered if Ward had told him of the phrase 'terrible blow', and the letter's emphasis on the invisibility of that blow? He was never to know, never to see the letter and destined only to hear about it from a frightened servant relying on memory. That particular estuary received no dam, and its water trickled along unhindered down the path Fate had set.

'We'll know soon enough if we're discovered. Do you think if any of us are suspected Cecil and the King will leave us to go about our business? Fawkes can keep a watch on the cellar. If there's any interest in it, then we'll know we're truly discovered, and plan accordingly. But before that, look at what this letter must mean.'

Wintour looked blankly at him.

'A traitor, Tom, a traitor! One of us must have written that letter. We've a snake in our little garden.'

The redness had begun to recede from Wintour's face, but it came back with a flood. 'Tresham! That bastard Tresham!' he roared.

'Possibly – but be cautious. Digby and Rookwood have more to lose than most of us, and wives who may fear they will lose their husbands and their livelihoods. Perhaps one of the other women . . . a priest who's heard too much in confession . . . a servant who's overheard his master . . . perhaps even your brother.'

'Robert! Never in a thousand years! He may be nervous, but if he isn't loyal then the Pope's not God's appointed.'

'We've to consider everyone, haven't we?' It was as if Catesby was discussing a game of cards.

'You'll call Tresham here? Now?' Wintour's face made it clear that Francis Tresham would be walking into his death when he came to White Webbs.

'Call him, yes. But not now. We're due to meet at Temple Bar on Wednesday. Tom, we must keep silent about this letter at least for a while. We must! You know the others. We can't let them think it's all over yet. Let's wait and see if a hue and cry starts. There were no names in the letter, were there? It will take time to examine, time in which we'll know if we're being followed or watched. Let's tell the others on Wednesday, and watch Tresham as a man has never been watched. Then let's decide.'

Wintour's face made it clear what his decision already was. As far as Tom Wintour was concerned, Francis Tresham was a dead man. The four conspirators ordered a bottle of wine. Catesby doubted there was more to discuss, yet there would be support in the wine and in the companionship of its drinking.

Francis Tresham, unaware of the plot being hatched on his life, and blissfully unaware of the Monteagle letter, lay in his rooms at Lincoln's Inn Walk. There was a knock on the door. He leapt as if for his life, grabbing the sword that lay by the bed. His servant, the learned but dilatory Vavasour, was out buying wine. There was another knock on the door, loud and urgent. Tresham held his sword poised, and wrenched it open. Something hit him, and he was suddenly on the floor with a ringing head, his sword held in the left hand of his visitor. It was the ox of a servant, Selkirk's servant.

'My master sends you the first down payment.' He tossed a package towards Tresham. 'And I wouldn't open doors suddenly, with a sword in your hand, if I were you.'

It was a passport, a travel warrant from the Government. It permitted him to travel abroad for two years, with horses, servants and other necessaries.

'The money, and the details of the ship, come when he's finished with you. Don't run out on him, will you? I'd hate to ruin that fine doublet you're wearing.'

'Why so long?' Gresham's scalp itched so that he longed to tear the skin off his head, his head was pounding as it had not done so since the river. 'Why is nothing happening?'

Gresham had revelled in the return to the House, and Jane had gone straight to her beloved library as if it were an old friend brought back from the grave. Yet as his impatience grew it was seeming more and more like a prison, more and more like the rooms in Alsatia.

There was the tedium of keeping up the pretence to cope with. The paste that kept his skin sickly-white needed to be re-applied twice a day, and Jane had to use a thin linen cloth rather than her hands, in case they too turned white. No lump in his side was necessary, the theoretical growth having been theoretically cut out, but it was necessary to keep a supply of fresh pig's blood to stain his shirts with, the amount decreasing every day very slightly, as well as suitably gory 'dressings' to be sent out with the servants. Gresham trusted the servants in the House more than he had let Jane know, but all it needed was for one to comment in the market or on the street about Gresham's miraculous recovery for unwanted attention to be directed on to him.

Yet the real worry was the lack of action on Cecil's part. It was as if the letter had never been received. The careful watch Gresham had placed on the cellar and house Percy had rented, as soon as Tresham had told him of it, had reported no untoward action or even interest in the place. The story of a plot being hatched in France was still current on the streets and gaining ground, but there was no hint to it of something closer to home, and no hint of gunpowder or mass murder or regicide. Tresham had been summoned to meet the conspirators again, but there was no sense of any special reason behind the summons. Sending the travel documents had been a gamble. They had cost him a small fortune, but as Jane had commented, quality never came cheap. In this instance, it was not quality he had paid for, but authenticity. The corrupt clerk who had charge of such matters had slipped the paper for signing into a heap so high that his master had yearned for it to come to an end with the intensity of a schoolboy wishing the end of school. Gresham needed his mole in the plotters' burrow to report. Had they noted men following them, questions being asked of the servants? Was the pressure on them to disband? Had the news of the letter reached them, through the servant, Ward, who was so close to the brothers Kit and Jack Wright, as Gresham had planned?

Gresham knew that impatience was his greatest weakness, yet the pressure of not knowing what was happening, coupled with the fear that nothing was happening, was near to destroying any peace of mind he might have. He called for music, and settled himself to listen as the lute dropped jewelled notes in the way of the long walk of the strings and the nasal urgency of the wind instruments. It helped, but not enough. In public he was still bed-bound for most of the day, so it was on his bed that he lay back and tried to let the music soak into his veins, as the musicians assiduously played for him.

It was dangerous for so many to gather at one time in London, but Catesby deemed it necessary. They had planned it long ago, for a week before the explosion. To cancel it now would cause panic. The presence of the others would lull Tresham into a false sense of security. He would hardly expect a gathering in London to be kept if his comrades knew the plot had been exposed, reasoned Catesby.

The taciturn Fawkes was there, inscrutable as ever. Rookwood had come down to receive his instructions, and to be fortified by Catesby if necessary. Tom Wintour was there, trying to hide the murderous gleam in his eye, whilst Thomas Percy, wild-eyed and stained from travel, had finally broken from his rent-gathering in the north to make it to London.

Tresham looked nervous, tense, almost distracted. Catesby raised an eyebrow, and Tom Wintour's hand stiffened towards the dagger in his belt. Rookwood had been given the task of buying dinner, not sensing the patronising ease with which Catesby treated him at one and the same time as friend and servant.

'Is all well?' Rookwood enquired nervously. Wintour flicked a glance at Catesby. These well-born, idle rich were food for Court and fine lace and fancy manners, he thought, but no good when push came to shove. The rich had time for a conscience. Men such as Wintour had time for action. That was the difference. Wintour cursed the day they hatched a plot which needed the money of such as Ambrose Rookwood.

'All's well indeed,' said Catesby reassuringly. The wine Rookwood had provided and drunk of so liberally had not calmed him, but if anything made him more nervous. 'We're not discovered.

The King hasn't hurried back from his hunting. None of us have felt ourselves watched, have we?' Heads were shaken in the negative, around the table. 'Stout hearts and courage are what we need now.'

No response from Tresham, who was turning continually to look out on the street, as if hoping for someone to walk by and rescue him.

'None of our number would betray us!' said Wintour, in far too loud a voice. Tresham started, but whether through guilt or simply the explosive noise of Wintour's interjection was difficult to say.

'What say you, cousin?' said Catesby to Tresham. 'You're strangely silent.'

'I'm sorry,' said Tresham. 'I've things on my mind. I shouldn't trouble you with them.'

Catesby and Wintour exchanged glances.

'I must have some of your money, cousin,' said Catesby easily. 'You know how pressing the need is.'

'Are you still set on this? Can't we at least delay until we know what legislation Parliament will pass?'

'You know the answer. As I know you won't betray us.'

There was a decided flicker across Tresham's face, a sheen of sweat across it. This was too public a place to kill him, thought Catesby. It would panic Rookwood, and draw attention to them. Not here. Not now.

'If you still have reservations, cousin, now isn't the time to discuss them. White Webbs, Friday, two days from now. Come and dine with us there. And, I pray you, bring some of your gold with you. My purse has been deep, but it's drawn dry. Until Friday then. I hope you'll come ready for a reckoning!' laughed Catesby.

CHAPTER 10

Though Gresham did not know it, the mood of William Parker, Lord Monteagle, was as destructive and tense as his own. He had waited for news every hour since his abrupt dismissal from Whitehall, yet none had come. The King was due back from hunting today, he knew. He could restrain his impatience no longer. Hurrying to Whitehall, he at least suffered no delay in being shown in to Cecil's presence. Indeed, barriers seemed to melt at his name. Gratified at the sudden power he seemed able to wield, he bowed in a rather cursory manner to Cecil, forgetting for a moment who was Lord and who was master.

'My Lord Monteagle!' said Cecil, an icy warmth in his voice. 'You must think I had forgotten you and your recent good service. Nothing could be further from the truth. These are weighty matters, matters we have let ripen on the vine.'

'You will tell the King, my Lord? Today?'

A flicker of annoyance crossed Cecil's face. 'In time, my good Lord, all in good time. Trust me, my Lord, as a friend, as well as an elder.' Cecil's tone softened, became almost caressing as his gimlet eyes fixed on the young man with his strong, straight body. 'You are beholden to me for a very large sum of money still outstanding against your name, are you not? You are beholden to me for restoring you and your family's standing and fortune, are you not? You have received those very great gifts in exchange merely for a little information, have you not? You may trust my judgement in these great matters of state, as I trust your judgement in lesser matters.'

Damn you, thought Monteagle. I am not your friend. I am your slave. As he left, his bow was deep and low.

'The men we sent out, they're still reporting, some of them.' Mannion stood by Gresham's side. 'They say these Papists are back in London, mostly. Gathering together for some devilry, I guess. Do you want to see three of them? Percy's booked dinner for three at The Mitre, in Bread Street. It's a haunt of theirs. Bold as brass. Our men say there's no sign of anyone else watching them.'

Why not? Gresham agonised. Why were these men gathering in London, instead of fleeing for their lives? Why was every Catholic sympathiser in London not being hounded down?

Could Gresham risk being an onlooker at this devils' supper? He was driven to it by his own demon, the frustration tearing at him as a real growth in his side would have done. Even the basic questions that were grist to his survival seemed irrelevant. Should he change his complexion from its deathly white? What disguise should he wear? Should he slip out of a side door of the House, or go as if to an appointment with his surgeon?

Why hadn't this powder plot folded in on itself? Had Monteagle been so unconvincing in his presentation of the letter?

Had he even presented the letter at all?

Robert Cecil knew little about warfare. It seemed to him that it excited men of a certain type, that it was costly beyond belief and that its results were unpredictable. It also seemed that an army large enough to fight a war was necessary to accompany the King on one of his hunting expeditions. The already astronomical expenses of the Royal household rose by the minute, and Cecil sighed as the endless train of horses and carts and assorted wagons brought back His Royal Highness King James I from his pleasures.

He waited until the afternoon following. Friday was an unlucky day in common belief, but also the first of the month, symbolic perhaps of a new start. King James was in his Gallery at Whitehall, alone.

Cecil approached, bowed, and offered the Monteagle letter, without comment. James raised an eyebrow, took it and read it. He looked up at Cecil, who made no comment again. He read it a second time, taking more care.

'It was delivered at night, sire, to my Lord Monteagle. He brought it straight here, to me.' And it was undated, thank God, thought Cecil. Would James be angered at the length of time it had taken to bring this letter to his attention?

'Clearly, my liege,' said Cecil, 'whoever wrote this is a fool.'

'In which case,' said the King, 'it were as well not to receive it likewise as a fool.'

Intelligence and experience, thought Cecil, his heart racing behind his composed exterior. Never forget this man has survived by his wits as King of the Scots. Never forget that conspiracies are second nature to him. Never forget there is no-one as wise as a fool.

Where were the others? thought Tresham as he entered White Webbs. He was shown to a room he had never entered before, and before he knew it the door had slammed behind him and he was facing Robert Catesby. Tom Wintour stood behind him. He drew both bolts on the door.

It all hinged on one sentence, Tresham was to realise later. If Catesby had said to him, in that terrifyingly calm voice of his, 'Why have you betrayed us?' Tresham's face would have broken down into a confession of guilt. He had betrayed the plotters to 'Selkirk', as well as betraying his marriage vows, his religion and, for all he knew, the God he had never properly worshipped.

But Catesby did not ask why Tresham had betrayed his friends.

Instead, he chose to ask, 'Tell me, cousin, why did you send the letter?'

The letter? What letter? The last letter Tresham had sent had been a peremptory demand for unpaid rent from one of his newly acquired tenants. Genuine confusion crossed his face.

'What letter? I've sent no letter!'

The instant vehemence of his response caused Catesby to pause. Even Wintour, poised behind him, shuffled uncertainly. Catesby spoke again.

'Don't pretend ignorance. Who else would send a letter to Lord Monteagle – *your brother-in-law* – warning him not to attend Parliament if he wished to preserve his life?'

'Now you mention it, I'd gladly have sent such a letter, if I'd only thought of it! You know what I think. We won't build our faith by this act, we'll destroy people's faith in it. I confess I'd thought of writing a warning, not to Monteagle, to one of the King's secretaries, but I never sent any such letter. Do you hear me? *I never sent a letter!*'

Sincerity strikes its own note. Sincerity uttered with a man holding a drawn dagger at your back strikes an even deeper note. It was picked up by Catesby and Wintour.

'If not you, who else?' It was Wintour this time, almost hissing in his intensity.

'How would I know? And can the condemned man at least sit down? It's not much of a last request!'

Tresham's genuine exhaustion, physical and mental, came to his aid. His tiredness was clearly no counterfeit.

If I can keep saying what I know to be true, I might yet walk out of here alive, thought Tresham. That would be an irony, for a man who was a congenital liar.

Gresham was exhausted, though mentally rather than physically. The strain of having to act the invalid in front of every servant, the strain of waiting, had all taken its toll. Standing to wash that morning he had felt himself shivering, something he had never done unless he had a fever. Mannion had said nothing, but Gresham noted the fire had been stacked higher than normal when he went to eat his breakfast.

Mannion had arranged the next meeting with Tresham in a stew, or brothel.

'It makes sense,' he had remonstrated. 'There's more control over who comes into a whorehouse than there ever is in a tavern. It's across the river, so we can get you over in a covered boat from our own jetty.'

In the meantime, Mannion had surpassed himself at The Mitre. Pretending to be searching out a room for his master and finding out which room Percy had booked, he had taken the adjacent one for an hour earlier. By the time Percy occupied his room the servants would have finished bringing the food and have left them to their bottles. Even better, an iron hook from which a lamp had hung had worked loose from the rough plaster of the dividing wall in Percy's room, and been fixed anew an inch or so up, leaving a hole. It had taken Mannion a split second with his dagger to drive through the hole and leave a clear mark on the wall of the adjacent room. It was the work of a few seconds to enlarge the hole so that one man could look through. Yet he worked with the utmost care at it, as the tap boy left their room. The plaster was old and rotten, and too much pressure would not open an eye hole, all but invisible in the other room, but rather tear out a great gaping hole.

Reluctantly Gresham had allowed Jane's importunings, and taken her with him, heavily hooded. At the inn it was just another well-bred lady coming to an assignation with a gentleman. They extinguished the lights in their room as they heard Percy and his guests enter. Mannion was first to look through. He had the descriptions of the others from Tresham and from the agents he had sent out.

'That's Percy,' Mannion whispered, 'the tall one with the white hair and beard. They say he sweats all the time. The other big one, red beard and hair, he must be Fawkes. The third one . . . he might be Grant, Robert Grant . . .'

Gresham took over from Mannion, peering through the tiny hole to the well-lit room beyond. How normal they look, he thought as the men started their meal. How much easier things would be if those determined to bring mass destruction to nations somehow looked different from their fellow men.

Tresham realised that his life had hung in the balance at White Webbs, but it took time for the shock to hit him. He had swaggered his way through the meeting, but gone into a near collapse afterwards when he had realised what had so nearly happened to him.

The smell of bodies and stale sweat in the room they used suggested it had only recently been used for a different purpose. They had come by separate routes, the most devious way possible, Gresham in a closed boat over the river to Southwark. Tresham had not been followed, Mannion was prepared to swear.

'Tell me what happened.' Gresham spoke calmly, sensing the rising terror in his spy.

Slowly, with much prompting, Tresham told his story. There had been a letter, to Lord Monteagle. It had caused Wintour to panic, but left Catesby strangely calm. The plotters had not been named. No action seemed to have been taken. The powder was secure. They were meeting tomorrow again, a group of them, to discuss the situation.

'And I'm the prime suspect,' he confessed. 'If they'd asked me a different question there might have been a different ending. Catesby . . . I don't know about Robin. I think he believes me when I say I've written no letter. Tom Wintour, now there's a different story.'

Gresham thought for a moment. 'Are you prepared to be arrested for your part in this plot? Taken to the Tower?'

Tresham gaped at him. Even Mannion started and showed surprise.

'Arrested? Taken to the Tower? Is the world gone mad, and am I the only sane person left? If either happens then I'm a dead man! I might as well throw myself off the boat home and into the Thames.'

'An understandable conclusion,' said Gresham, 'but not necessarily true. Think on it. If you're arrested peacefully and can claim to have used your best endeavours to stop the plot, that'll give them pause to think. You're a late recruit. Persuade them of that, and they'll leave you 'til last. With any luck you'll escape torture. It has to be sanctioned by the King, and that'll take time.'

'Escape torture if I'm lucky! Hell's fire, man, what do you think I am?'

'Someone who might prove very lucky in his friends. I said imprisoned in the Tower, not die in the Tower. Do you realise that when the news of this plot breaks you'll be a hunted man all your life? Well, our two interests come together. I need you to report to me for as long as possible, and that carries the risk that you'll be caught up in the exposure before you can get away. You need a new life – and you'll only get that if the world thinks you're dead.'

'And you can arrange that?' said Tresham incredulously.

'Did you realise that you've been receiving treatment for a complaint for some years past, from my good friend Dr Simon Forman?'

'Forman? That quack! I'm no woman wanting to miscarry quietly or to poison her husband, nor no idiot paying a fortune for a false horoscope.'

'Leave ranting to your friend Catesby. Forman is a better doctor than many who claim more training in that science. Now listen . . .'

Raleigh had told him on his last visit that he must drop the escape plan. He would never use it. His wife had pleaded with him. He had looked at her in that special way, the way he used for no-one else, and had stroked her head gently. 'A man does not run away,' he had said. 'A man lives by his honour, and if then he needs to die for his honour, then that too is part of the bargain.' What more fitting than that a plan that had been refused because it was not an honourable course of action should be used for a man who had lost all claim to honour?

It could be done, Gresham knew. Simon Forman could produce almost any symptoms to order. A urinary strangulation, he had favoured. Easy to fake with potions, easy to act. Forman could also produce substances that would slow the heartbeat down almost to nothing, make the body appear cold. The tricky part was getting the corpse diagnosed as dead, and into the coffin. Weeping women helped, flinging themselves on the corpse and keeping the doctors from a lengthy examination. They let the women in if the prisoner was seriously ill, knowing a man received better care from his family.

What would Cecil's reaction be when this plot was exposed? If it was done quickly and quietly, if the credit could be given to Cecil, who knows? He might save Gresham all the fuss and pretence and have Tresham declared dead in the Tower. If, that is, his gratitude to Gresham outweighed his hatred. Well, time would tell. With good fortune they would have these madmen cured of their plot and dispersed before Francis Tresham found himself a prisoner.

'Why not let him get himself arrested and then just leave him to die in the Tower?' Jane had asked sourly.

'Because I don't particularly want him implicating me in this business, and there's always the risk that he's seen and knows enough to find out that Alexander Selkirk is actually Sir Henry Gresham. But more important, I made an agreement with him. In exchange for his services I agreed his survival, as well as his wealth.'

'With scum? With people who make a rat look civilised?' said Jane.

'His personality is one thing. An agreement is another. It's a matter of honour. It wouldn't matter if the agreement was with Satan. Agreements must be honoured.'

If the truth be known he was more worried about the letter. Francis Tresham should have been able to be up and gone by now, the plot vanishing like smoke in the air. So the letter had been

265

received and reported. Yet no action had sprung from those facts. What had happened? Had his letter been simply too vague to ring the right alarum bells? Had the King dismissed it? Had Cecil dismissed it as a forgery, a ploy to distract attention away from a more real threat, such as a foreign invasion?

Back at the House the itching in his scalp was unbearable. He called for water and a basin, dipped his head and scrubbed at his hair with the beautifully scented French soap. The first and the second buckets, drawn as he had insisted from the sweet water of the House's own well, had been brought by servants. The third was brought by Jane.

'Are we washing out the stains of the world?' she enquired, pouring the contents on a head still half full of suds. Her fingers massaged his scalp, moving slowly and firmly through the tangled hair, easing the froth down and into the basin. A reddish tinge was still occasionally visible amidst the white suds.

'I must go to Cecil,' he said quietly.

There was no gasp of breath, no exclamation, only a slight faltering in the pressure of her fingers on his scalp, before the smooth, fluid motion recommenced.

'The letter's failed,' he said. 'I'd thought to spare bloodshed by naming no names, thought to spare Raleigh, thought to be honourable to Tresham, thought to disperse a plot before it could act. Well, I've failed.' He sat back, feeling the cold droplets of water course down his neck and back before Jane placed the towel on his head. 'One man has visited the cellar, our watcher swears, a man answering Fawkes's description. No man else. That cellar must be identified, emptied. Without the powder there's no plot.'

'How will you do it? Empty it yourself?'

'And have them fill it up again? Or be arrested as chief plotter? No thank you! I'll simply tell Cecil that on my sickbed I received notice that a certain cellar below the House of Lords is crammed full of gunpowder. I'll make it impossible for him not to search it. And you, Jane, will make sure it's searched, should I not return.

Searched and exposed. With the powder gone there's no powder plot.'

'And Raleigh?'

'He once told me that honour was the difference between a man and an animal. Is it more honourable to preserve my old master against a harm that might not come to him, or to preserve the nation from another blood bath that certainly will come unless I can stop it? I must take a gamble with the man I'd least willingly put at risk. How long have we been meddling with this plot? In all that time we've found not a whisper, not a syllable that could link it to Raleigh. Oh, I know, they can fabricate what evidence they wish, but I've been thinking.'

At times it felt as if he had been doing nothing else, lying awake for most of the night, the thoughts churning through his head.

'Raleigh has had one trial where there was no true evidence, and what there was consisted of lies. It was unpopular, hugely unpopular. I think it surprised Cecil, shocked him even, as only a threat to his own power would shock him. There's no real evidence to link Raleigh to any of this. I have to gamble Cecil won't risk another false trial with false evidence so soon after the last.'

'You're a stupid man, Henry Gresham.'

'Why so? Am I putting Raleigh at too much risk?'

'No, it's not Raleigh. It's you. You're never content, are you?' She knelt at his feet, wiping the shreds of soap off his shirt and hose. 'You say that survival is all a man can hope for, yet you put your own strange form of honour far beyond mere survival. You say you can influence nothing, yet you seek all the time to exert just such an influence. You think yourself ruthless, and you are ruthless with those who let you down or stand in your way, yet you'll risk your own life in the name of honour.'

He drew her hands gently off him, and stood up. 'Today, I ceased to be ill. Life is for living, isn't it? And when I see Cecil tonight, I'll at least know I'm alive, in every pore of my body, even until that life's extinguished. And after, I doubt my corpse will care.'

'No,' said Jane, 'but my living body will care. And the mind it contains.'

They looked at each other in silence.

The letter is confirmed,' said Catesby. It was Sunday, November 3rd. It was the last planned meeting of the conspirators, or such as could be mustered in one place. The news of the letter had shattered the peace of mind of those who had heard, as if there had not been tension enough already.

'Are we lost, then? Do I ride to Dunchurch?' It was Everard Digby, ever the dandy, leaning nonchalantly on the table in a doublet double-slashed in yellow and purple. In the morning he was due to ride to Dunchurch, where a 'hunting party' was to gather at The Red Lion. This party was a crucial element in Catesby's plotting. It was from here that Digby would move to Coombe House, a mere eight miles away, and capture the Princess Elizabeth, and this gathering was to be the base of the three hundred horsemen Catesby believed he could muster.

'I urge delay.' It was Tresham who spoke, causing an uneasy stir and a poisonous glance from Tom Wintour. 'Here, see these.' There was a slap as the package containing his travel papers landed on the trestle. 'I'll pay for some of the same, for all of you. Let's wait out this Parliament, see what comes to pass both with the law and the letter, take ourselves to France for some month or two. We can come to no harm in France, and we preserve ourselves to act when we think fit, when there's no cloud of suspicion over us.'

'Your cloud of suspicion will easily be dispelled with a cloud of smoke, smoke shot through with fire! Is it conscience that makes you speak, or fear?' Tom Wintour spat the words out.

Tresham rose to his feet, as did Wintour. Tresham felt a hand on his shoulder, pushing him back down on to his stool.

'Peace? If we fight ourselves how can we fight others! You ride, as we planned!' It was Thomas Percy, his vehemence startling the others. 'Yet we're cautious as well. We've two days to wait, and to watch. We've a ship moored on the Thames, ready and waiting our presence. We can be there as quickly as it takes to hail a wherry, and drop down the river before any hue and cry can catch us. You, Guido, you can keep an eye on the powder, report back any mischief there. Granted, we can't be rash. But nor should we waste years of planning before we have to.'

A heated discussion followed, but Tresham could see that Percy's passion had won the day.

Percy knew he had dominance. Yet it seemed he wished to cap it all:

'I've the means to test whether we're discovered. I'll use it.'

'What means?' It was Digby.

'The Earl of Northumberland's a member of the Privy Council, isn't he?' said Percy. 'I'll go to see him, at Syon House, tomorrow, on the excuse of needing a loan.' He barked out a laugh. 'It's not a new thing for me to do. If the letter's caused any serious problems, I must hear it. They'll detain me, for certain.'

'You'll take that risk?' Catesby seemed genuinely moved.

'It's a lesser risk than many we've taken,' said Percy, 'and yes, I'll take it.'

There was actual applause round the table. Yes, thought Percy, smiling through clenched teeth at his easy victory. I shall go to see my Lord the Earl of Northumberland at Syon House, and make sure that every servant at Syon House sees and hears me there, and that we talk in the Hall alone, out of earshot of all others. And then I shall go to my nephew Josceline Percy, in the employ of my Lord the Earl of Northumberland, and similarly make it known that I have been there. And then, he thought with a warm glow of vicious satisfaction in his heart, then see if my Lord the Earl of Northumberland can escape being implicated in what is to happen. Then, having steadied the plotters and unbeknown to them signed the death warrant of his kinsman, he left them. He had business, he said, to attend to in town.

Had Percy and Catesby worked it all out before the meeting?

thought Tresham. There was no way of knowing. If only they had taken his bait and gone, now, there and then.

It was dark as Gresham rode to Whitehall, the lantern Mannion bore before him giving out a pitiful light as it swung back and forth with the rhythm of the horse. Cecil must be getting tired of late-night interruptions, thought Gresham, though at nine o'clock he must at least by now have finished his supper. Prime fillet of baby, perhaps, with a snake's venom sauce. He felt a strange inner calm, as he always did immediately before an action of great risk.

In Walsingham's day the spies and agents had used a small, private door, just off one of the jetties that served the Palace. Its use had lapsed, with Cecil preferring to work with ambassadors and the gentry abroad who came in through the front door, rather than the lowlife Walsingham acquired in such large (and effective) numbers. Gresham called out to Mannion, and reined in as the glow of Whitehall appeared before him, the flaring torches still lighting the main drive to its gate. Some inner voice spoke to him, and he dismounted, handing the reins to Mannion, asking him quietly to wait where they stood. A tavern with some sign of life still in it was nearby. Normally Mannion would have jumped at the chance. This evening, he seemed uneasy.

'Don't you need me there, with you?'

'He'd never grant you admittance. And I might need to leave in a hurry.' Mannion nodded, reluctant, undecided but as always obedient.

Instead of the main path, Gresham broke off to the left, by the river. The vast expense of the Royal Household did not spread to employing enough gardeners, Gresham noticed in the dim light that spun off from the Palace. A handful of weeds, drooping from the winter but still virulent, were invading the edge of the path.

A gate barred his way, with two guards standing by it. They were cold, stamping their feet, and they let Gresham through with only a cursory question. He was finely dressed, and not for the first time

Gresham realised how much stress his age placed on dress and outward appearance. He gave his name as 'Sir Alexander Selkirk', with a grin of memory. The path kinked round out of sight of the guards, and there was the side gate. It was unguarded. He approached it, noting the signs of neglect, the wild grass lapping the bottom of the door. He looked round. A household of thousands was here each going about their particular business, but none looking out at this particular spot at this particular time. He tried the door. It was locked. He had not thought of entering secretly before that moment, but the slight give on the door put the idea into his head. His inner voice, that very calm commentator who seemed to live in his brain and talk to him only at moments of high drama, whispered to try the door again.

The frame on the outside was covered in mildew, probably the result of the proximity of the river. Gresham took his dagger and poked it into the wood. It sank in a great way, meeting almost no resistance from the spongy, rotted timber. He looked round again. Nothing. There were a series of narrow, unlit windows running off on either side of the door. Storehouses, if Gresham remembered correctly. Iron bars had been placed over them, too small for even a monkey to climb through. He examined the nearest window. The mortar was crumbling, the workmanship old, and shoddy. He picked at the base of the nearest bar with his dagger, and a chunk of mortar fell away, revealing the red, rusting base of the bar. A few minutes' more work and it was completely exposed. He eased it from its setting, leaving a neat, round hole in the better-textured mortar at the top where the bar had lain. The bar was heavy, perhaps a finger's thickness. He eased it into the gap between the door and its frame. The door's timbers were still relatively sound, but the rotten frame allowed him to push the bar, half an inch, then a whole inch in. Gently he forced the bar back. He could feel it bending, just as he could visualise the screws on the inside of the doorframe coming loose from the wet timber, the screws that held the iron box into which the lock fitted. He stopped, reinserting the bar into the even larger gap that now existed, and forced it away from his hand. There was a gentle tearing noise, and the door gave, shrieking on its rusted hinges. He slipped inside, pushing the door to. There were bolts top and bottom, he noticed, the topmost bolt seated in what looked like firm timber. They had not been pushed in.

He knew his way up the stairs, which had a layer of dust on them with only a few footmarks. He stumbled in the almost complete blackness, feeling his way with a hand on the walls. The chamber where Cecil met spies was at the top of the stairs, with three corridors branching off it. One led up to the main and State apartments, one was the access route that Gresham had used and the other he had never trodden. In addition there was a door in the panelling, leading to not so much a secret as rather a private passageway, part above ground and part tunnel, to Westminster.

Torches burnt in the passage, throwing a garish light on the unadorned walls. This was a business area of the Palace, shorn of frippery. Gresham advanced to the door, expecting to feel silence and emptiness at this hour of night, and that he would need to go up a floor to the State rooms where, no doubt, Cecil was still ensconced.

He froze as he heard low voices from within the chamber, inaudible and no more than a dull rumble. There was a scraping as of stools being pushed back. Gresham dipped back into the doorway from where he had emerged, wrapping its shadow round him. The door ahead of him opened. A blaze of light splashed out into the corridor. Cecil himself emerged, gave a brief glance along the corridor, and stood aside. Two figures followed him, glanced themselves up and down the corridor, and moved over to the door in the panelling, opening it and vanishing.

The figures were unmistakable. Gresham had seen them only the night before. Both were so tall as to have to duck under the lintel of the door as they entered the private passageway.

Guy Fawkes. Thomas Percy.

Gresham leant back, his head resting on the cool brickwork in darkness, controlling his breathing.

Guy Fawkes and Thomas Percy. Discoursing in the room the King's Chief Secretary used for his spies and agents. Discoursing with that same Chief Minister. Two of the leading agents in this powder plot.

And allies of Robert Cecil.

CHAPTER 11

'Fool! Fool! What a complete fool I've been!' Gresham's anger was uncontainable. It surged through the House, seeming to shake the very walls, threatening to tear him and all it came into contact with apart. The candles had been out, and hurriedly relit. They guttered, smoking from where there had been no time to trim the wicks.

'Do be quiet, will you?' Jane seemed angered by his anger. 'It's not foolishness I hear, it's self-pity! If you're a fool then we're all fools! Who could've dreamt of the King's Chief Minister wishing to blow up the King and Parliament?' She was scared. The rampaging thing that was Gresham was like a wild creature. She felt her world falling apart, torn by forces beyond her control.

The accusation of self-pity stung him like a slap across the face, because it was correct.

'That's where we've all been fools. How could I not have seen it? He doesn't want to blow up Parliament. *He wants the credit for discovering the plot to blow up the King and Parliament!* Can't you see? He's been in control of this from the start. The only people who benefit from this are the King and his chief henchman.

'It all makes sense now,' he continued. 'Unpopularity – I said

274

that was the key. The King's increasingly unpopular, and Cecil's never been popular. The Raleigh business gives them a permanent thorn in their side, which they can't remove, and the Treaty with Spain's laughed at. Everyone knows the Court's awash with Spanish pensions and bribes. When this so-called plot is exposed, at the last minute, Cecil will go down in history as the saviour of the nation and the Protestant faith, and James receive a huge backlash of sympathy. They'll ride on the back of this for years to come. It's all too easy for them.'

'But I'm still not clear,' said Jane, her brow furrowed in thought. 'Did Cecil start the plot off?'

'I doubt it. Catesby probably gave it to him on a plate. A God-given hothead, on whom Cecil placed a saddle without him even realising he was being ridden. Catesby must have walked straight into the arms of one of their agents overseas when they were looking for someone to deal with the powder.'

'And Fawkes?'

Gresham started to rampage among the vast pile of papers he had hurled on to the table when he returned. They were the reports of the spies and informers they had engaged at the start of this business, page after page of painstaking notes.

'The agent he walked into, of course. Either turned years ago, or suborned latterly. Look at his record! Born to a fine Protestant family, sells up his inheritance to go and fight in the Netherlands. All right, when he gets there he chooses to fight for Spain. So? Who has the money and the gold in the Netherlands? Who's paying a pension to nearly every one of James's courtiers at this very moment? The Spaniards. To Catesby and Wintour he's been a soldier of conscience. What if he's only ever been a soldier of convenience? A mercenary, fighting for the side that gives him most and pretending a religion to win promotion? Whilst taking a fat purse from Cecil to spy on the Spaniards, his employers, in the meantime!'

'So Catesby walked unbeknowingly into a trap set by Cecil?'

'Catesby triggered a series of thoughts in Cecil's mind, more like. The idiot goes blundering through Europe, looking for someone to blow up the Houses of Parliament, and latches on to one of Cecil's double agents. What a stroke of luck for Cecil – he has a real, a genuine conspirator to make the plot look real, and all the while he's paying the man with his hand on the fuse. It can't go wrong for him, provided he keeps a sufficient distance. No wonder he wanted me somewhere else.'

'What about Percy?' asked Jane.

Gresham threshed around among the papers again.

'Just look at *his* record. As wild as they come. Where is it . . .' he pounced on a piece of paper, '. . . *thirty-four charges* of dishonesty proven against him by Northumberland's tenants. He's nothing more than a bully boy, and then all of a sudden he marries a woman and converts to Catholicism – what a miraculous conversion! I'll bet anything you care to put down that was when he was grabbed to spy on the Catholics. What a bargain – he could tell them about the grand Earl of Northumberland, as well as the lesser kind. If you think about it, a Percy must have seemed like God's gift. Being a traitor is poured into them at birth, and what better guard against a northern rising than to have one of Northumberland's kinsmen on the inside!'

'I . . . I just can't take this in,' said Jane. 'Is *everyone* in the spy or a double agent in this world? Is there no-one . . . *normal*?'

'Oh, yes,' said Gresham, 'there're plenty of normal people. They die young.'

'Well,' said Mannion. 'That's all fine and well. A bit of philosophy always helps at a bad time, as I'm first to admit. But now that's over, can we decide what we're going to do?'

'What indeed,' said Gresham.

He looked almost devilish, his face receiving the light flung up from the lamps on the table. Jane felt a shiver of fear run through her body. How well did she know this man?

'I'm sorry,' she said, 'forgive me for being a stupid woman.' She glared at Gresham. Wisely, he said nothing. 'But how do Fawkes and Percy get out of this? The plot has to be discovered for James and Cecil to get the benefit, but if it's discovered it's death for Fawkes and Percy.'

'Fawkes just makes sure nothing does actually blow up, and then he's off on the nearest ship on the Thames. New identity, new life and a great deal richer than ever he was before. As for Percy . . . how do you think a knighthood and some fat manors would do him? The brave discoverer of the infamous Gunpowder Plot! The man who risked life and limb to ensure that every man involved in this blasphemous endeavour was brought to justice. Or he could simply take a fat purse and a different name . . . but I doubt it, somehow.'

'So what do we do now? Expose Cecil's involvement? Or just let the plotters walk into Cecil's trap, and pretend we never knew?'

'There you have it. It's Machiavelli's choice, isn't it?'

'Machiavelli died some years ago. We're still alive, in case you hadn't noticed. So, for that matter, are the plotters, King James and Robert Cecil,' said Jane acidly. 'I think we can keep Machiavelli out of it. After all, he played the wrong game and ended up being tortured and put out to grass, didn't he?'

'But the basic quandary he posed lives on, as it lived before he was born and as it will live on whilst humans seek and abuse power.' Gresham was lecturing her, unconsciously adopting the pose of a Fellow of his College talking to a young student. 'You see, Machiavelli said that truth wasn't necessarily worth very much, if it meant thousands of people dying. Good rulers put the welfare of their people above such minor things as truth and morality.'

'You're not a ruler,' said Jane, practically.

'No, but I could bring down Cecil and King James, I think.'

'Do you have evidence?'

'I could gain it easily enough. Men like Fawkes and Percy were paid to be traitors to their kind once. Pay them enough and they'll turn on Cecil as easily as they turned on their supposed friends.'

'So what will you do?' asked Jane, the anxiety cracking her voice.

'What will I do?' mused Gresham. The fire had smoked badly on being re-lit. In their panic to reawaken the household some wet timber had been placed on it. Now it had caught, and the cheery red flicker of the flames reflected in Gresham's eyes.

'What will I do?' he repeated. He turned towards Jane, with a thin, broad smile on his face. 'I shall be Machiavelli.'

The instructions to Fawkes had been clear. The frightened messenger was the same ambitious little rabbit Fawkes had showed the powder to an age ago. Fawkes was Cecil's safety catch, his half-cock on the pistol. Fawkes had to remain on guard until the last possible moment before the discovery of the powder, in case one of the other plotters decided to take matters into their own hands and light the fuse. Also, Cecil could not appear to know too much. A search party could not simply go directly to the cellar and find the powder. There had to be two searches, the first of the whole area. It would be told simply to observe and to report, to take no precipitate action that might trigger off the plotters. As such there would be no risk to Fawkes, particularly if the barrels were well buried under the faggots and firewood. If questioned he could claim quite truthfully to be servant to Thomas Percy, the tenant of the house. Who would distrust the servant to someone so recently appointed a Gentleman of the Bedchamber?

Suffolk would do to lead the search party. And Suffolk would be told to arrest no-one, to take no action that might start a panic, thought Cecil. He would summon that fool Monteagle to go with Suffolk in the first search party. Let Monteagle report that the pile of brushwood really was very large for the size of house above it, so they could go back to it later. It would all add credibility.

The second search, the one that would go back to the cellar, would take place at one o'clock in the morning.

'One o'clock!' whispered the frightened rabbit, though there was no-one nearby to hear or to see. 'The time is most important! My

Lord says you may leave after midnight, but not before! If a hothead such as Catesby were to hear the plot exposed he could still seek to blow up the building and so provoke rebellion.'

My Lord may go and fuck himself, thought Fawkes, if he has enough red blood in him to fuck anything, which I doubt. An hour was cutting it too fine, but he did not doubt that my Lord would have a watcher in the vicinity. Cecil was right, of course. With a gaping hole where Parliament had been the rumours could fly, and who knows what might catch seed in the confusion.

The rabbit scuttled out of the cheap lodgings, and did not notice the figure in expensive doublet, hose and short cloak detach himself, after a decent interval, from the wall and tuck in behind him on his route back to Whitehall. The figure could not fail to notice that two other men, in rough jerkins and with pockmarked faces, were also following the courtier, ahead. Typical of his type, the courtier stuck his chin in the air and barged his way through the common people, a testy 'Make way! Make way!' issuing from his lips. Suddenly he came upon two working men who, instead of moving aside in the busy, narrow street, put shoulder together to shoulder. He cannoned into them. Did one flick his heels to help him down into the mud? It was difficult to see, but certainly one of the men caught him a heavy blow on the head with his foot as he walked past the figure he had just helped knock over. Almost instantly, the two other men came up to the prostrate figure, and knelt down as if to offer help. There was a momentary flash of steel, so fast that no-one watching could be certain they had seen it, and the two men stood up and moved on, becoming lost immediately in the crowd.

The courtier's throat was cut, his life-blood ebbing away into the mud and staining the fashionable yellow starch of his ruff. Cecil had closed off one possible leakage of information in advance of the final act of his great play. The courtier gaped up at the figure in doublet and hose, gasping, terror in his eyes.

'They . . . they have stabbed me!' he croaked, unnecessarily.

'On your master Cecil's orders, be sure. If you wish a surgeon,' said Henry Gresham, bending down and whispering into the courtier's ear, 'you must first tell me what you said to Master Fawkes.'

The search party had seemed as inept as the rabbit had promised. Lurking outside, Fawkes had given his name as Johnson and told the leader he was Thomas Percy's servant and this Thomas Percy's rented house. The senior Lord in all his finery had seemed to be in a hurry to be anywhere except where he was, and the other young popinjay had tried to ask more questions but been hauled away by the other.

At eleven o'clock he took a simple lantern and materials to make the fire and light the fuse. The rabbit had been insistent that these were left by the powder, as if to suggest that everything was ready to ignite it at a moment's notice. He dressed carefully for the cold night, the spurs jangling as he walked for the last time to the cellar and opened the ancient door. Keyes had given him a watch, to time the fuse, as he thought. He had little realised that it would time Fawkes's escape. He sat on the stool he had lugged down into the cellar, not lighting the lantern, just letting the darkness and the silence enfold him. The dust, the ancient smell of decay, had become almost a comfort to him. So much danger in these barrels, so much threat, yet so much silence and peace here, underground. A broad grin lit his face in the dark as he thought on his master, Cecil. He wished he could see the expression on Cecil's face when the surprise was delivered. A pity he would be long gone.

He dimly heard the church bells strike midnight, and rose stiffly to his feet. He needed no light to walk to the door, the path learnt off by heart. He stopped, suddenly. A noise? From outside? He waited. Silence. A dog, or the wind. Nevertheless, he was careful in drawing back the door. Silence. He poked his head round the door for one final inspection. There was the tiniest flicker of light . . .

A roaring yell, and the full weight of the door was flung against his unsuspecting body, hurling him back into the cellar. He was down, and three, four, five men were on top of him . . .

'Leave off!' he screamed. 'I am under the orders of . . .' A sixth sense made him close his mouth. Something had gone wrong, horribly wrong. Yet these men – King's men, he saw by the uniform – were clearly not going to kill him or it would have been done by now. My Lord Cecil could not bear to have his part in this exposed . . . No, while he was alive he had power. This must, must be a mistake. He could surely stave off the truth until Cecil found a way of releasing him . . .

As the bound figure of Fawkes was bundled away by his men, Sir Thomas Knyvett mopped his brow, despite the cold of the night.

'A dreadful business, Sir Henry, dreadful business. You note the man was booted and spurred for flight? Cloak and hat and all! Had you not come in all haste with the message to commence our search early I fear he would have escaped! A dreadful business, dreadful . . .'

'It was, Sir Thomas, a pleasure to be of service to you, to my Lord the Earl of Salisbury and to His Majesty the King,' replied Sir Henry Gresham.

Kit Wright could not sleep. He envied any man who could do so, on this night of all nights. He was uneasy at being parted from his brother. As children the others had always joked that they hunted in pairs, and without his brother he felt strangely incomplete. Essentially a pious and a decent man, Wright prayed with his bare knees against the splintered boards for half the night. He failed to find his usual consolation. The same deep anger was there still in his soul for the seeming death of the religion he loved in the country he loved, the anger that Catesby had seen and tapped into. Until now that anger had killed any qualms of conscience he might have, but now, with the terrible thing so near, he could not rid his mind of screaming, the screaming of those buried under the rubble of Fawkes's powder.

He gave up sleep, dressed, and lay on his cot, fully clothed. There was a noise, surely? He got up, and opened the shutter. His heart stopped. A tide of torchlight was coming up the Strand, twenty, thirty, maybe even forty men. For him! For him! They must be coming for him! He turned and grabbed a cloak, buckling his sword as he flung open the door of his room. Even in his haste, he was not the first. The landlord, ludicrous in long nightshirt with offensive stains round its middle, had already unlocked the door and was standing, barefoot, gaping at the outside. Wright pushed past him, and halted as a dazed and half-dressed Lord Monteagle thrust past him, to be hailed from horseback by a finely dressed noble. 'My Lord! My Lord!' the noble was saying, as Monteagle's servants tried to put him in contact with his horse in the increasing melee of people. 'We must call up Northumberland! Now! With haste!'

There could be only one reason for every noble's house on the Strand to be being woken up this long after midnight. The plot had been discovered. How long did he have? Keeping as close to the sides of the houses as he could, Wright ran to Wintour's lodging, at The Duck and Drake. Breathlessly he gasped out the news. Wintour, as ever, kept control, pulling his clothes on as he spoke.

'Go to Essex House,' he commanded. 'Listen; they'll have the true story there, if they have it anywhere. If it's as we fear, go to Percy's lodging. Tell him to leave, now. It's his name on the cellar lease. He'll be the first warrant they issue – *and find out if Fawkes is taken!*'

'He's a calm one, my Lord!' The first questions were being asked of John Johnson, the man found in the cellar. 'He tells us nothing except his name, and that he's a servant of Thomas Percy. I didn't expect to see such calm in one so evil.'

Why had that fool Knyvett gone so early? Why?

He was here now, bustling in his own importance.

'Your messenger came most timely, my Lord.'

Messenger?

282

'He did?' replied Cecil.

'Sir Henry Gresham made fine speed to inform me of the change in plan.'

A great darkness opened up in front of the Chief Secretary.

One by one the plotters were roused, and, bleary-eyed, headed for the stables where their horses kicked and rose, sensing their owners' nervousness. From over London, they drove their mounts furiously, heading north, following the route Catesby, Bates and Jack Wright had taken the day before, the route to The Red Lion at Dunchurch. It was there they had planned to meet, to rally the band of armed, mounted Catholics who would sweep through the West Country raising a fire of rebellion as red as that burning at Westminster. Fear made them flee, some homing instinct sending them to where they had planned to go all along. No-one raised the alarm with Francis Tresham, and not only because he was a newcomer. The further away he was, the more belief in his guilt spread like a cloud of smoke among the plotters.

Meet at Dunchurch. It was the only security they had left.

If there were legends to be told about this affair, thought Ambrose Rookwood, his ride would be the greatest legend of all. He had left London last, except for Tom Wintour. He had supplied the horses for the others, but kept the best for himself. Thirty miles in two hours, on one horse! His head was aflame with the power and the exhaustion of it. His every limb ached, and he could hardly distinguish between his own sweat and lather and that of his present horse. He had overtaken Robert Keyes just beyond Highgate, then Percy and Kit Wright. Catesby, John Wright and Bates he saw on the horizon just beyond Brickhill.

They reined in. Catesby looked calm, but his eyes noted the state of Rookwood and Keyes.

'Well, Ambrose, your horses have done you proud to stand the pace! But why so fast?'

Rookwood had no other words. He blurted out, 'We're discovered! Fawkes is taken . . .'

Catesby. Bates. Jack Wright. Kit Wright. Keyes. Percy. Rookwood. The seven men stood in silence, the loudest noise the breathing of the horses, its steam stretching out in the cold air. The six scarves the men wore fluttered gently in the morning breeze. They were fine work. Rookwood had provided them. The weaving contained representations not only of the cross, but of items used in the Mass. Tom Bates had none, of course. He was a servant.

Silence. It was broken first by Jack Wright. His reaction was to start to curse, slowly at first, but with a rising voice of fear. The others looked, instinctively, to Catesby.

'Hold your noise, Jack!' Catesby's voice was like a whiplash.

'All is lost only when we all lose heart! There's chaos in London, isn't there? Confusion? Signal enough for all good Catholics to rise up on our side. We have horses, we have armour, we have weapons, don't we? We have men gathered at Dunchurch, don't we? All we need is stout hearts!'

Despite themselves, the men felt the warmth of his magic work its way back into the freezing bones. They rode, the Devil behind them and the Devil in front. Percy and Jack Wright tore at their cloaks, hurled them off into the hedgerow, as if by that small loss of weight they could drive their horses even faster.

Catesby yelled something back at them, in a delirium of speed and pounding hooves. They grinned insanely back through the blinding sweat and muscles that ached as if it was the men's feet driving them forward.

The furore outside seemed to bend the timbers of the house. Francis Tresham waited for the door to be flung inwards, to feel the hands round his throat, the blows to his body and head or even the stinging slash or probe of a blade. He waited. Why had they not come for him?

*

284

'Are you wishing to go the way of Lord Walsingham?' Mannion asked Gresham, glumly. Walsingham, Elizabeth's spymaster, had nearly bankrupted himself keeping a web of agents up and running. Gresham had placed one, two men on each of the plotters, one to watch, one to report wherever possible. The cost was appalling.

What was Tom Wintour playing at? The plotters were running now, running as he had hoped they would do when the letter was delivered to Monteagle. Gresham had nearly followed Catesby out of London, but to follow a man on those lonely, deserted roads without being discovered was almost impossible, and Gresham's instinct was to stay in London at least for a while to keep track of the anarchy he had unleashed. He had tracked Tom Wintour, choosing him instead of Thomas Percy because Wintour was the closest of all the conspirators to Catesby and, Gresham suspected, the born leader among them.

Gresham had witnessed Wintour issuing instructions, and then expected him to run for the stables where he kept his gelding. Instead Wintour had headed purposefully towards Westminster itself, the seat of the crime. Was it him escaping discovery by sheer bravado? Had he so much faith in Guy Fawkes resisting interrogation?

He saw Wintour stop and listen to a group of excited men in the street, and then followed him as he headed down King Street. There a crude barrier had been erected across the road, and a soldier barred his way. Wintour showed immense control, his shrugging manner, his easy craning of his head to look down the street perfectly those of the idle man caught up in a flood of gossip, speculation and interest.

Or was his gazing down the street simply the act of the vacuous onlooker? What *was* it that he so clearly wished to gain sight of? Whatever it was, he was unwilling to give it up. He walked round almost the whole perimeter of the Palace of Westminster, but there was a pattern to his ramblings, Gresham noticed, always returning to the one spot.

Whynniard's house. The phrase came back to Gresham from something Tresham had said. The plotters had started by hiring a house in the precincts of the Palace of Westminster, a house owned by John Whynniard. They had started a tunnel from there, Tresham had said, but given up the idea as beyond their physical and technical skills. That was when the cellar under the Lords had become vacant, allowing them to ditch the unfinished tunnel.

There it was. Whynniard's house. Gresham had been sufficiently interested when Tresham had mentioned the house to walk past it himself, and keep a watcher on it for a week. It was shuttered, empty. Yet now the empty house seemed to be the common denominator in Tom Wintour's appallingly dangerous trek round Westminster, even though the cordon thrown round Westminster meant he was unable to get closer than a stone's throw to it.

A soldier was starting to look suspiciously at Wintour. He had stopped for the third time in the same spot, the one nearest the house. Without seeming to notice, Wintour began to melt towards the back of the crowd, breaking off from it and heading in the direction of the livery stables when Gresham knew he kept his horse. The house, thought Gresham, might repay some attention. But now his most urgent aim was to keep up with Tom Wintour. Had the plotters dispersed? Or had they run to some assembly point, from where they would try to rouse the nation? The game was still being played, and Gresham guessed the next rounds would be decided out of London.

'You will leave us!' Cecil spoke with a fierce intensity, hating the dullness of the guards as they looked fearfully back at him. They were below ground level, the dismal, dark room set into the very foundations of the White Tower. He knew what the guards were thinking. Leave Robert Cecil, Earl of Salisbury, alone with this blackguard, this Devil on earth, this Guy Fawkes . . . fear of what would happen to them if the Chief Secretary was attacked fought for a brief moment with fear of the Chief Secretary. Fear of Cecil won. They backed away, bowing. Cecil closed the door. The bottom of it grated on the filthy floor.

Fawkes was huddled on the floor, rubbing his shoulder where the guards had hurled him to the ground. His head was badly gashed where he had been thrown down, the blood half-dried, fresh seeping through the caked residue. The cell was lit by the flames of a rough torch hung in an iron bracket. Even by its light the wetness on the walls glistened and sparkled on the five-hundred-year-old stone.

'Why did you betray me?' Fawkes's voice was rough, but steady enough. Cecil was caught off guard. It should not be Fawkes, the prisoner, opening this conversation.

'I did not betray you!' hissed Cecil through clenched teeth. The cold was penetrating even through the thickness of his rich cloak. 'You were betrayed by the fool who brought the orders for the search forward by an hour.'

'My Lord, we had a bargain.' There was fear in Fawkes's voice, but also resolution, and a tone Cecil could not quite track down.

'The terms and conditions appear to have changed very significantly!' he snapped.

'You'll have to have me testify, my Lord,' said Fawkes. The blow to his head must have disorientated him. He spoke in starts, as if suffering from momentary losses of concentration. 'I think it wouldn't be in your Lordship's interest to have me testify the truth.'

Fawkes's body was shaking now with the cold, Cecil noted with satisfaction.

'Many better than you have died in this Tower, without word and without testimony,' said Cecil, looking with loathing at Fawkes. 'Many have screamed for weeks in this Tower before they welcomed the sweet release of death. Have a care what you threaten.'

'No,' said Fawkes, 'have a care what *you* threaten.' His teeth were chattering now. 'If someone knows enough of your plans to bring the time of the search forward an hour, then someone knows enough of your perfidy to place you, my Lord the Earl of Salisbury, in this Tower, to die or to scream for your death alongside me. You need me, you need me to give a confession that will confirm your version of events, to name your other conspirators. If I stand firm, my Lord, many can challenge your honour's actions. None can prove them false.'

How grating was that accent of Yorkshire, how ludicrous the Spanish lilt laid over it.

'As you seem so much in control,' Cecil said as his eyes flicked over the manacles that chained Fawkes's feet to the wall, 'you will certainly be able to tell me what you wish me to do.'

Fawkes was shivering heavily now, his arms clasped round himself in a feeble attempt to keep warm.

'Move me to a secret chamber, a chamber with warmth and food. Many who have been tortured here have never been heard. Now may one be tortured who never was. Put out that I was steadfast, then that I was put to the torture. Write me a confession, what you will. I'll testify to your plot, as you'll have me do.'

'And then?'

'And then I shall die, weakened so far by the unspeakable pain you put me to that my constitution gave in. Here, in this Tower. Out of sight. And you will get me to France.'

There was something of desperation in Fawkes's voice. As well there might be. Cecil's mind was racing.

A live, testifying Fawkes would be an asset, if he testified correctly. The Keeper of the Tower, Waad, had incriminated Mary Queen of Scots. Hiding the nature of what was happening to Guy Fawkes was a mere biting-on compared to the meals that man had eaten. As for France, it was a long journey from London to Dover and across the Channel. A long and dangerous journey.

'Guards!' Cecil shouted. 'This man is no good to us dead with cold. Take him to a chamber with fire in it – warming fire, not the torturer's brazier! And keep his legs in chains!' he said viciously, as he left to discuss matters with Sir William Waad.

Robert Wintour had been having supper with Catesby's mother. Catesby had determined to tell his mother the truth before riding on to Dunchurch, but as he sat on his sweating horse outside his home he felt for the first time a chill wind blow through the heat of his self-belief. He could not face his mother, not now. He sent Tom Bates to summon Wintour to a field outside the house. Robert Wintour had always been a baleful recruit at best, unlike his fire-brand younger brother. Now he was totally downcast.

'We should surely throw ourselves on the King's mercy,' he said, 'and with God's grace some mercy might be shown.'

Catesby hardly bothered to answer.

'There will be no mercy. We must ride on to Dunchurch, to meet with the company. Only then can we decide.' He did not give a single backward glance to the house under whose roof his mother fretted.

There were over a hundred people gathered in and around The Red Lion. Brothers, cousins, relations, younger sons of Catholic families, all had gathered. Catesby had hoped for more, at least a hundred and fifty. Yet even now it might be enough. A babble of voices greeted Catesby's arrival. His heart began to beat faster, as it always did when he stood in front of a crowd. The blood began to speed through his veins. He held his hand up to command silence.

There was silence.

Briefly, quickly, he told them of the plot, that the powder had been discovered, but that London was aflame with rumour and suspicion.

'Are we sheep or cattle, to troop gently to our slaughter? Or are we men, men with a faith to be fought for? We have horses, we have guns, we have powder. If we ride now, ride for our freedom and our Faith, hundreds will join us from the west, the west where the Faith has always lived and flourished. We must strike now, strike while confusion reigns. Are we men of faith, or are we cowards?'

He was shouting now, standing up in his stirrups.

There was silence. They looked at him in the feeble light of a few torches. Then one, then a second, then a third turned away from the light, edging their horses off into the darkness. There was a pause, then a fourth, a fifth and then a stream. A muttered, muted babble of conversation rose between those left. Just as it seemed the departures were ended, another two or three would turn and move away, like rows of infantry having remorseless gap after gap blown in their line by withering cannon fire as they waited for a charge.

Robert Catesby had failed. For the first time in his life, he had spread the cloak of his character, the fire of his personality, out to a group, and seen it fall on stony ground. Soon, there were hardly forty left in the square outside the inn, making it seem almost deserted.

The fire cooled in Catesby, leaving a solid, hard dark nugget of cold in its place. He would die now, he knew. Perhaps he had always known. In a strange way the realisation took a dread weight off him. He was certain now, certain in a different way. He owed himself a good death. Himself, and the others he had brought along for all these months and years. They would want, would need to die with him, he knew.

He smiled, disconcerting even more those nearest to him. He allowed the runt of his rebellion, the rebellion that never happened and never would happen, to eat and rest a while. The sulky landlord and servants were desperate to be rid of them, desperate to avoid the taint they knew their association would provide. Even now they were remembering the detail they would so willingly give to the King's men and the Sheriff's men when they arrived, as they most assuredly would arrive.

And then, shortly after eleven o'clock at night, they began the ride. It should have been told of in some ancient saga, become a story to read out by the fireside on late, cold winter's nights, to frighten the young children. It was a ride of despair and desperation, of harsh and stupid courage. It was helpless and hopeless, madness in human form, a ride of the Valkyrie where only the horses had hope and their riders were dead men already.

From Dunchurch to Warwick Castle; the stables there raided, ten fresh horses taken to relieve the mounts of those who had ridden from London. Robert Wintour wringing his hands – 'It will make an uproar in the country!' – Ambrose Rookwood disdainful, his supply of fine horseflesh inexhaustible. On, on to John Grant's house at Norbrook, to pick up the powder, shot and muskets hoarded there. Through Snitterfield, across the treacherous ford of the Alne, on to Alcester. Through Arrow, then out along the Worcester Road, and then on the back roads and by-ways to Huddington. Two o'clock on Wednesday afternoon. Fifteen terror-driven, bone-crunching, muscle-wrenching hours. Sleep. Mass at three o'clock on the Thursday morning, then down to dress in armour, to pick arms and take ammunition from the long tables loaded with weaponry, the remainder hurled into carts. Six o'clock on a bleak morning, bodies crying out in agony at seating again on a saddle. To Hanbury, across Bentley Heath to Hewell Grange, Lord Windsor's house. The house empty, glum villagers standing by as they broke in, taking armour, more weapons, powder and money from a trunk containing over £1,000. Burcot. Lickey End. Catshill. Clent. Hagley. The names reeled off like so much flotsam passing a watcher by a riverbank, the names blurring into one another, increasingly meaningless. Sullen people, watchers, onlookers. 'We fight for the Faith!' No response. Occasional yells, muttered reply, 'We live for King James!' Onwards. Stourbridge. Heavy rain, drenching men, animals and powder, the ford racing, dangerous for fit men, perhaps lethal for tired men and horses. Holbeache House, the home of Stephen Littleton. Enough. They were exhausted. Sixteen hours to travel twenty-five miles. Rookwood had galloped thirty miles in two hours, earlier, on the one horse. Catesby had made over ten miles an hour, on his ride out from London. They were slowing, had stopped.

They must have rest.

They were pathetically fewer now. Servants had deserted, snapping off the road and away from the cavalcade when an opportunity arose. They had boxed in the party at front and back, but there were not enough of them to guard the sides and length as well.

Catesby had withdrawn into himself, even Percy seemed to be quiet. Only Tom Wintour, who had joined them late, had energy, walking, talking, organising a defence. They needed more men, if they were to fight off the likely assault on Holbeache and live to ride again. An outrider had reported a party, probably the Sheriff of Worcestershire, trailing them. Not one Catholic had joined their progress, which had leached men like a sandbag leaching out in the rain. John Talbot lived ten miles distant, at Pepperhill. He was Robert Wintour's father-in-law. Would Robert go to ask for men and support? 'How may I go, when he'll guard my wife when I am dead?' Tom Wintour looked with contempt at his brother. Without a word, he put his aching body on his horse again, and rode out to John Talbot's house, seeking the help he knew in his heart would not be offered.

Gresham rode harder even than he had ridden on that day from Cambridge to London. They had spirited Tresham out of his lodgings, placed him in a safe house. Dunchurch, he had said, repeating it as if it were a litany. They must go to Dunchurch. It is where they planned to gather, under cover of a hunting party, to raise the country up in rebellion. They will go to Dunchurch.

Gresham arrived at The Red Lion as the rump of the party was leaving on its mad, foolish dash across the country.

'Where are they heading?' he had hissed to an ostler, trying to thrust coin into the man's hand.

'To Hell and beyond, as far as I cares!' the man had replied, thrusting the money aside and running back into the inn, distrust visible in his every gesture.

Catesby's crew had rested, taken food. Gresham had no time. With an inward groan he remounted. At least following was not difficult, despite the driving rain. Servants and other riders peeled off from the party at regular intervals, to much shouting and yelling. At the start their leaders tried to give chase, but soon exhaustion crept in, and they simply tried to box in the cavalcade with their own horses. Still the leakage from the party continued, still the numbers, dimly visible sometimes, audible always, diminished. They were slowing down all the time, like a drowning man whose flapping at the water becomes more and more feeble as his strength leaves him.

Gresham had never felt more tired. He was soaked through, shivering violently with the cold, his teeth chattering so that he could hardly bite on the hard-baked meat he had flung into his saddlebag as he had left London. Yet he had to keep on guard. The servants and gentlemen who had escaped Catesby's party flew past him on the road, drawing their swords if they had them and fearing he was a pursuer. One had even taken a scything blow at Gresham's head with his sword as he had passed, Gresham blocking it only at the last second with a clang of steel. Finally, just as his horse was about to expire beneath him, the tattered, pathetic remnant of the party had come to rest at Holbeache. They could enter the house, with its warmth, its fires and its food. Gresham was examining the lay-out of the courtyard and steps up into the main house, wracked with icy cold, when his passport into Holbeache emerged from inside. The courtyard gate opened, revealing another horse and rider. The horse was a thoroughbred, a beautiful animal, but its rider was clearly a fleeing servant, whose riding experience was limited to sitting on the back of a cart on its way to market. The man was bouncing violently up and down on the back of the horse, clearly terrified. Gresham forced his own mount out into the roadway with perfect timing, taking his foot out of the stirrup and giving the rider a hefty boot as he was at the top of his bounce and halfway out of his saddle already. He fell with a yelp, escaping being dragged along only because his feet had never properly found the stirrups of his own horse.

Gresham took the rough jerkin and trews from the stunned man and sent him, half naked, bouncing along the road on his own exhausted mount. Liberally covering his disguise in mud, he walked into the house, or rather stumbled and gasped into it.

'A bite of bread and ten minutes by a fire, I beg of you?' He did not have to feign exhaustion. 'I've ridden from Dunchurch, but my master, he took off without me just outside the house. Help me, please. I've no master, no home and like to have no head when all this comes out . . .' The harassed woman he had spoken to had hardly listened, glancing all the time nervously over his shoulder, pushing him in the direction of the kitchen.

He was inside. The kitchen was a babble of noise. Servants shared their master's fate, and there was real terror in their ranks. Old campaigning instincts took over. Gresham grabbed a fistful of greasy, half-warm meat from a stone table and a mug of small beer that appeared somehow out of the chaos, and crammed both down his throat. The plotters were together in the Hall upstairs, he heard. They would not be leaving now, he thought, with night coming on. They were blown, exhausted. There was enough of the real Henry Gresham left to light a tiny smile in the corner of his mouth. He was inside the lions' den. It was about time he decided what use to make of his achievement.

Thomas Percy looked at the sodden crowd of his fellow plotters and cursed the luck that had exposed Fawkes. Clearly, Cecil's plan had misfired. Or had Cecil betrayed them? He doubted it. If Cecil had wanted both of them out of the way Percy would not have been let to go with the others to end up in this dreadful hole of a house. Percy caught the tail of his fear, which was starting to fly up and away like a kite out of control, and brought it back down to earth again with an effort. He had to assume that his job remained what it had always been, to kill Catesby and as many of the other con-spirators as possible. Cecil had always feared Catesby, recognising in him the capacity to lift and sway an audience. He had been willing to use him, the perfect unwitting foil for a plot that would bring Cecil nothing but credit, but yet he had always feared his power to incite. Cecil had been too much scarred by the ability of Sir Walter Raleigh at his trial to win hearts and minds by the power of his words and the attraction of his figure. He did not want Robert Catesby standing at the Bar, weaving the same spells with his audience that he had woven with the conspirators. Catesby had to die decently early, and that was Percy's role.

He had considered killing him on their journey, but no chance that did not threaten his own life had presented itself. The life of Thomas Percy was a very important thing, and soon to become even more important. Once Catesby had been disposed of, and the other plotters either killed or handed over to authority – Cecil had wanted some two or three at most, no more, if possible – then Percy would return in triumph to London bringing Catesby's body slung over a horse. He had thought on that, and thought that it would look best stripped to its shirt, as it would have been for an execution. He had reminded himself that he must drape the body over a horse as soon as possible after Catesby's death, before it froze in death and stuck out on either side like a bar across the saddle. In the midst of that triumph, he and Cecil would discuss the details he would give about the treachery of the ninth Earl of Northumberland, how the evil Earl had unwittingly placed in the hands of his kinsman the details of the treachery and the revolution he planned – his kinsman, who having handed the fate of the ninth Earl over to Cecil would, of course, become the tenth Earl of Northumberland. Had he not always claimed, even to the ninth Earl himself, that his branch of the family was older than that represented by the ninth Earl? Well, now he would prove it.

The powder they had taken from Hewell Grange had been loaded into an open cart. The drenching rain had soaked it. Their plan now was to rest for as long as it took to get their breath back, and then dash into Wales to gather support and await news of the landings and the Spanish troops that Percy had lied about to

Catesby. There never were any plans for invasion, and never any knowledge of any part of the plot by the ninth Earl – a delicious irony which Percy intended to savour when he became the tenth Earl.

Yet they might have to make a stand at Holbeache. The Sheriff of Worcestershire was on their trail. A servant who was probably running away had run into the Sheriff's party, over a hundred men, and gone back to Catesby as the lesser evil. Catesby and Wintour were convinced they could beat off the Sheriff's party, who would be untrained men in the face of a determined, well-armed opposition fighting defensively and for their lives. It was a classic situation – thirty men defending who were fighting to keep their lives, a hundred or so attacking who could only lose them.

'The powder from Hewell Grange is soaked through. If this place is put to siege, we might have need of it.' Percy spoke gruffly, in the old-soldier manner he had adopted from the outset with the conspirators.

'What do you suggest – warm it with a match?' It was Digby, a pale imitation of himself.

'Almost. It's wet enough to make spreading it out before the hearth safe enough. If Tom manages to bring back some extra people, the more dry powder we can show them the more likely they are to think we've a chance.'

He was surprised they agreed to it, but it was exhaustion speaking through their actions, and despair. Any action seemed to put back the tide of hopelessness.

They spread the powder out on to the stone hearth, moving the rushes aside first. The fire was well established, the wood seasoned and long since past spitting. Catesby, Rookwood and Grant took seats at the long trestle table to one side of the fire, hastily drawing up plans for the defence of the house. Henry Morgan, one of the few from the Dunchurch 'hunting party' who had stayed with them, joined them, as did Percy, for a while. Robert Wintour was huddled in a corner.

'I had a dream last night.' His sepulchral tones startled the men by the table, all of whom looked up.

'I saw church steeples bent awry, and sad, terrible faces inside the churches, looking out. Faces of despair.' Was he talking to himself, or to them? It could have been either. The men turned back, one by one, to their crude plans for defence. The problem was that few of them knew the house, and the owner was out of it with Tom Wintour.

Percy stood up, announcing he was going to piss. As he went to the door, it opened in his face, and the frightened figure of a servant came into the Hall, a huge pile of fresh logs held in front of him, half covering even his face. Percy pushed him aside, causing him to stumble and drop the top two or three logs. The servant mumbled apologies, as scared as the rest of the Holbeache servants, placed the remnant of his load on the floor and scrabbled to pick up the lost logs. A few of the conspirators glanced his way, disinterested, and looked away. Very carefully the servant made his way to the side of the hearth. He stopped as he saw the powder laid out, carefully moving round the black earth piled on the floor. He bent to lay his logs on top of the others on the side of the hearth, but the top log seemed to leap out from the pile of its own accord and fell into the fire. It crashed into the flames, dislodging embers that flew almost gently through the air and landed red among the black of the powder. The servant, who could see what was coming, flung the rest of his logs forward and dashed for the protection offered by the side of the jutting stone fireplace.

There was a blinding flash, and a sucking roar. For a brief instant Holbeache was turned into Hell. From a scene of almost peaceful domesticity the Hall was reduced to smouldering ruin. Panelling had caught fire, and those upright in the room were rushing to smother the small flames. The peculiar, acrid stench of powder mingled with the stench of burnt flesh and smouldering wood. John Grant was sitting on the ground, making small keening noises, rocking backwards and forwards, his hands clutched to his eyes.

They were burnt out, even blacker than the surrounding skin in his crisped, baked face, his hair, eyebrows and beard half gone and scorched. The man Morgan still had some sight, but was badly burnt. Catesby and Rookwood were badly scorched, both in obvious severe pain.

The two Wright brothers had been dozing in a corner, now jerked into wakefulness by the blast of fire. Percy rushed back into the room. Robert Wintour had escaped the worst of the searing heat, huddled in his corner. He was standing now, staring wild-eyed at the devastation. He stuck his arm out, a shivering finger pointing at Catesby and the others.

'The faces! The faces!' he said. 'The faces in my dream! These are the faces!' He waited, as if for an answer. His hand dropped to his side. He raised his eyes, locked them on to the pain-filled vision of Catesby. 'Well,' he said, in a low voice of total hatred, 'you have your blast now, cousin!' He turned and left.

There had been exhaustion, some despair and fear in the room before, but also some bravado. Now there was nothing. It was as if they realised it was over. It had to be God's judgement. Those who had intended to blow up their enemies by powder had themselves been blown up. The link was too clear, too obvious.

Catesby was recovered enough to speak. The fire had caught the one side of his face, pulling up his lip so that it seemed he had a permanent snarl. Robert Catesby. Jack Wright. Kit Wright. John Grant, writhing on the floor, hands fluttering at the wet bandage round his destroyed eyes. Ambrose Rookwood, moaning as the cold of the bandages touched his burnt flesh. Thomas Percy. With the exception of Rookwood and Wintour, the men stood at the end of the affair almost as they had stood from its outset.

'We are too few to fight.' Thomas Percy spoke the obvious.

'Then we must die fighting.' It was Catesby. No-one raised his voice against him.

Tom Wintour stopped as he entered the hall, his face draining of all blood in shock. He ran to Catesby, looking in horror at his ravaged and twisted face. If only he had brought good news! There was no help coming. Sir John Talbot had not even let them inside his house, but shouted them off as he might a carrier of the plague. A fleeing servant had told them of the explosion, and Stephen Littleton, the owner of Holbeache, had slipped away from his side. Everard Digby had gone. Tom Bates, the ever-faithful servant, was also missing.

'Where is my brother?' It was Tom Wintour, his eyes roaming the room.

'Gone.' It was Kit Wright. 'With all the others.' Robert Wintour had waited this long in his life to take a decision of his own.

Henry Gresham had picked himself up from the side of the fireplace, where the blast had thrown him. He was bruised badly enough, but nothing was broken. The heat had singed the back of his head, in between the collar of his jerkin and his bonnet.

He had intended only to eavesdrop on the plotters. The smell of the powder had hit him even through the door. In an instant he was back in the Netherlands, and it was as if the pain that had been his constant companion then for months came back to hit him also. Picking up the logs strewn outside the door and going in had been a terrible thing for him to do. When he had met Percy his heart had stopped, but Percy was not the type to recognise a lowly servant.

He had wanted to be sick as he had contemplated the fire, the powder and the need to fling his log into the midst of the fire. Yet the irony, the awful, dreadful irony, of firing these men up with powder, the sheer justice of it, had driven him. Loose powder does not explode, he knew, but burns off in an instant, developing a searing heat and light.

Those who know an explosion is about to take place can profit in the seconds immediately following. With no mental shock to add to the physical, Gresham was able to pick himself up in the immediate aftermath, scuttling through the door before anyone thought to ask of the servant who had caused the blow. He doubted any realised even that it had been the servant, so great was their confusion. What a pity Percy had chosen that moment to leave. Gresham was surprised by how little damage the fire had done. He could not judge at that moment the damage it had done to the spirit, as well as the bodies, of the plotters.

Gresham knew that the Sheriff of Worcestershire was hastening to lay siege to the plotters. The servant whose clothes he had taken had babbled of little else. Percy had to die at Holbeache, that much Gresham now knew. The question was how.

Thomas Percy was much taken at that moment by the other side of the question. How to preserve his life? He had believed they could beat off the Sheriff's men easily enough, with a pistol ball in the back for Catesby in the dying moments of the fight, or on their flight into Wales. That damned explosion had killed no-one, but merely increased the odds for their attackers and made the plotters vow to fight to the death. Well, so be it, mused Percy. There was risk in all things. He was playing for an earldom. He would wait for the siege, kill Catesby and then prove his credentials by firing a ball into one of the others – Tom Wintour by preference – and shouting that he was an agent of the King's. Far better than an agent of Robert Cecil for these country bumpkins.

The call to arms came some time before eleven o'clock. They propped the blinded Grant up in a corner, still moaning. Rookwood declared his intention to fight, though God knew if he could see enough to hit anyone, thought Percy. At the windows, they could see that it was more than a hundred men gathering outside. Torches lit those out of range, whilst movements in the shadow showed men running up under cover of the darkness to hide close to the walls, there presumably to make an assault through the main gate into the yard. Suddenly, a flickering light showed them more. Someone had lit a fire, almost under them. They were being smoked out. Damn! If they had more men they could have mounted a guard on the outer perimeter.

Catesby turned his head stiffly, and looked at Wintour. The

latter nodded, the briefest of gestures. Grabbing their weapons, they moved out and down into the yard.

Torches had been thrown over to give light, and lay guttering on the cobbles. It was too late. Enemy men were already in the yard. As Wintour burst out of the door shots rang out, most ill-aimed and wildly high. One caught Wintour, shattering his shoulder. He shrieked, a weird, unearthly noise, fired a wild round from his pistol and hurled it to the ground, dragging his sword up to defend himself as men with pikes started to circle warily round him.

Catesby had come down the stairs hanging on the arm of Percy. Jack and Kit Wright leapt out through the door and more shots rang out. Both dropped to the ground. As if by accident it was Catesby's body that swung round and forward as they came out of the door, moments later. One shot banged viciously into the night air, but the others had fired at Wintour and the Wrights, and were clumsily reloading. It looked as if Catesby and Percy were standing back to back, but Catesby had swooned as they hit the night air and was only half-conscious.

Gresham was standing by the side of the courtyard. He had floored one of the first soldiers to creep up over the wall into the yard with one blow from the stock of the hunting rifle he had taken from the house. The helmet was too large to fit, the leather jerkin hanging off his frame. Other men flooded into the yard. Gresham saw Tom Wintour rush out and spin round in response to a fusillade of shots. Then the Wright brothers were dropped like gamebirds. Rookwood was clearly wounded, as was Morgan, stumbling around with the injured Wintour. There was a pause in the firing, partly through the need to reload, partly through the growing realisation that this pathetic band posed no threat.

A trooper had run to Gresham's side, his eyes full of the glazed fear that Gresham had been so familiar with in Flanders. His musket was unfired, waving wildly in the air. Gresham decided he might as well act to stop the boy shooting him.

'Soldier!' he snapped. 'Come to it, man! Give me your name!'

'John . . . John Streete, sir,' mumbled the boy, regaining a grip on his musket.

Wintour yelled, for Catesby, Gresham thought, and the soldiers turned towards him. Catesby emerged in the doorway, hanging off Percy. As if in slow motion, Gresham saw Percy place his pistol against Catesby's side, saw the flash and the body of Catesby stiffen and slump, mouth agape. As if in one single smooth movement Gresham brought up his gun, aimed and fired, the crack of the rifle almost simultaneous with that of Percy's pistol. Percy's mouth was also agape, he was about to shout out and cast Catesby's body to the ground. The bullet caught him and he jerked violently backwards, his inert body almost bouncing on to the cobbles.

Gresham turned to John Streete, standing gaping by his side. He pulled the boy's musket arm towards him, yanked the trigger and caught the gun as it recoiled, firing into the air.

'There, boy,' said Gresham. 'Two birds with one shot. Go on, claim the credit.'

Gresham turned, and saw Catesby crawling back into the house. The pack of soldiers were advancing on Rookwood, Wintour and Morgan. Wintour made a mad dash forward. His sword was knocked out of his hand, and a soldier, crazed with fear, was about to plunge his pike into the wounded man's midriff. There was a barked command.

'Hold. Hold! Some of these are better kept alive for His Majesty!'

Catesby had crawled just inside the door. He was holding his gold crucifix, sobbing with pain and exhaustion. He half turned as Gresham clattered through the door.

'Selkirk!' he moaned, in frightened recognition. Then the light went from his eyes. He slumped to the ground, dead. Gresham heard the noise of advancing men. Quickly, he tore a picture of the Virgin Mary off the wall where it adorned the entrance to Holbeache House, and wrapped Catesby's still warm fingers around it. As the first of the other soldiers burst in through the door, Gresham retreated into the shadows.

The soldiers were out of control. They were stripping the corpses of everything they bore. Even Kit Wright's boots had been taken, and the silk stockings he wore under them. Percy's body, half naked, lay on the cobbles, mouth open, eyes staring. A soldier who had missed the best of the plunder gave it a vicious kick as he passed by. His head lolled back with the blow, slack, empty.

Gresham gazed back at the lights, the shouting and the smashing noises as the house was torn apart. He turned, and without a word he started the ride back to London.

CHAPTER 12

'Be careful,' said Jane. 'He fooled you once.'

'Fooled me?' said Gresham. 'I prefer to think he left me asking the wrong questions for a short period of time.'

Gresham was putting the final touches to his dress. It would be his fourth visit to Cecil. He felt more in command of this one than he had with several others.

Gresham arrived, without appointment. It was a different clerk from the last time, a biddable, pleasant-mannered figure, clearly rushed off his feet and worried. The usual crush of humanity was stinking the place out, shouting its case to be the only person with a real need to see the King's Chief Secretary.

'I shall take your request to the Earl, Sir Henry,' he replied to Gresham, 'but he is monstrously busy, I fear to say . . .'

'I do understand. Tell him Sir Henry Gresham wishes to see him, and that it concerns matters of high treason.'

The clerk's eyes opened wide, and he waddled off. He was clearly surprised on his return, and bowed low.

'Sir Henry! The Earl will see you immediately. Please follow me.'

Cecil was crouched at the head of the table. A litter of papers filled its top half. Among them, Gresham noted, was an unsigned letter in a familiar hand. It was already known as the Monteagle Letter. Gresham had heard of its new name with a wry grin.

'Sir Henry.' Cecil's voice was flat, expressionless.

'My Lord.'

'I see you are recovered. Please accept my congratulations.'

'I was never ill. It was merely a ruse designed to divert your Lordship's unwelcome attentions away from me, while I discovered what you so clearly wished to keep from me,' Gresham answered, in a brisk tone.

'Indeed?' Cecil raised an eyebrow, maintaining his icy control. 'And did you discover this great secret?'

'Yes, my Lord, I did,' said Gresham.

'Which was?' asked Cecil, not entirely able now to keep the tension out of his voice.

'Guy or Guido Fawkes, otherwise known as the servant John Johnson, was a double agent, supposedly working with Catholic forces in Europe for some years, but in practice working for you. Robert Catesby, the true leader of the Gunpowder Plot or whatever you will choose to call it, either stumbled into him, or was directed his way by another of your agents, when Catesby and a group of Catholic hotheads needed someone who could lay a slow train of powder. You knew about the Gunpowder Plot from the start. You used Fawkes as one of your inside men for the whole duration of the plot, allowing it to ripen so that you could discover it amidst the greatest public attention and so win a lasting popularity for you, and for the King. I believe – though I have no evidence for it – that you let it blossom also in the hope that it would reveal a leading noble as one of its leaders, perhaps one you saw as posing a threat to yourself. Did you hope to implicate Raleigh? Or was it simply Northumberland? In any event, you encouraged another of your double agents, Thomas Percy, to become involved and to work again on the inside of the plot on your behalf. Fawkes, I suspect, was to be bribed with money and a free passage out, perhaps even to go back to Europe as a hero and remain on the inside of the

Catholic rebels over there. Percy was to be bribed, perhaps even with the Earldom itself.'

'And how do you know all this . . . fantasy? This . . . invention?'

Cecil's eyes had never seemed more dangerous, his hunched body more ready to pounce.

'I have had my own man on the inside of this plot. I wrote that letter you have on your desk, to splinter and disperse the plot before harm was done. I brought Knyvett out an hour early, so that Fawkes could be found. It was I who caused the powder to ignite at Holbeache House. Oh, and by the way, I shot Thomas Percy.'

'You dared to challenge my will?' Cecil was roaring now, the first time Gresham had ever seen him lose his control.

'Challenge your will? Are you God, as well as Secretary to His anointed?'

'You have no evidence of this. No evidence at all.' Cecil's voice had dropped, his body fallen back into the chair.

'I have a story that men will believe, because it fits so many facts and fits the hatred and suspicion they have of you. I have the drafts of that letter you have in front of you – and a devil of a time it took, I can tell you – in the same hand and in a manner that progresses so convincingly that all will believe the authorship. And I have a plotter. Francis Tresham, to be exact, kept where you will not find him.' Gresham doubted that last comment, personally. If Cecil pulled out all his resources he could find anything, even a clean spot on the King's body. 'And several signed accounts by Tresham, undeniably in his hand, and witnessed, hidden also where you will not find them.'

'What is it that you want from me?' hissed Cecil.

'A chair would be pleasant,' said Gresham, with a polite smile. He was still standing. Angrily, Cecil motioned him to sit, never once taking his eyes off him.

'Do you hate me, Henry Gresham?'

It was an odd question, coming from the source it did, but Gresham paused to answer it.

'Yes, most certainly. More so than perhaps any man alive or dead.'

'Then you wish to destroy me?'

'Oh, no!' Gresham's laugh so startled Cecil that he fell back a little, and blinked owlishly. 'You see, only a person whose soul stinks like the foulest sewer could run a country such as this. A murderer, a torturer, an abuser, a liar, a cheat and a lost soul before God. These are necessary in a ruler. Some people have to die, of course, some have to meet the rack and some have their guts sawn out in front of crowds to make peace happen. Some, it is true, have these things happen to them who do not deserve them, or who are unlucky, or who happen to be in the wrong place at the wrong time, but all things come at a price. Peace and stability carry a higher price than many. And they carry the highest price of all for the ruler, the leader of that midden we call politics and human life. They carry the price of a lost soul, and eternity spent in Hell. Yes, I hate you, Robert Cecil, Earl of Salisbury. Because I hate you, I am happy for your soul to be the price of peace in this country. I would like to kill you, to see you suffer and writhe in front of me as you have seen so many others. But I must make Machiavelli's choice, and go for the greater good at the expense of some of the lesser pleasures.'

The silence extended for a minute, perhaps more.

'So what it is that you want from me?'

'Nothing.'

'*Nothing?*'

'Well, nothing really. I wanted to have the pleasure of your knowing what I knew, that your attempts to gag and mislead me had failed, as well as your pathetic attempts to blackmail me. I suppose I ought to have your oath that you will take no steps to harm me, or those closest to me. No strange deaths in alleyways, or long decaying illnesses from poison.'

'Is not the Papal archive enough?' asked Cecil, his hatred of Gresham beginning to infect his voice.

'I thought it might be, but you proved me wrong. And it's not just the Papal archive where I keep papers, believe me. But you see, there is something strange about you, rotten and corrupt as you are. I have never known you go back on an oath you have sworn. Quite extraordinary. But this oath will be special. You will swear it on the life of your son.'

'On the life of my son . . . but I . . .' Cecil was almost speechless, grabbing for words.

'You had better pray for a long and peaceful life for me, my woman and my servant. Because if we die, in any way that might lead back to you in any way, your son will die.'

'You would not . . .'

'Yes, I would. You cannot lock a child away from life. Unless you can hide it away completely you cannot lock it away from the reality of death. Look at me, Robert Cecil. And then tell me if you think I lie.'

Unwillingly, Cecil found himself looking straight at Gresham.

'You have sought to bring your full power against me. You have failed. You will swear to do everything in your power to ensure that no harm of any kind comes to Henry Gresham and those nearest and dearest to him. And if you break your oath, your son will die.'

There was no lie in Henry Gresham's eyes. There was a look that told of all the innocent children those eyes had seen slaughtered, the women raped, the babies with their throats slashed. There was a look that told of the plotter Kit Wright, fighting for his religion, leading a mad, hopeless and courageous charge into the yard at Holbeache. Kit Wright, the stolid, dependable Kit Wright, the man who thought quite genuinely that if one believed in something then one had to be prepared to fight and to die for it. Kit Wright, who could in many respects have been Mannion, if Mannion had chosen to give his total loyalty to Catholicism instead of to Gresham. Brave and foolish Kit Wright, lying in the filth of the courtyard, with a rough soldier frantically yanking at the silk stockings on his dead legs for booty.

Yes, thought Robert Cecil, my son will die at this man's hands if

I break my oath. The hatred gleaming in his eyes, with every word dragged out of him as if by red-hot pincers, Robert Cecil swore his oath.

'Well, that was good,' said Gresham lightly. 'Every good boy deserves favour, and so I'll give you something else for your pains, and as a gesture of my goodwill. I wouldn't have you deposed, Chief Secretary. It amuses me to have that in my power, but it's a power I won't exercise. Someone less evil might come along to run the country, and perhaps if you were deposed you might have time to take a part of your soul out of the Hell it so richly deserves.'

'Cease this jesting!' said Cecil. 'Have you not had your satisfaction?'

'This isn't jesting,' said Gresham, 'and if there's any satisfaction in the air, it will be your own. You hold Guy Fawkes, don't you, in the Tower at this very moment?'

Cecil did not answer. He knew Gresham knew the truth.

'Wondering what to do with him, no doubt. What jolly talk there must have been between you both, when he was brought in by Knyvett's men. Has Guy Fawkes ever mentioned to you his relationship with the ninth Earl of Northumberland?'

'His *relationship*?'

'Yes. You thought Fawkes was your man, didn't you? It never crossed your mind that he was someone else's. Before he started to receive money from you he'd been employed by Northumberland. From the outset, in fact. It was Northumberland who spotted him as a young man, sent him over to Europe and paid to settle his wife – Maria, I think she's called – and their son Thomas, in his absence. You see, Fawkes never was a soldier of fortune. He always was a soldier of conscience. When you came along with your offer for him to turn spy, Northumberland encouraged him to say yes. Northumberland always despised you, never trusted you. It amused him to have one of your spies in his pay.

'And then Catesby came along. Northumberland knew the plot was a disaster, knew it would turn the country against Catholics.

And he knew exactly why you were urging Fawkes to go along with it. So he planned a little surprise all his own.'

'Are you seeking to tell me that this Guy Fawkes was in the pay of Northumberland?' said Cecil.

He was a clever man, thought Gresham, you had to admit. He had never actually admitted to any involvement in the plot, or that he had employed Guy Fawkes. Even the oath he had sworn had not been an admission of guilt.

'*Is* in the pay of Northumberland.'

'And what was my Lord of Northumberland's aim in all this?' To his credit, Cecil recovered quickly. Gresham could almost see the machinery of his brain grappling with this latest problem.

'Very simple, really,' said Gresham. 'He was going to let you expose the plot, take all the glory and revel in it. He was going to wait until you put on trial whatever few pathetic plotters you had managed to keep alive.

'And then he was going to blow up the House of Lords.'

Cecil's face went as white as a full moon.

'Oh, don't worry,' said Gresham cheerfully, 'he wouldn't have killed anyone. Or at least no-one important, just a few servants. He'd have blown the mine when the House was empty. And because of where it was, it wouldn't have been the whole House of Lords. Probably just one wall or so of it.'

'The mine?' Cecil could hardly force the words out.

'Remember? They tried to dig a tunnel under the House of Lords, before they found and hired the cellar. It came to grief against the foundations; they simply couldn't drive through them. You thought they'd abandoned it, didn't you? Well, the plotters did, but Fawkes didn't. Northumberland brought some miners down from the north-west. They were kept in isolation for a week, never told what they were doing, and sent home with a fat purse. Probably dead by now, if Northumberland has any sense. They widened the tunnel, secured it. Didn't have to dig all the way through the foundations, just part way in. Enough to bring a wall down.

'They packed it with barrels of powder. Fawkes used some of the good powder from your cellar. You'll find the stuff in the cellar is all decayed, more or less. The rest they bought in. If the powder held out, they were going to blow up the mine on the day you had your first show trial. Robert Cecil, Earl of Salisbury, and the hero of the Gunpowder Plot! Except the Catholics fooled him, kept another mine hidden from him and blew a wall out of an empty House of Lords just to prove how little Robert Cecil was actually in command on the very day he was bragging just how wonderful he was.

'You'd have been a laughing stock, forced into immediate resignation. The King would survive, the laughter rebounding on him and blowing a hole out of his authority. If I was them I'd have had pamphlets printed, pointing out that the Catholics could have blown up the whole farce with the people inside it if they'd wished, making it clear they had the power to provoke a rebellion, but had chosen not to use it. James would almost certainly have had to call in Northumberland as his Secretary after that, to make peace with the Catholics. Beautiful, isn't it? Let you make all the running, let you blow yourself up to maximum height and then prick your balloon with a gentle little explosion where the only physical casualties are a few bits of stone, and the only other casualty is one of the Papists' most bitter enemies: you.

'It's still there, of course. I mean the mine, and the powder. I set my servant guard over it when we found it, but called him off when I came here, just in case you sent someone and he got arrested as a conspirator. We wouldn't want old Mannion to find himself being nabbed like Guy Fawkes, would we? So I suppose Northumberland could have sent someone down there right now to blow it up, since you appear to want to implicate him in the Gunpowder Plot.'

Gresham stood up easily. He looked out of the high window in the direction of Westminster, as if for a cloud of smoke.

'I'd get someone down there pretty quickly, if I were you. Someone to secure it, take the powder away. Someone you can

311

trust not to talk. We wouldn't want London knowing there was a plot you knew nothing about, would we?'

Gresham made as if to leave.

'Oh, by the way,' he said, 'there is just one other thing. I'll make Francis Tresham give himself up, so you can have your full set of conspirators. But I want no torture, and I want a fake death to get him out of the Tower and out of England. He won't trouble you again, I guarantee. Are we agreed – on that oath you swore? Tresham has just become both near and dear to me.'

Cecil nodded, a curt, hard nod. Gresham nodded ironically back, and left the room, almost casual in his manner. As he reached the nearest wall out of sight of Whitehall, he leant back against it, and breathed for what seemed like the first time in an hour.

Why had Gresham remembered Tresham's talk of the tunnel Fawkes and the others had tried to dig from the house they had rented, the tunnel they had given up on when the cellar under the House of Lords became available? Perhaps it was simple curiosity, perhaps it was the realisation that a secret tunnel leading up to the walls of the House of Lords was an open invitation for the future, a hostage to fortune and a loose end that simply needed to be tied up. Perhaps most of all it was Wintour's staying on in London, for far longer than was reasonable, and Wintour's obsessive attempts to reach the street in which the house was situated. Had he been trying to hide in the tunnel? Or had he hoped to re-open it himself, ironically wishing to stage the same embarrassment for Cecil as Northumberland had planned all along?

It had been easier than Gresham had thought to gain access to the house from where the plotters had started. A desultory guard was on duty now the first excitements were over, easily bluffed into allowing Gresham and Mannion entry by the obvious wealth of Gresham's clothing and his casual use of Cecil's name and title. Gresham had half expected to find nothing, or at best the caved-in remnant showing what happened when amateurs tried to play at being miners. They had found the shaft under the floor, despite the

312

care of the miners in re-laying the boards their work had scuffed and splintered.

Mannion had been voluble in his insistence that Gresham should not enter. Gresham had ignored him, stripping down to his shirt and crawling through the surprisingly spacious tunnel. This was no work of amateurs, he realised, noting the simple yet effective pattern of timber framing that held up the roof of the tunnel. At its end a positive chamber had been hollowed out, the powder stacked neatly in the seven- or eight-foot-deep hole that had been made in the old foundations, rumoured to be some eleven or twelve feet thick in total. Nothing had been left to chance. Lanterns, tinder, flint and fuse had been stored there, awaiting whoever came to blow the mine. There were two pointers to the originators. A napkin or towel was stuck behind one of the barrels, pinned between it and its neighbour, as might have happened if it had become trapped as a man manoeuvred the one barrel into place by the side of the other. It was simple stuff, of the sort that would be put at table to wipe a guest's hands. Embroidered into the top corner was the Percy crest. Gresham knew that Northumbrian miners worked naked in the tunnels, sometimes discarding even a loincloth, but wrapped a piece of towelling round their brow to wipe the stinging sweat off before it reached their eyes. They must have given the miners napkins from Syon House to take the place of the towelling. Gresham had worked with the moles in the Netherlands, which was why he looked carefully on the ancient stone of the foundations. Those who cut through stone like to leave a mark on it. Eventually he found it, scratched on to a stone, perhaps with the edge of a pickaxe. '*AK for God and HP*'. HP. Henry Percy. Perhaps the ninth Earl had deliberately recruited Catholics to work his mine, and perhaps even given whoever had supervised them a hint of what it was all about.

Gresham had guessed at much of it, of course, but Cecil had not denied it. He had known Fawkes had to be a triple agent as soon as he had seen the completed mine. It was Fawkes who supervised the mine early on, Fawkes who put the powder in the cellar and kept watch on it. The activity needed to finish the mine would never have escaped him.

Mr Fawkes, thought Gresham, was about to have an interesting exchange with Cecil.

They had come upon him at midnight, dragged him out of his sleep and from his comfortable chamber and down into the bowels of the White Tower. What had gone wrong? His grim-faced gaolers would not speak in answer to his entreaties. He knew they showed prisoners the rack, the mere sight of the obscene contraption enough often to break men. His hope died as they strapped him to the machine, still without a word being spoken.

The pain was the most terrible thing that had ever happened to Guy Fawkes. There were no words for the appalling agony that drenched through every fibre of his being, the pain that defied all experience, the pain that made his scream simply a tiny little thing heard far away on the winds of his destruction. They did not take him from the rack when finally he lost consciousness. They threw filthy water over his tortured, strung-out frame, and waited for part of him to emerge from the dark. When he did so he could hardly think. In losing its absolute top, searing edge, the pain had almost worsened, spreading out in equal measure to every limb and every extremity of that limb. It had broken his body, that he knew. He would never walk properly again, stand up like a man. It had broken his spirit too, that he knew.

The face of Cecil loomed over him, devilish in the torchlight.

'You did not tell me about Lord Percy,' he said. 'That was a pity.'

He turned to the gaoler.

'Rack him. And then rack him again. Yet keep him alive. He must walk or be carried on to the scaffold.'

The screams followed Cecil as he swung out of the chamber.

Cecil and Guy Fawkes met only once thereafter, alone. Fawkes had been tossed like a rag doll on to the rough cot in his cell.

Courteously, Cecil had asked one of the gaolers to straighten out his limbs as they lay on the bed, contemplating his fingernails as Fawkes screamed and sobbed as each limb was gently rearranged. Cecil waited. Patience was something he had always had plenty of. When there was something resembling a light of intelligence in Fawkes's eyes, he spoke.

'You are a dead man, of course. You must realise that?'

Something that might have been a nod came from Fawkes.

'So the issue is not whether you die, but how. We could arrange for you to be kissed by the rack again . . .' A shudder passed through Fawkes's frame. 'Or, of course, we could arrange for a clean break at your execution.'

Those sentenced to be hung, drawn and quartered were first of all hung, and then had their entrails dug out before being chopped into pieces. If the prisoner made a suitable confession and prepared to die in a manner that pleased the crowd and the executioner, he was let to hang until he was either dead or wholly unconscious, and only then cut down and dismembered. Other prisoners would be cut down almost immediately the halter had tightened around their neck, and left to experience the full pleasure of the executioner's crude surgery.

'Now,' said Cecil, almost gently, 'let us consider. Is it the rack, or a slice through the tongue to render you speechless and a long death on the scaffold? Or no more meetings with the rack and a quick death? Well, it will mean a trial, of course. And we could always try to speak out there, couldn't we? And an execution, too, where we might wish to speak more than the people should hear. But it would be good, very good for Guy Fawkes to go to his death and say nothing. What talk can there be of conspiracy if the man who was set to blow the powder says nothing of it? Oh, they will talk and conjecture, for a thousand years for all I know. But with you silent, my friend, they can never know, can they? No, my friend, much as it grieves me, we are in a bargaining situation. You have something I need – your silence. I have the power to grant you an easy death, little though you deserve it.'

Fawkes stirred on his cot. A croak emerged from his mouth. Cecil gazed carefully at the prostrate figure, checking that no knife or weapon was lurking on his person, and bent down close to listen.

'Ah, my Lord of Northumberland? You are still loyal to him, are you? A very praiseworthy thing in a servant.' He bent down again, to listen to the muted whisperings. He stood up, a colder and darker tone in his voice. 'Agreed. I swear on my oath that Henry Percy, ninth Earl of Northumberland, will not be brought to execution by any power or inaction on my part. Strangely enough, as another has recently pointed out, I have never broken my sworn oath.

'Yet I wonder if your concern for the ninth Earl might not be linked to his support of your wife and child? Yes, I know of it. And of them, though a devil of a time it has taken me to find them. So I will swear another oath, swear that they will both die, most horribly and at most great length, should you break your oath of silence.'

Why take the risk? thought Cecil, as he swept from the room, leaving the broken figure behind him.

Gresham would have told him. Gresham would have said that he was a man whose whole life had been based on control, on having the strings of the puppets in his hands. Then a figure, Henry Gresham, had come along and shown that those same strings, the strings Cecil thought he held, were in fact held by another man, a man who had taken control completely away from Cecil's hands. Could Robert Cecil, by force of will and by imposition of pain, bend this man Guy Fawkes to obey him, to take the secrets he held to his grave? Cecil needed to know he could do this thing. If he could then his power was undiminished. He was like the mighty Mark Antony, whose power failed him only in the face of the one man, Octavius Caesar. He would block Gresham from his mind. Yet hidden from Cecil's own sight, he and Gresham knew that the secret of Cecil's survival lay in one man alone, and that was not the man who would go to his death on the scaffold with the other plotters.

*

There had been a brief flurry when at the trial Fawkes had pleaded 'Not Guilty'. Cecil's heart had started to beat louder, but he had kept his outward calm and merely looked at the broken man in the dock. Fawkes had mumbled – he could hardly speak – that he had not understood some of the charges, and the crisis had passed. In fact, Cecil mused, it had probably been not so much a potential rebellion against Cecil, but more an attempt to protect some of the Catholic priests implicated in the plot, and Father Henry Garnet in particular. It was to no avail. Garnet would die, in agony, as was right.

It had been a bitterly cold morning when the first four had been dragged through the streets. The sentence had been for the traitors to be hauled at the tail of a horse, heads dragging on the ground. Amusing though the humiliation was, interpreted in its simplest form it meant the prisoner was likely to drown in the filth of the streets, or have his head banged so much as to make the executioner redundant. The crowd must not be deprived of their sport, so the prisoners were placed on a wicker hurdle for the first part of their ordeal. Would Jane wait and watch for him in a nearby house as he was dragged through the streets? wondered Gresham. He hoped not. You were best seen as already dead at this stage in the proceedings, and no dignity was to be acquired from any part of what went on.

Everard Digby's wife and children had managed to find a spot on the roadside. One of their little boys had cried out 'Tata! Tata!' as their father was dragged past, the baying crowds silent for a moment, the clods of earth ceasing their hurtling towards the traitor. Did the little boy notice the spit staining his father's shirt and body? wondered Gresham. Tom Bates's wife had dashed out to him on the street as well. He had apparently told her where some money was stashed, practical to the last.

Poor Digby, innocent baby that he was. He had played the romantic fool at his trial, and he spoke at length, and to very little purpose, on the scaffold. It had not helped him. He had been cut down almost as soon as he had hung, and carved up fully conscious. Immediately after the crowd had gone its way, the rumour had started that when the executioner had held up the bloody lump of flesh that was Digby's heart, with the cry 'Here lies the heart of a traitor!', Digby had cried out in his death pangs, 'You lie!' Well, Gresham reflected, someone might have heard those words. All he had heard was Digby's final agonised screams. Old Robert Wintour and John Grant had died decently enough, Tom Bates needing to make a speech.

The second batch of executions contained Fawkes. Tom Wintour, now recovered enough to die, Ambrose Rookwood and Robert Keyes went along with him. Keyes cheated the hangman at the last, hurling himself off the scaffold and breaking his neck the minute the halter was around it. Fawkes was last to go. He mumbled a few words – 'forgiveness' and 'the King' was all Gresham could hear, near as he was. The pathetic figure had to be helped on to the scaffold. His neck broke cleanly as he was hung. Strange, thought Gresham, that the crowd were denied the full bloody rites of this perceived ringleader. Stranger still that he had made it to execution, knowing what he knew. Or was it the real Fawkes? For all Gresham knew, some village idiot had been acquired in the place of the man who had died on the rack. He hardly cared. All he did know was that Cecil would never allow Guy Fawkes to live.

Mannion had come with him on both occasions. 'Nothing like a good execution!' he had stated with enthusiasm, and even now he was comparing the eight deaths with others he had seen, for all the world like a man comparing plays or sonnets. He munched on a mutton pie as the conspirators were put to death, one by one. Jane had not come. 'I've excitement enough in my life,' she had said, 'without needing to smear my eyes with blood.' Gresham had found her crying, the night in between the executions.

'Why are you crying?' he had whispered to her, reaching out in the night.

'For the women,' she had sobbed, 'and for the children. For the innocents, left behind with no inheritance, their lives ruined by these *stupid* men. These men who care only for their great cause, and leave behind them weeping the only true great cause a man can have.'

Gresham could have said how those damned were only a tiny proportion of those who would have suffered if rebellion had broken out, if the plot had not been smashed and exposed. Yet was it so? Would more, or fewer, men have died, women been widowed and children been orphaned if Gresham had kept out of the whole affair? Cecil had it under control, did he not? Fawkes would have lived on, Percy been ennobled, a few plotters executed.

So what had Henry Gresham done, except send Guy Fawkes to the rack and Thomas Percy to his grave?

Gresham lay awake, the occasional ripple of a sob still passing through the beautiful body lying next to him. Was it Machiavelli's choice that he had made, to keep a corrupt ruler in his place? Or was it simple vanity?

EPILOGUE

It was a cold wind blowing across the marshes. The small boat that would take them out to meet the tiny pinnace was rocking in the water, the slap-slap of its hull loud in the night. Gresham wondered if there were troops at that moment searching the south-coast port where he had let it be known that the embarkation would take place. He doubted it, but it would be a good test of Cecil's word.

The priest, Father Garnet, had been arrested. He had tried to defend himself at his trial, but he had no defence. What did a court of King James care for the secrecy of the confessional? If he knew of treason and a plot to murder the King, his duty as a subject was to report it, never mind whether he heard it in a wooden box with incense all around him. He was a dead man from the moment they laid hands on him, and Garnet knew it as well as the court.

Francis Tresham slipped out of the fisherman's hut in which he had been waiting. Gresham and his men had needed to check the area, to exchange the password with the two sailors in the small boat. He could smell the fear on Tresham, as well as the drink with which he had been filling himself for days. Spiriting him out of the Tower, supposedly dead, had been ease itself with Cecil's word behind the conspiracy.

'Here,' he said, thrusting a parcel at Tresham and forcing himself not to speak in a whisper. 'Money, and your papers. You are now Matthew Brunninge. Your passage to Spain is booked. Congratulations. Like Jesus, you've risen from the dead.'

'Will he live happily ever after?' asked Jane, snuggling up to him as they watched the boat move gently out through the creek.

'I doubt it,' said Gresham. 'But then again, who can say who'll live happily ever after?'

'Sir Henry,' said Jane, stepping away from him, 'I think it's time I became your wife.'

For once, Gresham let his shock show on his face. What the Devil had this woman? To talk of *marriage*? On a windswept Norfolk coast, surrounded by potential enemies and busily involved in spiriting away a traitor and sworn enemy of the Crown, not to mention someone who had supposedly died of a urinary infection in the Tower!

'God help us!' exploded Gresham. 'I . . .'

'You see,' said Jane, ignoring him completely, 'it's one thing for me to be your whore. It is another thing for our son to be born a bastard.'

DRAMATIS PERSONAE

Francis Bacon, 1st Baron Verulam and Viscount St Alban (1561–1626), failed to establish himself at Court under Queen Elizabeth I, probably because Lord Burghley saw him as a rival to his son, Robert Cecil. His career blossomed after the death of Robert Cecil in 1612, but he fell from grace in 1621 when he was convicted of bribery, briefly imprisoned in The Tower and then allowed to retire in disgrace.

Robert Cecil, 1st Earl of Salisbury (1563–1612), was the creator of Hatfield House, and died 'much troubled in mind and body' after a long and painful illness.

Moll Cutpurse (c. 1570–1650), known also as Mary Frith and Mary Markham, was the daughter of a shoemaker, and died of dropsy in Fleet Street. She is the basis for the play *The Roaring Girl* (c. 1607) by Middleton and Decker, and appears as a character in *Amends for Ladies* (1612) by Nathan Field. She was prosecuted in 1605 for appearing in man's attire at The Fortune Theatre, uttering lascivious speeches and singing bawdy songs whilst playing the lute. Among her many achievements, she robbed General Fairfax of gold during the Civil War, shot him in the arm, was pursued and arrested and sentenced to be hung. She bribed her way out of this at a reported cost of £2,000.

John Donne (1572–1631) is recognised as the leading light of the Metaphysical school of poetry. Finally ordained in 1615, he became Dean of St Paul's in 1621.

Dr Simon Forman (1552–1611) was a notorious self-taught physician and astrologer who among other things predicted the day of his own death. Linked to Sir Walter Raleigh's 'School of Night' and a famous poisoning case featuring the Countess of Essex, his 'play books' contain the first eye-witness accounts of some of Shakespeare's plays in performance.

Inigo Jones (1573–1652) was a designer and architect whose partnership with Ben Jonson in the presentation of Court masques was to last from 1605 until 1631. Jones played a major part in introducing the proscenium arch to English theatre, and was responsible for the original layout of the piazza in Covent Garden.

Ben Jonson (1572–1637) was the leading playwright of his day after Shakespeare, and wrote a fulsome prologue to the published version of Shakespeare's plays. His partnership with Inigo Jones in presenting masques for the Court of King James I was long-standing and successful. As a Catholic and someone who had dined with members of the Gunpowder Plot conspiracy, he was questioned following the plot, but not accused.

William Parker, 4th Lord Monteagle (d. 1622), died peacefully and prosperously in his bed.

Henry Percy, 9th Earl of Northumberland (1564–1632), was imprisoned after the Gunpowder Plot and not released until 1621.

Thomas Phelippes was a key figure in Walsingham's spy empire for Queen Elizabeth I, specialising in 'deciphering', code breaking and formulation and forgery. He was reputedly able to break ciphers in five languages and was instrumental in the conviction and execution of Mary Queen of Scots. He fell out with Robert Cecil when Cecil inherited the remnants of Walsingham's empire.

Sir Walter Raleigh (c. 1554–1618) spent thirteen years imprisoned in The Tower, before being released to go on one last ill-fated expedition. He was executed by King James I, largely on the urging of the Spanish Ambassador, in 1618. His eldest son, Wat, was killed in 1618 in an heroic engagement against the Spanish-held village of St Thome in the 'Indies'.

THE CONSCIENCE OF THE KING

Martin Stephen

The Conscience of the King - the second gripping Henry Gresham adventure - finds the courtier and spy embroiled in one of the deadliest, most exciting and most dangerous parts of Jacobean society: the theatre.

It is 1612, and when word reaches Gresham that Robert Cecil, Chief Secretary to the King, is dying, he knows he should be rejoicing. But even in his final hours his archenemy can still cause him trouble. Summoned to Bath, Gresham is given one final order, a command from Cecil's deathbed that could find Gresham joining the Chief Secretary sooner than he'd like . . .

King James I has been a little too indiscreet in his liaisons with Robert Carr, Viscount Rochester, and now an unknown Cambridge bookseller has got hold of their potentially devastating correspondence. Is Cecil's request to Gresham for help because he knows that he is the only man who can return the letters, saving the monarchy from the sort of scandal that could prove its downfall? Or is it Gresham's downfall that Cecil seeks?

Gresham's fate is soon linked not only to the missing letters but also to stolen manuscripts by William Shakespeare that have already cost two men their lives. Drawn increasingly into a world where nothing is as it seems, Gresham is haunted by a mysterious play, *The Fall of Lucifer*, rumoured to be so incendiary its performance could cause riots. It's a play whose twisted creator has been thought dead for twenty long years: a creator who is in fact alive and plotting terror of his own . . .

From the depths of the River Thames to the heights of King's College Chapel, from the terror of the Tower of London to the strutting glory of the Globe Theatre, Henry Gresham moves inexorably towards the truth behind the world's greatest playwright, a literary mystery that has obsessed the world for over 400 years. Yet for Gresham, the truth could guarantee nothing but his own destruction.

To be published by Time Warner Books UK in autumn 2003.